'The absurd situations through which the hapless and avaricious Ian tumbles in his attempts to protect his illicit fortune from the real Millennium Bug unleash countless comic observations. Some of these are convincing and genuinely funny, some puerile or simply off the mark, but the tale of borrowed identities and karmic payback is in the main a success' *The Bookseller*

'A painfully funny thriller . . . part Mike Leigh grimness, part Hollywood action flick, expect to see the film of the book in a multiplex near you soon' *Heat*

'*Snakeskin*'s compelling tale depicts the adventures of Brummie Ian Gillick, a man struggling to save his own neck while simultaneously destroying his own identify . . . While the readers are invited to laugh at the obsessive behaviour of each character, they are also coaxed into reflecting on how real they actually are. Scary stuff. *The List*

'Thoroughly entertaining, topical novel . . . McCabe's devilish sense of fun wakes up amongst the pocket protectors and low-nutrient junk food – and has the last laugh. Hilariously misanthropic, with all the nasties finding their comeuppance at the end of a tale that's half bile, half smiles' *I.D.*

'McCabe has woven an intricate but absorbing tale of deception and betrayal. Like his previous two books – *Stickleback* and *Paper* – it's cleverly written with a strong sense of place' *Birmingham Post*

Also by John McCabe

STICKLEBACK
PAPER
SNAKESKIN

and published by Black Swan

John ~~McCabe is the author of~~ three oth~~er acclai~~med novels, *Sti~~ckleback, Paper~~ and ~~Snakeskin~~. His latest novel, *Herding C~~ats, is now available in Transworld paperback*

STICKLEBACK

'Witty and incisive about the preoccupations of modern life'
Observer

'Not only do you have a compulsive read on your hands, you also have a fascinating profile of the ritualized mediocrity of contemporary living'   *Big Issue*

'This fine first novel . . . makes a very welcome break from the norm'   *The Times*

'A must-read for all fans of Nick Hornby, James Hawes and Ben Elton'   *Bookseller*

'A witty, fast-paced novel'   *Glasgow Herald*

'A novel about habit and memory and more Hornby than Proust'   *Spectator*

'*Stickleback* is a promising début and provides an enter-taining read'   *Examiner*

'A rampant roar through the stultifying world of office life. This is a wonderfully funny little thriller with a firm grasp on the frustrations of everyday life. McCabe is a terrific new voice'   *Midweek*

PAPER

'I could say that McCabe writes as Nick Hornby would if Nick Hornby were locked in a laboratory for a year. But that would be glib. The writing is original, entertaining and compelling' *The Times*

'A fine and highly original thriller. Hitting you with a series of unexpected outcomes, it provides us with an interesting twist in this well-used genre' *City Life*

'Through the unlikely medium of farce, *Paper* puts real flesh on the truism that science is a cultural enterprise. Not cynical so much as "slightly bruised", McCabe perfectly captures the intellectual and institutional frustrations that oppress the "poor bloody infantry" of science'
New Scientist

'With its grungy setting, down-beat style and depressed male protagonist, it places itself right at the centre of its genre' *The Times Literary Supplement*

SNAKESKIN

'Coincidence is just another tool of fate. And John McCabe uses this tool like a master craftsman, creating a thoroughly enjoyable comedy of errors ... Every twist and turn of *Snakeskin* makes you wonder just how many sub-plots McCabe can introduce into one book and it's a pleasure to watch the whole story unfurl' *Punch*

'McCabe's madcap third novel is Carl Hiassen meets John O'Farrell by way of Leslie Neilsen. Hi-octane hi-jinx'
Mirror

BIG SPENDER

John McCabe

BLACK SWAN

BIG SPENDER
A BLACK SWAN BOOK : 0 552 99968 7

Originally published in Great Britain by Doubleday,
a division of Transworld Publishers

PRINTING HISTORY
Doubleday edition published 2002
Black Swan edition published 2003

1 3 5 7 9 10 8 6 4 2

Set in 11/12pt Melior by
Falcon Oast Graphic Art Ltd.

Black Swan Books are published by Transworld Publishers,
61–63 Uxbridge Road, London W5 5SA,
a division of The Random House Group Ltd,
in Australia by Random House Australia (Pty) Ltd,
20 Alfred Street, Milsons Point, Sydney, NSW 2061, Australia,
in New Zealand by Random House New Zealand Ltd,
18 Poland Road, Glenfield, Auckland 10, New Zealand
and in South Africa by Random House (Pty) Ltd,
Endulini, 5a Jubilee Road, Parktown 2193, South Africa.

Printed and bound in Great Britain by
Cox & Wyman Ltd, Reading, Berkshire

For the real John McCabe and his Three Rules of Life

BIG SPENDER

Speed Bumps

Jake Cooper slammed over the last speed bump before work, cursing the planet and most of its problems. As his seatbelt tensed, he finally decided the world was now just too safe. In fact, it had probably never been this harmless in its short, treacherous history. Speed bumps. Air bags. Crumple zones. Security cages. Everything in his previously exciting existence was becoming disturbingly predictable.

As Deputy Executive Hazard Prevention Officer for the mediocre town of Bridgeton, Jake appreciated that the world's growing reliability was partly his own fault, but it didn't make him any happier about the situation. And it wasn't as if he craved danger. Instead, he felt hopelessly trapped on a planet that was increasingly unadventurous. The radio news was in full flow and Jake turned it up, screeching into the speed-limited car park. As he did so, he engaged the central locking of his shiny new car. Safe as Bridgeton undoubtedly was, he was about to enter the only truly hazardous territory in town.

It was an interesting morning for world events. A

plane had crashed into a hillside in Peru. Two factions of the same Balkan country had woken up and decided to kill each other. A Spanish ferry had put to sea without closing its doors, and had promptly sunk. A lorry had shed its load of sheds near Shepshed, and was causing the newsreader problems. Truly, there were two worlds – Bridgeton, and the other bits. But the car park, as Jake made his rapid way through, might as well belong in Bogotá. This part of the planet was distinctly unsafe, a haven of chaos in an otherwise harmless town centre. Jake reversed into a space, keeping his seatbelt tightly fastened. So far, so good. And then, out of nowhere, a fist banged down on his bonnet.

'You fucking fucker!'

Jake checked the central locking and remained inside the vehicle.

A bang on the roof, a crazed face at the window, spitting as it swore. 'My fucking space!'

He turned the radio up and looked away. Best not to antagonize them. The litany of catastrophe continued on the news. A coach had fallen off a mountain in France. Hurricanes in the Midwest of America. A mud slide in Brazil. If someone died these days, no matter how far away, we were going to know about it, whether we wanted to or not. This was the obvious side effect of our world becoming safer – we have to go further and further afield to hear about interesting death and destruction.

'Come on, you wanker. That's my fucking space!' the face screamed.

Jake killed the engine and remained resolutely in his car, thinking. No longer are our children going to waste away through malnutrition. No longer are people from our village going to be buried alive in a collapsed mine. No longer is the entire Smith family next door going to be consumed by the plague, more's the pity. Disaster, on our small part of the map, is further removed from us than ever before.

A final flurry of swearing and a last malevolent punch of his car, and the man retreated. Jake waited a couple of seconds before climbing out and heading towards the squat, grey lifelessness of the Hazard Prevention building. The high-tech entrance could only be brokered when a security guard had checked that nobody was leaving at the same time. This reflected a recent initiative to minimize door-related incidents. So if we've achieved one thing, he said to himself, glancing up at the CCTV camera and sighing, it's predictability. And if we've achieved another, he conceded as the door finally opened, it's the radio, television and newspaper means of informing us that the world isn't predictable.

In his office, Jake stared at the poster he had faced every day for eight years. *Safety Is No Accident*, it proclaimed. Next to it, this week's Hazard Prevention slogan advised *Make Danger a Stranger*. Each slogan came with a statistic attached, as a grim reminder of society's evils. Jake read the frightening piece of information again. *Last year, 91 bread bin-related incidents required hospital treatment*. He walked to the window which overlooked the car park. The door opened, and Roger, his colleague, sidled in and headed for his desk. Roger was a six-foot-two streak of unadulterated caution. Even his clothes looked worried, with their paranoid creases and maniacally furrowed folds. His eyes swam wildly around behind fish-tank lenses, darting back and forth, searching out danger, and his nostrils flared as if he could smell oncoming disaster. Jake enjoyed sharing an office with him because next to Roger he felt calm. He was able to measure his own mildly racing pulse against Roger's obvious panic, and usually came off best. While it is undoubtedly noble to be judged alongside the great and the good, it's far more rewarding to be compared with those who are obviously lacking.

13

'Anything this morning?' Roger asked, sweating lightly.

'Some minor fist work, bit of interesting language,' Jake answered. 'Nothing special.'

Roger joined him at the window and they monitored proceedings with interest. Hazard Prevention shared part of its site with the County Psychiatric Unit. Literally, all that separated Jake from insanity was a narrow, elongated strip of tarmac with white lines on it. Through a genius of forward planning, two of the Psychiatric Unit's more attention-grabbing departments formed the other sides of the uneasy rectangle. As a result, patients of Anger Management and visitors to the Tourette's Syndrome section regularly vied for parking spaces within the confined area. Jake passed hours in front of his window watching as people with particularly short tempers rubbed up against patients with a penchant for uncontrollable swearing. He appreciated that the problem was not easily soluble. The Psychiatric Unit had to care for all its patients, whatever their difficulties, within a single building. Extremes of the mental spectrum were therefore likely to antagonize each other in every conceivably wrong way. The distinctly nervous encountered the thoroughly agitated; the permanently anxious met the utterly uptight; the pleasantly psychotic bumped into the desperately troubled. The degree of chaos contained within the walls of the Psychiatric Unit could only be guessed at by those on the outside, whose single glimpse of the potential bedlam occurred as patients jostled each other to park their cars.

Jake and Roger continued to watch while a red Metro reversed into a space. Around the car park, they could just make out other dedicated voyeurs in their various workplaces, holding mugs, peering hopefully at the tarmac in front of them, delaying the start of another inevitable day. As Jake checked the time he was blissfully unaware that the comings and goings of the Psychiatric Unit were about to feel tame compared with the rest of his life.

'Right,' Roger said during a lull in the action, 'ready to go?'

Jake looked away from the window. 'You bet,' he said.

'Let's do it.'

'Who is it first?' Jake asked.

'Research and Development Two.'

'Poor bastards.'

'Lights,' Roger said, facing him.

'Camera,' Jake replied.

'Satisfaction!' they shouted in unison. Roger aimed for a high five.

With his missing finger, Jake only managed a high four.

The Pornography of Violence

The unknowing innocents of Research and Development Two were herded into a small stuffy lecture room in the Hazard Prevention Unit. Cups of coffee were distributed and dunkable biscuits circulated. Jake and Roger did all they could to provide a comfortable environment. There was an element of the condemned man's last meal about this ritual. Jake tried to imagine what the staff in question expected as they travelled to his department. They usually arrived in high spirits, aware that although safety lectures were invariably tedious, they sure beat working. Away from their offices, factories and building sites, they were child-like, giggling, joking around, unsure how to relate as a group outside their place of work. Roger lowered the lights and set the projector up. Research and Development Two slowly quietened down and Jake stepped up to give the standard introduction.

'Right, everybody, this film will last about twenty-five minutes, and raises some basic safety issues. When we've finished we'll have a discussion about what you've seen. OK?' There were a few uninterested nods. Jake slipped a knowing wink to Roger. 'Enjoy it,' he said.

The film was called *Office and Laboratory Catastrophes*, and was the Safety Team's current favourite. As Jake dimmed the lights still further and the audience settled down, he couldn't help wondering who made safety films any more. Someone seemed to have made a job lot of them in the early seventies, most likely at the Hammer studios, before giving it up as a bad idea. But not without having had some fun. To Jake's mind, safety films were to violence what pornography was to sex. They were badly acted, with poor dialogue and transparent plots. And yet they were utterly compelling and sickly funny. There was a brutality, a distance, a sense of voyeurism. Rather than medallions and moustaches, there were overalls and safety glasses. But the premise was the same. Here is an aspect of human behaviour in its crudest form. Take your eyes off it if you dare.

Besides their inherent depravity, the other great thing about safety films was that they were scarier than horror movies. As soon as you know you are going to be scared, horror flicks lose most of their terror. A safety film, however, is another matter. When an audience trots in half-heartedly as they had just done, expecting an unchallenging infomercial, glad to be away from their desks or machines for an hour or so, their guard is lowered. They are vulnerable. And when confronted with some of the most sickening special effects ever assembled – ones even horror makers shy away from – then, Jake smiled to himself, you really do have a captive audience.

The dated whirring and flicking noise of the projector was gradually drowned out by introductory music, which led into the first title.

Office Surprise

The film ran as follows:

> Close-up on a pleasant, middle-aged secretary, female. She is chattering away and opening mail. The camera zooms to her hands, which have peeled open an envelope. She thrusts several fingers inside. Then she stops. There is a bone-shaking scream. She removes her fingers, which are drenched in blood, with red stuff spurting everywhere over her dress. We pull out. One digit is hanging off. She stands up, panicking, blood spraying forth and stumbles towards the first-aid sign. Camera pans down to feet level. There is a handbag on the floor. We see her high heel catch on the bag. Long shot. The secretary loses her balance and grabs at a heavy filing cabinet, which topples onto her. There is the distinctly unpleasant sound effect of a body being slowly crushed and ribs snapping. All movement ceases. Focus in on her shoes, one high heel broken, blood seeping from under her body.

Onscreen message: *Beware of Staples Lurking Inside Envelopes.*

The audience began to look sceptical, some of them obviously wondering whether this was an elaborate practical joke. Roger grinned through the half light at Jake. While the next scene started up, there were a couple of nervous coughs and the odd murmur. Meanwhile, the second title appeared.

Food for Thought

> Full-length shot of a scatty scientist, no cliché left unturned (overflowing beard, woollen tie, crazy hair), fiddling with a beaker housing a nasty chemical. Close-up of his lab bench. Next to the beaker is a cup

of coffee. Long shot. The scientist calls to another on the far side of the lab. Back to the bench. Without looking, the scientist reaches for his coffee, but his hand wraps instead around the beaker. Close-up as he swigs liberally from the beaker of toxic chemical, before standing up and grabbing his throat. We see acid burns appear through his skin, and a stomach-churning green fluid pulses through the wound. Pull out, to see him stagger around, still clutching his neck. He spills forwards towards a Bunsen burner, his unkempt hair catching the flame and bursting alight. The scientist is now clutching his scalp. On fire, he runs blindly through the lab. Long shot. He spots another beaker, large, uncovered, and containing clear fluid. Assuming it to be water, he douses his hair in it. Close-up on beaker label. 'Highly flammable. Keep Covered.' Unusually realistic footage of a human ball of flames running through the lab, flesh burning, hair blazing, screams echoing, a trail of blood behind him.

Onscreen message: *Do Not Eat or Drink in Laboratories.*

The audience were now distinctly restless. Some appeared pale, their white faces shining out of the dark. Jake caught Roger's eye. There was an air of anticipated disaster in the lecture theatre as the next scenario began, and a collective intake of air as the title appeared.

Ladders and Screwdrivers

Two workmen in overalls are manoeuvring a large stepladder in front of a building. There are sharp railings at waist height around the building's periphery. One climbs the ladder while the other holds it, using a long, pointed screwdriver to tighten a loose rung. [A couple of whimpers from the audience.] Workman

A makes it safely to the top and climbs onto the roof. Close-up of Workman B, who tucks the screwdriver into his front pocket and shifts the ladder to a new position around the corner. Pan up to A, who has finished his job, and turns round to climb back down. He steps back without checking the position of the ladder. Pull out to observe the razor-sharp gothic railings. [Several screams from the assembled masses.] Shot of a man falling backwards off the roof. We watch as the arrow-head railings pierce his body, blood gushing forth, the man vainly struggling to free himself, his skewered body spasming. Cut to Workman B, who has heard the commotion. He comes running from around the corner. A quick shot of his boots, neither of which has its laces tied, panning up to the long screwdriver he is carrying in his hand. [Obvious mild hysteria in the lecture theatre.] Back to the shoes. He steps on a lace, stumbles, falls forwards and impales himself on his screwdriver, coming to rest inches away from his colleague's writhing form. As he does so, the palm of his hand crashes down on one of the railings, which tears through his flesh. We follow a trickle of blood from the railings man as it mingles with a rivulet from screwdriver man. Both take their dying breaths.

Onscreen message: *Be Careful with Ladders and Sharp Objects*.

By now, the audience were not happy at all. Some appeared close to vomiting, others almost in shock. Still the film rolled on. People scanned wildly for exit signs, which, in the interests of safety, Roger and Jake had turned off. The fourth and final scenario began to rear its very ugly head. This was the mother of all safety scenes, the summation of all the previous catastrophes. Roger usually described this one as, 'The end of *An American Werewolf in London*, where they couldn't think how to end it, so just had one enormous pile-up of traffic crashes.' Jake called it 'The

Exterminator' or 'Arma-fucking-geddon', depending on how optimistic he felt on the day.

Acid, Base, Fire, Knives

Quick scan around a busy research and development laboratory. We see the following clues to the disaster which is about to unfold: someone wearing open-toed sandals; a woman with long, free-flowing hair; a man smoking a cigarette; a woman perching precariously on a stepladder with a hefty bottle of something nasty in her hands; a workman sharpening a large knife; piles of loose and presumably very flammable papers; a huge flask boiling over with orange goo; a female secretary in high heels carrying a parcel; an uncapped bottle of ether; an unsupervised student pouring a container marked 'Acid' into one marked 'Base'. There is an ominous pause. [One of the viewers shouts, 'For Christ's sake, run for it!' in the direction of the onscreen student.] Slow motion. The secretary slips on something and goes over on one of her heels. We follow the parcel, which shoots out of her hands and knocks into the student. He tips the acid into the base. A short lull followed by a colossal bang. The workman pushes the knife clean through his hand with the shock of the explosion, and stumbles into the stepladder. The woman at the top of the ladder holding the nasty-looking bottle is shaken off balance and drops it. It shatters on the ladder before landing on the open-toed sandal of the scientist below. A toe detaches as the thick glass embeds itself into his foot. He hops forwards, gushing blood, and crashes against the large distillation flask which spills over the bench and floor, trailing noxious fumes in its wake. The cigarette-smoking man jumps out of the way, but drops his fag into the orange goo, which ignites. A pale blue flame runs over the lab surface and makes straight for the bottle of ether, which goes up a treat, cutting off the single exit from the developing Armageddon. The woman with the long hair bends down to help the man with the knife through his hand, and in doing so manages to dip her mane into the fire. She screams and runs to the far end of the lab, towards a sink. There, she manages to spread the flames from her head onto the pile of loose papers, which again eagerly catch light. The camera pulls slowly out as we see smoky and burning figures limping and running around and crashing into each other, flames creeping higher, until the film stops.

Roger turned the striplights back on, which flickered into life. Research and Development Two blinked in time with the neon tubes. Paleness abounded. A nervous female at the back was stifling tears. 'Right then,' Jake said, standing up at the front. 'Any questions?' Muffled crying aside, there was a universal silence. Jake and Roger were defending an unbeaten run of seventeen showings of *Office and Laboratory Catastrophes* without a single coherent enquiry from the audience. Jake goaded them once more. 'Nothing at all? No issues you feel like raising?' A couple of cleared throats, a scraping chair. Slowly, unsurely, a hand trembled its way into the air. 'Yes?' Jake asked, taken aback, noticing that the hand was connected to a slender arm, which itself was attached to a willowy girl, who was unusually attractive for Research and Development Two.

'Well,' she faltered, 'I just wondered what the procedure was for reporting unsafe situations, like the ones we've seen in the film.'

'What sort of unsafe procedures?'

'All of them.'

'All of them?'

'All the ones you've shown us.'

'Specifically, what concerns do you have?'

'OK.' She cleared her throat. 'Blocked fire exits, open beakers of dangerous chemicals, sharp objects, frequent explosions, people with long hair—'

'Frequent explosions?'

'Yes.'

Something occurred to Jake. 'Which workplace are you from?'

'Peril and Sons.'

Roger and Jake exchanged furtive glances.

'So you know about Peril and Sons?' the girl asked.

'Oh yes,' Jake said, 'we know about Peril and Sons.' This was tricky and would take some careful handling in front of an audience. 'Look, why don't you stay behind and we'll discuss your concerns? The rest of you, remember, safety is no accident. Hopefully this session will have put things into perspective, and you're now free to go.'

When the new recruits had risen unsteadily to their feet and shuffled out, Jake took the girl to one side. 'There's a couple of things we have to tell you about your employer,' he said. 'Roger, dim the lights and run the next scene of *Office and Laboratory Catastrophes*.'

'But we never show the fifth scene!'

'Trust me.'

Roger appeared even more apprehensive than usual. 'But . . .'

'She has a right to know.' Jake sat down behind the girl and took his laser pointer out. 'Roger, roll the film.'

Nerd-flirting

At home later that night, Jake called out to his girl-friend Kate, who was surfing the Internet. Kate was always surfing the Internet. She seemed to have taken up residence there, in one of its many chat rooms. Their quarterly phone bill told the real story, and a sorry one it was. He would watch her sometimes, chewing the ear-end of her glasses, typing quick approximate sentences, scanning the screen im-patiently before eagerly typing another reply. Twenty other people across the country, lacking the com-punction to get off their arses and enter real life, also sat around in front of monitors, tapping away at key-boards, pretending to be young, blond and vivacious, and neglecting to mention that they were old, knackered and lazy. Not that Kate was old or knackered, he appreciated as he looked at her. Lazy, though, yes, he thought, kissing her on the head.

Jake worried about the amount of time his girlfriend spent in solicitous chat with sad computer geeks. These were people who passed their days convincing others they weren't lonely, insular nerds by typing emails. Surely this was a self-defeating exercise, like borrowing money to pay off your debts. After all, if his girlfriend was going to chat other men up, Jake felt she should at least have the decency to target the vaguely desirable. Occasionally it would get to him and he would provoke her into an argument.

'Oh come on,' she used to say, 'it's just like flirting. And who doesn't flirt?'

'You,' he would reply. 'Not with me any more.'

But she would already be typing again.

Jake threw his briefcase down on the sofa as noisily as possible.

Without looking up, Kate asked, 'Is it six thirty already?'

Jake always arrived home at six thirty. He wondered why she hadn't seen through this yet. Surely some days he should be later and others earlier. But no, it was always six thirty, on the dot, and she had never once commented. Neither had she ever asked why, seeing as he finished work at five, and the journey was only two and a half miles, he wasn't home an hour earlier every night.

'I'll do the tea,' she said, 'just let me finish up.' Twenty minutes later, Kate dragged herself away from the computer and slouched into the kitchen to warm a ready-made meal. Somewhere, Jake told himself, things were going wrong.

He knew the overwhelming odds were that his relationship was doomed. Not just because it was so obviously failing, but because of the sheer statistical unlikeliness of any relationship succeeding. Even if you are happy, even if things are solid, the odds are hugely stacked against long-term happiness. Jake had been in ten previous relationships, give or take. Mainly take. But all ten had failed. Why should this be any different? In the midst of other relationships he had never envisaged an end. This was it. This was the one, the one that lasted for ever. Until it ended. And even if he married Kate, as she suggested with alarming regularity, the chances of them remaining together to their final days, without affairs, divorce or death splitting them up, weren't so much slim as dying of starvation.

Maybe it was the Statistics of Safety that had first made Jake think like this, seeing all events as cold probabilities of risk as he did all day at work. Or maybe it was because they had stopped making love. But either way, when he returned to Kate each night, it was with a heavy sense of doom. Which is why, at five thirty, he pulled his car to a grudging halt in a street four hundred yards away, a quiet road frequented only by resting taxi drivers escaping the public for a few precious moments. And while they switched their engines off and reclined their seats, safe from being directed left, right and straight ahead, Jake would turn up his stereo and try to imagine he was about to go home to a woman who loved and respected him. He would watch the dashboard clock, occasionally glancing up as another taxi eased to a halt, its driver stretching, yawning and rubbing his face. This was his hour, the sacred hour of the day when he was neither working nor sitting in silence with his girlfriend. They were the happiest five hours of the week.

But unlike the taxi drivers, Jake wasn't resting any more. These days he was engrossed in something. He had a notepad, a calculator and an assortment of papers. What was increasingly dawning on him as he beavered away was that something had to be done about his situation and soon. And when 18:25 flashed up in green dashboard digits before his eyes, he would start the engine, forget all about it and drive slowly around the corner to their cul-de-sac to meet his six-thirty curfew.

While Jake realized that parking in side streets for long periods of time was not necessarily a healthy thing, he also appreciated that relationships impose these necessities on you. They expose you, get under your skin, force your defences up. So placing a buffer between the thing which paid him and the thing which spent his money was far from a good sign relationship-wise, but to do something about it would be more worrying. He and his girlfriend had invested years in each other. They had sacrificed their freedom, had pooled their resources and had rejected the occasional advances of attractive strangers. To walk away from this was to admit that all those things were wrong and that each stranger could have taken them on a journey which was a lot more fun than the ghost relationship they had now. What was keeping them together was the refusal to admit that they had misjudged each other.

Occasionally, very occasionally, they made love at the weekend and things were all right again. They would make more effort, they told each other as they hugged afterwards. They never did though, and in many ways Jake's relationship came to mirror the fortunes of the local football team, which generally managed plenty of possession but very little penetration.

Kate trudged back from the kitchen with a suspiciously square lasagne. She took her own plate over to the computer and resumed typing, one handed. Jake glared at the computer. He was becoming jealous of a plastic box, and this annoyed him even further. An off-white plastic box half-full of unimpressive components. He wanted to take it outside for a thorough kicking. Not the men she corresponded with, but the box she spent hours alone with. He realized he was shooting the messenger, but when did she ever look at him and smile? When did she ever run her fingers over him? When did she ever give him her full, unadulterated concentration, except when telling him off? But as he was well aware, cohabitation can be tricky territory. Bad situations persist because to change them is often more painful than putting up with them.

And to make matters worse, it was Friday night. With no chance of escaping to work, weekends were fast becoming dangerous territory.

Issues

Jake sighed as he climbed into bed. A pattern had been established, over which he had little say. Work seemed to own him during the week, and Kate owned him at weekends. Saturday mornings usually panned out as follows:

Kate wakes up early.

Kate's brain: Seven jobs need doing. Repeat, seven jobs need doing. Wake Jake. No other alternative, must wake Jake.

Jake's brain: It's the weekend. Oh yes. Stretch, yawn, smile, roll over.

Kate's brain: Prod Jake.

Jake's brain: Saturday morning. Slight chance of a good poking.

Kate's brain: It isn't working. Jake still enjoying himself. More prodding needed.

Jake's brain: Am being poked somewhere. Doesn't matter – someone else will sort it out – it's the weekend.

Kate's brain: The following jobs are not getting done. Window of the spare room won't open. The hallway needs repainting. New chest of drawers is still flat-packed. Grass in the back garden is over half an inch long. Two pictures require

29

	putting up. There are leaves on the front drive. Several items must be brought down from the loft.
Jake's brain:	Fried breakfast. *Football Focus*. Afternoon drinking.

Kate gets up, sighs loudly, flushes toilet twice.

Jake's brain:	More room in bed suddenly. Adopt star shape, hog every spare inch of mattress. Fart loudly. Revel in it.
Kate's brain:	No jobs are being done. Grass is growing as he sleeps. And the front door needs fixing. Eight jobs now. Must wake Jake. Will remove the duvet.
Jake's brain:	Duvet is slipping off me. Doesn't matter – someone else will sort it out – it's the weekend.
Kate's brain:	What the hell is that smell?
Jake's brain:	Hang on, I've been here before. Trouble is brewing. Pretend to be asleep.
Kate's brain:	Don't think you're fooling anyone. You are mine, and I shall use you as I see fit. Shake partner violently.
Jake's brain:	Am being shaken. Battle is being lost. Try pleading. Beg for another half hour.
Kate's brain:	I am holding all the cards. Negotiate a grossly unfair compromise. 'Five minutes.'
Jake's brain:	'Fifteen.'
Kate's brain:	'Ten, and then I'm getting the flannel.'
Jake's brain:	Fuck this for a game of soldiers. I might as well start working weekends. At least then I'd get a bit of peace. Try desperately to muster a pre-emptive fart of protest.

Jake climbed out of bed and began to dress himself in quiet melancholy. His real concern was that he never woke up unreasonably early on a Saturday morning, fixed his girlfriend with a beady eye and said, 'There's a long list of chores I want you to waste your weekend doing for me.' There just didn't seem to be any fairness to it. However, he let this remain a silent gripe. That way he could enjoy it more. If he voiced it out loud, it would become an issue, and would be sullied by counter-arguments from Kate. As it was, silent and unsaid within his brain, it was pure, a grievance untainted by an opposing perspective, free to fester away and swell to gigantic proportions. Occasionally Jake would feed it with new injustices, stoking its fires, filling its belly. But there was another issue, a much wider issue. As far as Jake could see, none of the jobs really needed doing. For a few months now he had begun to suspect that rather than find fault with the relationship, his girlfriend was merely finding fault with the location in which the relationship took place.

Today, Kate was even more insistent that Jake allowed his meagre two days off work to be blighted by menial household tasks. There were, as she mentioned approximately two thousand times, visitors coming in a mere five hours, visitors who would doubtless tramp out of the house in disgust if, for example, any chests of drawers hidden in the spare room had yet to be assembled.

Later, as Jake pieced together the flat-packed item of furniture, swearing liberally at the MENSA-level instructions helpfully provided by Ikea to increase your brain power, he conceded that he was actually quite excited about the visitors. They rarely had people over, and when they did it was never anybody even remotely related to him, for Jake came from the world's smallest family. Two only-child parents who only had one son. Grand total of three. Number of surviving grandparents: none. Number of cousins: none. Number of uncles and aunties: none. Number of half-uncles: one. Number of half-uncles with a severe allergy to spending money: one. Uncle Norbert. And he was coming today with his wife Elizabeth. Christ, it was almost a houseful.

Half-uncle Norbert

'Come on, Norbert, get on with it,' his wife Elizabeth urged him.

'I'm going as quick as I can.'

'Well do it quicker.'

'How about that?'

'A bit better, I suppose.'

Norbert moved his fingers with as much dexterity as he could muster. 'Is that the right spot?'

'It looks right, but it's not doing anything.'

'I'll try something else.'

'Jake and Kate are expecting us.'

'Let me just fiddle with it a bit longer.'

'Well hurry up then.'

'Do you want to have a go?'

'Me?'

'Maybe you'll have a bit more luck.'

'I doubt it.'

'Suit yourself then,' he said sulkily, 'I'm coming out.' Norbert slid himself out from under the car and rubbed his hands on a rag.

'I said you should have taken it to the garage. It's been getting worse for months.'

'You know how I feel about garages. Anyway, I think I've tightened that nut. Turn the key again.'

'Nothing. Come on, we've got to do something.'

Norbert stared at the car in silent dismay. 'Right, we'll get the bus,' he said.

'The bus? It's miles and we've only got twenty minutes. It'll have to be a taxi.'

'We are *not* getting a taxi. You know how I feel about taxis.'

'Well what then?'

'Don't panic. I'll ring them, say we're going to be late.' Norbert strode into the house before his wife had time to protest and picked up the receiver.

Jake was surprised by a vaguely familiar noise, which took a couple of seconds to pin down. Then he realized it was the phone. Its ringing was a rare event, not because he and Kate were especially unpopular, but because his girlfriend's Internet addiction meant that the line was almost permanently downloading messages like: 'R U m/f, age, * sign?' or 'Send pix 1-2-1 m23'.

'Hello,' he said. A female voice answered.

'Hello. This is the operator. Would you accept a reverse-charge call from, um, your uncle Norbert?'

Jake sighed. 'Yes,' he replied.

The female voice was replaced by an older, drier, male one. 'Jake? It's Norbert. We're running late. Spot of bother with the car.'

'Right.'

'So we're a bit stuck. Elizabeth wants us to take the bus, but you know me, I wouldn't see any wife of mine in anything but the luxury she deserves.'

'Get a taxi, then.'

'I would, you know, of course. But . . .'

'But what?'

'You know how I feel about taxis.'

Jake sighed again. 'Or the train.'

'We would, really we would . . .'

There could only be one winner in a struggle like this, and Jake saw that it wasn't going to be him. 'I'll come and get you,' he said, quickly conceding defeat.

'I couldn't—'

'I'll get you,' Jake repeated.

'Right-o,' Uncle Norbert replied. 'See you in a bit.'

Jake put the phone down and called to his girlfriend, 'Kate, I'm going to pick them up. Lock up the valuables – they'll be here in half an hour.'

Slow-motion Explosion

Bridgeton was a market town, small enough that your business could be known by people you didn't care for, but large enough that you could lose yourself among strangers. Like a slow-motion explosion, the town was gradually erupting outwards, leaving a vacuum at its epicentre, as supermarkets you had to drive to sucked people out to the periphery and town-centre shops you could walk to closed. One of the reasons people preferred to use their cars rather than their feet was that Bridgeton abided by the Universal Law of Small Town Transportation – the more isolated the place, the greater the preoccupation with cars and motorbikes, as if these vehicles could one day take you far enough from home to be happy.

The drive to his uncle's house would usually have taken fifteen minutes, but a large queue of traffic for the colossal new Safebury's hampered his progress. Small-town frustrations aside, Bridgeton was far from an unpleasant place to live, Jake thought to himself as he changed from first to second and back to first again. On the contrary, it had many advantages over the cities he had spent varying amounts of time in. London, Leeds and Manchester had all been very interesting places. In fact, if you liked high property prices, never being able to park, gangs of rough youths, indecipherable graffiti, eternal congestion and not knowing anybody, they were ideal. But Bridgeton's overriding bonus was that it was easy. Everything, apart from his uncle's house, was close, convenient and accessible.

Obviously its amenities weren't exactly cutting-edge, but Jake saw this as a plus. Who wanted to see a film the day it was released? Far better to wait a couple of weeks until the rest of the country could ring you up and tell you not to bother. And what was the point in having a ballet or opera house? In fact, what was the point in ballet or opera anyway? Touring bands rarely troubled Bridgeton with their presence, and again, this didn't bother Jake, who was too old to waste his time standing at the back of a large room with a pint of warm beer worrying about his hearing. All in all, Jake believed, access to cultural events only made you feel bad that you weren't as cultured as you thought you should be. And because such facilities were there, you got suckered into doing misguided things like standing in front of a blank canvas for twenty minutes vainly wondering what the artist was trying to say – 'I've got no paint' would seem the obvious message – or listening as some bearded wonder painfully tried to get 'Blair's Britain' to rhyme with 'drowning kitten' at a poetry night. So for Jake, no amenities and very little culture meant no guilt. And no guilt meant he could devote his time to fretting about other inconsequential matters, like picking his uncle and aunt up for a lunch which would be, to say the least, interesting. In fact, as his uncle Norbert finally climbed into the car and began a minor rant about the extortionate cost of mobile phones, Jake appreciated that he should have spent more time reminding his girlfriend about the potential bedlam to come.

On the drive back, Jake reflected that one area of the arts that Bridgeton did excel in was creative drinking. There were more pubs in the town than in almost any other place Jake had ever lived, London included. A pub crawl in Bridgeton could be a dangerous and expensive venture. Jake drove past the Lime Kiln Inn, carried on to the Goose, turned left at the Three Cheers Wine Bar and carried straight on at the Nag's Head. There were thirty-eight drinking venues within a half-mile radius, and they were always full. Given the relatively modest population of the place, this seemed to defy logic. Either most of the people were drinking most of the time, or punters were being bussed in from neighbouring towns to make up the numbers. As Norbert continued to complain, Jake reflected that the only time Bridgeton really got together as a community was at pub kicking-out time, and then it was a very literal getting together, with all too real kicking.

When Jake, Norbert and Elizabeth eventually returned, Kate was on the phone, rustling up a take-away for lunch. 'I hope you don't mind me not cooking, it's just that I'm so busy at the moment,' she lied. 'And the French restaurant in town delivers for free if you order wine as well. Should be here any minute.'

Norbert was ushered to the table and sat down. 'You bought wine from a restaurant?' he asked. There was a keen note of interest in his voice.

'What's wrong with that?'

'Well I would have thought with the money that restaurants charge—' Elizabeth, sitting to his right, appeared to nudge her husband.

'Yes?'

'That you could have bought several—' He was nudged again, this time more painfully, and decided to leave it there. 'Nothing,' he answered irritably. It had occurred to Norbert some time in his late teens that all women were annoying to greater or lesser degrees. The more time you spent with them the more annoying they became, and the less time you spent, the better. To confuse the picture, a short time with some women was very annoying, while a long time with others was only mildly vexing. Elizabeth fitted the latter category. Norbert found he could tolerate her sometimes for up to several continuous hours without needing to leave the house. This was good, since they had been together now for eleven years, a grand total, he calculated, of over ninety thousand hours.

'Still, if you don't want wine, Norbert, you can always have some orange juice or something,' Kate said.

'What make is it?'

'Make?' Kate regarded him quizzically. 'Diamonte, I think.'

'Ah well, there's another example. You see, current thinking suggests that a small number of manufacturers produce most of the different brands of foods available. So supermarket orange juices are generally made in the same factory as posh drinks. The man from Diamonte he say, "Yes! Kwiksave economy grapefruit juice? We'll do that. We'll just water it down a bit." That's why it always pays to buy economy-brand groceries.'

'Right,' Kate said slowly. She glanced at Jake, who raised his eyebrows slightly. He really should have explained about Uncle Norbert. Although his girl-friend had met him a couple of times before, both had been fleeting visits, with little time for his eccentricities to make themselves obvious, eccentricities which appeared to be becoming ever more extreme. 'Or you could have some mineral water, if you like,' Kate offered. Jake winced at the suggestion. They were already deep enough in the conversational minefield.

Elizabeth spiked her husband with a menacing glare, which he chose to overlook. 'Mineral water?' He seemed agitated, and was almost twitching. '*Mineral water?* Here – pass me the bottle. Why would anyone buy . . . look, answer me this, Kate. When was the last time you came across a naturally sparkling spring in the Mendips bubbling over with two quid's worth of minerals? And "Filtered through layers of rocks". What's that all about? Personally I'd pay *not* to drink something which has been swilling around a load of manky boulders and stones. And naturally carbonated. *Naturally* carbonated? How often is water fizzy? Is the ocean fizzy? Do streams effervesce? Do lakes have bubbles in them?'

Norbert's momentum was interrupted by the doorbell. Kate seized the opportunity to answer it, taking Jake's credit card. A couple of minutes later, during which Jake tried to steer the conversation away from anything involving expenditure, Kate returned with the takeaway, and proceeded to serve. As they ate, Kate and Elizabeth chatted, and Norbert leaned across to Jake.

'Your energy bills high here, Jake?' he asked quietly.

'Phone and electricity are killing me,' he said, glancing at his girlfriend, who was deep in conversation with Elizabeth.

'You know, Jake, between you and me, I once discovered an entirely efficient and totally renewable source of energy.'

'Really? How did that work then?'

'Electrical Perpetual Motion.'

'How do you mean?'

'What I did was this. I adapted as many of our household gadgets as possible to run on batteries. Easy for small items – Walkmen, remote controls, radios, torches et cetera, for which battery power was the only option. But it was the bigger ones that were draining current from the mains and racking up the bills. The iron, the CD player, the toaster, the upstairs portable television, the kettle. What I needed to make the leap from the small to the large was to get the big items working on batteries.'

Jake smiled at his uncle. He had a certain enthusiasm which was infectious. Saving money was his passion, his zeal. Jake imagined other people missed this quality in him as he bemoaned the cost of virtually everything. As long as you weren't married to him for a protracted period, he was engaging company. 'Yeah?'

'So I used car batteries. Which worked fine for the black and white portable and the CD player. The toaster and the kettle were more of a struggle, but I got them going in the end.'

'Surely you're still using electricity, which you had to pay for?'

'Not, and this was the clever bit, if I recharged all the batteries at work. I was effectively smuggling electricity home with me, and was therefore using free energy.' Norbert drank some mineral water. Despite his moral objection to the stuff, he was still willing to consume it, provided someone else had paid. 'It was while recharging my car battery one evening in the office, hidden under my desk, that I came to realize the possibilities of the scheme. If you were patient, you could watch TV, listen to music, have a cup of tepid tea and some warm bread, and all for free. Except for the bread and the tea bag. And then – hey presto! – bring the battery back into work the next morning, and charge it again. Perpetual motion.'

'And does it save a lot?'

'Not any more, since I stopped working. But there was potential.'

'And now?'

An irritable twitch flared around Norbert's mouth. 'Elizabeth, for some unknown reason, refuses to take car batteries into work with her to recharge.'

Jake watched his aunt for a moment. She was probably the wrong side of forty, but there was still a spark about her. It was there in her eyes, playful and yet standing no nonsense. She was a teacher, one you would have hated as a pupil but respected as an adult. Taking in her tightly pinned-back hair, Jake knew who wore the Oxfam trousers at home. Norbert was silent, having imparted enough wisdom to be happy. Eventually the afternoon petered out, and Jake once again followed the trail of pubs and supermarkets to his relatives' house, where he dropped them off. Norbert shook his hand and thanked him for the lunch, suggesting that he should come over for a meal some time soon. Jake asked whether Norbert would require a contribution for the food. His uncle simply smiled before trailing Elizabeth up the drive. Jake returned slowly via the ring road, hoping most of the washing-up would be done by the time he arrived.

A couple of days later, he realized he should never have driven them home. Instead, he should have kept them at his own house, safe and secure, away from the dangers of a sporadically dangerous world. It would have spared them all an enormous amount of suffering in the long run.

Secret Acts of Sabotage

Monday 8:20 a.m.

At home on Monday morning, Norbert called up to his wife, 'Tea, dear? I've put the kettle on.'

'Yes,' came the reply. 'But I want a fresh bag.'

'Right-o.' Norbert stood in the kitchen, watching the kettle eagerly. It was getting hotter, and his finger hovered over the mains switch. The last thing on earth he wanted was for it to come to the boil. As he often told his wife, if you're boiling, you're wasting. Steam is an expensive luxury, the by-product of heating water past the temperature necessary for making tea. We don't drink steam – we drink water. He also pointed out that it was folly to make a drink too hot, when you only had to wait for it to cool again before you could consume it without taking the roof of your mouth off. And so, with the first whiff of vapour, he unplugged the kettle and emptied its entire contents, which filled the mug exactly. Again, it was wasteful in terms of time, energy and money (especially money) to heat more water than you absolutely needed. He prised a used tea bag from the sideboard and partially resuscitated it in the water. Exhaustive experimentation had told him that tea bags would make four cups each if treated with respect. Next, Norbert plucked a tiny carton of milk substitute from a carrier bag stuffed with similar items plundered from fast-food restaurants, and bravely battled with its foil lid. The small amount of UHT extra-skimmed low-fat guaranteed-milk-free milk which didn't spill over his fingers was poured into the cup. Happy with the operation, he took it up to his wife, who examined it suspiciously.

'Nice meal at Jake's over the weekend, don't you think?' he said, sitting down on the bed.

'Nice? You mean free.'

'I mean he's a nice chap. Don't see enough of him.'

'Yeah. He's OK.'

'Interesting day ahead?'

'Lesson after lesson of ungrateful bastards,' she answered, taking a wary sip from the mug.

'I've made you some sandwiches.'

'Right.'

'Only you might want to check they're OK. The fish paste said eat by yesterday.'

'So why did you put it in?'

Norbert stared at her in surprise. 'It was a special offer.'

Elizabeth appeared close to words but remained mute, putting the mug down and combing her hair with masochistic force. 'And you?'

'There's a sale at Aldis. Got to get there early before the grannies.'

'Competing with grannies, eh? You're really up against the big boys these days.'

Norbert thought he might have detected an edge of sarcasm but let it pass. He wasn't very good with irony, and deep down he knew he had been right to quit his job. 'They've got a nose for it, old people,' he said. 'Ageing seems to ruin all your faculties apart from the important one – bargain hunting.'

'Important?'

'Vitally important. Where would we be without economical goods?'

'Enjoying ourselves somewhere decadent instead of just scraping by?'

Again, Norbert overlooked his wife's retaliation. She would see, one day. He just had to convince her. 'Not drinking your tea?' he asked.

'What tea?'

'On the side there.'

'That isn't tea.'

'What is it then?'

'At a rough guess, warm puddle water infused with some sort of white stuff – Tippex, maybe.'

'It's long-life milk. Lasts for ever, actually.'

'So will you, by the look of things,' she said, putting down her hairbrush. 'And I don't see that as an advantage.'

'Well, waste not, spend not,' Norbert countered, enjoying the opportunity to antagonize his wife with one of his favourite expressions. He picked up the much criticized beverage. Taking an optimistic swig, he grimaced as its sheer tastelessness sucked the moisture from his mouth.

'Anyway, I've got to go. Year Ten aren't going to teach themselves Human Reproduction. Mind you, looking at some of them . . .' Elizabeth glanced out of the window towards the bus stop. 'Ah, Eric's awake already,' she said.

'Well, it's not as if he's got much of a bed to lounge around in.'

Elizabeth gave her husband a weak smile, and trotted out of the house with the sandwiches safely tucked away.

Eric, the tramp who appeared to live perpetually in the bus shelter, was pleased to see her, as he was every day. 'Morning,' he said, stooping slightly more than was natural even for him.

'Hello, Eric.'

'What's on the bloody menu today?'

'Fish paste,' Elizabeth said, dragging the sandwiches out of her bag and handing them over.

'Fuckingsmashing,' he replied.

'Right, there you are. I'll see you tomorrow.'

'Ah, youbastardbloodybastard!' he shouted as a car drove by. 'Yes, tomorrow. Wankingfuckingwanker.' Another car was greeted with his fist. 'Tomorrow. Good.'

Over the last few months, Elizabeth had been conducting an unofficial experiment into the nutritional dangers of Norbert's sandwiches. So far, Eric didn't seem any the worse for wear, though in fairness, it would have taken a major downturn in his health for him to appear noticeably iller than he already did. He was a large man who oozed disease and ruin. He drank and smoked as much as he possibly could, and constantly swore at passing motorists. Although intimidating, Eric knew which side his bread was buttered on, and Elizabeth was always more than happy to hand her food over to him. Besides, it wasn't as if fish paste would be the ideal accompaniment for the glass of champagne that she always, always had with her lunch, even if she was only grabbing a cheese sandwich. The joy this hidden ritual brought Elizabeth verged on the orgasmic. She would feel a tingle down below, at the front, in that special spot, the place she carried her purse, as if it was suddenly shedding weight and floating away empty. And if she felt spent afterwards, it came from a very tangible sense of handing over money, money which Norbert couldn't get his hands on, rather than any sexual fulfilment.

Elizabeth often thought about her husband. Balance was what a marriage required. It might have seemed out of kilter from the outside, but her secret acts of sabotage more than compensated for Norbert's spendthrift ways. She glanced at Eric's clothes. They had once belonged to her husband. As well as food, she palmed random items of his wardrobe off on the tramp when she felt herself going under, a small but buoyant lifejacket that kept her sane and prolonged the marriage. Without these minor revenges for her husband's meanness, the relationship would have shattered years ago. The thought that a homeless man was walking around in Norbert's clothes, and was considerably better dressed than her husband most of the time, gave her a feeling of quiet victory.

A bus arrived and Elizabeth stepped aboard, day-dreaming while it juddered her in the direction of work. Eric sat down on a nearby bench and put the sandwiches in his pocket. He opened a can of Tennent's Special, and began swearing at as many cars as he could.

Norbert waited a minute or so after his wife's bus had departed, and made his way into the spare room. Locking it from the inside, he bent down and felt about under the bed. His hand gripped the small bundle he kept there, which he pulled out. Glancing up at the lock to double-check he was safe, he unwrapped his sacred possession, which was housed in an oily cloth. The gun stared back at him, full of promise. He picked it up and straightened in front of the mirror, watching himself with the object. He pointed the gun at the mirror and pulled the trigger. It wasn't loaded. Then he wiped it down with the rag before unlocking the door and walking downstairs. Picking up his coat, he slid the gun into one of its deep front pockets. He was going shopping and would be needing it today.

Risk Assessment

Monday 8:23 a.m.

Roger Johnson had a burning ambition he had nurtured since adolescence. While the ambition was not particularly unusual, the stringency with which Roger devoted himself to it bordered on the pathological. It was his overriding goal in life not to be maimed, killed, harmed, injured, wounded, hurt, impaired or otherwise damaged in any way. What Roger did at home and in his spare time was governed by this single objective, and when he had chosen himself an occupation, this too had satisfied his rigid criteria. By the time he finished college, Roger had already consulted the statistics. He had discovered that the three most common fatal injuries at work were falling from a height, being struck by a moving vehicle and being struck by a moving object, and that the most common forms of serious mutilation were multiple fractures, concussion and internal injuries. These risks obviously precluded a number of occupations, such as directing traffic at busy intersections, handling explosives, cleaning skyscraper windows and running a corner shop without a weapon.

Next, he found out that the fatal-injury rate for the self-employed was twice that for employees, which ruled out setting up his own business. In terms of sector, agriculture, manufacturing and construction had almost suicidal rates of fatal and non-fatal injuries compared with service industries. For those still alive, the most common injury events − 120 per 100,000 people per year − were slips, trips and falls, closely followed by lifting, handling and carrying. Statistically, offices were safer than almost anywhere. Within a typical office-based environment, the following locations were increasingly hazardous: the sales area, the entrance or exit, the kitchen, the staffroom, the car park, the warehouse and, to be avoided at all costs, the loading bay.

Assuming you were able to stay in your office, it was still reasonably likely that you would trip, fall over an obstruction, fall from a ladder or chair, be struck by a flying object from a shelf, walk into a fixed object, have a door slammed in your face or damage yourself lifting something once every ten years. What this would do to you, in reverse order of popularity, was fracture your arm, shoulder, collarbone, wrist, ankle, leg, hip or thigh; internally injure your head or torso; sprain your back, leg, ankle, wrist or thigh; lacerate your finger, leg, hand or head; or, if you were especially unlucky, any combination of the above. All in all, therefore, Roger had decided from an early age that what he needed was a job in a service industry, working for someone else, well away from moving vehicles or heavy objects, with good clear walkways, no carrying, no heights, no agricultural or manu-facturing responsibilities, in an office or sales area, well away from shelving, doors, sharp objects and, most of all, loading bays.

Only one career path could satisfy such a rigorous set of criteria. And thus the door to Hazard Prevention opened gradually and carefully in front of Roger without damaging any of his limbs. The thing about Hazard Prevention, Roger had concluded after studying the statistics, was that it was undeniably safe.

Peering apprehensively through the window of his bungalow (*Domestic Safety Rule One: Stairs are more likely to kill you than snakes*), Roger wished the rest of the world was equally predictable. 'It's a jungle out there,' he said, sighing loudly.

'That's what I've been telling you for ages, Rog,' his wife Pauline said, joining him at the window, 'but you won't listen.' Pauline was a pale, insipid woman whose colour had long since run. She often thought she should have run along with it, but it was too late. Protracted marriage to Roger had seen to that. And besides, with her colour had gone her nerve.

'Something's got to be done about it.'

'So why don't you do something?'

'It's just not safe any more.'

'But we can't go on living like this for ever,' she said, following the direction of her husband's gaze.

'There's no point taking needless risks though.'

Pauline continued to stare irritably at the waist-high grass of their garden and felt her patience wane. 'Look, it's only a bloody lawnmower!'

'Do you have any idea how many people are injured in this country by faulty lawnmowers?'

'None?'

'No. Considerably more than that,' Roger replied.

'Get a gardener then.'

'I don't think that would be very sensible. Asking an unregistered workman to use an electric mower that we haven't even had any checks done on . . .'

'But I can't use the garden.'

'Darling, as I've told you before, research has shown that you are three times more likely to die in your garden than in your house.'

Pauline looked as though she might scream. Instead

she sought to remove the source of her irritation. 'You'll be late for work,' she said encouragingly.

'Yes. But better to arrive late than dead on time,' her husband replied. He always said this, a half pun which worked safety into travel. Indeed, whenever he lectured bored workers on the dangers of transportation, he did his best to mention it. In the joke-free environment of Roger's seminars, it rarely failed to stand out as a beacon of wit.

'Here,' his wife said, briskly passing him his motorcycle gloves. Roger dropped them, picked them up again and then put them on. Then he struggled into his helmet, squeezing his ears through its padded interior. Pauline zipped up his leathers and Roger dipped his head so she could kiss his helmet. This used to have altogether different connotations earlier in their marriage, but now was as close to affection as they came. 'Be careful,' she said, ushering him towards the door.

'What?' he asked, his voice muted through the layers of protection.

'Be careful!' Pauline shouted.

'Right-o. You know me. Careful is as careful does.' He strode purposefully out of the front door and opened the garage. Inside was his gleaming silver dream-machine. No matter how many times he gazed at it, he was still in love. He ran his gloved fingers over its sleek metal surfaces and felt a tingle of excitement. Whatever your views on safety, Roger said to himself, extracting the key from his pocket, you had to have some fun.

Slips, Trips and Falls

Monday 8:36 a.m.

'You OK?' Jake asked.
 'I'm bored,' Kate told him.
 'Bored of what?'
 'Bored of everything.'
 'Like what?'
 'Like your relatives.'
 'They've only been here once.'
 'Like everything else as well,' she said.
 'Name me one thing.'
 'I can't.'
 'Try.'
 'I am.'
 'Try harder.'
 'You.'
 'What?'
 'I'm bored of you and your questions.'
 'You're bored of me asking you why you're bored?'
 'Aha.'
 'I was only trying to help.'
 'Well you're not.'

'But don't you think this has stopped you being bored?'

'What?'

'This argument.'

'Who's arguing?'

'We are.'

'You might be, but I'm not.'

'I can't be arguing with myself.'

'Sounds like it to me.'

Jake rubbed his face. 'I'd better go,' he said.

'I guess you had,' Kate replied, turning round and heading for the computer.

'Back at six thirty,' he called after her.

First thing Monday morning was not a good time for safety, because it meant dealing with the mess that was last thing Friday afternoon. And last thing Friday afternoon was a twilight zone inhabited by half-pissed secretaries and feckless factory workers stumbling blindly around, dreaming of the weekend. Jake had a bad feeling about this one from the moment he saw the message on his posterboard. Roger still hadn't arrived, and Jake had therefore been unable to palm it off on him. It didn't sound the most onerous site visit, but it was always the small errands that caused all the trouble. As he left a memo for Roger, he noticed that the weekly safety slogan above his desk had changed to *Drinking Stops You Thinking*. Surreal data was presented below it. *Nationally, 537 Casualty visits last year resulted from loofah-associated mishaps*. He left the office disturbed that so many people could possibly be injured by a bathing accessory.

One of Jake's duties was to catalogue workplace accidents in the Bridgeton area, and a sorry collection of misadventure it proved to be. Every quarter the Safety Team published vivid descriptions of all incidents occurring within this period in an attempt to prevent future mishaps. Jake had been instructed to make each event an interesting story in its own right and to leave no incompetent detail unexplored in order to make the bulletin an attractive read. As a laudable aim, it failed miserably. It was just far too entertaining. The Safety Bulletin had become a cult read throughout the town. Every time an administrative assistant caught his or her finger on a paperclip, or a workman dropped a hammer on his foot, or a machinist sewed part of herself into a piece of fabric, Jake was forced to fill in a form and write up a report, which was used for the department's statistics and the general amusement of Bridgeton.

At the offices of a small legal firm on Warward Lane, between two of the town's rougher pubs, a fussy middle-aged Perm Queen ceased her typing as Jake sat down and shook her hand. He saw the look of curiosity in her eyes, an expression he encountered daily from people who didn't know him. 'Why the fuck are you missing a finger?' their faces screamed. For those brave enough to ask, Jake had a standard reply which covered all angles but stayed well away from the truth. The Perm Queen let her nosiness remain silent, however, and so he continued with his business. 'Tell me in your own words what happened,' he said, taking out his clipboard.

'Well, I was carrying this file from my desk to my boss's, when I slipped.'

Jake scribbled a note on the form in front of him. 'And what surface was this on?'

'Carpet.'

'Carpet. Right. And you say you slipped?'

'Yes.'

He looked up. 'It's just that we tend to find people trip on carpet, rather than slip. Too much friction, you see.'

'What's the difference?'

'It's hard to slip on carpet.'

'No, I mean, what difference does it make to my injury?'

'Unfortunately, on my form here, I've got to put a single tick in either "slip", "trip" or "fall" if I'm going to report your injury accurately.'

'I definitely fell, then.'

Jake's biro hovered over the box for 'fall'. 'What would you say you did first, though?'

'I slipped.'

Jake pushed the nib of the pen into the paper.

'And then I tripped.'

Jake stopped. 'You slipped, and then you tripped?'

'Yes. And then I fell.'

'So you slipped, tripped and fell?'

'I think so. Hang on.' The Perm Queen turned to a nearby colleague who was monitoring proceedings with interest. 'Alan, you saw me hurt myself on Friday after the pub. Would you say I slipped or tripped?'

'I'd have said you stumbled more than anything,' Alan replied.

'So you slipped, tripped, stumbled and fell?'

'From where I was,' Alan answered, 'she stumbled first, and then slipped and fell.'

'But she didn't trip?'

'I didn't see it.'

'No, I *definitely* tripped,' the Perm Queen insisted. 'And then I stumbled before the slip.'

'What did you trip over?'

'The carpet.'

Jake tried to remain calm. He could only tick one box – that was the rule. Two boxes and the computer, which automatically assessed his form would, apparently, implode. He was all for ticking any random box and getting back to his office. And yet he had to be accurate. The team, under his supervisor's inspired leadership, was trying to answer the vital question of whether to target slips or trips in their next mission statement. 'So the carpet had a bump or something in it?' he persevered.

'I don't think so. My shoe just sort of jarred on it, making me stumble and trip . . .'

'And slip and fall.'

'Yes.'

'Mind you, now I think about it,' Alan piped up, 'it wasn't so much a stumble as a lurch.'

'A lurch?'

'Yeah. She kind of lurched to one side, and that's what made her trip before she slipped.'

'So let me get this clear,' Jake said, taking a deep breath. 'She jarred, lurched, stumbled, tripped, slipped and then finally, eventually, when she could go on no longer, fell over and sprained her wrist?'

'Yes.'

'Only it's not so much sprained as strained.'

Jake took another deep breath. This was a whole other ball game. On page 11, section C, lurked two ominous and empty boxes, one marked 'sprain' and the other 'strain'. He recalled Roger insisting during a meeting of gigantically tedious proportions that the department's inspectors differentiate between the two. Due to the imminent unconsciousness of all present, it was voted through.

'And you can tell the difference?' Jake asked.

'A sprain is more of a weakness, isn't it?'

'And a strain?'

'Well, it's more strained, if anything. Stands to reason.'

'Yep, she's right,' Alan agreed helpfully.

'So it's strained.'

'It throbs as well.'

'Throbs?'

'And might be broken.'

'I think you'd know if it was broken,' Jake answered, patience rapidly ebbing.

'Why? I'm not a doctor, you know.'

'I just mean—'

'Are you a doctor?'

'No.'

'Then how do you know it's not broken?'

'Because you were typing with it when I came in,' Jake said quietly to himself, flicking through the other fourteen pages of the form. This was going nowhere.

'And I'm thinking of suing,' the Perm Queen added.

'You're going to sue your employer?'

'Yep. That carpet is dangerous.'

Jake ran his eyes over the innocuous floor covering and blew slow air out of the side of his mouth. 'So you're going to sue the solicitor you work for?'

'I've got a good case. Someone's got to be to blame . . . might ring one of those claim companies you see on TV.'

Jake peered through her glasses and into her eyes. Another Claim Blamer. For some people, there were no accidents, just malicious acts perpetrated by a world that was out to get them. He anticipated her next question.

'So what do you think my chances are?'

'For returning to work from the pub, falling over and suing the legal expert who's your boss?' Jake stood up and closed the form triumphantly. 'I advise you go for it.'

The Perm Queen smiled sycophantically. 'Great,' she replied.

'Look, I've got what I need,' he said. 'I suggest you walk carefully to your local surgery and have a doctor examine your wrist, being careful not to jar, lurch, trip, slip, stumble or fall on your way.' Jake turned round and walked out, having administered sufficient sarcasm to meet the needs of the situation. He ticked a few boxes as he made his way back, and then, at the back of the form, wrote POP in large letters.

Worthlessness

Monday 6:12 p.m.

In a side road close to his house, surrounded by slumbering taxi drivers, Jake Cooper, thirty-two, finally came to the conclusion that had been eluding him for so long: he was utterly worthless. His recent quest was at an end, and he put his pen down and scoured the piece of paper he was holding, running over the summary of the situation. He had been working for twelve years. During that time he had earned roughly 210,000 pounds – a very reasonable sum when lumped all together. In fact, it was a fifth of a million pounds. And that was just the legitimate stuff. There was more, but he didn't like to remember the other cash. With its memory came a dull ache of dread.

Still.

Taking his income as a whole, a bystander may therefore have believed that he had something tangible to his name. A savings account, some investments, positive equity. They would, as he now appreciated, be very much mistaken. And worse than this was that having calculated his net worth, he discovered he was worth nothing at all. Actually, he was worse off than

57

that. He *owed* money. Twelve years of mildly taxing labour and he was more impoverished than when he had started. Working was literally making him poor! Surely something was wrong. He went through the financial summary again on paper, and then double-checked using the laptop he had bought to determine precisely how much in debt he was. Eighteen thousand, eight hundred and thirty-one pounds, eleven pence, including the computer, which was a good one, with a price to match.

The problem, Jake appreciated, was the disparity between his ability to spend and his ability to earn. As far as he could see, there didn't appear to be anything inherently wrong with his spending skills. Indeed, these were very much at the peak of their form. He could still buy like there was no tomorrow, as the laptop and recent new car testified. No, the real issue was that his salary rarely raised its game in line with his purchasing requirements. If anything, he was being let down by his pay packet. Sitting and staring at the small grey digits on the screen, displaying the number 18831.111111112 with a minus sign hanging ominously in front of it, superimposed on a graph with a suicidal downhill slope, Jake realized for the first time that something had to change. He had been badly off-balance for a number of years, and things were beginning to catch up with him.

The obvious solution was to earn more money, although this was easier said than done. There wasn't so much a career path in safety inspection as a single lowly step, from Deputy Executive Hazard Prevention Officer to Assistant Executive Hazard Prevention Officer. Roger, one day, might make Assistant Executive level, at a push. Jake, if he was entirely honest with himself, was facing a protracted – if not permanent – stint at Deputy level.

He started the engine of his efficient German car and drove round the corner to the house he shared with his thoroughly inefficient girlfriend. Although Jake had always been useless with money, at least it had been his own money. But now he had a partner in crime. Two disasters spending one salary. The maths weren't good. He pulled into the cul-de-sac and as he glanced through the living-room curtains on his way into the house, Jake told himself that from now on, money was going to become a new thing to argue about. Persuading people to fill in the correct form before embarking on a mildly risky endeavour was by no means an extravagantly well-paid job. Kate had never professed much of an interest in working, and he couldn't blame her for that. But it was time for change. Very painful change. Still, tonight was the single night of the week that Jake genuinely looked forward to. It was DangerClub night. A cup of tea, a dubious lasagne, a couple of phone calls and a pulse-racing escape to his friend Tim's house. And, best of all, it was free.

Inside, Kate was typing. Without looking up, she said, 'Do you fancy fish fingers for tea?'

'Have you been out shopping?' Jake asked, taken aback that lasagne wasn't on the menu.

'No. Someone posted them through the door.'

'Seriously?'

'Seriously. A few minutes after you left for work.'

'Sounds a bit weird.'

'They'd been opened as well.'

'We definitely won't be eating them then.'

'Why not?'

'It's not exactly safe to eat food which has—'

'You know,' she said, turning to face him, 'you're becoming a real bore about safety.'

Jake ignored the jibe. 'Where's the box?'

'In the freezer. Why?'

'I just want to have a look.'

In the kitchen, Jake pulled the fish fingers out from under a pile of lasagne boxes and frozen-chip packets. He examined the package suspiciously. On the front

59

the label said, 'Ten Prime Quality Fish Fingers, Made with Real Fish'. He opened it and tipped the contents onto the worktop, frowning. Why the hell would someone have posted fish fingers through the letterbox? Jake might be in financial trouble, but cod-based snacks were unlikely to cure his ills. He began to replace them in the box, and as he did so a nasty thought occurred to him. He counted the crumb-coated foodstuff. Nine. The digits of both his hands were spread across the kitchen surface. He examined the stump of his ring finger. Nine indeed.

Sex and Beards

Monday 10:07 a.m.

As Norbert stood at the bus stop, being eyed suspiciously by Eric the tramp, he caught sight of himself
in the glass of an adjoining phonebox. What he saw
didn't please him, and he wondered momentarily
whether he was looking at a reflection of the vagrant.
On closer inspection, however, the tramp appeared
considerably better dressed than he was. There was
something vaguely familiar about his clothes as well,
he fancied. Maybe they bought from the same charity
shops. Either way, Norbert was forced to admit that there
was a faded look about his own mirror image, as if he
had been put through the wash once too often. His hair
was three-quarters grey, the remainder having given up
the ghost and fallen out. His skin was weathered, not by
a glowing sun but by a leaching wind, and his clothes
had been around too long and needed a rest. He also had
a beard, and with good reason, for beards, Norbert
had calculated, were cheap. It didn't cost anything to
grow one, and as long as you didn't mind the mess, the
smell and the dandruff of food, it could be left for
months without being clipped.

Norbert had spent a lot of time looking into the economics of beard clippers. On the face of it, clippers were a good thing. According to his extensive research, having a beard trimmed at the barber's cost between two pounds eighty and seven ninety-nine in the Bridgeton area, depending on where you went. Clippers, on the other hand, retailed for about twenty quid. So several trims and you were quids in. So far so good. All sound common sense. But what about the batteries? What about the maintenance? What about depreciation? What about mechanical failure? At this point, Norbert had decided clippers might not be such a good investment, and had switched his attention to scissors. A decent pair of scissors? Four ninety-nine. A decent pair of scissors after twenty minutes of haggling in the corner shop? Four eighty-nine and a free can of slightly expired beans. So there you are – a lifetime's beard care for four eighty-nine and a free can of slightly expired beans. No razors, no aftershave, no moisturizer, no brush, no blades, no nothing.

And with more of your face covered in hair, Norbert had discovered, came other knock-on benefits. Toothpaste, for example. No point in cleaning your teeth as much if they weren't going to be seen. Of course, you didn't want to leave yourself liable to dental bills, so not cleaning them altogether was a bad idea, but even if you concentrated more on your molars than your incisors, toothpaste savings would be appreciable over a number of years. And there were other pluses. First, more beardness meant less facial area to wash and hence lower soap usage. Second, the greater the beard the lower the chance of sexual intercourse.

The bus arrived and Norbert begrudgingly handed over seventy-five pence after unsuccessfully asking for a pensioner's discount. He continued to ponder. On the superficial level, he was well aware that less sexual activity might not appear to be an advantage.

Sex was a beautiful act, if performed correctly. And by this he meant cheaply, which of course meant without flowers, meals or contraception. Which was dangerous territory given the potential for accidents and the subsequently exorbitant cost of rearing children. So whatever you tried, sex was an expensive business, even if you were married, and was to be avoided if at all possible. In fact, as he thought about his wife, he couldn't help feeling that Elizabeth represented poor value for money on this front more than almost any other. Still, they were stuck with each other now, and divorce was far from an attractive financial proposition. The bus staggered to a halt and Norbert gave up his musings on the economy of sex and beards in favour of making rapid progress towards Aldis. This morning was Red Sticker morning. There were serious bargains to be had.

That Norbert found himself trekking to low-grade supermarkets on Monday mornings was down to a realization that had dawned on him almost seven years previously in his job as an accountant. Sitting at his desk and examining his bank account details, he became conscious that it wasn't what he earned that determined how rich he would ever be, it was something else, something which would always be holding him back unless he addressed it head-on. Everything he had ever learned as an accountant told him that all gains are tempered by losses. Your balance, at the end of the financial year, is the net result of profits minus deficits. If your losses are high, then your profits are low. He watched workmates kill themselves for an extra two grand a year, at the same time raising their net losses by spending an extra three on making themselves feel better, thereby more than cancelling out any gains they had made. Promotion appeared merely to make most other accountants worse off. They worked harder to earn more so that they could spend more, and in doing so felt they could now afford to borrow more. They bought flasher cars, bigger houses, more luxurious gadgets and more Pringle jumpers, and all of these sought to undermine them. Flasher cars cost more to run, bigger houses meant bigger mortgages, luxurious gadgets depreciated more quickly, and more Pringle jumpers meant that you would be forced to take up golf at some stage.

By consistently not being promoted he hoped to become richer, purely through minimizing his losses. And so while his colleagues slaved long hours in the desperate hope of higher wages, Norbert devoted his spare time to shifting the balance of his finances. He started at home. They had savings. Norbert used them to pay off part of their mortgage because borrowing money always costs more than you can gain from saving it. Elizabeth was appalled. What about our holidays? she asked. So holidays became the second area of rationalization. Instead of long-haul flights to areas of the world where taxi drivers charged a year's salary to circle the airport pretending to find your hotel, they would stay at home and sit in the garden for a week. And then he sacked the gardener and let the grass grow, persuading Elizabeth that holidays would be more exotic surrounded by waist-high vegetation. And so on, until inevitably Norbert made straight for the heart of the issue. He gave up his job, and decided to devote himself to Red Sticker days.

Aldis was packed with coffin-dodgers. It always was on Mondays. There was a knack to Red Sticker shopping, and these were Norbert's tactics. He hung around near the staffroom entrance, monitoring comings and goings for several minutes. Then he found what he was looking for. A shopfloor worker with a pricing gun. Norbert sprang into action. The woman scanned her clipboard and made her way carefully up and down each aisle, with Norbert a couple of paces behind. Wherever she marked an item down, he dived in quick – before the hardcore bargain-hunting pensioners – and snatched what was going. If it was something undesirable, or the discount wasn't high enough, he rejected it and let the wrinklies fight over it. Whenever the product was something good, he lowered it carefully into his basket and smiled in satisfaction. But there was one more money-saving step to take. After he had parted with his cash, he peeled the red stickers off and disposed of the receipt, so that Elizabeth wouldn't notice the disparity between what he had spent and what he said he had spent. This way, Norbert could pocket the difference. And it was important to keep Elizabeth in the dark as much as possible.

How Much It Costs to Run a Wife

Norbert had performed extensive research in the field of Wife Economics. For his own part, he could, he had discovered, live on seven pounds twenty-six a day. This included food, clothes, drink, bills and beard-trimming. A weekly total of around forty-four pounds. However, as he left Aldis and stood next to a dustbin peeling red stickers off his recent purchases, he rued the fact that he and Elizabeth spent around one hundred and eighty pounds a week on the above luxuries. Deducting his expenditure gave a grand and exorbitant total of one hundred and thirty-six pounds for his wife. Sharing the same house and eating the same food somehow cost Elizabeth three times as much as it cost him. And she didn't even have a beard. He had been through the sums again and again and there were no two ways about it – his wife was costing him one hundred and thirty-six pounds a week to run. That was seven grand a year! A lot of football teams cost less than that, Norbert muttered to himself, struggling vainly to remove a sticker that had attached itself to his finger.

When he first looked into the rough figures, Norbert had been on the verge of pointing this inefficiency out to his wife. However, he quickly realized that she might counter his argument by suggesting that as she was the only one working, technically Norbert was costing her forty-four pounds a week. This would have been a difficult comeback to deal with, so he had decided to let things go until he could construct a foolproof argument. In the meantime, he set about trying to discover how Elizabeth could be run more economically.

Several aspects of his wife's finances were beyond his control. Her lunches, for a start. Norbert knew very well that Elizabeth's school had a canteen which was subsidized for its staff, should she choose for some insane reason not to eat his sandwiches. They were virtually giving food away. But this wasn't, he suspected, good enough for her. She had to eat out. And although, despite repeated questioning, she would never tell him how much she spent, he knew it wasn't cheap.

The second sphere of spending Norbert had little influence over was her habit of buying from catalogues. Since this didn't involve actually shopping, there was no way he could follow her around and censor her outgoings. The only thing he did know was that every few weeks a package bearing her name arrived at the door. Norbert had valiantly tried refusing to sign for them, but the delivery man was always very insistent, and if he didn't comply, simply turned up later when Her-in-Debt was back from work.

Sometimes Norbert felt his wife had been put on the planet purely to undermine him. She was given to the ways of Satan, and was able to strike right at the heart of his being. In short, she didn't just like to spend, she positively revelled in it. Norbert had nothing against shopping per se, as long as it involved either windows or supermarkets, or both. And he, too, liked to spend. It wasn't that he was stingy, just that he was careful. There was a difference. People said so themselves. They told him that he was *careful*. Not tightwadded or mean or less likely to buy a round than a particularly religious Arab, just *careful*, and he took great pride in this. It was as if he cherished his notes and coins gently, with a father's love, or caressed each plastic card, afraid his rough fingers might rub their silver numbers away for ever. Friends told him they didn't think he was mean, as such, always with a substantial pause after the 'as such', and then a long intake of breath, just that he was – sigh – *prudent*.

His wife didn't share their optimism. While she rarely said what was undoubtedly on her mind, a number of occasions had served to reveal her thoughts on the matter. Besides, she had more devious means. She once gave Norbert's middle name as Ebenezer on the electoral roll. She signed him up to buying a crate of champagne a month from a magazine until he found out the terrible truth. She bought him a box of moth pellets. For your wallet, she screamed, slamming the door. And all because he was trying to balance their budgets, tighten their belts, put a bit of money away for a rainy day. Elizabeth said it would have to be fucking pouring before her husband got his hand in his pocket. She said they'd be swimming for their lives before he coughed up. She said Noah would have sailed on by in his huge fucking ark before Norbert got round to paying for something. In fact, she said a lot of things, mainly around a theme, with some fairly unhealthy language to boot. But, Norbert told himself, heading for the bus stop with a damaged tin of pineapple rings, some low-grade mince which needed eating today and a bottle of conditioner for heat-damaged hair, which leaked slightly, she would see in the long run.

The bus ride home was quicker than the outward journey, the morning traffic having tailed off. Norbert glanced over the details of the till receipt, as he always did. Twice in as many years he had been wrongly charged. Although both occasions represented accidental undercharging, the principle was still there – you could never be too careful. The bus slowed and Norbert muttered to himself, his stop approaching. It wasn't always easy doing what he was doing. True pioneers were generally misunderstood. He ran his eyes over the receipt he was still holding, and stood up. As the doors opened and he shuffled off the bus, he looked up from the piece of paper and spied Eric the tramp, crossing the road. Eric swigged from his can and gave him another funny look. And then something on the receipt dragged his eyes back. The fuckers! They had diddled him out of thirty pence. He calculated again, standing in the road, behind the bus, a sense of injustice consuming him. The bastards. He would return and complain. Might even be some compensation. In fact, he thought as he fingered the gun through the lining of his overcoat pocket, there was going to be more than just a refund. Serious action was called for. Just let them try to rip him off this time. He wrestled his calculator from his pocket and gave the receipt one final check.

Safety Scene #6

Close-up on a man's face. He is bearded, and his features have a dryness about them. He looks angry. One of his hands is holding a small piece of paper, which he appears to be reading. In the other, he has a calculator. We notice that his clothes are shabby, and his hair unkempt. Pan back. He is standing behind a bus. There are very few people around. A vagrant is on the opposite side of the road, drinking from a can and shouting at cars. The traffic is sporadically busy, the street a suburban A-road. We see that the speed of passing vehicles is brisk. We stay with the main character as he concentrates all his attention on the scrap of paper, before taking his calculator in the same hand and tapping its keys with the other. In the background, a couple of elderly people board the bus, which closes its doors with a hiss. The man glances up at the noise, and then returns his attention to the calculator. We hear the engine note of the vehicle rise, and glimpse one of its indicators begin to flash. We return to the man's face. His brow is still furiously knotted, and he is muttering to himself. We hear the muted sounds of calculator keys being tapped. Cut back to the traffic. A few cars pass close by and at speed, weaving around the bus. The man takes a step forward from behind it.

A few moments later there is a sharp screech of tyres and the sickening thud of flesh against metal.

A pause.

Two more quick thuds as heavy tyres pass over the body.

It is all over.

Fade slowly out from the scene, watching a rivulet of blood run over into the tarmac.

The Danger Club

Monday 7:32 p.m.

Jake left the house and all his domestic troubles and called Tim en route.

'You got the necessary?' Tim asked.

'Oh yes.'

'Anything tasty for the discerning punter?'

'Special import. Under-the-counter stuff.'

'Great. I've called the boys.'

'OK, but Adam's not coming this time,' Jake stressed, passing a multitude of pubs on both sides of the road.

'Why not? He's all right, isn't he? Keeps his mouth shut.'

'He's too highly strung. It annoys me, makes me uncomfortable.'

'Too late. I've already asked him.'

'Well, un-ask him.'

'I can't. And anyway, he's *your* friend.'

'No he's not. He's my workmate Roger's friend. It isn't the same thing.'

'Well, *you* introduced him to the club.'

'I had no choice. Roger lumbered me with him.' Jake

pulled up at a set of traffic lights. 'So, who else is coming?'

'You know. The suspect usuals. Quiet Jez, bald Si, gobby Pete.'

'Good. And Tim, get some proper beers this time.'

'Any special requests?'

'Something with a bit of alcohol in.'

'I'll see what I can do.'

Twenty minutes later, Jake pulled into a steep crescent of respectable modern houses, each one complete with a respectable modern car. Tim's drive was littered with four or five such vehicles. The boys were obviously eager tonight. Jake double-parked, and entered the house with a small package under his arm. Inside, the other members of the DangerClub were drinking and chatting. Jake was handed a beer, and decided to get the evening's proceedings started.

'Right, what have we got? Are we all in?'

'What's the stake?'

'Minimum stake is a fiver.'

'Bit rich, isn't it, Jake?'

'This is a quality event.'

'How about two?'

Jake glanced around the eager faces. 'Any objections?' A collective shrug. 'Right, cheapskate bets it is. Two quid minimum, you know the rest of the rules.'

'I'm a bit strapped,' Pete said in explanation.

'No problem. Now, who's in? Let's see the cash. How about a kitty of ten quid each?'

'You banking, Jake?'

'Yeah. I might as well stay neutral on this one.'

One by one, the DangerClub players unfolded notes and passed them to Jake, who stood up and walked over to the video player.

'Here it is, then,' Jake said, proudly holding the film aloft. A small cheer went up. He inserted the tape and opened his can. Pete, Si, Jez and Adam sat down on whatever they could find and made themselves comfortable. Presently Tim lowered the lights and a general air of excitement spilled through the living room. The title came up, and was greeted by another cheer.

Madams et Machinerie

'French one, Jake?'

'Nothing but the best for you lot.'

'I like the Asian ones myself,' Jez ventured.

'Nah, for your real enthusiast, it's the German films,' Si said.

'Can't go far wrong with the Scandinavian ones either,' Pete added.

A general murmur of approval went around.

'All right, settle down,' Adam urged, 'it's starting.'

Close-up on a woman. She is young and vivacious, and is moving her hands up and down slowly and rhythmically. A man is standing close behind her. He says something in French to her. She looks up guiltily and ceases what she is doing with her hands. We track down her body and see that she is holding some sort of tool in her long, slender fingers.

Jake paused the film. 'OK, gentlemen,' he said, 'let's have your offerings.'

'Filing cabinet,' Adam shouted.

'Stapler.'

'Fiver says she loses a finger.'

'I'll see your fiver and raise you seven – blade goes through her palm,' Si countered.

'You're on.'

'No way. You watch the filing cabinet.'

'OK, everyone in?'

'The man trips,' Jez predicted quietly.

'I'm sitting this one out,' Tim replied.

Jake pressed play and the frozen image came back to life.

The woman resumes what she is doing, staring intently at the man, who continues to talk to her. Again, we pan down to her fingers. It is obvious that she isn't watching what she's doing. The tool slips and slices into her palm. The woman stands up and screams, fairly realistic blood gushing out. Fade out. Onscreen message in French.

'Was that it?'

'That was crap.'

'She could at least have had the decency to pull the filing cabinet on top of herself,' Adam complains, his overeagerness ebbing.

'That's a fiver you owe me.'

'Double or quits.'

'Live with it,' Jake says. 'I've heard along the grapevine that this is a classic.'

'It better be. It's bollocks so far.'

'Right, here we go again.'

Two workmen are assembling some scaffolding. One is balanced precariously at the top, several storeys up, and is hauling sections of scaffolding aloft on a length of rope. The other, at the bottom, has his back to the structure and is watching a woman walk past. He wolf-whistles.

'Nice touch,' Jez pipes up.

'It *is* French,' Pete says.

Jake pauses the tape. 'Any offers?'

Various predictions are made, and small bets distributed. When everybody has voiced an opinion, Jake allows the film to proceed.

The scaffolder's colleague stops to view the passing woman, and also decides to compliment her, using the fingers of one hand to whistle. The rope slips through the palm of his other hand and the large, heavy scaffolding pole plummets downwards. The ground-level scaffolder turns round, but is too late. The vertical pole gathers momentum and nosedives towards his head. He is not wearing a helmet. The pole passes straight through the upright scaffolder, who is skewered to the ground.

'Jesus,' Jez whispers, shocked. 'I didn't see that one coming.'
'Nor did he.'
'What is this? Some sort of feminist safety film?'
'Nah. He hasn't been castrated yet.'
'Give it a chance.'
'Sorry, boys, no winners there. It's a rollover. I'll give you twenty seconds on the next scene.'

An efficient building site. No women in skirts. Workmen are hod-carrying, bricking walls, mixing cement and digging trenches. A foreman directs proceedings. From the top of the picture, a small digger drives onto the site.

The film stops.
'JCB into the ladder,' Pete shouts.
'No – the hod-carrier's going to drop his bricks,' Adam answers, rocking back and forth in anticipation. Jake and Tim exchange glances.
'Bollocks. JCB–ladder. Tenner.'
'Tenner it is,' Si says, scratching his hairless scalp.

The digger begins to reverse slowly. The driver is talking on a mobile phone.

'Come on!' Adam screams.

Pete joins in, the financial incentive biting. 'Back that baby into the ladder!'

'Hoddy. Come on, hoddy,' Si encourages. 'Drop those bricks.'

We see the back wheel of the digger closing in on the foot of the ladder.

Pete and Adam are becoming very animated.

Pan up to the driver who is unaware of the potential peril. He takes his hard hat off to scratch his head. Above him, the hod-carrier totters up his ladder. Finally, the digger hits home, unbalancing the workman, who spills his bricks into the air. We follow the bricks as they stream down onto the digger driver, who slumps forward unconscious, knocking his vehicle into first gear. The digger lunges forwards and catches the foreman, pushing him into a trench and falling in on top of him. There are realistic French screams.

Adam is at the point of orgasm.

We see the hod-carrier lose his battle to stay on the ladder, and tumble two storeys into the trench as well. None of the three men stirs. The wheels of the digger come to a slow halt.

'Let's see the money then, Si,' Pete says.
'You're joking.'
'What? The JCB smacked into the ladder.'
'Yes, but the hod-carrier dropped his bricks.'
'Only because my man bumped into him.'
'Looked pretty simultaneous to me.'
'Jake – you're the expert – what do you think?'
'A draw, I'd have said,' he replied. Besides, a new scene was starting, a new situation of dangerous practices, a new cast of actors pretending to be injured,

and more money to be won and lost by members of the DangerClub.

An hour or so later, when the film had ended and the group had calculated their gains and losses, Jake took the film and drove home. There, Kate appeared even more miserable than usual. In fact, as Jake looked at her, she seemed positively upset.

'What's wrong?' he asked, putting his arm around her.

His girlfriend burst into tears, and Jake checked his mental calendar, wondering whether some facet of the female reproductive cycle might be to blame, or whether he had forgotten some significant date. Kate opened her large brown eyes and a tear slithered down her cheek, cutting a wet line through the vast dusting of foundation. 'It's Norbert,' she said.

'What did he steal?'

'Nothing. This is serious. Elizabeth rang.'

'What's wrong?'

'I'm so sorry. He . . . he died today,' she told him, more tears arriving thick and fast.

Jake jerked away from her involuntarily. 'Seriously?' Kate's face confirmed the worst. 'How?'

'Run over coming back from the shops.'

'Fuck.' He gripped his temple, his cold fingers lying across his brow. 'Fuck fuck fuck fuck fuck fuck.'

'She said he mustn't have been watching where he was going.'

'But they took him to hospital?'

'He passed away at the scene.'

'Shit.'

'It was a bad accident. Elizabeth didn't go into specifics, but she said at least it was instant.'

Jake gripped Kate again, almost hurting her, and buried his head into her neck.

Live Chicken

Jake was upset by his uncle's death and spent the day at home. He rang Roger, who had already devoured a rough copy of the accident report, and was able to tell him that Norbert had been badly damaged by a moving car and a following lorry. For a moment, the cartoon violence of the previous evening's safety film made him shudder, standing jarringly at odds with the reality of accidental death.

He passed the hours silently grieving, the stillness of the house broken only by the clatter of typing. This was why he had gone into safety in the first place. To prevent accidents, to stop people dying. He could see now that his efforts had been half-hearted, lost in paperwork, swallowed by a lack of immediacy. There used to be a time when he believed in Providence, but that had passed. What was important now was that he had lost someone he cared for. It was sickening, and Norbert's death permeated the indifference he had painstakingly built up around himself in the years since he discovered what real suffering meant.

As quiet periods seeped away, Jake turned his

attention to Elizabeth. She was the one left behind, having lost her husband of eleven years. Jake had met his half-uncle just ten or so times, but it was obvious that only those very close to him were going to miss him. Norbert had been his dad's cousin, and even his father, when he finally managed to contact him, didn't appear too overcome by the sad news. His penny-pinching had, by the end of his life, endeared him to few.

Jake went to work the next day in a mild trance. To look on the positive side, he tried to summon up all the good things about his uncle's life. He pictured the many thrift shops Norbert had kept in business, and the numerous downmarket supermarkets that had relied on his custom. Most of all, he thought of the nest egg his aunt would now be able to fall back on in her time of need.

During his silent homily, Jake was forced to carry on his faintly ludicrous duties. Besides showing comically gruesome public information films, he was required to perform statutory safety inspections, which did little to cheer him up. Neither did they bring much light into the lives of the people he inspected. In fact, the whole business was hollow, particularly on a day like today. In the afternoon, Jake and Roger were scheduled to inspect a factory on a nearby industrial estate.

'What time's it happening?' Jake asked Roger, putting thoughts of Norbert on hold.

Roger flicked through his diary. 'Two.'

'Should be fun,' Jake said miserably. Above him, yet another new slogan had appeared. The bloody things must be reproducing.

'Yeah. But we've got a film first.'

'A film? Who is it today?'

'Builders Four.'

'You got a suitable movie?'

'Oh yes. Something right up their street.'

Jake read the words of the poster. *Better to Be a Live Chicken Than a Dead Duck*. Below the text, a healthy chicken looked vacantly into the camera. Next to it stood an obviously stuffed duck. At the bottom lurked the dreaded statistic. *Research shows that peer pressure accounts for up to 5% of all injuries in the 16 to 25 age group.* Jake shrugged, mildly perplexed, then peered over at Roger, who was waggling a video tape around for him to see.

'A cheeky little German number,' Roger said.

'You've watched it?' Jake asked.

'Thought I'd better take it home and check it out.'

'And?'

'Let's just say *Office and Laboratory Catastrophes* is last year's news.'

'Thank fuck for that.'

'Yah. Und eet ees wunderbar.'

'What?'

'Wunderbar. Wonderful,' Roger explained. 'You know, in German . . .'

'Right,' Jake said miserably. That was all he needed. A roomful of builders, Roger and a Teutonic splatter-fest to cheer him up.

After shocking a suitably unprepared shambles of builders and returning from the inspection, Jake pulled up in Restingtaxidriver Street. And instead of mulling over the financial mess of his life, he allowed himself time to think about his uncle. The funeral had been set for a few days' time. With a slight shiver, Jake realized that Norbert's cold body would be parked in a funeral director's somewhere, doubtless being dressed, measured and fitted for a coffin. The chill air his uncle lay in would be suffused with a quiet dignity, as the business of death was conducted by sombre men in dark suits. That at least was a comfort.

Coffin Dodges

'Yeah, but what I'm saying, boss, is that we could save nine inches, a foot on the coffin, and nobody'd be any the wiser.'

'Run me through it again, Bob.'

Bob Walsh was a stolid man who wore stolid clothes. It had never been his overriding aim to work with dead members of the public, but having laboured with living ones, undertaking was by no means a step in the wrong direction. In fact, he had tried his hands at a number of professions, some of them more legal than others, and was happy until any better opportunities came along to keep his nose, and those of the bodies he embalmed, very much clean. He surveyed the torso in front of him. In several years as an undertaker he had rarely seen a mess like this. 'This chap – Norbert Flint – he's got no head, right?'

'Right,' Malcolm Dabner, the chief undertaker of Dabner and Sons, Funeral Services, Bridgeton, replied, resting his ashtray on the deceased's chest.

'Well, with no head, he's only five foot long, max.'

'So?'

'So we pop him in one of our short ones, which, let's face it, we've got loads of, given that everyone's getting taller, and no one's going to know any different.'

The head undertaker took a deep drag on his cigarette and brushed some ash off torso-man's chest. 'But what's the point, Bob?'

'Small coffin four hundred pounds. Large coffin six fifty.'

'Two hundred and fifty quid, eh?' Malcolm took a sip of his coffee and screwed his face up. It hadn't been stirred properly and he couldn't taste the sugar. 'Won't anyone notice?'

'Probably not, if we play it right.'

'I mean, in real life he's a strapping six-footer. When we come to put him in the ground he's suddenly circus dwarf material.'

'It's deceptive, a length of wood,' Bob replied, swigging from a mug of tea, which he set down besides his boss's ashtray and coffee on the deceased's chest.

'Not that fucking deceptive.'

'So we get some small pall bearers. It's all about perspective.'

'This is getting out of hand.'

'All I'm saying is he's got no head, so we can't do an open coffin anyway.' Bob took another mouthful of tea, noting with interest the circle of red skin the boiling-hot mug left behind.

'S'pose not.'

'Relatives aren't going to want to travel large distances to come and view a neck. The coffin is therefore closed. So while we're at it, why not save a few quid?'

'And we charge full price?'

' 'Course.'

Malcolm used one of the cadaver's fingers to stir his coffee, and sipped it again. That was better. 'And what about the hole?'

Bob glanced over the body. There was a gaping

chasm at the neck, but other than that the remains of Norbert Flint appeared to have the normal number of openings. 'What hole?' he asked.

'The one you'll be bloody digging.'

'Oh, right. What about it?'

'Well, will that be dwarf size as well?'

'Definitely. I mean, if we lower him into a normal-sized grave, there'll be room for the fucking vicar as well.'

Malcolm was quiet for a second. 'Right, get one of the short-arse ones dusted down,' he said, making a decision. 'And have a word with Jimmy and Dave. They're not going to win any awards for gigantism.'

'Good thinking, boss.'

'We'll use the smaller hearse as well.'

'I'll book it out.'

'And Bob.'

'Boss?'

'Not a fucking word to anybody. All right?'

'Right.'

'We've got our reputation to think about here.' The chief undertaker stubbed his fag out in the ashtray, which sank very slightly into the cadaver's skin. 'And get this one embalmed when you've got a moment. The bugger's starting to go off.'

Eulogy

Uncle Norbert's funeral was the most interesting one Jake had ever been to. Seemingly caught somewhere between grief and hysteria, his widow had put in a performance which both unsettled and entertained the assembled mass. Whereas most eulogies tread a fine line between benefit of the doubt and downright optimism when summing up a person's character, Uncle Norbert's was a pack of gleeful lies steeped in irony. Elizabeth had delivered a marvellous act of comedic grief, mastering the hysteria that always exists at a funeral and can take you into unpredictable territory. It is not uncommon for grief-stricken mourners to fight back laughter during the service, and for people who barely knew the deceased to find themselves overwhelmed by perplexing tears.

If Jake was being unkind, he would have said that Elizabeth seemed almost glad to see the back of her husband. There was a maniacal spark in her eye as she slowly murdered Norbert in front of his friends and family. Every reminiscence served as a backhanded swipe, and she had steered the mourners – many of whom Norbert had owed money – firmly away from unhappiness.

'As I cast my tearful eyes over all of our wonderful friends and family,' she said, 'I'm moved to think of the joy Norbert brought to all of us at some time or other. Anyone who ever shared a taxi with him, went drinking with him or split a restaurant bill with him will know how he spent his money.' Nods of recognition, a few puzzled faces. 'Charity was his middle name. And many people say charity begins at home. But not for Norbert. No, Norbert never spent any money at home. Or abroad for that matter.' The vicar perked up at hearing the word 'charity' and smiled supportively. 'Moreover, any of you who ever had business dealings with my late husband will recall the extraordinary lengths he went to to broker a good deal.' Cough. 'For himself. And Norbert worshipped only one god,' Elizabeth nodded towards the vicar, who smiled again, 'and paid homage not just once a week, but every day the banks were open. Any of you who ever sent him a Christmas card, lent him money or took his financial advice will appreciate the need to bury him with the dignity he aspired to. Which is why I've cleaned out our current account and have spent all of it – except what he owes his creditors – on a lavish burial. Norbert would have been thrilled to know his money was literally being buried with him.' By now there was some light embarrassed sniggering, mourners catching on to Elizabeth's motive. 'And many of you who will have seen my late husband dressed in what he used to refer to as "an economy of style" – which allowed him to generously keep many Oxfams and Sue Ryders going,' another knowing nod from the vicar, 'will be heartened to hear that I ensured that the funeral directors – who've done a smashing job – buried him in the finest suit Norbert's money could buy. So what I really want us to do today is not to grieve the passing of a great man – that wouldn't be appropriate under the circumstances – but to celebrate instead the life of someone who made us all think at one time or another of what it means to be truly rich . . .'

Elizabeth paused, and Jake sensed the attack was about to become more brutal. 'But it was Norbert's unflinching efforts on behalf of the environment that I shall really remember him for. I recall one time I caught him hanging his used dental floss over the bathroom radiator. What are you doing? I asked him. Protecting the environment, he answered. And I'll be buggered – sorry, vicar – if he didn't make one roll of floss last almost a decade. In his latter years, he began to follow the great German environmentalist Uter Cant, and adopted the Cant philosophy. And in a way, he ended up just like his idol. In short, he became another Uter Cant. He was a Cant when he got up in the morning, and a Cant when he went to bed. He was a Cant when he turned the pilot light of the boiler off, calculating that the flame would consume forty-two pence worth of harmful gas over the summer, and he was a Cant when he discovered he couldn't restart it. He was a Cant when he said he didn't want to inconvenience a plumber, and a dedicated Cant when instead he took plumbing classes at night school. And by February, when he had finally managed to light the thing, I'm sure he felt a righteous Cant. But his Cant-ish actions didn't end there. He was a man of principle who felt the need to share the earth's resources. He sold my exercise bike and bought a manual lawn-mower with the cash, telling me in his Cant-like way that mowing the lawn would improve my fitness. And so the list goes on.'

As Elizabeth stepped up her underhand assassination, the mood in the church changed entirely. There were more tears of suppressed laughter among the mourners than water in the font. The vicar, misreading the situation entirely, saw a large number of people desperately trying to contain their grief, stuffing hankies in their mouths to quiet themselves from wailing, hysterical anguish rampant throughout the women, men hunched forwards, reddening with pain, their shoulders shaking silently. He was even moved to attempt to lighten the proceedings with philosophical platitudes about Norbert – whom he had never met – a man whose generosity of spirit and determination to help his fellow man had warmed the hearts of all before him. This only seemed to encourage the grief of the assembled mourners. Little did the vicar know that Norbert would have grudgingly put five pence in his collection plate, and taken change.

Elizabeth played a blinder. There was nothing in the sensibility of her clothes or the quiet dignity she carried with her to suggest otherwise. But she must have practised. Jake dragged his eyes away from his aunt, who was still in full flow, and risked a look at the coffin. There was always something unreal about the presence of an empty body, devoid of life, lying in a wooden box, as though all the energy, triumphs and warmth of one person should need a far larger vessel to contain them. As Jake stared at the coffin it appeared especially disproportionate, as if his uncle couldn't possibly have been crammed into such a tiny space. Beside it, two pall bearers who wouldn't have looked out of place in a circus fidgeted uneasily, doubtless having sat through more eulogies than could really be healthy. Elizabeth began summing up, and Jake thought he detected an air of relief about the congregation.

'So if anyone wishes to donate any money to charity on Norbert's behalf, well, you know what he'd have done with it. And as he always said in what became his motto to his dying day, "*Aldis netto lidl co-op kwiksavum*".' The vicar, whose Latin may have been a little ropy, struggled to translate, and decided a knowing smile would cover the tracks of his ignorance.

After singing a final hymn, the congregation filed outside. At the nearby cemetery, the coffin was lowered into its hole, which again, to Jake's eyes, seemed to contradict the memory he had of his uncle as a man of more than average height. Jake looked up and surveyed the mourners. Most were friends, with relatives sparse on the ground. To make matters worse, Jake's parents had disappeared for a year, travelling the world on an extended mission to gloat about their early retirement. The sorry truth was that Norbert had isolated himself from the majority of his family through the obsessive desire not to spend money. In the old days, as an accountant, relatives had looked to him for financial advice, which he had gladly given. He had been mildly popular, through profession if not through personality. But three or four years ago, Norbert had changed course, and instead of sensible advice on tax issues, had begun to ramble and rave about the need to minimize expenditure. He had been taken at his word for a while, until family members gradually came to the conclusion that something was wrong. One by one, they had fallen by the wayside. And when Norbert started returning their Christmas cards, simply scribbling 'vice versa' on the inside and 'return to sender' on the outside, things really deteriorated. But with a family tree of Bonsai proportions, Jake had been intent on staying reasonably close to his uncle, no matter how painful that might be. Now, though, his quest was over, and his family shrunk still further. The coffin was lowered into the ground, a few words were mumbled and Jake turned and walked away.

The Bible

Jake felt slightly unsettled after the funeral. For a start it didn't seem as if they had buried his uncle so much as crucified him. Clearly his aunt had been overcome with morbid humour during the ceremony, and Jake and the other mourners had been swept along with it. But there was a small debt of dignity owing. The following day, he went to pay Elizabeth a visit to ease his conscience.

'Sniffing round, are you?' she asked, after ushering him in. She was tired and gaunt.

'Sorry?'

'Like all the others, sniffing round to see what he was worth. Claiming back long written-off debts?'

'No. Honest. I came round to pay my condolences.'

'You'd be the first to pay for anything round here.'

'Really – I didn't even know him that well.'

'Did yourself a favour there.' Elizabeth slumped on the sofa.

'It might sound like a daft question, but are you OK?'

'Fantastic.'

'I mean the funeral was . . .'

'Was what?'

'Well, a bit caustic.'

'Can you blame me?'

'I'm not really sure I understand.'

'Eleven years and what has he left me?'

'I dunno.'

'Bugger all.'

'He didn't have a will?'

'Nope. No will, no savings, no nothing.'

'But I thought he was, well, not given to excessive spending.'

'Now you're getting it. You'd think there would be a lot of it knocking about. I mean, we're talking about a man who could make one tea bag last a week. A man who would slink into jumble sales just as they were about to end, when prices were cheaper. A man who would only buy car parts from the scrapyard. A man who believed taxis and credit cards were the work of the devil. A man who hung around people moving house, asking if there was anything they didn't want to take with them.' She shook her head. 'And it wasn't as if I didn't earn a fair wage as well, especially in the last few years. So when Norbert died, I naturally expected to be a wealthy woman of leisure. If we'd spent most of the last decade working hard and constantly scrimping, it stands to reason that there would be quite a few thousand pounds to show for it.'

'And there isn't?'

'A few hundred, at a stretch.'

'What about life insurance?'

'The bastard cashed it in. Four years ago, apparently. Never even said anything. And I continued giving him half of the contribution every month.'

'He got you to pay for his life insurance?'

'The way he argued it, I was the sole beneficiary if he died, so it would be a kind of investment.'

Jake was filled with respect for Norbert. Just when you thought he had achieved a new low, he managed to better it. 'Where do you think all the money has gone? If you don't mind me asking.'

'You've asked now. I don't know. I wish I did. We only had two bank accounts. And he didn't have any bad habits or expensive hobbies. I've looked under beds, on top of wardrobes, everywhere. And not a sausage.'

'I suppose at least . . .'

'But I'll tell you what I *did* find. A carrier bag full of carrier bags. A box stuffed with rubber bands. A container crammed with used toothpaste tubes. A jar of half-pences. A suitcase bulging with old shoes he swore he'd thrown away. A holdall chock full of spent light bulbs, for Christ's sake. I mean, what's the point? The man never got rid of anything. Except, it seems, his cash.'

'I suppose at least you aren't in debt,' Jake said, trying again at an earlier point.

'Don't you see though, Jake, I *am* in debt. I've spent my married life in bloody debt. I've been forced to conserve, recycle, penny pinch and make do, and now I want paying back. I've forsaken holidays, cars, clothes, perfumes, the bastard lot. I feel some sort of compensation package should now kick in. I want to be lying on a beach somewhere, drinking rare liqueurs, being waited on, throwing my money around like there's no tomorrow.'

'I guess there isn't much chance of that now.'

'I'd have more chance of winning the lottery. Which, incidentally, I've started doing. Norbert's always been dead against it. But now he's dead, and against it, which is a different matter. He used to say the statistics were all wrong. Sod him, I'm buying tickets like there's no tomorrow.'

'You never know.'

'No, I think I do know. That's not the point though. It's just a cheap way of spiting him. And as for holidays, the most I can hope for these days is a week arsing about in the back passage of Cornwall. Some fucking payback, if you'll excuse my French.' Even in the midst of mourning, Elizabeth had an uncanny ability with swearing.

'You know, if there's anything I can do . . .' Jake hoped there wasn't, but felt he ought to offer anyway.

'No, bless you, Jake, there isn't. As I said, I'm not poor so much as deprived. I still have my job, and teachers, despite what you may have heard, aren't actually that badly paid. I'll get by. And you've got money problems of your own. In fact, if what your mother told me on the phone is true, I should be offering to help you out.'

'Oh don't worry about me – I'm beyond help,' he replied.

'But at least you enjoy your cash.'

Jake was quiet for a second. Although he liked to spend there was nothing particularly joyous about protracted debt. 'I used to enjoy it. Now I worry. Listen, I just thought I'd, you know, say that if you change your mind, Kate and I are only too willing to help.' He stood up and walked towards the front door.

As Elizabeth opened it, she said, 'You know, there is one thing I can give you.'

'Honestly,' Jake answered, 'I didn't come for anything.'

His aunt disappeared upstairs and returned a couple of minutes later. 'Here.' She thrust something at him, which he examined suspiciously. It was, on a good day, a manuscript. On a mediocre one like today, it was a bundle of papers threaded loosely together with a length of green garden twine. The title page was inscribed as follows:

FIRST OUT OF THE TAXI,
LAST TO THE BAR
by
Norbert H. Flint

Jake flicked through it as he left Elizabeth's house and headed up the road. Inside were a hundred and three pages of poorly typed prose which alternated between descriptions of Norbert's life and gems of his advice. The paper itself was cheap enough to be almost transparent – there was less paper than ink – and with its pages tied at their corners, it resembled a wad of newspaper used for bum-wiping purposes in the days before bathroom tissue. But it was obvious from the first line that there was a theme to *First out of the Taxi*.

At home, Jake spent an avid hour studying it in detail, and became more and more fascinated with every crinkly page. And as he read the manuscript, piecing together its haphazard sections, it started to make some sort of sense.

The Foreword read:

Comrades

It is true that money makes the world go round. But it will also spin of its own free will if you ask it nicely. It is also said that the love of money is the root of all evil. This, however, is patently untrue – the love of spending money is the root of all evil. My money, in particular. So in the following pages I present a guide, a distillation, if you will, of a lifetime's skill within the field of spending.

Please do not borrow, photocopy or otherwise harm the earning potential of this book.

Yours in anticipated riches,

Norbert Flint.

Safety Scene #7

An Accidental Life

July 1960. Saturday 8:48 p.m.

Interior of a small enclosed area. The walls are thick and red. It is hot. Nothing happens for a long period of time. Slowly, we are aware of indeterminate changes in the vessel. Then we see movement. Pan out. The walls are changing position, sometimes coming closer, sometimes receding. There is an opening at one end. A large object enters, filling all available space, and then moves away again. This happens repeatedly. Suddenly there is an influx of fluid. We move through a tight aperture into a smaller enclosed area. Very powerful close-up of one of the walls. A spherical egg comes into view. Even more detailed close-up. The fluid surrounds the egg. Pan out completely, from dark to light. There is a couple in a bedroom. The curtains are half closed. One of them speaks.

Are you sure the rubber is OK?

Looks all right to me.

But you're sure?

Well, I guess.

Shouldn't you blow it up?

Nah. It'll be OK.

It had better be all right. I don't want to get pregnant, you know.

I know. Yawn. Everything will be fine. Just fine.

The female drinks from a glass of water. Do you ever think, though?

What?

You know, if we had a baby.

Not really.

I mean, what would we call it?

I don't know.

Cheryl, if it's a girl. I've always loved that name.

Yeah? And if it was a boy?

I'd have to think about it. I've always pictured a little girl. What do you think?

A pause. Given what we've just been doing, how about Roger?

A short giggle. Roger. Well it's certainly got a ring to it. Either way, let's hope not, eh?

Too right.

I mean, my dad will kill you. We're not even married.

It won't come to that.

Now you're sure that thing is OK?

The man sighs and closes his eyes. Yes. It's fine. Everything's all right. Everything is just all right.

Marriage and the Undercarriage

Roger cautiously examined his face in the bathroom mirror. He had cut himself shaving, but reckoned he would live. Statistically, shaving was very rarely a cause of death, though mild infection was an outside possibility. As he monitored the injury from subtly different directions, he spotted a new blemish on his skin and cursed. Almost every week now a fresh imperfection made itself at home on his face. And although small, it was noticeable, a tiny patch of whiteness showing through the black. For Roger suffered from vitiligo, which had been apparent from his late teens. It had been triggered, he now believed, by an unpleasant incident he had buried beneath a mountain of safety statistics. Although this idea wasn't apparent to him at the time, the two distressing events had been almost simultaneous.

For white people, vitiligo is a mildly vexing condition, but nothing more than this. Roger, however, wasn't vexed so much as very fucking annoyed. Every time he looked in the mirror, a new piece of him had disappeared. He was being eaten away, a sort of race leprosy which was gradually and inevitably leaching his essence.

But at least he was confounding his critics. Before, kids at school had called him Coconut – black on the outside, white on the inside. Now what were people going to say? he wondered miserably, still staring at his reflection. Peanut? Light on the outside, light on the inside. And here was the real fucker about vitiligo. It was an auto-immune disease, the doctor had told him, with some satisfaction, enunciating *auto* and *immune* a clear two seconds apart, so that the meaning sank in. This was the body attacking itself from the inside. There was no pathogen here, no external invader assaulting his skin. There was only his immune system, his coconut immune system, slowly whitening him from the inside out, progressively taking him captive. And it was definitely getting worse of late. Much worse. Before, there had been a few isolated spots across his face like drops of bleach. Now, they seemed to want to join the dots and spell out Race Traitor for all to see.

In white people, vitiligo often remains hidden, the effects delicate, the lack of pigment only really becoming obvious after the rest of your skin has enjoyed a long hot summer and has browned a shade or two. In an Afro-Caribbean though, the effects were noticeable straight away. Fortunately, it had started on his feet. He had been reluctant through most of his university days to change his socks or shoes in public. Sandals had been right out. Swimming was a no-no. The beach had been a disaster area, and the sandy Caribbean of his not-so-distant ancestors had felt a world away. If Roger was brutally honest with himself, which he tried not to be as far as possible, foot shyness was one more reason that he ended up in Safety. In very few professions were you less likely to bare your toes. On the contrary, stout work boots with immovable steel toecaps were the minimum level of protection.

Gloves, safety goggles, face masks and lab coats all had to be worn with ruthless disregard for fashion. Roger wouldn't have gone as far as to say that he was hiding particularly, just that Hazard Prevention provided a certain dignity for a black man slowly turning white.

And while he was running himself down in the bathroom mirror, it wasn't only his face that gave him away. Black man, relaxed man. That was what they said. He should be cool, laid back and hung like a donkey, and yet he was none of these, and knew it. Not by a long stretch. And Roger had certainly tried stretching it. This was when stereotypes crucify you not because you conform to them, but because you don't. It was when others looked at you quizzically, wondering why you didn't live up to the labels they had already attached to you, questioning what the hell must be wrong with you. Roger's problem with stereotyping, therefore, was not the shallow assumptions strangers made about him because of his colour, but the assumptions he wished they would make. In short, Roger aspired towards typecasting.

The cut was bleeding more freely now, and he dabbed at it with some antiseptic gauze to minimize the risk of bacterial contamination. He wrestled a plaster from its packet, and attempted to trim it with a pair of alarmingly sharp scissors. Roger clenched his teeth. He was now bleeding from his finger. Cursing, he dropped the scissors and managed to stab one of the toes of his left foot. Now he needed three plasters. At this rate, he was going to have to call an ambulance, provided he didn't bleed to death first. While he dressed his various and multiplying wounds, he returned his thoughts to his wife. Surely this was where the support of a good woman made all the difference, loving her husband despite all his visible failings. And although his wife Pauline certainly did love him, and even on occasion championed him, she didn't always help matters. She had an unnerving ability to cut to the very source of his insecurities, particularly when they rowed. 'If I wanted a boring bloke with a small cock,' she had once said in the heat of battle, 'I should have married a white man.' Roger ought to have divorced her then and there. But no, he had taken it on the chin, walked away and stared mournfully into the mirror, watching himself slowly turning pale.

Before meeting Pauline, Roger had flirted with the idea of never getting married. After a quick glance at the statistics, the single life appeared to have a number of life-prolonging benefits. Most murders, for example, are domestic. The smaller your family, therefore, the lower the chances of having your wife poison your tea or attack you with a bread knife (a kind of bread knife attacking you with a bread knife situation). Also, along with domestic strife came children, which were inherently dangerous items as far as Roger could garner. When was the last time a child put safety goggles on? As opposed to leaving roller skates lying on the stairs? (*Domestic Safety Rule Two: Children cause four times more accidents per capita than adults.*) So the single life had things going for it.

But then as Roger investigated more fully, he came to appreciate that bachelors die younger than their married counterparts. Their lifestyles, apparently, were more detrimental to their health. They ate poorly, drank efficiently, and were neither sober nor nourished enough to attempt any exercise. Bearing in mind the fact that physical activity was intrinsically dangerous, the prudent thing to do therefore was to get married to someone who didn't appear likely to attack you, and who wasn't particularly bothered about your general condition. Roger felt he had achieved these dual aims, and, despite his wife's biting tongue, was therefore satisfied. As with many things in his life, nothing inspired Roger more than a thorough lack of excitement.

Finally, his shaving injury clotted, and he slunk away from his own reflection, sensing for some reason a small wave of relief.

Sex Live

As Jake approached his car in the world's most dangerous parking area, he noticed something unusual about its aerial. A small pink object was attached to the end. Walking closer, he realized what it was. He reached up and pulled the plastic novelty finger off. On its underside, three words had been inscribed. 'Property of Ronnie' stared out at him in black marker pen. The name made Jake stand very still for a couple of seconds. He glanced around the car park, and then climbed into his car and flicked the central locking. He drove to Restingtaxidriver Street, jittery, and recalled a few events he tried not to think about these days.

Things weren't quite right at home either. As soon as he opened the front door, Kate made her way into the kitchen unprompted, and without asking for directions. It wasn't as though he expected her to cook his dinner, more that he couldn't understand what else she had to do all day. And if she was going to blight his weekends with menial jobs, he thought he might as well return the favour when he could. With an unnatural absence of microwave sounds, Kate shouted from the kitchen, 'I'm going to prepare you a special meal tonight.' Jake kicked off his shoes and entered the kitchen, wondering what might be up.

Kate said, 'It's the thirtieth today,' handing him a glass of wine.

'Aha.'

'And that makes it the thirty-first tomorrow.'

'Yes.'

'So how much have we got?'

And then Jake twigged why Kate was being nice to him. 'I dunno,' he answered.

'You don't know? Look, I'll sort the food out while you get on the Internet and check the balance.'

'But—'

'But what? It's tradition. It's what we do. And I've been looking forward to it all month. Now get in there and see what we've got left.' And with that, Kate gave Jake a firm nudge towards the living room.

Jake padded around the front room in his socks. As he sat down at the computer, he noticed it was still switched on. The screen was blank, except for a line of text at the top.

TRADER68: R U OPN 4 CH@ STILL?

What the fuck? It looked like a message of some sort, presumably typed by TRADER68, whoever that was. Mind you, it was a woeful communication. Jake wasn't very good with computers, but he could at least type straight. He read it again. Maybe it was some sort of code. He tried it phonetically. Are-you-open-for . . . CH@. Ch-at. Chat. Are you open for chat still? He typed a response. 'Y. CH@ AWAY.' As he pressed return, he saw his message appear below the last entry for TRADER68, preceded by the ID BIGSPENDER. Apparently this was Kate's on-line name. There was a rapid reply.

TRADER68: B/F NOT BACK?

B/F? Boyfriend? Jake sent a swift answer.

BIGSPENDER: B/F @ WRK
TRADER68: U STILL HORNY?
BIGSPENDER: N
TRADER68: DON'T WANT AGAIN?
BIGSPENDER: WANT WHAT?
TRADER68: LIVE S*X

Things were beginning to make sense. Jake had an idea, and searched the hard drive for files called TRADER68 or similar. Sure enough, a couple appeared. He opened them. They were picture files. An early-thirties man, dark hair, passably handsome, reasonable teeth, brown eyes, stared back at him. The second picture was the same man laughing, mouth partially open, hand stroking his chin. Jake closed the files, quickly checked his bank balance, swore under his breath and then returned to the chat window.

TRADER68: ?????????
BIGSPENDER: N
TRADER68: OK/ JUST CH@
BIGSPENDER: TLK 2 ME

Jake was getting the hang of this half-language. Besides, this was becoming interesting.

TRADER68: TIME 2 MEET SOON/ 1-2-1/ THNK IM READY NOW
BIGSPENDER: WHEN?
TRADER68: NEXT WK? WK AFTER?

Jake stared into the blank screen. This was something. Kate shouted incoherently from the kitchen. 'Be there in a minute,' he yelled back. Presumably she hadn't met TRADER68 in the flesh yet, though it did seem as if they had probably fucked through their computers. Although this disturbed him greatly, there was nothing to be gained from confronting Kate directly. She would say it was merely a flirtation. Clearly it was more serious than the chat-room banter which consumed most of her waking hours. They had discussed getting together, after having sex. Usually the other way round. But as he thought about it, a plan stitched itself together. It was time to have some fun with TRADER68.

BIGSPENDER: MAYBE
TRADER68: SAY Y
BIGSPENDER: MAYBE

'You hungry?' Kate asked over the clatter of cack-handed kitchen activity.

'No,' Jake muttered in return.

TRADER68: PLS/ DESPERATE
BIGSPENDER: OBVIOUSLY
TRADER68: WHAT D'YA MEAN?
BIGSPENDER: NOTHING

'Shall I bring you some wine in?'

'It's OK – I'm coming. Just give me a second.'

TRADER68: CAN'T WAIT 2 MEET U
BIGSPENDER: LIKEWISE. GOTTA GO
TRADER68: TEASE

'So it's teasing you want?' Jake said to himself. 'Well, it's teasing you're going to get.' He stood up, and smiled. He was, he decided, going to have some satisfaction with TRADER68.

Lurking

Elizabeth sat at the bottom of the bed and cradled her head in her hands. She turned round and ran her eyes over the queen-size mattress one more time. Which side was she supposed to sleep on now? It just seemed so big. Before, they had allotted sides, which they doggedly stuck to, even when sleeping in foreign beds. Norbert on the left, Elizabeth on the right. On the rare occasions that Elizabeth slept alone, she had spread herself across as much of the mattress as she could. This made her feel uneasy now. To spread would be to encroach on her husband's space. And although Norbert's bony limbs were no longer going to poke her as she tossed and turned, he was still with her when she slept.

Throwing the duvet back, Elizabeth made a policy decision. She would remain on the right, unless she rolled over in the night, in which case she would take things as they came. She was about to lie down when a noise in the garden stopped her. Over the last couple of weeks, the house had suddenly come alive with suspicious sounds. This one was different though.

Everything else had turned out to be accountable – the central heating, loose doors, the fridge freezer kicking into life – but what she had just heard was a clear crash of wood and glass. Elizabeth turned out the light and crept towards the window. She edged the curtain back and peered into the surrounding gloom. The sky was blue-black and oppressive. A streetlight pushed a slim shaft of orange between the two houses behind. She slid the window open an inch. All was silent. The shed at the bottom of the garden crouched in the shadows and was surrounded by long grass. She listened intently and stared at the ground below her. Nothing. She waited, sure that she couldn't be seen. And then there was a movement. The door of the shed opened slowly. From her vantage point, no one was visible. The door couldn't be opening of its own accord. It continued to swing until it was gaping in the darkness. Elizabeth could just make out a few of the items which were stored inside – tools, implements and the other usual shed detritus. She continued to stare, fixed to the scene. Then there was a glint of light. Someone was in there. The garden was a long, slender one and the shed was twenty or thirty yards away. The telephone was downstairs. Her nearest relative lived on the other side of Bridgeton. Elizabeth suddenly felt scared. Another speck of light. She realized whoever was in there was smoking. Drags on the cigarette lit the intruder's face. She was too far away to pick any details out of the murkiness.

The sounds of activity picked up. There was rummaging around. Elizabeth remained rooted to the spot. As her eyes became used to the half-light, she saw that the figure was a man, and that he was collecting things in one corner of the shed. After a couple more minutes, he emerged with a holdall, and pushed the door shut. Then he began walking towards the house. He stared through the downstairs patio doors, and then glanced up at the bedroom window.

Elizabeth shrank back. He was going to break in. She risked another peek. He was directly beneath. His hands cupped against the glass, looking into the living room, maybe even, Elizabeth realized, spotting the phone. She stood utterly still, female, vulnerable, alone, scared, waiting for the smash of glass. Seconds passed by, each one witnessing several heartbeats. Nothing. Maybe he was trying the doors. Still no obvious bangs or crashes. And then came the sound of the door lock being tried. Elizabeth ceased breathing.

The phone was out, then. She was cut off. A man was about to enter the house. Elizabeth had an idea. She ran into the spare room. It was packed with random clutter. She grabbed a pan, a hammer and a whistle and sprinted into the front room. Opening the window, she began to bang the pan frantically with the hammer while blowing the whistle. It was a suitable racket. In addition, she shouted, 'Help, call the police, burglar!' A few seconds later, the man dashed down the drive, and ran into the road. He looked back as he was running, before crossing over, diving through a garden on the other side and vanishing from view. Elizabeth kept making a noise for several minutes, the adrenaline still surging, until a neighbour stood in front of the house and asked her to stop.

Big Spender

On Saturday, Jake sat alone in the Hog's Head, the same high-street pub he always sat alone in at the end of the month. He surveyed the other punters gloomily. His heart really wasn't in it today. At five to twelve he ordered a second pint and a glass of Babycham and his mobile phone chirped into life with its pre-programmed tune, a tinny rendition of their favourite song.

```
parp   parp   parp parp   beep beep
parpparpparp   parp   parp   parp
beep   beep   beep   beep   beep
beep   parp   beep   parp
```

It was Kate. 'I'm just about to walk in the joint,' she said.

'Right,' Jake replied.

'Well, put some life into it.'

'I'll try.' He turned his phone off. It was time to begin the ritual. He slouched over to the dormant jukebox, slid fifty pence into the slot and selected C112 twice —

to be on the safe side – before walking out of the back door. Jake hung around in the car park for a couple of minutes and heard the song swagger into life. One minute to twelve. She would doubtless be inside already, eagerly anticipating his arrival. He used to look forward to the ritual himself, but the sting had gone from it now. In truth, he was faking it, following through for the enjoyment of his girlfriend. Twelve o'clock on the dot. If he'd been a smoker, he would have taken a deep drag and let out a long, mournful smoky sigh. Instead, he headed towards the main pub entrance, where he composed himself. He was a bad actor in a poor play which had lost its direction. He fingered the small wad of notes in his pocket and pushed the door open with his foot before striding purposefully into the main lounge again.

Kate was sitting in the usual place, close to the juke-box, dressed in a fake fur, and for an instant Jake remembered why he had fallen in love with her in the first place. Her heavy brown hair shone through the gloom, and her mouth and eyes came alive as she smiled up at him. Shirley Bassey's *Big Spender* boomed around the pub.

'Hey, Big Spender,' she said. 'Care to spend a little time with your girlfriend?'

Jake sat down and kissed her cheek. 'If I must,' he answered.

'Oh you must. So what's the grand sum?' she asked excitedly.

'Seventy-four pounds, twenty pence.'

'Jesus. That's not going to go very far,' Kate complained, some of the sparkle dulling in her eyes.

Jake was tempted to mention that if she didn't spend all her time electronically fucking anoraks, and actually went out and got a job, the sum of money they had left at the end of the month might actually be worth spending, but he refrained. Besides, it wasn't as if he was any better with their finances. Jake also didn't have the heart to tell her that this month they had overspent, rather than underspent, by seventy-four pounds, twenty pence.

'It'll do for a start.'

'Any ideas?' Kate asked, sipping her Babycham.

'Not really. You?'

'Underwear would be nice. Something a bit slinky.'

Jake was about to voice his approval, when he thought suddenly of TRADER68. Maybe the underwear was destined for her virtual – in many senses – lover. He sat silently and pondered while Kate reeled off a list of potentially bankrupting purchases.

'Or a DVD player. Mind you, we could do with a wider TV. I was watching it the other day, and ours seems, well, a bit on the narrow side. And my mobile isn't WAP compatible, apparently. Could always upgrade to a better phone that does WAP stuff, what-ever that might be. Or – and this is a big one – how about putting a deposit down and buying a second car?'

Their end-of-month tradition had originally been Kate's custom. She had been single and earning reasonable money faking dramatic vacuum-cleaner demonstrations in large shopping centres. Jake had inherited it the way people pick up bad habits from their partners. She had been in the same pub almost three years earlier, about to go out and squander the remnants of her disposable income, when Jake had entered alone, and, as luck would have it, in time to the song. She had caught his eye – beautiful, confident and singing to herself, and they had struck up a con-versation at the bar. He had followed her shopping, and had immediately been impressed by her ability to haemorrhage money.

'So what do you think? Deposit on a TV or car or something?'

The tradition had stuck and things were starting to get out of hand. Having spent the last couple of weeks examining their financial status, Big Spender now appeared like a frivolity too far. Jake put his drink down and stared into his girlfriend's eyes. 'Kate, this thing – our game – don't you ever think we should *save* some money?'

'Save? You've never saved a penny in your life.'

'I know, but . . .'

'As you've always said, saving is for dullards.' She placed her hand on his and squeezed it. 'The way I see it, we could die tomorrow, and then where would a few hundred quid in the bank get us?'

'Might pay for a decent funeral.'

'Which we wouldn't appreciate.'

'But at least we wouldn't leave the planet in debt.'

'So what? Everyone's in debt, one way or another. And look, this is how we are. Our disposable income, we dispose of it. That's how we live. We're happy enough, aren't we?' Jake smiled weakly. Inside his head he screamed the words 'Fucking Ecstatic'. Kate drained her minuscule Babycham. 'Come on,' she said, 'I'm double-parked. And I don't park our car for any boy I meet.'

Safety Scene #8

A calm summer morning. Not yet hot enough for T-shirts but getting there. A feeling in the air that anything is possible today. Close to a school a ten-year-old boy runs a stick along black-painted railings. Small for his age, he has to reach up on tiptoes. The clatter of the stick reminds him of a xylophone. Or is it a stylophone? He doesn't know. He is wearing short trousers, and the cool air tickles his legs. His laces are untied but it doesn't bother him. Everybody always says if you don't tie your laces you'll fall over, but he hasn't done yet. Two days of leaving them undone, and not so much as a stumble. Mind you, grown-ups talk about a lot of things which never happen. The bomb which never drops. Bees which never sting. Rusty nails which never give you lockjaw. Cigarettes which don't kill you. Strangers who never harm you. All in all, he thought, if you listen to adults enough the world is a dangerous place.

But his world was different. Despite riding his bike non-handed, climbing trees, hanging around building sites, playing with matches and swinging on rope swings, he never had a scratch on him. While his friends had cut themselves, or gone home bruised, or had injections after being bitten by dogs, he had walked through unscathed. He began to wish for minor injuries. His friends had plasters, slings and stitches to show for their adventures, while he had nothing. They were cool, and the more often they had been to Casualty and the more they had been smacked by their parents, the cooler they were. And the less harm he came to, the more he came to believe someone was watching out for him. And if the untied laces weren't proof, then what was?

Maybe it was God. He was always there, and was all-powerful, so it could have been him. He had decided to let God know how he felt, in the hope that he would stop looking after him. But when he plucked up courage to shout 'God is a dickhead' nothing was done about it. He had waited for the clouds, for the lightning, for he didn't know what, but nothing happened. He had tried harder, accusing God of a lot of things he barely understood, words and actions he had heard in the playground, and still the Almighty remained silent. And then he began to wonder whether he had misjudged him. Maybe God looked out for you whether you wanted him to or not.

Closer to the school, he abandoned his stick and thought about doing his laces up, before once again deciding against it. He could see that he wasn't really putting enough effort into things. That's what the teachers had told his parents and his parents had told him. Doesn't apply himself. Gives up too easily. And as he saw the playground of his school in the distance, he had an idea how he could prove everybody wrong. He was going to put God to the test, beyond shoelace level. He started to walk quickly, and then to jog, and then to run, and then to sprint. He closed his eyes and a big smile spread across his face. He counted paces. One, two, three, four, five, six, seven, eight, nine – and then he speeded up to flat-out, his eyes still tightly closed, ten, eleven, twelve, thirteen, fourteen, fifteen – he felt a slight step down onto the road – sixteen, seventeen, eighteen, ninet— A bang, a stabbing pain in his legs, a sudden change of direction. Scuffing against the tarmac. Moving against his will. Stillness. Stillness. Eyes open, taking nothing in but flashes of light. Tyre noise. A car pulling away at speed. He looked up into the blue above him and saw a cloud shaped like a cow. Silence. Peacefulness. Nothingness. He closed his eyes. Nothingness. Someone screamed somewhere. Nothingness . . .

Fireworks

Twice a year, on a predetermined day and at a mutually convenient hour, Jake paid a surprise visit to the factory of Peril and Sons, sole manufacturers of fireworks in the Bridgeton area. He walked around the virtually empty building, chatted with one or two managers and workers and scribbled barely decipherable comments onto his clipboard which he didn't type up back at the office.

Peril and Sons was of particular concern for Jake and all the Safety Team. Life expectancy on the factory floor was roughly two decades below the national average, and explosions and blazes were so common the local fire brigade was on constant standby. And yet there was always a queue of fresh, eager employees lining up to take the place of workers despatched to different corners of the industrial unit by particularly ill-advised experimentation.

Peril and Sons traded under the brand of Bulldog Fireworks. Robert Peril, the MD, was on a one-man mission 'to make UK fireworks more interesting'. Not that fireworks were boring, he explained time and time again to Jake, just that they were crap. 'British banger? More of a fucking whimper,' he would say, stroking his bearded double chin and laughing out loud. So Peril and Sons pioneered experimentation into increasingly surprising, spectacular, bizarre and deafening fireworks. As a result, most of the injuries occurred in the research department, where explosives were mixed like inexperienced cocktails by underage drinkers. Inevitably, the research department attracted danger freaks. Long-term staff had a kind of swagger about them, on a par with fighter pilots in the Second World War, and formed close sects with private languages of danger-banter.

While Jake had no real idea what went on in the research section, he also had little enthusiasm to find out. Ignorance meant he might live a bit longer. But the entirely random and bizarre nature of the accidents meant that Bulldog Fireworks were difficult for the Safety Team to police. Besides, there were other issues. Peril and Sons was a large local employer. Many of its products were exported, to countries where Catherine wheels which took off like dangerous frisbees were the norm rather than the exception. They paid agreeably high wages which kept local shops and pubs happy, and the hospital busy. Indeed, the nature of the accidents at the factory meant that Bridgeton Infirmary was rapidly gaining a national reputation as a specialist burns unit. The workforce was content to trade financial gain for the slight chance of losing a couple of toes. All in all, everyone was happy. Even the Safety Team wasn't too put out. After all, as Jake's boss often said, 'No Bulldog Fireworks, no job.'

'So we've doubled the thickness of the perspex,' Robert Peril continued. 'And no one's allowed in the research room without first attending your course.'

'Right.' Jake scribbled furiously and pointlessly on his pad.

117

'And lost limbs are down twenty per cent this quarter.'

'Good.'

'And we're looking into implementing survival suits which will withstand fairly healthy blasts.'

'Robert, you're always looking into implementing survival suits.'

'They're just so bloody costly.'

Jake glanced up from his clipboard as someone he vaguely recognized walked past him and entered the research room. She was slim, even in a lab coat, and had beautiful eyes, even through safety specs. He rewound through several possibilities, wondering where he had seen her before. 'Lives are costly,' he said, returning to the point. 'Not safety equipment. And modern survival suits can make all the difference. Between you and me, Robert, it's a dangerous factory. You're not negligent and your workers know the risks, but please, try to protect them as much as you possibly can. OK?'

'OK.'

This fruitless admonition over and his conscience cleared, Jake moved on to the next part of his routine. 'Now, I'd like to chat to one or two of your staff. That worker there.' He pointed at the girl. Robert motioned for her to join them from behind the perspex.

'I'll leave you to it.' Robert sauntered off, whistling.

'Hello,' the girl said. 'Still showing those terrible films?'

The penny suddenly dropped and Jake recalled showing her the forbidden fifth scene of *Office and Laboratory Catastrophes*. 'You remember me?'

'I remember the film,' she answered.

'You had some concerns at the time about your workplace. Is it still as bad as you thought?'

'Worse.'

'Really?'

'But the money's great. And you get used to the danger.'

'That's not necessarily a good thing,' Jake replied, examining some of the doodles he had been perfecting on his notepad.

'Isn't it? Don't you think life's got so dull these days?'

Jake shrugged. 'Maybe.'

'Look, our cars have air bags, our houses have smoke detectors, our fags have health warnings, even our food is labelled so we don't eat more fat than is absolutely safe. Where's the danger? Where are the Marie Curies, the Scotts of the Antarctic, the Donald Campbells?'

'Dead?' Jake suggested fatuously.

'Wrong. Gloriously dead.'

'So what are you saying?'

'They didn't die from eating too many saturated fats.'

She had a point. He'd had similar thoughts himself recently. 'Jake Cooper,' he said, offering his good hand.

'Louise Mathers,' she replied, smiling.

Safety Reports

Tuesday 10:14 a.m.

'Elizabeth? It's Jake,' he said, as his call was answered.

'Hi, Jake.'

He glanced up at the posterboard above his desk. A new motto had replaced last week's effort. 'You know what I do for a living?'

'You're some sort of safety person.'

'Right.' *Lethargy Is Your Liability* bore into his eyes. Underneath, the sorry story was spelt out in numbers. *5,945 trouser-related mishaps resulted in Accident and Emergency visits in the year 2001*. These doubt- less included people who ironed their trousers while still wearing them. 'And part of my duty is hazard prevention,' he continued.

His aunt let out a slow breath. 'So?'

'Well, one of the accidents I've been asked to in- vestigate is Norbert's.'

'I see.'

'And, if I'm honest, I asked if I could look into it, rather than being forced to.'

'Why would you want to do that?'

'Aside from my parents, Norbert was my only proper relative. I think I owe it to him.'

'Thanks, Jake, I appreciate that.'

'Besides, I didn't want to think of a colleague sitting next to me at work and doing it, creeping around trying not to offend me.'

'I'm sure you'll do a good job.'

'You never know. Anyway, I'll let you know what I find, that's if you're interested. I'll be in touch then.'

'Jake, before you go, there's something I should tell you.'

'What?'

'Something distressing happened the other night. Someone broke into my garden shed and stole a few items.'

'You're joking.'

'I'm not. The frightening thing is that they also tried to get into the house, while I was in. I've had a few days to calm down, but it's still under my skin. I'm having real trouble sleeping. Doctor's got me on some tablets.'

'You should have told me. Look, why not come over and stay with us?'

'No, Jake, it's OK. I'll be all right.'

'Did you see the burglar, then?'

'Actually I did. It was dark and from a distance.'

'And?'

'And nothing. But you know . . .'

'What?'

'I felt unnerved. It was like I'd seen him somewhere before.'

Later that morning, Jake saw the paperwork which told the story of his uncle's haphazard death in controlled words and ordered sentences.

Police Report

Mr Flint was knocked down by a car and then run over by a lorry. The angle of the latter insult was such that the victim was, to all intents and purposes, decapitated. One witness, Mr Eric Jones, who has subsequently been untraceable, gave a preliminary description of events at the scene to the first arriving police officer. However, his address has now been identified as a false one. According to the officer, Mr Jones was of scruffy appearance, possibly a vagrant.

Mr Flint apparently crossed a busy road, heading from a bus in the direction of his house, without checking it was safe to do so, leaving neither the driver of the car nor the driver of the articulated vehicle any chance to take preventative action. It is not anticipated that charges will be pressed at this time.

Safety Officer's Report

Tyre marks suggest that neither vehicle was travelling at excessive speed. Conditions were fair, visibility was good and the ground dry. The deceased was of good health and sound mind. There is no evidence of contributory slippage, trippage or falling. In the absence of a reliable witness, the police report will have to suffice.

Post-mortem Report

The deceased sustained massive head and internal injuries as the result of an RTA. The entire cranium was detached by the sheer forces of a large wheel, probably from a lorry. Primary cause of death – decapitation.

Verdict: Death from injuries consistent with a severe road traffic accident.

Spend and Save

With the accident reports all pretty straightforward, Jake resolved to visit the scene after lunch. He was far from relaxed. For a start, a nasty wound from his previous life appeared to be tearing itself open. He wasn't sleeping. Every time he had drifted off over the last few nights, images of severed fingers prodded their way into his slumber. His unconscious mind seemed to go looking for trouble, and was increasingly finding it. When he awoke, he was on edge, waiting for the next sign that all was not over and done with. Added to this, there was the pressing matter of his finances. He had reached the point where his salary was struggling to pay off the interest on his credit card, car loan, bank overdraft and mortgage. And when you can't even manage the interest that your borrowings have accumulated, you know you're in danger of going under.

He sat in a high street pub studying his uncle's manuscript for some sort of salvation, and as he did so, one thing nagged away at him. Other than a few hundred pounds, Norbert had left no savings behind.

123

To a man like Norbert, spending and saving were opposing forces of good and evil. If you did one, you couldn't do the other. He had said as much in the first few pages of his book, which Jake had been carrying around with him since inheriting it. He re-read the relevant section, seeing it now in a new light.

At the end of the day, it's a question of what money can do for you. Sure, it can buy things, transient things, things which fade and die. It can take you places and furnish you with memories, memories which will grow dusty and vague with age. It can gain you access to places you couldn't otherwise get into, places which, it often transpires, weren't really worth the price of admission anyway. Spending is temporary, as is the pleasure it brings.

Saving, in contrast, is a lifetime of fulfilment. Any time you want to be cheered up, forget hazy memories or instant purchases – go to the bank and demand a balance. A free balance. Clutch the slip of paper to your breast and feel the warmth flow through your clothes and nestle against your body, the zeros circling your heart, the ones pricking your skin with pleasure. You will never be alone in the world if you have money. Not because money attracts people – which it obviously does – but because on the coldest night, in the most desperate hours, somewhere in a metal vault, snug against the elements, cuddling tightly up, is a large bundle of notes, silently yearning for your touch.

So surely Norbert had stashed something away for a rainy day. Maybe Elizabeth just hadn't found it yet. He had been secretive enough about his finances that an illicit bank account could have slipped through the net. Jake drained the froth of his drink. Money was especially on his mind because in ten minutes he was meeting a financial adviser. He was taking this drastic step on the advice of Roger, who, cautious by nature, had almost choked on his biro when Jake let slip the extent of his negative equity. Since it wouldn't be wise to discuss the state of his finances in front of Kate, they had agreed to meet in the pub.

Jake scanned the bar, which was littered with lunchtime boozers. Dire Straits was on the jukebox, which struck him as a poor omen. For the first time in his life, he wished Status Quo was playing. Before he stood up to order another drink, a thought occurred to him and he flicked briskly towards the back of Norbert's manuscript. He remembered seeing a section on drinking. Fairly quickly, Jake found it. This was more promising.

Bar Tactics

Golden Rule Twelve: First out of the taxi, last to the bar. Count the number of people you are with. Assess the number of hours you are likely to be out. Work to the Standard British Imbibing Law of one drink every forty minutes, and position yourself in the round as follows:

Drinkers	Hours	Drinks	Position
2	3	4	2
3	3	4	2 or 3
3	4	6	3
4	3	4	4

i.e. in general, always get as close to the end of the round as possible. If you are out-manoeuvred and end up first, either leave after one full round, or insist everyone stays until the end of the second — otherwise your beer:money ratio will be low. Remember — the aim here is to maintain the highest possible alcohol to cash index.

This was gold dust. Why had he never had these thoughts himself? Jake was usually so happy to be out of the house that he would barge his way through the crowd to order the first round. What a fool he had been. As he thought about it, he had friends whom he'd never witnessed buying a drink. No wonder people were always eager to go drinking when Jake was there. He had been bankrolling them for years.

Instead of going to the bar, he sat and pondered. There was going to be a new Jake Cooper in the many pubs of Bridgeton, a leaner, meaner, cheaper one. It was time to let Norbert's manuscript guide the way. He looked at his empty glass and then at his watch, and decided to kick-start his new initiative by trying to manoeuvre the financial adviser into buying the drinks.

Right Place, Wrong Time

Unsurprisingly, the financial adviser had not brought good news. In fact, Jake had detected a momentary glance of disbelief as they had completed a grim post-mortem of his assets. The look had been caricatured, magnified by her large, all-conquering Deirdre Barlow glasses. She had been professional enough not to say, 'Look, you're a fucking idiot and you're going under,' but the message was there all the same, lit up in bulging blue eyes. At least she had bought the drinks.

The adviser, who met what she termed 'unrealistic spenders' on a daily basis, could offer no obvious salvation. Jake was living beyond his means, beyond most people's means, and had to do something about it. Spend my way out of trouble? he had suggested as a joke. She had merely raised a single eyebrow, which curved up like a cat arching its back.

At his desk after lunch, Norbert's manuscript of thrift was burning a hole in Jake's expensive bag. He locked the door, and continued to plough through the battered collection of his uncle's musings. The financial adviser had implied a painful couple of years of debt management. Norbert, however, promised the earth, as long as Jake stuck to the wisdom contained within the hallowed pages.

Part of the problem was undoubtedly Kate. As well as not working, she drained his resources and encouraged him to empty his pockets at the end of the month. Jake knew that he was useless with money, but it was much easier to focus on her shortcomings than his own. Besides, she provided a thorough reciprocal service, whether he wanted it or not. On page 32 of the great book, just after 'How to Deal with a Shared Bill', a particularly mangled section offered him the kind of guidance he was looking for.

The End of a Relationship: How to Leave Someone But Take Your Bank Balance with You

Most relationships end. That's the fact of the matter. But even if love ends, money endures. And the trouble is that your money and your partner's money might not be quite so happy about the thought of you splitting up. They might still be jointly invested in a comfortable bank account somewhere. So you need tactics. If your relationship is floundering, start thinking about the following options to let you walk away with what is rightfully yours. And, if you're especially cunning, a good deal of what isn't.

Wait until your partner is out or away, and have your house valued. It won't cost anything, and estate agents will be falling over themselves to do it. Get bank statements and find out what your investments — if you have any — are worth. Set up a new account at a new bank, and keep the details secret. Channel anything you've tucked away that your partner may be unaware of into this account. Slyly move a few quid from the joint account here as well. Calculate the approximate value of shared belongings such as furniture, cars etc. Work out your likely losses if all your assets are divided and then use Norbert's Golden Rule 21: Never end a relationship if it will cost you money to do so.

Being unhappy is a terrible thing, but being unhappy and

skint is a catastrophe. However, if you calculate that your net worth will be unaffected, or even enhanced, then by all means call it a day. Negotiate hard, knowing that having done your sums, the advantage lies with you. With careful bargaining, you should be able to leave your lover but retain your lolly.

This was more like it. What did financial advisers who looked like Deirdre Barlow know anyway? Jake could now consider whether his problems might simply be overcome by finding a more economical girlfriend. There was a knock at the door, and he tucked the manuscript under a pile of safety literature, before unlocking it. Roger entered purposefully in his leathers, with his helmet under his arm.

'How come you locked the door?' Roger asked. 'You know that sprained wrists and broken noses are twelve times more likely when someone assumes a closed door is unlocked than when—'

'Doing something private,' Jake answered, scrabbling about for the reports on his uncle's death, and holding them up.

'Ah. Sorry,' Roger said.

'No problem.'

'You must still be pretty upset.'

'Yeah. I am. It's hit me quite hard,' Jake replied, sighing. 'That's part of the reason I asked to handle his report.'

'You've had time to read it then?'

'Yes. What did you think at first glance?'

Roger dropped his helmet and picked it up again. 'Pretty straightforward RTA. When're you doing the scene visit?'

'I'm just on my way there now.'

'If it's any consolation, you know, me and Pauline, we were very sorry to hear . . .' Roger ran out of the right words.

Jake put him out of his misery. 'Thanks,' he said, standing up and monitoring the car park for potential conflict. Spotting a lull in the action, he left the office and headed for his car.

Later, Jake loitered at the scene of the accident. Norbert died within yards of his house, the reports suggesting he was heading there. One of the statements included a diagram of what happened. Using its scale, Jake stood at the exact point his uncle breathed his last breath. A couple of short skid marks pointed out the spot in black rubber. He scuffed the tarmac with his foot. There was still a faint reddish hue to the surface. All that remained. Stains on an indifferent road. Cars flashing over, oblivious, taking minute particles of Norbert away on their tyres. Slowly being worn to nothing, carried to random destinations across town, dispersed around the whole of Bridgeton. And then even the skid marks would fade, lost rubber reclaimed by scuffed wheels.

Two weeks earlier, Jake could have called to him and told him to watch out. But that was the bugger about time. You could have all the distance measurements in the world and be in precisely the right place, but without the correct timing it amounted to nothing.

Jake scribbled a few notes confirming the police findings, and walked over to his aunt's house. It was a mid-fifties semi with neglected window frames and a peeling front door. The brickwork was cold and damp, and Jake shivered as he ran his eyes over it. He rang the doorbell and Elizabeth opened the door.

'Just been doing the final paperwork,' he explained.

'Everything OK?'

'Fine.' His aunt invited him to sit amongst piles of Norbert's boxes and carrier bags which she was evidently sorting through. 'It's just a bit frustrating because usually we'd talk to the witness,' he continued.

'So why aren't you?'

'Gave a false address. It happens. People who

shouldn't have been where they were, you know, having affairs or skiving off work and the like, not wanting to incriminate themselves.'

'A bit selfish.'

'Mind you, this one seems a bit different. The police thought he might have been a vagrant. Probably panicked when they asked him where he lived.'

'A vagrant? Could have been Eric.'

'Eric?'

'The tramp who lived in the bus shelter. Haven't seen him since . . . Norbert . . .'

'Well, when he turns up, give me a ring. The powers that be don't like accidents with no witnesses.'

Elizabeth smiled, but her eyes were wet. 'Bit like that falling-tree thing,' she said. 'Is an accident an accident if no one sees it happen?'

There was an uncomfortable silence which Jake felt he should interrupt. 'So how are you bearing up?' he asked. 'You know Kate and I would love to have you over . . .' He became Roger and quickly ran out of the right sort of words. Where did women find them? They were so much better at comfort. Men like Jake and Roger just seemed to flounder in the face of tears. Should he hug his aunt? he wondered, but his arms stayed in his lap and fidgeted.

'I'm fine,' Elizabeth replied after a few slow seconds.

Keep talking, Jake said to himself. Do anything that doesn't involve hugging a weeping middle-aged woman you don't know very well. 'I hope my investigation hasn't upset you. I just wanted to make sure everything was done properly.'

'No, that side of it is bearable. It's been good of you.' Elizabeth blew her nose, and Jake sighed with quiet relief. The tears had stopped. He was out of the Hug Zone.

'And no more break-ins?'

'No. But it's got me spooked. And why the hell do people steal garden implements, for fuck's sake?'

'It's easy, I guess.'

Elizabeth was quiet, staring over Jake's shoulder. He glanced around. There was a photo of Norbert above the TV. 'I know I bad-mouthed my husband almost constantly . . . even at his funeral for Christ's sake,' she said after a gaping stillness, 'but I still miss him. And yes, I'm bitter about the money and hate him for his miserly ways, but the house is so damn quiet without him muttering to himself or hammering away on his calculator.'

'Hmm,' Jake replied, eager not to see his aunt upset again.

'Not that *you're* ever likely to starve a woman half to death in the interest of scrimping and saving.'

Jake gave another neutral grunt. Chance would be a fine thing.

How to Deal with a Shared Bill

A few nights later, Jake asked Kate whether she fancied dining out. His girlfriend tapped non-committally for a few seconds, turned to him and asked him to repeat the question. Before he reiterated the idea, she had swivelled back to the screen and was once again typing. 'Mmm,' she answered. 'Yeah.' Tap tap tap. 'I think . . .' Tap tap tap. 'Yeah.' Tap tap tap tap tap. 'Whatever . . .'

Jake changed out of his work clothes and ran a bath. While the water rose, he opened his uncle's manuscript. In the steam of the bathroom, the pages became almost transparent. It was an unusual document. Half diary, half manual, it was a series of mental jottings all running and screaming away from anything involving expenditure. Some sections were child-like in their use of language, some were funny, some were burdened with unappetizing accountancy jargon while others surged with evangelical joy. There was conviction, a system of beliefs, religious almost, a bible for those of an economical – rather than ecumenical – persuasion. And Jake had to admit that he was rapidly becoming a believer.

As he caressed the frail pages, momentarily picturing his uncle lying in a wooden box beneath the ground, he searched for further inspiration. Tonight was the night to confront his girlfriend with the stark reality of their finances. And that meant dragging her away from the delights of her chat rooms, out into the real world, where people sat and faced each other, sensed body language, intonation, nuance and used actual words formed from actual letters, rather than strings of clunky keyboard characters. He quickly found what he was looking for. A section devoted to the potential hazards of eating out.

Bistro No-Nos

In essence, eating out achieves all of the things that eating in achieves, but with more expenditure and less convenience.

Part of the problem lies with starters. I mean, what's the point? Do you rustle up a starter at home before your egg and chips? Do you prepare an ornate, expensive and frankly not very filling appetizer before tucking into your baked beans on toast? Of course not. So why should you feel compelled to do it when eating at a stranger's table?

Drinks are another issue. Take the following examples. A cup of coffee – upwards of one pound fifty. Each. The same coffee at home, using Aldis own-brand economy-grade instant granules and Lidl UHT fat-free milk – nine pence. A glass of wine – two fifty. A *bottle* of wine at the supermarket – one ninety-nine. And so the list goes on, all the way to the brandies. Robbery. Sheer robbery.

One way to avoid this is to dine only at unlicensed establishments. Take a cheap bottle of plonk (you may, if the situation arises, use your price gun (see Chapter 3) to label it with a £7.99 tag), and you're already quids in. That's if they don't charge corkage. Now, there are crimes against mankind, and then there's corkage. Two quid to open a bottle? That's the kind of job I'd like. My only suggestion is to open the bottle before you arrive, and try to argue the toss. A restaurant's going to be hard pressed to charge you for uncorking an uncorked bottle. Or take a box of wine with you, and tell them you'll gladly pay if they can find a cork to remove. If both of these fail, another idea is to drink cans of beer instead — there isn't, as far as I'm aware, a fee applicable to ring-pullage.

Jake made a mental note to buy four cans of lager on the way to the unlicensed Italian restaurant in the high street. He tested the bath water using the body's in-built toe thermometers, and stepped in. Kate shouted something he didn't quite hear, and Jake picked the manuscript up and continued reading. The next dining-out section detailed his uncle's opinions on tipping.

To Tip or Not to Tip

Take the Burger King approach. Point out that if you were going to tip, you should at least be consistent. Seeing as you don't tip in fast-food restaurants, why should you tip in slow ones? Surely you would only be rewarding sluggishness, which can't be a good thing. Take that to its logical conclusion and we'll all be giving large sums of money to DSS counter staff, builders and local government officials.

If you are ever in the nightmarish situation of having to hand over an appreciation for the service you have just received, try Norbert's sure-fire Tip Buster. This of course presupposes that the following disasters have all occurred: you have been forced/tricked/coerced into eating out; you have been forced/tricked/coerced into bringing your wallet; you have been forced/tricked/coerced into paying the bill; and that all exits are blocked.

OK, here's the Tip Buster. Pay by VISA and don't leave a tip. Prevent your partner observing this. Leave the restaurant. Never visit the same place twice. Simple. The only obvious drawback is if said wife/partner/Her-in-Debt insists on returning. This takes some skilful negotiation, but will be worth it in the end.

Jake decided to dust one of his credit cards off for the occasion. He submerged his head and allowed a stream of bubbles to escape to the surface. Tonight was the night. Telling Kate they were in perilous financial shape was almost as bad as finishing the relationship. In many ways, it was worse, because Jake needed to tell her something else, something distasteful. He had attempted to put it off, but it was no good. She had to know. He rehearsed the line underwater, saying it through bath-water bubbles. Kate, you're going to have to get a job. He surfaced. It was the only solution. Two incomes instead of one, and they could begin to dig their way out of debt. But Kate would be less than excited by the idea. He spat some water over his stomach. Very much less than excited.

Jobs

Saturday 7:11 a.m.

The weekend again. A small ache of dread began to seep through Jake's body. He rolled over, trying to get comfortable, and, failing, rolled back again. Maybe it was the meal sitting heavily on his stomach. Either way, something was gnawing away at him, bringing him struggling and fighting with the bedclothes towards consciousness. And then it became obvious, as the duvet was slowly tugged off him.

Kate's brain: Jobs. Jobs. Jobs.

Jake's brain: Fuck. Here we go again.

Kate's brain: Jobs. Jobs. Jobs.

Jake's brain: Pretend to be asleep.

Kate's brain: Jobs. Jobs. Jobs. I don't want a fucking job.

Jake's brain: Pull duvet slowly back up body.

Kate's brain: But there is one sort of job that might help.

Jake's brain: Duvet battle is being lost. Girlfriend moving into position to wake me. Bugger.

Kate's brain: Blow job. Blow job. Blow job.

Jake's brain: Something weird is happening.

Kate's brain: Blow job. Blow job. Blow job.

Jake's brain: I must still be dreaming. This can't be right.

Kate's brain:	Blow job. Blow job. Bloody blow job.
Jake's brain:	Open one eye slowly. See if you're in the right house.
Kate's brain:	Persevere. New tactics. Operation Be Nice to Boyfriend.
Jake's brain:	Right house. Yes! Correct girlfriend. Yes! Saturday morning. Jesus.
Kate's brain:	Jaw aching. Wrist cramp. It will all be worth it in the long run.
Jake's brain:	Yes! Why? Yes! Oh Christ. Yes! She wants something.
Kate's brain:	Come on, I'm waiting. Let's be having it.
Jake's brain:	Yes! What does she want? Yes!
Kate's brain:	Shit! I've just had a better idea. A baby! We ought to have a baby!
Jake's brain:	Oh yes! She's scheming something. Yes! This is very unnatural behaviour. Yes!
Kate's brain:	I'll just let him enjoy this one, and then there'll be no more sperm wasted around here.
Jake's brain:	Yes! But what is she after? Yes! Oh fuck it. Yes! Who cares?
Kate's brain:	Dum dee dum. Oh hurry up. I can't remember it taking this long.
Jake's brain:	Yes! I'll worry about it later. Yes! Kylie Minogue! Yes! Kylie Minogue. Yes!
Kate's brain:	Ah, here we go. Brace yourself. Sound enthusiastic.
Jake's brain:	Yes! I'm going to pay for this. Yes! But what the hell. Yes! Kylie. Yes! Yes! Yes! Yes! Yes! Yes! Yeeeeeessssssssssss!!!!!!!!!!!!!!!
Kate's brain:	Mmmm. Gag. Yes. Gag. Mmmm. Yeugh.
Jake's brain:	Heaven.
Kate's brain:	Hellish. Why does it taste that bad?
Jake's brain:	Fantastic.
Kate's brain:	Maybe it was the asparagus he ate last night at the restaurant.
Jake's brain:	The only thing that could possibly improve the situation is a kip.
Kate's brain:	Right. Phase One over. Time for Phase Two. Let him sleep. He's going to need his energy when he finds out what I've got in store for him.

138

Jake's brain: Seem to be slipping back into a coma. Floating, but pleasantly heavy. I am really going to pay for this. Still, name your price. I'm willing to cough up.

Kate's brain: Go to bathroom, and cough it up.

When he awoke, Kate had left her computer for a rare minute, and was in the bath. Jake wandered aimlessly around the living room, and then had an idea. He logged on to the Internet, and was soon inside his girlfriend's chat room. There, he began the ritual mating call of the single nerd.

BIGSPENDER: TRADER68? U STILL THERE?
TRADER68: Y. U BATHED?
BIGSPENDER: N. STILL DIRTY
TRADER68: OH YES!!!!!! ☺ ☺ ☺ ☺
BIGSPENDER: WANNA C U
TRADER68: WHEN?
BIGSPENDER: SOON
TRADER68: WHEN/WHERE??????
BIGSPENDER: HOGS HEAD PUB
TRADER68: N. DON'T ♥ HOGS HEAD
BIGSPENDER: Y NOT?
TRADER68: LONG STORY. CYBER CAFE?
BIGSPENDER: WHERE?
TRADER68: HI ST, NXT MCDS
BIGSPENDER: RIGHT/WHEN?
TRADER68: THIS WEEK?
BIGSPENDER: MAKE IT NEXT
TRADER68: WHENS GOOD 4 U?
BIGSPENDER: LET U KNOW
TRADER68: Y. ☺ ☺ ☺ ☺ ☺ ☺

With a little careful planning, he was going to conspire to make TRADER68's life a misery. No point in rushing in. He would take his time, see just how serious Kate felt about him first. And then, the set-up.

Jake figured over the course of the weekend that he

might as well start enjoying himself. Everything else was either complicated, expensive or very little fun. Or all three, he muttered on Sunday afternoon as Kate called for him to hand her a paintbrush. She was acting strangely. As well as decorating the spare bedroom, she had initiated more sex over the last two days than in the previous six months. The novelty was beginning to wear off. Jake had a mild sense of foreboding as he climbed the stairs. She was going to seduce him again. Four times yesterday, twice today already. He just wasn't used to this sort of action. His body, well past its alleged sexual peak, had slowly become adjusted to once-a-month capacity. By the top of the stairs there was a noticeable ache in his testicles. 'Bring it in, will you?' Kate shouted. Jake grabbed a paintbrush from his toolbox, sighed, and entered the spare bedroom. She was painting in her knickers.

While his girlfriend was by no means unattractive when virtually naked, her sedentary lifestyle was taking its toll, with her expanding backside telling the true story of her inertia. Her breasts had drooped a little, he fancied, and her stomach divulged the sins of a thousand ready-made meals. 'See anything you fancy?' she asked him coyly, in mock *Carry On* style. 'Only you,' Jake answered, as positively as he could. He had always envied the men you heard about who had sex three times a day every day. Now he began to see that it wasn't that clear-cut. Seven times in a weekend? Lunacy.

Here Comes the Bride

Afterwards, as Jake stared up at the ceiling wondering what the hell – aside from his penis – might have got into his girlfriend recently, Kate leaned over and brought her mouth close to his. She kissed him passionately, and Jake did his best to reciprocate. In truth, his lips weren't really interested. Ten minutes previously, as they notched up their seventh respective orgasms of the weekend, their lips and tongues had been very pleased to know each other. Now though, they were stale lovers who weren't bothered about staying in touch when the fun was over.

'Jake,' she said, 'you've never really told me what you feel about marriage, have you?'

'No,' he replied, happy to leave it there.

After a substantial pause which her boyfriend declined to fill, she continued, 'Well, don't you think you should at least talk about it some time?'

Jake smiled. Not because the situation amused him, but because of a section he remembered from Norbert's manuscript.

The Tightwad's Guide to an Economical Wedding

Financially, weddings make no sense at all. They are simply a convenient way for florists, hoteliers, caterers and tailors to take a large step towards their retirement bungalow at your expense. In fact, if there is another means by which you are likely to spend money so unwisely that it borders on the illegal, then I would like to hear about it.

Kate slid off the bed and went downstairs for a glass of water. Jake reached quickly inside a nearby drawer and dragged out Norbert's manuscript, scanning his ramblings and musings on the subject of marriage.

Certain cultures have commendable approaches to the temporary madness of the wedding day. Guests bring money and give it to you. If performed correctly you could almost make a profit from such a venture. However, British events substitute the cash for things which will never, ever be of any use to you, or else items which, seeing as you've probably been cohabiting for several years, you already have at least two of. Which brings me to the conclusion that the traditional wedding gift is no longer relevant in our society. Instead of giving the happy couple what they really need — money to pay for the one hundred and twenty free-loaders who turn up because it's a cheap booze-up — we present them with deep-fat fucking fryers or chocolate fondue sets, while they struggle to repay the loan they took out to have you come and palm them off with a cheap and unwanted gift.

However, there is some good news. As with everything, there are shortcuts, starting with the ring. Steady nerves as well as the element of surprise are what's important here. Buy an expensive diamond engagement ring at least four sizes too large for your fiancée-to-be. Take your intended on a long walk on a summer's day. Go down on one knee (bring a plastic bag along to save on laundry bills). Stare joyously into her eyes and ask her to marry you. Show her the ring. Allow her to try it on. Soak up the glory that only a substantial diamond can bring. Go home a happy, fulfilled man. Encourage her to show it off to as many friends as possible, and watch their eyes for sudden jealousy as the carat-laden beauty sparkles before them. Then, and this is the important part, return to the jewellers the next day. Ask for the ring to be adjusted to match your fiancée's delicate finger. Demand to keep the spare gold. And insist that the diamond be swapped for a zirconia stone of equal size. Pocket the difference in cash. Return victorious with the ring. No one will ever know, and besides, you have witnesses. All your friends have seen the diamond with their own eyes.

Kate was approaching, and so Jake tucked the hallowed document back in its hiding place. He propped himself up on his elbows. Outside, the summer rain was doing a fair impression of its winter counterpart.

'What are you smiling about?' she asked, climbing back onto the bed.

'Weddings.'

'What about them?'

'Oh, you know . . .'

'No I don't. You never even talk about it.'

Jake held his left hand up. 'Look, what's the point? I couldn't even get a ring to stay on. I mean, I'd have to sellotape the bloody thing to my stump.'

'You could use another finger.'

'That's not the point. I thought I spelled out our financial problems. A wedding is the last thing we could afford.'

'OK. How about children?'

'Children?'

'Yes. Wouldn't it be great? We could start a family.'

'A family? I mean a wedding's bad, but children? Have you any idea how much kids cost?'

'Cost? You're bringing money into this?'

'I'm the only one bringing money into this house.'

'Meaning?'

'We talked about you getting a job. We're skint. And I don't see you doing anything about it.'

143

'That's right – blame me.'

'I'm not blaming you.'

'I mean, I'd love to get a job. It's just not that easy.'

'Not if you sit on your arse all day faffing about on the Internet.'

'There's lots of jobs advertised on the web these days. I'm looking. Really, I am.'

'And I do like the idea of children, it's just . . .' A nasty thought suddenly came to Jake. Sex. They were having lots of sex. She was seducing him, and even being nice to him. If she became pregnant, she wouldn't have to get a job. So that's what was going on.

'Just what?'

'Nothing. We'll talk about it later. I'm going to have a shower.'

'Want me to come with you, lover boy? Think you could handle some more?'

Jake declined the offer, and not just because his gonads were doing fair impressions of raisins. It was time to re-establish his celibacy. A new strategy was called for. This would take some fairly underhand tactics of his own.

Human Biology

Monday 4:57 p.m.

Elizabeth opened her front door and stepped out of the rain. She was cold and the house's warmth surged forwards to meet her. Since Norbert's death she had been running the central heating almost constantly, in a futile attempt to compensate for years of underuse.

Fucking pupils, Elizabeth swore to herself as she slung her handbag down next to the sofa, deciding to blame her job for all her woes. 9B. Bastards. 8C. Cunts. 10A. Arseholes. That was the problem with secondary-school education. You had the full range of adolescence to confront every day. Just the biological words spelled it out. Pubescent, juvenile, immature, teenage, infantile. She shook her head rapidly. It wasn't as if she had a lot of contact with the adult world either, since the death of her husband. And Mondays were always the worst, as if the kids had spent all weekend saving up their hormones to release into her stuffy classroom.

Elizabeth slumped on the settee with a cup of coffee and kicked off her shoes. She inhaled the heavy aroma of her drink and some heat began to return to her body. As she breathed it in again, she detected something else as well. Skulking within the sweetly seductive odour was an altogether less pleasant smell. She put her coffee down and stood up. There was a mustiness about the room, and, as she wandered around, a suggestion of stale tobacco.

The problem with the sense of smell, Elizabeth recalled from the human-biology modules she taught, is that it decays rapidly. After several seconds of detecting the same smell, the nose loses interest and demands a replacement. It soon found one. Alcohol. She walked through the house sniffing. In her bedroom, a can of Tennent's Special sat on her bedside table. She picked it up and shook it. A dull rattle came from within. Elizabeth headed into the bathroom and tipped the can upside down over the sink. A soggy roll-up butt flopped out of the empty can. She went to the telephone and called the police. 'Someone has been in my house,' she told them.

While the police made their way over, Elizabeth nosed around, on edge. It was possible that the intruder was still inside. She crept through each room silently. Her eyes saw the living spaces differently now. They were tainted with the presence of a stranger. She searched for signs of disruption. A chest of drawers in the back room appeared to have been opened. Upstairs, the spare room looked considerably messier than usual. Her bedside drawers had also been moved. She didn't touch anything, aware of ruining potential forensic evidence. At last she mustered the courage to shout, 'Look, if there's anyone here, I've called the police. They'll be here any minute. Just tell me what you're after.' Silence. Elizabeth screamed, 'What the fuck do you want from me?' Her words echoed around the walls. 'Please. You're scaring me. What are you after? I have nothing.' Again, there was no reply. 'There aren't any valuables. There isn't anything worth having here.' She slumped on the sofa. 'Not any more,' she said to herself. And then she began to weep inconsolably.

The police arrived over an hour later and began to examine the house for evidence. After twenty minutes of noisy investigation, one of them sat down with Elizabeth on the tatty sofa to tell her what they'd found.

'The first thing to state, Mrs Flint, is that there's no sign of a break-in. Whoever got in here, if they got in here, is either a professional or . . .' The PC left his sentence hanging, to bring home the weight of what he was going to say next.

'Or what?' Elizabeth asked.

'Or has a set of keys.'

'Oh my God.'

The copper wiped away a layer of sweat from his forehead. The house was an oven. Quite why Mrs Flint felt the need to inhabit a subtropical environment in the middle of summer was a mystery. 'I think you'd better change the locks. Failing that, keep your doors bolted.'

Elizabeth frowned. 'But the keys . . . You know my husband was run over?'

'The decap—' The PC stopped himself short. All of Bridgeton's seventeen policemen and women knew about her husband's death, and in intimate detail. A few of them had attended the scene. Accidents that nasty weren't easily forgotten.

'Yes. Well, that's another funny thing. There were no keys returned to me with his effects.'

'So they're missing. And he definitely had them on him?'

'Must have. Otherwise he'd have been locked out. And I haven't come across them in the house.'

'What are you saying exactly, Mrs Flint?'

'I don't know. Just that a man breaks into my shed

and then my house. The house requires keys, keys which have gone astray.'

The PC studied the notes he had written. 'Tell you what I'll do,' he said, standing up, 'I'll get on to the investigating officer for your husband's death, see if I can find out where his keys might have ended up. That seems to be the important thing here. In the meantime, keep your doors and windows bolted, and ring us if anything happens.'

'And next time you'll get here within the hour?' Elizabeth asked, unable to keep fear and sarcasm from mingling with her words.

'Next time we'll be here in seconds.'

After the police had left, the enormity of her loneliness came to Elizabeth as a series of cold sharp breaths. She picked up the phone and dialled Jake's number. It was engaged. Thirty minutes later, she finally got through, and told him what had happened. And then she said what was really on her mind.

'I think it's Eric,' she began. 'The shed and now the house.'

'But why would Eric start to threaten you? I mean, you gave him his lunch every day.'

'He's a vagrant. Maybe things aren't that simple. I mean, you've got to ask why someone is living rough in the first place.'

'A lot of homeless people do seem to have personality disorders,' Jake agreed. 'Though whether that's cause or effect is another matter.'

Elizabeth was quiet for a second, and Jake could hear her rapid breathing. 'All I'm saying is it's a bit weird he should go missing after being at the accident scene where Norbert presumably had his house keys.'

Jake turned from the phone. Kate was in her underwear and was rapidly advancing. 'It's possible, I suppose,' he answered. 'Look, I'll pop those reports round to you tomorrow. Maybe we can talk about it then.'

And with that, Elizabeth put the phone down and made herself another cup of coffee, while Jake was dragged up to the bedroom for some more unwelcome sex.

Fat Is Dangerous

Roger lowered the copy of the *Lancet* that had occupied him for fifteen avid minutes, and started muttering to himself.

'What is it?' his wife asked.

He looked up at her, and snapped back to reality. 'Fat!' he said.

Pauline frowned. 'If you're going to start name-calling . . .'

'No. Fat. That's the thing.'

'That's what thing?'

'Fatness. Obesity. The statistics . . .'

'Roger, please start making sense.'

He tried to calm himself. This was a revelation, and excitement, fear and apprehension coursed through his veins. 'They've done a massive study—'

'Who?'

'Some scientists and doctors. And if you look at the figures, the one thing that's more harmful, more dangerous, more likely to kill you in the long run than smoking, drinking and anything else, is obesity.' He was almost shaking with agitation.

'Being fat is dangerous, Pauline. In fact, it's positively lethal.'

'Worse than smoking and drinking?'

'You're more prone to injury, to heart disease, to skeleto-muscular problems, to . . . well, you name it. Look at the life-expectancy figures, the morbidity and mortality data.' Roger held the article up and pointed to a confusing graph, where coloured bars accounted for a host of problems Pauline would rather not know about. 'Then there's hygiene issues, greater likelihood of strained and sprained joints—'

'What's the difference?'

'Well, a strain is more . . . Look, the point is, it's futile taking precautions with your life, if you let yourself get out of shape. I mean, I could be a walking time-bomb of infirmity.' He stood up and searched the living room excitedly.

'On the bed,' Pauline suggested.

Roger came out of the bedroom clutching his coat.

'Where are you going?'

'To the gym.'

'Which one?'

'I don't know. I'll find one.'

'But you're not even a member.'

'Pauline, you're witnessing a new birth. From now on I'm going to be fit.'

'You *are* fit.'

'Fitt-er. Healthier. Less likely to be obese.'

'Roger, you're not likely to be obese in a million years.'

'That's the spirit. Helmet?'

'On top of the wardrobe.'

He returned to the bedroom and very carefully retrieved his protective headwear (*Domestic Safety Rule Three: Objects falling from heights are the fifth most common cause of household injury*). For some unfathomable reason, his wife carried around with her an *A to Z* of the exact location of every possession they had ever owned, which could be called upon day or night when he couldn't find what he was after. The attic, the shed and the garage were similarly catalogued. Even items which hadn't been used for years could be accounted for in an instant. Outside the house, however, his wife could barely find the car, and frequently got lost on minor shopping trips. Although this struck him as something of a contradiction, he had never said anything, except once, when he suggested that she ought to secrete various useless household objects in random shops around town, which she would then be able to track down easily as she collected the groceries. And then, for personal safety reasons, he had never mentioned the idea again.

He entered the living room, pecked his exasperated wife on the cheek, and embarked upon his search for a gym. 'Remember, you'll be seeing a new me from now on,' he shouted as a parting gambit.

Pauline picked up the *Lancet*, flicked half-heartedly through it, and hid the magazine somewhere her husband wouldn't look. Then she collected her coat and left the house, glad that Roger had made it easy for her. No excuses were needed tonight, which was a relief, because she was running low on them. There were only so many evenings out she could have with her alleged Book Club or her non-existent friends.

Climbing into her car, she checked the time. She had arranged to meet Simon at a nightclub in nearby Taunsley. Revving the vehicle harshly, she pulled out of the drive at speed. As long as she was back in a couple of hours, Roger would be none the wiser.

Two days later, there was indeed a very different Roger knocking about the bungalow. His wife had noticed the change the day before, but had kept quiet. Today the situation was, if anything, even more pronounced. As a master stroke, she flicked the kettle on in the kitchen, before joining him in the living room.

'So you'll be off to the gym tonight?' she asked

her husband as he sat in front of the TV eating his tea.

'Better not,' he answered, keeping his eyes firmly on the screen.

'But all that cholesterol . . .'

He turned to her, swallowing a mouthful of food. 'The body does need fat, you know.'

'Ah, kettle's boiled. You couldn't make me a cup of tea, could you?'

'I'm eating.'

'Oh go on, I've hardly sat down all day.'

'But—'

His wife flashed him an annoyingly unrefusable smile. Roger sighed, and attempted to stand up with something approaching dignity. Although simple just a couple of days previously, it was now no easy matter. His joints ground together as if they'd had their cartilage replaced with grit, and all his muscles ached as if they'd been punched repeatedly. To make matters worse, he had a heavily strapped foot and his left hand was bandaged.

Pauline monitored proceedings with interest as her husband hobbled towards the kitchen. 'Do you think you'll be able to manage?' she called after him. Her husband grunted. 'Only it might not be so easy with your broken finger and sprained ankle.'

Roger grunted again. His left index finger – the only part of his body that wasn't aching – began to throb as he once again pictured himself dropping a large weight on it. 'I haven't sprained it,' he replied curtly. 'As I told you, it's strained.'

'Either way.'

'Sugar?' he asked.

'I'm dieting. Don't want to get fat.'

Roger shuffled back with the drink and handed it to his wife.

'So you'll be looking into the gym's safety licence?' she suggested, mock seriously.

'No,' he replied meekly.

'Why not? Surely it wasn't your fault the weight fell on you and that you twisted your ankle?'

Roger lowered himself gingerly into his chair. 'Sometimes,' he said, knowing that this wouldn't be the last he heard about it, 'you've just got to accept that the world is a dangerous place.'

Pauline sipped her tea and smiled to herself. With a husband like Roger there was always some fun to be had. And with Simon always available, she certainly had both ends of the excitement spectrum.

Guilt

In the car park of potential death, Jake noticed that something was wrong with his car. One of the windows didn't seem to be reflecting any light. Closer, there was a sprinkling of square, chunky pieces of glass on the passenger-side tarmac. He pushed his hand through the gaping window and swore. Some Anger Management case had obviously had an argument with his Audi. Maybe the car had looked at him funny. He walked round and climbed in. There was more glass inside, and as he picked a few of the pale blue fragments off the seat, he noticed an object on the dashboard. It was a circular-saw blade, covered in red. Jake slid it off and let it fall onto the upholstery. The blade was thick, and its teeth sharp and eager. Red paint had been splashed across the surface. He ran a fingernail through it and a small residue detached. Jake rubbed it between the finger and thumb of his good hand and a single name jolted through him. Ronnie. He shut the door and left the car park in a hurry, slamming over the speed bumps, his seatbelt unfastened.

At his aunt's home, Jake was about to post the safety reports through the door when he spotted some movement. She was attaching something to the windows. Elizabeth let him in. She appeared haggard. She rubbed her face often as she talked, a quick, irritable downward stroke, and occasionally scratched her scalp. Jake didn't know exactly how old his aunt was, but if he'd had to guess today he would have said about a hundred and twenty.

She began to fill him in on the details of yesterday's break-in. 'So when I got home, I realized that someone had been here.'

'And you're sure they didn't steal anything?'

'I don't think so. The police asked the same question. After they'd gone I started hunting around. There was nothing obvious, just drawers that looked as if they might have been opened, that sort of thing.'

Jake began to sweat. It was unreasonably hot. He glanced at the bay window. For some reason, his aunt had covered it in clingfilm. 'And?'

'This is really weird. Although the intruder appears to have had a good rummage around, I can't think of a single item that's been stolen. And there were valuables – you know, the video, a camera, watches, some jewellery, all of which were worth having.'

'So what did the police say?'

'To bolt my doors. They were a bit sceptical at first, but there you go. Maybe they think I'm just a middle-aged woman who's lost her husband and is cracking up.'

Jake glanced guiltily away from his aunt, the same thought having crossed his own mind. 'What's with the clingfilm?' he asked.

'Insulation.'

'From what?'

'From draughts.'

A large drop of perspiration nose-dived between his shoulder blades and down his back. 'But it's summer.'

'Just compensating,' she murmured.

He sat and pondered. Against his aunt's unsettled behaviour, he was by no means calm and sane either. Something he thought he had left behind was rearing its very ugly head again. Just as an intruder had forced his way into Elizabeth's house, an unpleasant object had been rammed into Jake's car. The difference was that Jake wouldn't be contacting the police. 'Anyway, I've brought those reports, if you want to have a look,' he said, dragging himself away from his own troubles.

Elizabeth took the documents and scanned them thoroughly. Something in the cold description of events appeared to unsettle her. Viewed from certain angles, she looked close to tears, and Jake once again felt the icy grip of hugphobia render his arms limp and useless. Oh Christ, here we go again, he whispered to himself, regretting his decision to come around. What if she started to cry again? He was trapped. He made a desperate bid to change the subject. Children — apparently middle-aged women liked talking about children. 'You never had any kids, did you, Elizabeth?'

She glanced up from the reports. 'No, we never had children. Norbert was dead against it.'

'Why?'

Elizabeth gave him one of her teacher looks. 'Why the hell do you think?'

Don't know, miss, he felt like saying. 'The expense?'

' "Kids," he would say, "are just about the worst investment you can make. How much return is there? Where are the dividends, the perks, the tax breaks? Thousands and thousands of pounds, year after year, just to produce something that probably doesn't like you anyway and spends your money as if it thinks it's earned it." '

'I suppose you can see his point.'

'No I can't see his point. Look at me, I'm forty-two in three months. I'm past it, over the chuffing hill. No husband, no child, no savings. That bastard has deprived me of everything I should rightfully have, and all the while he said he was making me rich.'

He was quiet for a few seconds, cursing himself for choosing a topic which was even more upsetting than her husband's death. Jake wondered hopefully whether Elizabeth might be too dehydrated by the crushing heat to summon any tears. He decided to risk returning to the point. 'So what do you think about the reports?'

Elizabeth looked up at him. 'They're missing a vital piece of information.'

'What? I thought all the—'

'Let me explain something,' she interrupted. 'It's like this. On the day he died, Norbert made me some fish-paste sandwiches. I didn't eat them. I gave them to the tramp at the bus stop instead. And when they returned Norbert's effects to me, there were my sandwiches again.'

'I don't follow.'

'Don't you see? Norbert must have got the sandwiches back off Eric. I gave them to Eric and somehow Norbert retrieved them.'

'And why would he do that?'

'Obviously because he was the world's tightest man. But this has been eating me up since I worked it out, Jake.'

'What?'

'The last thing he ever did for me was to make my lunch. And what did I do? I gave it to a sodding vagrant. And Norbert knew. He died, knowing that I was throwing his efforts back at him. Maybe he had only ventured out to salvage my lunch. Maybe the only reason that he died was because he was correcting my ingratitude.'

Jake used the back of his hand to wipe away some more sweat. 'He did go to the shops as well.'

'But he could have been crossing the road on his way home when he spotted Eric and decided to demand his sandwiches back, and got distracted, and . . .'

'It's possible, I suppose,' Jake conceded, rubbing his chin. 'Eric was at the scene of the accident.'

'If only I hadn't given those sandwiches to Eric . . . And now it seems the bastard might be wandering around my house when I'm not in, for some reason.'

'We don't know for sure.'

'But we don't know he's *not*. Fat lot of good those reports were as well. And it could all have been my fault that Norbert's . . . Norbert's . . .'

Jake spotted the first signs of moisture in his aunt's eyes. Tears were beginning to gather in the corners, and it was only a matter of seconds before one of them made a bid for fame and leapt down her cheek. He had to say something comforting, and quick. What do you say to someone who has lost everything? Which thin, insipid words could possibly paper over the enormous chasm of death? How can you make light of the terrible, menacing emptiness? Overwhelmed by the sheer size of the task, he remained silent and awkward.

Elizabeth wiped her eyes and scratched her scalp again. She continued in a low voice, half whisper, half whimper. 'I feel like my last act was to betray him, and his last act was to be betrayed by his wife. And I know it's only sandwiches, bloody fish-paste sandwiches, but that's not the point. It's the principle. I mean, I've always slated my husband – even at his funeral – and yet, when it all shakes out, I'm the one in the wrong.'

Technical Merit

Jake surveyed the crowded, smoky room, and spotted a girl who made his pulse race. She was five-six, wore mainly white, sported open-toed shoes and had her auburn hair tied back. Louise. Attractive though she undoubtedly was, something about her appearance rankled with him, and although he tried to overlook it, eventually he decided he ought to do the decent thing and tell her.

'Louise, isn't it?' he asked, walking across to her and offering his hand.

The girl looked him up and down for a second, and then replied, 'Yes.'

'Jake,' he said, his hand remaining open to offers.

'I'd better not shake, if it's all the same to you,' she shouted above the music.

He glanced down at her fingers and nodded, realizing it would probably be better all round. 'No problem. Do you mind if I have a quick word?'

'Actually I'm waiting for someone.'

'Won't take a second, and it's important.'

'OK,' she answered reluctantly, looking nervously around her.

'It's about what you're wearing.'

She turned to face him. 'Yes?'

'Sandals are a no-no as far as I'm concerned.'

'Really?'

'Yes. The rest of your clothes are fine, it's just the open-toed shoes have got to go.'

'And what gives you the—?'

'Louise.' A tall, scruffy man approached and handed her a glass of something. 'Take this,' he said.

Jake felt a little awkward. He didn't like her friend's clothes either. 'Could I have a word with you?' he asked.

The man was gruff and unimpressed. 'What is it?'

'I expect certain standards of dress, and you don't meet those standards.'

The man snorted. 'Oh yeah, and who are you?'

Jake paused, meeting his eye. 'The Hazard Prevention Officer.'

'Shit,' the man said, glancing guiltily at the glass of chemical he had just handed Louise. 'I'll just go and put my lab coat on.' He left them, slicing rapidly through the dense gaseous atmosphere of the research and development lab, turning the radio down en route.

'I've got some protective shoes,' Louise blurted, 'in my locker.'

'Fine. And goggles, as well.'

'Right.'

'But at least you're wearing a lab coat, which is something, I suppose. In fact, you're the only bugger wearing one.'

'I'm still new,' Louise said.

'That would be it. So how long do you really plan to be here at Peril and Sons?'

'Two or three years, maybe.'

Jake couldn't help but inhale sharply. The average

limb expectancy of researchers at the firework factory was roughly eighteen months. Before too long, they would be carrying her out in a body bag. Or, if especially unfortunate, a series of body bags. Pity really. She was far too pretty to be dismembered.

'What?' Louise asked, reading his shock. 'As I told you last time, the danger side of things gets under your skin, makes you feel alive.'

A low, rumbling noise emanating from the far side of the room began to shake the table Jake was leaning against and interrupted their conversation. Workers continued calmly about their business, some of them struggling into protective clothing, having been tipped off that a safety inspector was in the vicinity. Suddenly he heard the single shouted word, 'Nagasaki!' Almost instantaneously, personnel flung themselves to the floor. A couple of ominous seconds later a heavy blast rocked the east wing of the factory. Jake, belatedly appreciating what the code word 'Nagasaki' implied, found himself lying on top of Louise, who had also failed to understand what was happening before the force of the explosion knocked them both over. His heart was racing, and only later did he realize that this had less to do with the blast than the position he found himself in. He hadn't been on top of a woman that he wanted so much for years. Instead, he had mainly found himself on top of women that he only half wanted, or on top of Kate, who, with the exception of the last few days, only half wanted him.

He rolled off Louise, the cinematic image of a cigarette being lit flitting through his mind, and helped her up. The smoke slowly skulked out of the room through the open windows, and the firework pioneers resumed where they had left off. An unidentifiable character piped up, 'Sorry,' and provoked a couple of cat-calls. Then one of the beards near the scene of the bang held up two pieces of paper and showed them around the lab. Jake strained his eyes. One appeared to say '5', and the other '6'. 'What's that?' he asked Louise. 'Technical merit,' she answered. 'Nice,' Jake said grimly. 'Very nice.' He had some fairly serious matters to raise with Robert Peril.

In the early hours of the next day, while Jake made a fumbled trip in the direction of the toilet to piss mainly in the bowl, he realized his ears were ringing. Even over the sound of his urine bouncing off the seat, ricocheting around the porcelain and drilling into the water, there was a clear buzzing in his head. As the source of the noise – yesterday's explosion – came flowing back to him, another sensation joined in with the muddle of his half-awake state. Something was gnawing at him. The bang, the aftermath, the calm shrug of the workers as they shook the brick dust off and started again. The black humour of those who had failed to be hit by any flying glass.

But among the accepting bravado he had also witnessed fear. There had only been a sliver of it, caught for a second in one person's face, but it had been there all the same. And then he remembered. Louise, as he peered into her eyes, had looked scared. There was genuine apprehension. And then another notion fought its way into his ringing mind, something altogether more serious. Louise wasn't just scared – she was in danger!

He opened his own eyes. A beautiful girl was in peril, and he could actually do something about it. How often did that ever happen in the real world? At last, Safety had provided him with a mission. He stumbled back into bed, and crawled in beside Kate. Lying on his back, he began to see that his job might actually have a purpose. OK, so other people were at risk, but how many of them, he asked himself, were slim and attractive? How many of them would he give

163

anything just to lie on top of in a shrapnel-ridden laboratory? How many of them wore such pretty (and unsafe) sandals? As he thought about it, he decided that things were going to change in Bridgeton. And, for once, for the better.

The Accumulator

On the bus to work, Jake held his uncle's manuscript close to his chest, before opening it and running his eyes over the section that had been swimming around his brain for the last few days. A lot depended on this. He had just taken a drastic step on Norbert's posthumous advice, and needed to see in black and off-white that he had done the right thing. The argument had been persuasive enough, but maybe he had been vulnerable. In the cold light, on a crowded bus, car-less, Jake began to have his doubts. He allowed his eyes to loiter, to take in the words they had been too agitated to absorb, to speed the message from paper to brain.

Cars

Let me frighten you with a few awful, shocking, depressing words. Brace yourself. You may never be the same again. OK, you've been warned. Here goes. Depreciation. Road tax. Wear and tear. Repairs. Petrol. Breakdown cover. Insurance. MOT certificates. Tolls. Oil filters. Air filters. Pollen filters. Servicing. Parts. Labour. VAT. CD multichangers. Car washes.

Parking tickets. Clamping fees. Speeding tickets. Theft. Batteries. Compulsory excesses. Clutch fluid. Brake fluid. Washer fluid. Towing. Wiper blades. De-icers. Parking meters. Shock absorbers. Spark plugs. Seat covers. Tyres. Deionized water. Air fresheners that look like cardboard pine trees. Snatch-plate stereos that still get stolen. Had enough? Well, this is only scratching the surface of the problems you have if you are a member of that penalized majority – car owners. Really, Amnesty International should launch an appeal.

The obvious trouble is that cars and cash are mutually exclusive. You have one, you won't have the other. So here are my tips on transportation.

First, sell your vehicle. I have done the calculations and can tell you that not having a car is substantially more economical than having one, even, and this is an enormous even, if you catch taxis everywhere instead. Obviously I'm the last person to encourage such financial insanity, but when you factor in the number of miles travelled against the yearly cost, taking taxis is, almost unbelievably, cheaper. When put into this sort of perspective, the sheer scale of the problem should send shivers down your spine. And by not having a car, many spending pitfalls are avoided. No one is going to ask you for a lift, before claiming not to have any petrol money. You are not going to be asked to drive to the shops to buy things you don't need. You will not be a glorified and unpaid chauffeur of convenience for your family.

Second, find someone with a car – a friend or colleague – and begin to spend a lot of time with them. Moan about the state of public transport, the cost of taxis etc. Because the only better invention in this world than a car is someone else's car. All of the warmth, convenience and speed, with none of the wallet-breaking costs.

Jake exhaled a long breath of relief. He could see now that he had done the sensible thing. At 9 a.m. prompt he had driven to the local garage and sold his car back to the person he had bought it from, at a considerable loss. As well as being a financial liability, the vehicle had been attracting unwelcome attention of late, as the missing window testified. The slight damage had lowered the trade-in price even further. It had cost him roughly two thousand pounds to no longer have any means of transport, and although the maths of the situation still rankled, Norbert's words convinced him that, in the long run, it was the right decision. In fact, everything the manuscript had advised so far had turned out to make sound financial sense. Cheap dining, the avoidance of tipping, bar tactics with the financial adviser, the joys of saving and wedding-phobia were all beginning to turn things around for him. And the more he read, the more he came to see that the thin straggly wedge of paper he had been consuming since Norbert's death had a beauty all of its own. It wasn't merely the ramblings of a tightwad, it was the expounding of a philosophy, a theory, a way of living. There was symmetry, grace and art in it, and Jake was fast becoming a convert. You used people as vessels to get you where you wanted to be. You steered them towards the bar, towards paying the bill, towards the front of the queue, towards giving you lifts in their car. You guided their money for them, always cushioning yourself from spending your own. This was a noble pastime which had kept the rich rich and the poor poorer. A nuance here, an evasive answer there, a protracted fumbling for your wallet at the critical moment – it was a craft of the highest order. And what gave people like his uncle a bad name, Jake came to see, was not the principle of what he did. It was, instead, the crude efforts of brass-necked tight-wads who attracted unwanted attention to the subtleties of Norbert and his ilk. The blatant misers with pursed lips, who said can't pay won't pay. The true craftsmen, who slipped silently through the night, guiding their pennies towards safety, all suffered because of the bad publicity gained from such amateurs.

And disciples of Norbert had a name. They weren't misers or tightwads or skinflints. They were accumulators. They accumulated the excess of life, trimmed the edges of what people didn't need or didn't want, mopped up the glut of money which spilled from the careless existences of others. They amassed it and saved it from waste. They gave the surpluses of life a proper home, and called them their own. They weren't scavengers so much as recyclers. It was a good fight, a just fight, an honest fight.

That is what he would tell Kate anyway. Standing up and shuffling off the bus, Jake appreciated that she might not be quite as sold on the idea as he was. But without a car, she could now only shop for small, easy-to-carry items, which could only be a step in the right direction.

Helmet

At five o'clock, Jake decided it was time to get the ball rolling. 'The buses are terrible these days,' he said.

Roger glanced up and grunted.

'And taxis are just so extortionate.'

'Mmm.'

The message wasn't getting through, so Jake tried a more direct approach. 'Roger. Have you got a spare helmet?' he asked.

Roger nodded and then said, 'Why?'

'I need a lift home.'

'Right.'

Jake frowned as he noticed a new safety slogan had been stapled to the posterboard. The poster stated, *The Best Motivation Is Self-Preservation*. 'D'you mind?'

Roger shrugged. 'I suppose not,' he said.

'What time are you going?'

'Now-ish,' he replied, retrieving his biro from the floor. 'Just give me a minute.'

Jake gave Roger a minute, then five, another five, ten more, and finally, after almost half an hour, he was ready to extract himself from his chair. Roger had been reading a new set of safety guidelines with evangelical enthusiasm. For his own part, Jake began by idly watching a couple of minor scuffles develop into fully fledged battles in the car park. Roger always parked on the far side of the unit, well away from the action.

Roger began to put his leathers on. Jake turned from the window and watched him. He spent several minutes carefully inching them over his bandaged foot, cursing every time his broken finger got involved in the action, before realizing he had the leathers on back to front. Roger started again, still in pain, and cried out as the padded trousers caught his ankle on their way off, and one more time as he put them back on. Next, he put his gloves on over his injured finger, before finding that he couldn't adjust the straps of his motorcycle boots. Jake made himself comfortable. This certainly beat sitting at home and watching TV. Roger removed his gloves, slid his injured foot gingerly into a boot, fixed both sets of straps with some difficulty, and then pulled his gloves back on. Then he stopped. His keys were still in his work trousers. Irritably, Roger pulled his gloves off and rummaged around beneath his protective pants. Jake looked away. Finally he appeared to be almost ready, and they headed out of the office together, largely in silence, having already exhausted a day's worth of conversation.

Jake was excited about a ride on Roger's motorbike. He had only ridden a bike once himself, and that was as a teenager on holiday. Over the time they had worked together, he had often tried to picture his colleague's motorbike. Roger never seemed willing to discuss it though, which only added to its aura of speed and danger. It was the one redeeming quality of his office-mate: although cautious to the point of spinelessness, he had a hidden streak of adventure in his bones.

As they entered the car park, Jake followed a step behind the creaking of Roger's leathers, and glanced quickly around for signs of the two-wheeled monster. Among the cars were two mopeds and one racing machine, which wouldn't have looked out of place pulling wheelies down the home straight at Donnington. He felt a quick surge of giddiness as they headed for the souped-up racer. And then, as they approached the bike, Roger did a curious thing. Just in front of it, he veered to one side and stopped.

'What are you doing?' Jake asked.

Roger pulled out the world's largest set of keys, which looked like a bunch of emaciated metal grapes, and pointed one at a Volvo in front of the motorbike. 'Spare helmet's in the boot,' he explained, the car beeping in robot recognition of its master.

'Right.'

Roger walked round and opened the boot. Inside was a full-face helmet and some more leathers, which he passed to Jake. 'Here,' he said, 'they're Pauline's, but they should fit.'

Although it seemed a little weird that Roger had a car and a motorbike in the car park, Jake took the protective gear and began to put it on. He asked him through the padding of his headgear whether his wife would mind.

'What?'

Jake repeated the question, most of which seemed to be absorbed by the headgear.

'Never wears the stuff herself,' Roger replied at the second time of asking. 'Can't understand it personally, but that's the way she is. I've given up nagging her.'

'So what cc is this machine of yours?' Jake asked, getting a little excited.

'Cc? I don't know. Sixteen hundred, maybe.'

'Sixteen hundred? Jesus. Goes a bit, I guess?'

'I suppose. Can't say I really push it though.'

'Fair enough.' He pulled his final glove on. 'I'm ready if you are,' he said.

'Good.' Roger climbed into the car and started the engine.

Jake peered through his visor at him in mild surprise. 'What are you doing?'

'Hop in.'

'But . . .' Jake pointed a thickly gloved finger at the high-performance motorbike.

'What?'

'You mean we aren't taking your bike?'

'What bike?'

A horrible thought came to Jake and he felt himself flush inside the protective gear. 'You're telling me . . .'

'What?'

'You put all this bloody stuff on to drive home from work?'

Roger glanced up through his visor with a semblance of curiosity. 'I would have thought that was obvious.'

'Not fucking likely. Come on, you must be joking.'

'Do I look like I am?'

'No, you look like . . .' Jake decided not to insult his way out of a lift. 'But why?'

'It's safety, Jake.'

'No. It's bloody lunacy.'

'Cars are dangerous. You are eleven times more likely to die driving to work than actually working. Depending on your job.'

Jake ran his eyes over the large silver Volvo estate. 'And if you work in Hazard Prevention?'

'I don't know the statistics for that. I'll look it up.'

Jake tried to remain reasonable. 'But I still don't get it. Why the hell do you dress up like you're about to go into combat?'

'Simple. If I have a crash, and the Side Impact Protection System, front air bags, side air bags, side torsion beams, pre-tension seatbelts, anti-lock brakes, collapsible steering column or steel cage of the car don't prevent injury, then the leathers

172

and helmet will provide a last line of defence.'

'From what?'

'From whatever reckless fool might crash into me.'

'So you wear all that just to drive about?'

'Of course. And it obviously works.'

'How?'

'Well, I'm still here, aren't I?'

Jake mumbled 'Un-fucking-fortunately' into his helmet.

'In the long run, Jake, a big car is going to involve fewer head injuries than a small one. And a helmet is going to reduce that risk even further.'

'You're a cheerful bastard, aren't you?'

'A cheerful worker is a safe worker,' Roger replied, missing the sarcasm.

'For fuck's sake,' Jake said, exasperated.

'What?'

'You're not interested in safety, Roger, you're just a fucking coward.'

'Same thing.'

'No it's not. Not by a mile.'

Jake climbed into the car with an overriding sense of defeat and Roger pulled slowly out of the car park in first gear. 'Look, you try being this accident-prone,' he said after a minute or two of muffled silence. 'Imagine how bad things would be if I worked somewhere dangerous.'

'You've got a point, I suppose,' Jake answered, taking his helmet off. 'Now are you going to drive me home?'

Roger risked second gear. After a laboured thirty minutes of strict adherence to speed limits and braking distances, the Volvo cruised into Jake's cul-de-sac. Roger bade him an incoherent goodnight, and, despite some impressive revving, pulled off at sub-pedestrian pace.

Spending long periods locked inside a Volvo, dressed in women's protective clothing, being driven

173

by an accident-prone safety freak, was the easy part, Jake told himself. Now it was time to confront Kate with the news that they no longer had a car. He strode purposefully into the house where, for the third successive night, he was ambushed by a semi-naked woman.

Lumps

Kate served the casserole in her underwear. Not literally, of course. Most of it was in a bowl, which wasn't necessarily a good thing. As Jake peered into the murky, lumpy brownness of her cooking, he became a little uneasy, and began to crave the microwaved perfection of lasagne and micro-chips. There was certainly a hint of meat to the dish in front of him, but what meat, and indeed what dish, remained a mystery. He bravely chewed his way through a difficult couple of mouthfuls, battling with gristle, chunks and still-raw vegetables, while Kate garnished the air with encouraging phrases like, 'Got to keep your strength up, lover,' and 'That'll put hairs on your chest.' On my arse, more like, Jake said to himself.

Although he had planned to rush his food, there was a disturbing friskiness about Kate's behaviour. He endeavoured to slow down. She was lining him up for another seeing to. This was becoming a nightmare. Morning and night, whether he was interested or not, Kate wouldn't take no for an answer. Previously, no was the only answer she ever gave, unless she was feeling particularly spirited, in which case she might have enticed him with the irresistible come-on, 'OK, if we must.' Kate took the opportunity to ply him with more wine, which he gratefully downed while making heavy weather of a stubborn carrot and lamenting his change in fortune.

Between his girlfriend and his workmate lay a land of partial sanity. Veer just a fraction into the direction of either of them, and the rules of normality wavered and diverted and tied themselves into messy knots. He took a moment to think, as a swelling of meat successfully battled the efforts of his teeth. He was sitting in his own living room in a woman's motorcycle leathers, facing a born-again nymphomaniac dressed only in her underwear, having sold his beloved car after being left surreal reminders of an incident he thought he had long since left behind, and was expected to inadvertently impregnate his girlfriend so that she wouldn't have to work and could sit around getting turned on flirting with some computer nerd she had never met, spending the money that Jake didn't have, and all the time he was going under, debts swallowing the earnings he made from trying to stop pissed people injuring themselves, earnings that were by no means extravagant, in a job which didn't really appeal, and even economizing was costing him money, with the end of the month rapidly approaching, and his panicking girlfriend doubtless assuming they would be spending the leftovers of another bad month . . . and— something snapped. He spat the gristle out and stood up.

'You ready, big boy?' Kate asked, also rising, misreading the signals.

'Oh I'm ready all right,' he answered.

'Great idea with the leathers.' She took a step towards him. 'Come on, Motorcycle Boy, deliver your message.'

'Message? There's a message all right. Look, today I—'

'Hang on, I've had an idea.'

'What?'

'I'll go upstairs and dress as an office girl. And you can come striding in—'

'I'm trying to tell you something.'

'And I'm trying to tell *you* something, Mr Sexy Leathers.'

'These are women's leathers actually.'

'Getting kinky, are we?'

'No. I'm wearing them because I've sold the car.'

'You've done what?'

'I took the car to the garage and flogged it.'

'For a motorbike?'

'No.'

'So why are you dressed up like Carl Fogarty?'

'Long story.'

'And you're not just dressing up for sex?'

'Not exactly.'

'Well, not to worry, we'll soon get you *undressed* for sex.'

Jake monitored his girlfriend's body with interest. Although he had seen a lot of it over the last couple of weeks, there was something eternally fascinating about staring at her near-naked form. The recent exercise they had been indulging in had done little to help matters, however. There was, he concluded after several seconds scrutinizing her neck, shoulders, breasts, stomach, hips, thighs and legs, something sloppy about her these days, as if she had been poured into a mould and had overflowed slightly. Her form had a looseness about it, where once there was only tautness. He glanced up from her body and into her face. 'Kate. I sold the car because we're skint.'

A brief look of panic spread across her features. 'Skint? What do you mean, skint?'

'I've been trying to tell you for a while.'

'Well, you said we had to economize, but I didn't think you meant we were in trouble.'

'Let me spell it out in numbers. We're nearly twenty grand in debt. Well, about thirteen now I've got rid of the car. We've got credit-card bills, an overdraft, a bank loan for the house deposit and our mortgage is considerably more than the property is worth. In short, we're fucked.'

Kate slumped down on a chair and pulled a jumper around her shoulders. 'Fucked?' she asked, the foreplay truly dead and buried.

'You've got to get a job. I know it's tough, and I know a lot of this is my fault, but that's the way it has to be.'

'But, Jake – a job? I'm not good at anything.'

'Bollocks. There's loads of things you can do.'

'Like what?'

Several ideas came and were dismissed without troubling Jake's mouth. Microwaving. Flirting. Spending. Parking her arse. 'Lots of things,' he said diplomatically.

'Look, why don't we go upstairs and we'll discuss this all later.'

Kate clearly wasn't listening, and Jake felt a surge of anger inside his leathers. 'Are you just being evasive, or do you always have to—?'

The phone rang, and Kate took the opportunity to escape from an unwelcome line of argument. 'Hello?' she said, picking it up. 'Oh right, yes, just a minute. It's for you. Elizabeth. I'm going for a bath.'

Jake cursed. Things were going nowhere. And this was all he needed. An aunt on the verge of a nervous breakdown to add to the personality problems around him.

'Jake. There's something else,' she said.

'What?'

'Something of Norbert's is missing.'

Jake stole a deep breath out of the side of his mouth. 'How do you mean?'

'His prized possession. A gun . . .'

'What sort of gun?'

'A price gun.'

'A *price* gun?'

'You know, the ones they use in supermarkets to put price labels on things. He didn't think I knew he had it.'

'And why did he have it?' he asked, rubbing his face.

'Devious sod used to alter the prices of things he'd bought, so I'd never know quite what he was spending. Anyway, the point is, it's missing and it wasn't in his personal stuff the police gave me.'

'Elizabeth, I'm really sorry. Maybe I'm being a bit slow here. What are you getting at exactly?'

'Look, we know Norbert was run over. We also know that for some reason he died with my sandwiches on him and that someone has got hold of his keys. But now I've discovered that his one item of luxury and necessity is missing. Don't these things strike you as odd?'

'Not really.'

'And think about it. Norbert was careful as anything.'

'Accidents happen.'

'OK. How about this. I've got another theory.'

'Have you?' Jake asked, with little desire to discover more.

'The tramp disappeared, giving a false address, and he was the only witness at the scene. Now, Norbert stole my sandwiches off him. Let's say a struggle developed. Maybe they fought, and maybe Eric took the price gun and the keys. Then Norbert was pushed into the road, got run over, and Eric scarpered.'

'Anything's possible.'

'You don't sound convinced.'

'I know this is probably difficult to hear, but I think it's time to accept what's happened, and to get on with reconstructing your life. People break into houses and sheds all the time.'

'I can't move on. These things are weird, Jake, and aren't in the least bit explained by the official events.'

Jake was forced to concede that it didn't all add up, and that there were inaccuracies, but that imprecision was far from unusual when it came to accident reports. He agreed to at least think about it. And with that, Elizabeth hung up, Kate slammed the bathroom door and Jake slumped on the sofa feeling thoroughly bewildered.

Changes

The following day, Jake cycled to his aunt's house at lunchtime. He had taken the morning off work to buy a bike, which would, in the long run, save him money. In the short run, however, the 21-speed, dual-suspension, active-braking, all-terrain aluminium Canondale mountain bike had done him few favours. Not so long ago you could have bought a small car for the price he had paid, and still had change to fill it full of petrol. And to tax it. And insure it as well. But the principle was there, and that was what mattered. As Jake pedalled up the last hill of terraced houses before Elizabeth's street, appreciating that the active braking and dual suspension were doing little to further his cause, he understood that once again in an attempt to economize he had gone out of his way to lose money. He had fallen victim to the inevitable spending philosophy that for just a few extra pounds he could have a vastly superior product, a logic which propelled him from an entry-level and perfectly adequate cycle to a top-of-the-range, state-of-the-art piece of machinery that wouldn't have looked out of place in a NASA laboratory.

He removed the clip-action wheels and the seat post, and U-locked what remained to his aunt's gate. Elizabeth was mildly surprised to see him, particularly as he seemed to be carrying half a bike shop with him. Inside, she asked whether he'd thought any more.

'A bit,' he told her. In fact, during the night, images and ideas had settled heavily within him like the lumps of gristle in his girlfriend's stew.

'That's a start, I suppose.' The house was still unbearably hot, and Jake noticed that she had been busy fitting draught-excluders to the doors and cling-filmed windows. 'But I want to show you something,' she said. 'Because of the break-in I've taken some time off work and have been sorting through a lot of things. And I realized that I never really examined his clothes properly. They just came in a bag, a bloody bag full of bloody belongings. I decided I ought to wash them and see if they were good enough to give to a charity shop. And that's when I spotted the shoes. They weren't too bad, all things considered. I mean, they were wrapped up in a shirt which was absolutely sodden with blood, but they were just . . . splattered. Anyway, I had a good look at them, and something struck me. They were small, much smaller than the rest of Norbert's shoes. He had large feet. So I carried them upstairs and opened one of his boxes, where, for some reason, he kept all his old footwear. I've got a pair here.' Elizabeth held up a pair of battered work boots, and opened them up. 'Look,' she said, 'size eleven.'

Jake declined the offer to inspect footwear that his uncle had spent several years in.

Then his aunt showed him the ones the police had returned to her. 'Size seven,' she pointed out.

'Maybe the police got his effects mixed up with someone else's,' he suggested.

'I don't think so. They were all in a bag, clearly marked with his name. I can't see it.'

Jake took one of the shoes, which appeared to be sweating. He ran his fingers over it. The sole was well worn, and the upper was coming undone at the seams. A label inside stated, 'Size 7, European 41, Made in Taiwan'. Hard as it was to admit to himself, his uncle's death was throwing up some difficult questions. But perhaps he was simply seeing the personal side of an accidental death, the side he never normally saw in the reports he filed or the films he watched. Maybe all accidents were like this. The truth was something written, words that relied on hearsay, interpretation and assumption. It was possible that for all events, if you took the sum total of evidence and shook it thoroughly enough, a few anomalies would drop out. He thought of the shooting of JFK. A president had died, an assassin had been arrested, but the truth lay somewhere within an enormous wealth of contradictory evidence. And there had to be a truth to everything, even if you couldn't see it. So a few irregularities were just about par for the course, even for events occurring in front of millions of witnesses, all of whom would inevitably have their own version of the facts. And yet, sometimes, a single discrepancy is all you need to appreciate that the version of the truth you have in your hands is not the right version.

'It's the tramp that bothers me,' Jake said after a few seconds.

'Why?'

'He's the only witness, he was there at the scene, some sort of interaction occurred between him and Norbert, and he's done a runner. Now the break-ins are probably nothing to do with him at all – just co-incidence, maybe. But either way, he's obviously got something to hide.'

'So what can we do?'

'I'll take the accident report over to the police station tomorrow – I've got a friend there – and we'll chat about it. Maybe they'll try and track Eric down for us, and we can find out what he actually knows. By the way, you know that manuscript thing you gave me?' he asked.

'Bloody glad to see the back of it.'

'Norbert didn't have a word processor, did he?'

'Spend money on a computer? Come on. Stop talking out of your hole.'

'So where did he get it typed?'

'Woman down the road.'

'Whereabouts?'

'Number Eleven. Norbert saw a card of hers in the newsagent's. She'd mistyped the word "typing" – put an "e" in it – so he thought she might be cheap. Turned out he never paid her anything.'

'Why not?'

'Well, she – Mary her name was – settled in the end for having Norbert do some odd jobs around her house. Couldn't get the bastard to change a light bulb in his own home, of course, and if he did, he wouldn't throw it away, but at Mary's, he practically rewired the place.'

Jake flicked mentally through Norbert's section on DIY.

DIY has one sole thing going for it. If you Do It Yourself, you Pay For It Yourself. So it's cheap. But other than that, to be avoided at all costs. Rewiring, for instance. What's the point? If it's already wired, why bother doing it again? I mean, who ever heard of re-plumbing? If it's plumbed once, then that's good enough for most people . . .

'Do you still see Mary around?' he asked.

'From time to time. Why do you ask?'

'No reason.' Jake had had an idea. After chatting a while, and making sure his aunt was at least partially sane, he left and walked in the direction of Number 11, where he found himself without a solid excuse for knocking. He would have to wing it. The door was several coats deep in glistening emulsion and had a smart brass knocker with matching letterbox and two ornate number ones. Jake pulled the knocker back and let it swing against its metal contact. After ten seconds or so, the door was yanked briskly open and he found himself facing a moderately alluring woman in her mid-thirties whom he thought he recognized from the funeral.

'Yes?' she asked.

Jake stood and stared at her, wondering what to say. 'Are you Mary?' he answered eventually.

'I am. And you might be?'

'My name is Jake. Jake Cooper.'

'So?'

'I'm a relation of Norbert's. I understand you two had an arrangement . . .'

'What sort of arrangement?'

'I mean that you typed his manuscript while he fixed up your house.'

Mary regarded him with continued scepticism, unsure of what he might be implying. 'That's true, I suppose. But why are you here?'

'I'm sorry to put you out. I was just upset that he's no longer with us, and wanted to talk to people who knew him.'

Mary softened. 'Cup of tea?' she asked, stepping back from the door and allowing Jake room to enter. The house was fussily furnished. It wasn't overly cluttered, but it also wasn't going to win any feng shui competitions. There were chairs where Jake would have had space, and space in areas he would have difficulty getting to. Mary pointed him at the sofa and walked into the kitchen, maintaining a half-hidden conversation from there. 'Is there anything particular you wanted to know about Norbert?' she asked.

'The only thing really is his manuscript.'

'What, that old thing of his?'

'Yes.' Jake crossed himself reverentially and whispered, 'The Bible,' under his breath.

Mary returned with a tray of assorted tea paraphernalia. 'Have you seen it, then?'

'Oh yes. It's magnificent.'

'Magnificent? There's no need to be polite, just because I typed it.'

'It is, though.'

Mary raised her eyebrows and pushed out her lower lip. 'You say so. I always thought it was a load of tripe. Norbert's little joke, I used to call it.'

'What do you mean?'

'Well, a bloke like Norbert having me type such a load of nonsense. Generous as the day is long, and he spends all his time scribbling down anecdotes about being a tight-arse.'

'*Generous?*'

'We became good friends. He was always bringing me things. You know, presents and the like.'

'*Presents?*' Jake asked incredulously, recalling his chapters 'The Giftless Christmas' and 'Birthdays Without the Birthday Money'.

'Not large things, of course. Just thoughtful ones.'

'Like what?'

'There was that consignment of storm-damaged underwear. And one time, a tennis racket. No strings, but he said he'd get hold of some cat gut, one way or another . . .' Jake had a fair idea of where that might have come from. 'Then there was the door knocker and the numbers. Took him ages to find them. Came over with them one night, all flushed with excitement he was.'

It was a good bet that some poor sods at Number 11 Other Street had woken to find they were minus a few items of door furniture. 'Did he spend a lot of time here?' Jake asked.

'Yeah. You could say that.'

'But when he wasn't here, and wasn't at home, do you know what he got up to?'

'Lots of things, I suppose.'

Something had been going on at Number 11. Judging by the state of Mary and her house, Norbert's money hadn't been swallowed up there. But Jake was beginning to feel that there was more to Norbert's life than met the eye. Whether his aunt's obsessive worrying was undermining him he wasn't sure. All he did know was that certain facts didn't add up, and that Mary, a woman who had actually enjoyed his uncle's company, and who had received presents from him, might well be a useful source of information. Jake left Number 11 and walked back to his aunt's house, where he unchained his bike and began to add the various components he had stripped from it, which took longer than his journey. He checked the time. Two o'clock. Fuck, he was late for work.

Pigs

Roger was quite excited as Jake strode in, breathless. Although 'quite excited' was hard to identify against the background of Roger's permanent anxiety, Jake nonetheless detected a minor air of animation about him. As he dumped some of his cycle paraphernalia, Jake noticed with dismay that a new safety poster had made itself at home above his desk. It announced, *Stay Alert and Nobody Gets Hurt*. Over a photo of a lorry driver dozing in his cab lurked the cheery message: *Roughly 10% of all road-haulage fatalities result from driver fatigue*. He turned his attention to the window, vainly searching for signs of commotion, before stretching and sitting down. Endless shagging, coupled with pedalling a mountain bike so advanced that it was hopeless on flat roads, was taking its toll. His limbs ached and he suspected he was suffering from a major salt deficiency. He vainly hoped that he was coming down with something dangerous which would prevent his girlfriend seducing him when he got home.

'Look what I've got,' Roger said, holding up a reel of film, 'hot off the presses.'

'Where from?' Jake asked wearily.

'Japan,' he proclaimed proudly.

'How did you get hold of that? Surely it hasn't been classified.'

Roger tapped his nose in conspiracy, and Jake noticed a new white patch trying to eat through his colleague's skin. 'Friends in high places,' he said.

'Right.' Jake knew Roger had no friends, in high places or otherwise.

'You cycling?' Roger asked.

Jake glanced at the cycle clips in his hand, the helmet on his desk, the seat post in his other hand and the two wheels he had extracted when he locked his bike up. 'Yes, Sherlock,' he answered.

'You do know, Jake, that you're seventeen times more likely to die on a bike than in a car?'

'Depends who's driving,' he said.

'Anyway, guess who we've got now?'

'Tell me,' Jake mumbled, dumping the rest of his various cycle-related accessories on the spare office chair.

'Chefs Three. And guess what the film's called.'

'Dunno.'

'*Safety Is First – Don't Be Losing Your Head.*'

'Nice.' Jake flicked through a few safety forms which needed sorting. The pornography of violence was losing some of its appeal. He had been aware over the last few weeks that he was watching less and less of the films, and more and more of the audience, to try and gauge their reactions. Were they as sick as he was? he wondered. And was he as sick as he used to be since his uncle's death? And something else had occurred to him. Because we are largely buffered against catastrophe and pain, we now pay to see it in films and on TV. And what's more, we enjoy it.

Jake picked up *Safety Is First – Don't Be Losing Your Head*, and followed Roger towards the viewing room. He continued to ponder as they walked. Violence stands alone in the field of human misery. There is nothing funny about footage of someone mourning or crying or being abused. However, show a person being shot at close range à la *Pulp Fiction*, or having bricks repeatedly smashing on their head in a Laurel and Hardy fashion, or using six-inch nails and a hammer for acupuncture in *The Young Ones*, and we all laugh.

In the lecture theatre, Chefs Three giggled and joked, glad to be away from their various kitchens. Jake extracted the film from its circular casing and mounted it on the projector. Still, he told himself, a new film was always interesting, and it was harder to find reasons not to watch it than to go with the flow. Roger encouraged Chefs Three to settle down and take note. Jake turned the projector on and sat down.

Safety Scene #9

Interior of a slaughterhouse. Large bovine and porcine carcasses are hanging from hooks. Well-presented Japanese workers quickly perform a variety of tasks including cutting, sawing, chopping and mincing. This is a good film. The director knows what he's doing. He is leaving it up to the audience. Several potential disasters are avoided. Unusual camera angles add to the sense of being inside the abattoir. This guy wants to direct proper films, Jake thought to himself. The tension is rising, as sharpened knives plunge through the air and cleavers catch glints of light. Despite his recent squeamishness, Jake became absorbed in the film. This wasn't pornography, this was erotica. Having set the scene and heightened the trepidation, the director was ready to allow the climax to begin, and Jake knew it. He braced himself. A worker at the edge of the picture is fixing a bacon slicer. The camera follows the electrical lead of the slicer to the plug. It is switched on. The worker unscrews some mountings, while all around him meat is chopped, diced and violated in every possible way. We see his gloved hand flick a switch and the blade of the slicer rotates very quickly. In slow motion, an artistic device rarely used among the instant carnage of safety films, we see the blade lift up, detach and set off menacingly across the room. Jake quickly acknowledged to himself where the title of the film was coming from. The blade leaps through the shot and cleanly decapitates a worker. His head rolls into a wheelbarrow holding pigs' heads. Beautiful symbolism. His blood sluices into a sump of cattle blood. Fade out in red.

Onscreen translated message: *Act like Pig, Die like Pig*.

Jake was moved almost to tears. Why watch people fuck when you could watch them make love? This was fantastic. It would be wasted on Chefs Three, and probably even on the DangerClub, but what the hell, maybe he'd transfer it to video and take it home with him. The second scene opened gently, sucking everyone in. Chefs Three fidgeted, scratched their heads and looked away. Jake was consumed. And not just by the film. A new idea came to him as he watched. Act like pig, die like pig. This was the central truth. As he thought about it, pieces began to fit. Fish-paste sandwiches. Small shoes. A headless corpse. A price gun. A missing witness. Death at the bus stop. Shed sabotage. An intruder. A bunch of keys. Eric the vagrant. That was it! Gruesome images flitted through his brain as they appeared on the screen. He looked at his watch. He would have to sit still for another twenty minutes. As he continued to think, he couldn't contain his restlessness any more than the squeamish members of Chefs Three could. He was excited and nervous, and desperate to exit the room.

* * *

'Well that was crap, wasn't it,' Roger said to him as he walked quickly out of the lecture room.

'Nope. It was fucking great,' Jake replied.

'Where're you going?'

'Got to nip out to see a friend. Be an hour or so. Can you cover for me?'

Roger nodded. 'If I must.'

'Oh you must. This is important.'

Panic at the Funeral Directors'

Dabner and Sons was rarely a cheerful place, even at the best of times. Not that there were many best of times to be had in a funeral parlour, but there was a certain darkness in the humour of its employees which eased the pervading atmosphere of death and futility. As far as Malcolm Dabner, Chief Undertaker, was concerned, death came with two conflicting and contradictory states: dignity and comedy. They were opposites that kept each other in sober check. All in all, it was a schizophrenic profession. A public face of sorrow, a private face of sick jokes and gruesome practices.

As he replaced the receiver, a horrible thought came to him and he summoned his second in command, Bob, who was busy embalming a recent corpse in the adjoining room. Embalming always seemed such a gentle word for what they did with long, thick needles, scalpels, suction pumps and liquids noxious enough to clear drains. Certainly, when Malcolm himself died, he wanted a quick cremation, and the less he was buggered about with by cheerfully morbid bastards like Bob, the better. Mind you, embalming was going to be a mild form of torture compared with the potential repercussions of the present situation.

Bob was rubbing his bloody hands on a rag, as a mechanic might clean congealed oil from his fingers after groping around under the bonnet. 'What is it?' he asked, sauntering into the office.

When he was nervous or flustered, Malcolm often attempted sentences which he had little hope of finishing. He tripped himself up, unerringly using words that left his mouth nowhere to run. 'What it is, is . . .' he began, 'is . . .'

'What?'

'Trouble,' Malcolm told him, cutting to the chase.

'What sort?' Bob wiped the remaining blood on his overalls.

'You remember that one we had a few weeks back with the missing head?'

'Hamlet, you mean.'

'Yes. And you'll doubtless recall your bright idea to bury him in a dwarf coffin.'

Bob shifted uneasily. This didn't sound like good news. 'Made us a couple of hundred quid,' he said, opening the case for the defence.

'The thing is with that is, is that . . .'

'Boss?'

'That that might be so, Bob, but now the fuckers want him dug up again.'

'You're joking.'

'Do I look like a comedian?'

Bob glanced at his boss. No, you look like a miserable old undertaking bastard who can never get his words out straight, he thought, allowing the question to go unanswered.

Malcolm was set on pursuing the matter. 'Do I?'

Quite why he was insisting on an answer to a rhetorical question, Bob wasn't sure, but he replied, 'No.'

'Right,' Malcolm answered, honour satisfied.

Bob shuffled his feet uneasily. 'Why do they want to do that?'

'I'm not really sure. The police wouldn't give me a clear answer.'

'The police? Christ. You don't think they've twigged that we pulled a bit of a fast one, do you?'

Malcolm thought for a second. 'It's possible.'

'So what are we going to do?'

'Well, I'll tell you one thing for sure. We're going to dig that coffin up, and then we're going to put Hamlet in a larger one before they get here.'

'When are they coming?'

'That is what it was . . . that they said . . . tomorrow morning. I told them we'd start excavating, and they let me know that a special exhumation squad would come and do the rest. I'm sure they won't object if we've already done the job for them.'

'And then when we rebury him, shall we put him back in the four-foot-sixer?'

'Why the fuck would we want to do that, Bob?'

'Because a full six-footer isn't going to fit back in a five-foot hole.'

'Fuck.'

'Indeed.'

'This is going to call for some pretty careful work. I mean, if the police twig what we've been doing, there's no knowing how many graves they're going to want dug up. And if people get to know that Dabner and Sons bury headless corpses in dwarf coffins while invoicing grieving widows for full-length ones, well, we're buggered. Tell you what we're also going to do, Bob. You and me are going to dig that fucker up tonight and get him out. Then we're going to write to Hamlet's widow explaining that we accidentally overcharged her, and return her money.'

'But, boss, I want to—'

'What you want to do . . . I don't care what you want

195

to do. We're staying late and getting this done. And, Bob . . .'

'Yes?'

'Next time you have a bright idea, keep it to yourself.'

Bob had just had the bright idea to try and push his boss into the empty grave and quickly fill it in if he got the chance, but he kept it to himself.

Later, Bob drove Malcolm to the town's largest cemetery. The ring road was disturbingly close, the suburbs sprawling relentlessly out to consume isolated stretches of calm. Queues of traffic often sat just yards from the mass of graves, motionless drivers peering gloomily across at their inevitable resting places. The road was quiet by the time they arrived, most people having retreated to the sanctuary of their new houses on modern estates.

Twenty yards through the gates, Malcolm turned to his reluctant assistant and asked, 'So, where did you put him?'

Bob stopped the car. 'Can't remember,' he replied, running a finger down the bridge of his nose.

'What do you mean, you can't remember?'

'It's not my fault – we've been doing six stiffs a week recently.'

'You make us sound like an old knackered hooker.'

Bob glanced at his boss. Old knackered twat, more like, he said to himself, lighting up a fag.

'So the book . . . why don't we check the book? You *did* bring it?'

'We could, only . . .'

'What?'

'We haven't been filling it in.'

'Why the fuck not?'

'Me and the boys couldn't see the point.' He turned the engine off. 'It's not like many people need digging up to be messed about with by the filth. And besides, rather than bothering us, the bereaved tend to ask the cemetery keeper where he's parked their loved ones.' Bob took a conclusively deep drag on his cigarette and summed up. 'So it's not our problem, boss.'

Malcolm appeared to redden. 'Well, it is now. I mean, how the hell are we going to find the mangled bugger?' He checked his watch. 'The cemetery keeper will be at home with his feet up, tucking into his cottage pie and chips.'

'We could give him a call,' Bob suggested.

'I don't know,' Malcolm replied, unfastening his seatbelt. 'Keep this quiet . . . I think maybe we'd better . . . any other ideas?'

'Not really.'

'Tell you what,' Malcolm suggested, 'why don't we just scout round for reasonably fresh graves?' He climbed out of the car. 'Shouldn't take too long.'

About an hour later, when the two men were on the verge of murdering each other, they finally came across Norbert's resting place. It was gloomy, and they stopped for a break. Bob soon detected an obvious problem.

'We haven't got any spades, boss,' he said.

Malcolm turned to look at him. 'Well, get some,' he replied.

'Slight hitch.'

'What?'

Even through the advancing gloom, Bob could tell that Malcolm's already ruddy complexion was darkening. 'All the tools are locked up.'

'Fuck.'

They stood and thought for a couple of eerie moments. They had to do the job tonight, or there would be problems. The light was rapidly fading. Neither of them could easily lay their hands on the proper equipment for the job, and both silently cursed the other for not thinking about this sooner. Bob scraped some mud off his boots and then stood up. 'Hang on, boss, I've had an idea,' he said.

Malcolm was not overjoyed. He had specifically asked Bob not to share his ideas. Indeed, the very reason they were stood in a cemetery in the dusk trying to dig up a headless man was because of an identical sentence Bob had uttered some weeks earlier. 'What?' he asked reluctantly.

'Wait here,' Bob replied.

Bob disappeared into the twilight and Malcolm leant against a nearby tombstone. He hated graveyards and cemeteries. It wasn't the death, it was the silence. One stiff lying quietly on an embalming table was fine, but a whole fucking field of them freaked him out. He wished they would make some noise, rattle some chains, anything. But no, they remained resolutely hushed, watching him eagerly, with litres of Draino coursing through their veins. The position of the graveyard also troubled him. It was at the very edge of Bridgeton, as if the town was excreting its dead, useless effluent pushed out into the rapidly disappearing countryside. He shivered against the cold stone, and then looked up as an unexpected noise filtered through the stillness. Over occasional crashes came the unmistakable sound of a large diesel engine. And then he saw it. A huge yellow JCB being backed towards him, intermittently running over graves, with Bob at the helm, almost in control.

Bob parked the beast next to Norbert's grave and jumped out. 'Problem solved,' he announced happily, crushing a display of flowers.

'What the fuck is that?'

'It's a JC—'

'I know what it is. I mean, where the fuck did you get it?'

'Noticed they're building some new houses over the other side. And look, there's a pneumatic drill on the end, boss.'

'Bit over the top.'

'You've got a better idea?'

'You know how to use it?'

'Easy.'

'And tell me again how you got the thing started.'

'Are you joking? A child could get an old JCB going. They don't exactly come with alarms or immobilizers.'

'You'll put it back, though.'

Bob glanced doubtfully at the ruin he had inflicted on the cemetery backing the digger in. 'Yes, boss,' he answered without conviction.

'Right. Best we'd get . . . we'd best get started.'

His assistant jumped back into the cab and revved the engine impressively. The digging arm swung round and flattened a couple of headstones. Malcolm crossed himself involuntarily. There was precious little left of Norbert Flint. By the time Bob had drilled him out, he guessed there would be substantially less.

Screwdriver

There was a movement, a small swish of material, the creak of a floorboard. She was not alone. Elizabeth lay perfectly still, instantly awake. A tiny fragment of light penetrated the curtains. A figure was standing over her. She fought the urge to scream, and forced her breathing to sound like sleep. He didn't move. Brown coat, a smell of alcohol and smoke. She squinted, her eyes three-quarters closed. It was too black to make out any more. Then he moved, turned around to scan the room. He was holding something. The light caught it. She stared through the gloom. And then it became clear. A long thin screwdriver. Elizabeth struggled to stay calm. Who was it? He moved slowly away. A seventies terrorist balaclava, long shabby coat, an object in his other hand. The telephone downstairs. Middle of the night. The house cold. Neighbours wouldn't hear a thing. Even the police would probably be asleep. What does he want? What the fuck does he want?

He moved again. Slow half steps. Creeping. He doesn't intend to wake me, Elizabeth realized, breathing out of synch with her heart rate. If he doesn't want to wake me, he doesn't want to kill me. Stay absolutely still. Rigid with fear. Pray. Please take what you want and fuck off. Maybe just casing the joint the other day. Has come back for something. She could smell him, hear his breathing. What was in his other hand? Stare at it in the dark. Cylindrical. Long. Metallic. A fucking can of beer.

Stands over her again. He is staring down at her. She closes her eyes, tries to hide the shivers which are shaking her body. He grabs the duvet and pulls it slowly. Oh fuck. Maybe he's after something else. The duvet begins to slide down her body. Elizabeth is paralysed. A single word lights up in her brain. Rape. Who? A pupil from school? It happens. An adolescent with unhealthy desires fixates on someone who teaches them Reproduction. Who? The duvet is almost off. She is naked. Has never felt more exposed. The telephone downstairs. Nobody around. A stranger taking her body in through the half light.

Action. He puts the screwdriver down. His hand moves slowly towards her. Action. Nothing to lose. Element of surprise. His fingers about to touch. A sudden burst of revulsion. Leap off the bed and scream. Run to the window. Scream. Wrestle with the catch. Scream. Look around. He is frozen. Scream. Then he picks up the screwdriver. Try the window again. Tug at the catch, hands useless, gripped by terror. Scream. Open it, finally. Yell out. Turn to look at him. He has gone. Nowhere. Keep shouting. The back door opens and closes. Scream. Shout. Yell. Cry. Sob. Break down. Lie on the floor shaking.

Reflection

Friday 8:24 a.m.

Jake slammed the front door and stood in the drive balancing his bike against one leg while he adjusted the straps of his helmet. He swore as he tightened the front fastening and nearly garrotted himself, while clipping the rear one into its bracket took a small chunk out of his ear. Kate made an unexpected appearance at the door in a short T-shirt, by far the most clothing she had worn for several days. Jake continued to fiddle, worried that she was about to ask him back to bed.

'It's the phone,' she shouted.

Jake swore again, put his bike down and strode into the house. Kate took the opportunity to pinch his bum as he passed, and made a crude helmet joke, which he would have laughed at before their extended shagathon. He picked up the phone. It was his half-aunt.

'Can I come over and spend the day with you?' she asked.

'I'm just off to work. Come and visit Kate if you like, I'm sure she won't mind. Why, what's up?'

Elizabeth told him.

'Fuck,' Jake said, when he had heard the story. 'I mean, pardon my—'

'This time I'm really frightened. He was in my room. There's no way I can stay there. No way at all.'

'Where are you now?'

'The police station.'

'What do they say?'

'Actually, they've finally agreed to take me seriously. They're going to keep a watch on the house.'

'How did he get in? I thought you were going to bolt all the doors.'

'I did. He used a screwdriver to loosen a window.'

'You're even scaring me now. This is terrible. Look, come straight over.'

Elizabeth was quiet for a couple of seconds, and Jake thought he detected a gentle hum of unhurried activity in the background. 'Something is strange as well,' she said. 'Some things are missing.'

'Like what?'

'Lots of little things. Small items of clothing, personal things, valuables.'

'You sure?'

'Never surer of anything. And I'm worried. Suddenly I'm living by myself and somebody has been in my house, while I slept. He even . . .' Elizabeth started crying. For once, Jake wished he could hug her. 'He even . . .' She couldn't get the words out. Jake studied his reflection in the hall mirror. There was a fakeness to his concern, as his aunt continued to sob. He tried to look more cut up, but the helmet spoiled the effect. He just gave the impression of a mildly apprehensive cyclist with ill-fitting chinstraps.

'You know one good thing about this?'

Elizabeth stopped sobbing. 'No. There is no positive thing.'

'Well, OK, I suppose not. All I meant was that it shows you've been right all along. And now the police are involved, hopefully we'll get everything sorted out.'

Dig Out

Phil Ryder was on the short side for a policeman. Even in Dr Martens with built-up heels and air suspension, he was barely average height. Neither, in the way of compensation, was he particularly broad-shouldered. Not that this mattered. Instead of police brawn he had detective brain, which had seen him promoted ahead of his sturdier peers to a position where he would hopefully never have to grapple with any well-built members of the public.

Phil's dad had been a policeman as well, a much respected one of the old-fashioned variety, who had a beat and knew people, rather than beating people and pretending not to know about it. One of his friends was Jake's father.

'Phil, thanks for this,' Jake said to him as they approached Dabner and Sons Funeral Directors on foot.

'No problem, Jake. It does all sound a bit strange.'

'I hope it hasn't been too much trouble.'

'Just the usual forms and procedures. Cleared it with my inspector, passed on what you've told me about missing witnesses, wrong shoes, keys . . .' Phil gave Jake a mock-serious look, 'fish-paste sandwiches, and he agreed. I mean, you need good evidence of possible wrong-doing to exhume a body. And when you've got something as concrete as fish-paste sandwiches . . .'

'OK, take the piss. But I reckon Uncle Norbert didn't die accidentally.'

'So you say.'

'I reckon there was a struggle. I'm not so sure that the tramp didn't push him, or grapple with him, or something.'

'Well, we'll see, once the forensic lot have had a good look. And I spent a couple of hours with your aunt earlier. All sounds very dodgy. We've been round and changed the locks. Plus we're going to keep the place under surveillance. She's staying with you for a while, she said?'

'Yeah. She's too distressed to go home.'

'Not surprising. And we've begun to circulate a description of the tramp. Turns out the boys at Taunsley think they know him.'

'Know him in what way? Socially?'

'He's got some previous history with them.'

'Why? What's he done?'

'I'm not sure. We're going to talk to them tomorrow. But I think from what the sergeant said, there might be a bit of a story.' Phil stopped and touched Jake on the shoulder. 'And Jake, for the sake of this being a fully justifiable and transparent procedure, please act in your capacity as a regional safety inspector, and not as a grieving nephew with a suspicious hunch.'

Jake smiled. 'I'll give it a go,' he replied.

As they reached the entrance, Phil suggested that Jake wait outside. 'It won't be pretty in there,' he said.

'What's going to happen?'

'We'll get the pathologist to have a quick look for marks, abrasions and the like, which might point towards a struggle. Forensics will take a few swabs for fingerprints – a real long shot, if the truth be known – and we'll look for anything else which seems appropriate.'

'Post-mortem?'

'No point. We know how he died. It's just the why which is open to debate. We'll only have him out for a couple of hours before we put him back.'

'Fine.' Jake loitered in the car park of the funeral directors' and sat down on a small wall.

Inside, Phil Ryder shook hands with Malcolm Dabner.

'In there he's . . . he's in there, on the table,' Malcolm told him.

'I understand you dug him up yourself,' Phil replied.

'Happy to help.'

'You didn't see anything unusual last night at the cemetery? People hanging about?'

'No,' Malcolm said, swallowing hard. 'Why do you ask?'

'Had a report of serious vandalism up there. It appears some yobs stole a digger and smashed the place up pretty bad. We think it might have been a satanic thing – you know, maybe the actions of a cult.'

A cunt more like, Malcolm thought to himself, picturing Bob careering about the place in the semi-darkness.

Phil's nose for discomfort sensed something uneasy about Mr Dabner, but he let it pass. People were always on their guard when talking to him. They would blush with the minor misdemeanours of a lifetime, feeling suddenly transparent, as if he was a psychiatrist or psychic who could see into their hidden sins.

They walked through to a plain clinical room used for the preparation of bodies. On a metal table was most of a cadaver. The remaining portion – the head – was absent, and Phil exhaled a long, slow breath in the cold air, the way he always did when he saw something repulsive, a way of dissipating the heavy sickness which threatened to climb his throat.

Jake's backside grew cold as its heat leached into the damp wall. He walked around and stretched his legs, encouraging some blood flow, before sitting down again. The exercise disturbed his stomach and he belched, an acidic reminder of the previous night's culinary catastrophe. At a guess, it had been a cheesy, fishy kind of dish, which also seemed to contain fruit, for some reason. Kate hadn't been too precise, and had mumbled something about an experimental delicacy. Certainly there was nothing delicate about the aftertaste which was burning his throat, though as an experiment in poisoning, it had been a resounding success.

Jake was tempted to go home, or otherwise to walk into the building, but he did neither. Instead, he bought a newspaper and some extra-strong mints, and waited. Phil emerged an hour later and Jake stood up as he approached.

'Well?' he asked.

'Too early to tell.'

'Surely you must have some ideas.'

'Oh, I've got some ideas all right.'

'Such as?'

'Nothing I can let you know right now. We'll have to see the results first, and they're going to take at least a week.' Phil took his mobile phone out and dialled a number, before holding it to his ear. 'But I'm not sure everything's quite what it seems.'

Cheap and Cheerless

Friday 2:09 p.m.

Jake headed to work, wondering what Phil might have been hinting at, making good progress as he approached the Bridgeton Hazard Prevention Unit. His attendance over the last few days had been patchy at best, and there were only so many accidents a week which could excuse his absence from the office. His boss didn't seem to have noticed, and Jake passed an uninspiring Friday afternoon translating POP – his shorthand for 'Passed Out Pissed' – into the safety form category of 'Suspected Alcohol-Involved Incident'. But as he did so, realizing that all over the town workers would be stumbling back from the pub dangerously intoxicated to spend the afternoon handling heavy machinery, it began to eat into him that filling in forms wasn't going to prevent a single accident. In an uncharacteristically rash moment, Jake decided to quit his job. He strode into his supervisor's office.

'I want to hand my notice in,' he blurted, before he had time to change his mind.

His boss, Geoff, locked the fingers of both hands

under his chin and told Jake to sit down. 'Why?' he asked after a few seconds of contemplation.

'It bores me.'

'Safety bores you?'

'Yes.'

A habitually restless man, Geoff stood up and paced over to his window. He was early fifties, and as grey as the carpet of his office. In fact, when he wore his similarly coloured suit he liked to imagine himself lying on the floor invisible to those around him, like a flat-fish on the ocean bed. 'But how on earth could it bore you?' A minor skirmish was developing in the car park. 'It's the fundamental stuff of life.'

'What, safety?'

'Danger.'

'But I don't see any danger.'

His boss span round to face him. 'Precisely! Now do you get what I mean?'

'Not really.'

'Look, what we do here is hunt danger down, capture it, imprison it, make it our own and . . . tame it!'

'Tame it? You make it sound like we're out there doing battle against evil.'

'Now you're getting it. Think of yourself as an explorer out in a wilderness of peril, tracking a vicious foe . . .'

'Geoff, I sit on my arse all day filling forms in.'

'Nonsense! You're out there! You're the hunter, the protector, the saviour of innocent people terrorized by an invisible evil!'

'I'm a paper shuffler.'

'Same thing.'

'It is not the same thing.'

Geoff sat down again. 'Just depends how you look at it,' he responded.

'I'm looking at it *realistically*.'

'Well, if we're going to do that,' Geoff shrugged, 'we might as well all give up now.'

Jake scratched his head. 'I've been thinking about things. Occasionally, I try to stop people getting injured. I do that by writing documents persuading them that harming themselves is a bad idea. But they go on doing it regardless. And when they've done it, I write a report which nobody takes any notice of, except to laugh about. And the next time they bang their finger with a hammer, they realize it isn't in the least bit amusing, and run off to complain to health and safety.'

'So?'

'It's hardly the stuff of schoolboy dreams.'

'Depends on the schoolboy.'

'You're not telling me you set out to do this for a living.'

'Maybe not,' he conceded reluctantly, shrugging again. If Geoff had a talent, it was shrugging. He could have shrugged for England.

Above his boss's head was an embroidered square in a wooden frame. Someone had taken a great deal of trouble to stitch a motto into the cloth with different coloured threads. Jake mouthed the words, and waited a second for the meaning to sink in. *Safety starts with an S, But begins with U.* He pictured Geoff's greying wife pushing a long blunt needle through the material in slow devoted concentration. Then he thought suddenly of Kate and remembered another source of grievance. 'And it's the money as well.'

'What about it?'

'It's hardly wheelbarrows of cash.'

'Shut the door, Jake.' Jake walked over to the door and closed it. 'Look, I know the money's not great. That's the public sector. I'm no happier about it than you. Tell you what I'll do. If you withdraw your resignation, I'll back you up for a discretionary pay award. You're doing a good job, despite what you say, and we should be able to get you bumped up to a higher grade. What do you think?' Geoff asked.

Jake sat and thought for a second, before making his way to the door. 'Can I think about it over the weekend?' he asked, opening it.

'Sure. But, Jake . . .'

'Yes?'

'Make the safe decision.'

Jake returned to his office and calmed down. He felt his impetuousness wane. Money was a real issue. He told himself it wasn't that he could be bought, just that, well, at the moment, certain things had a price. Maybe the unsettling events of the last few weeks were taking their toll. But a small salary hike would be a satisfactory end to the week. What wouldn't be a good finale, however, was the evening that lay ahead.

Jake hung around waiting for Roger to show up, with quiet misgivings. Adam, Roger's only discernible friend, was having a stag do, and as Roger's only discernible colleague, Jake had been dragged along for the ride. It was a bit like a chain letter of bad luck, and Jake had decided not to pass the misery on and invite any of his own friends. This could have got out of hand. But having introduced the vastly unpopular Adam to the DangerClub, he more than qualified as a close acquaintance and had found the event difficult to decline.

Roger finally returned, spent an unfeasible amount of time squeezing into his leathers, and drove with excessive sloth to the venue which Jake had suggested. Adam was already waiting outside the single-storey building and appeared agitated. After parking outside the East Bridgeton Conservative Ex-Serviceman's Club on Wallace Street, the trio entered and hung around the foyer. Roger appeared very unsure and glanced suspiciously at Jake. Adam had dragged his usual aspect of twitchiness up a couple of notches to the frankly jittery. A violently moustachioed pensioner began to sign them in.

'Should be a good one tonight, chaps,' he said,

handing Jake's membership card back. 'Got us a bit of a cabaret, you know.'

While it had never been a burning ambition of Jake's to join the Conservative Ex-Serviceman's Club of East Bridgeton, for reasons too numerous and idealistic to list, it did have one terrific advantage. It was easy on the pocket. His uncle had been a member, and by virtue of now being dead, had unwittingly proposed him for membership, which he duly accepted when it arrived in the post. Entry was free, beer was virtually at pre-war prices, seemingly to avoid confusing the pensioners, and if you didn't mind the occasional rant about homosexuals and the youth of today, the place might be almost bearable. But for a stag night, a dismal, dismal stag night, this was all he wanted. The company wasn't going to get any better, regardless of the surroundings, and as they would hopefully be drinking their bodyweight in beer, best to visit a place where a Pound-a-Pint promotion would be seen as blatant overcharging.

'Adam? What can I get you?' Jake asked, running his eyes over the shabby carpet tiles, brown curtains and tobacco-stained ceiling.

'A vodka.'

'Roger?'

'An orange squash,' Roger replied. 'I'm driving.'

Jake bought the required beverages and distributed them, taking a healthy swig from his own pint. He glanced at his watch. Seven thirty. The sooner this was over the better. The only proviso was that, according to Norbert's calculations, his beer to money ratio could be vastly enhanced by staying for two more drinks. The three protagonists, who really barely knew each other, sat at a small table and all felt uncomfortable, and for various reasons. Roger, for his part, appeared reticent about the tatty club, scanning for fire doors and checking for safety warnings. Adam was just overexcitable. This was his natural persona and he was admirably good at it. At the DangerClub, his restlessness took a more serious turn. He had an obvious fascination with death and mutilation which unnerved even Jake. Quite why Adam and Roger were such good friends, Jake had never figured out. Maybe Roger lived excitement vicariously through his friend. Either way, this wasn't going to be a heady cavalcade of fun, and so far, so awful. In fact, it was terrible.

A compère ambled on stage, tapped his microphone and announced that the evening's entertainment was about to begin. Jake shrugged at Roger, who shrugged at Adam, who looked eager. They were close to the action, and surrounded by a rabble of opinionated pensioners.

'And have we got something special tonight,' the compère continued. 'Let's have a big Conservative Ex-Serviceman hand for Paradise Knives.'

'Did he say "knives"?' Roger asked Adam.

'I think so.'

'In a confined area?'

'I hope so. This is beginning to sound like my kind of night out.'

'How do you figure that?' Jake enquired.

'You know, lots of blood and stuff if we're lucky.' Adam swallowed an eager mouthful of vodka.

A regimental burst of applause was followed by two shadowy figures walking on stage.

'Fuck me,' Jake said. 'I thought this sort of thing went out with tap dancing and ventriloquism.'

The thrower limbered up by throwing some long, heavy knives at a large circular target board. All around, former servicemen monitored the precision of his aim and murmured comments to each other, of which the decipherable highlights were: 'had him with a bayonet', 'don't like it up 'em', 'worked as a magician's assistant', 'rear gunner, apparently', 'not in my day', 'right between the eyes', 'nine-bob note', 'the iron lady', 'wouldn't have seen him on a dark day', 'hid the cards up you know where', and 'eighty-six pence a pint? Daylight robbery'. The knife thrower approached the stage and bowed, while the conversation died out in anticipation.

It was quickly apparent that all was not right with the act, however. His assistant, a small woman in a cape and mask, appeared increasingly reluctant to have sharp objects lobbed at her in the semi-darkness, and skulked around at the back of the stage. As a general point, this was very much understandable. For a knife thrower's assistant, though, such behaviour was a distinct career disadvantage. The pensioners became restless as the thrower retreated from the spotlight and remonstrated with his potential stab magnet. A few ashtrays were thrown and some impressive and imaginative swearing offered up for general consumption. After a couple of minutes, the man approached the microphone and said a little tentatively, 'We seem to be having a problem tonight. My assistant is, er, unwell, and unless a member of the audience volunteers, I'll have to cancel the show.'

Jake leaned forward and nudged Adam. 'It is customary on stag nights to tie the betrothed to something dangerous,' he said. Adam grinned back. 'Roger? What do you think? Save us getting a stripper.' Roger was reluctant to commit himself. 'Or maybe you fancy a go?'

'No, I do not fancy a go,' Roger answered firmly, leaning back and drinking a small measure of orange squash, as Adam sauntered over to inspect the knives. Then something on stage caught Roger's eye and put an idea into his head. He began to wonder about the possibilities.

Casualty

Roger tried to stem the flow of blood. Friday was not a
good time to be in Casualty. It was semi-organized
bedlam.

Jake was unable to fathom why they should have to
wait several hours to see someone. Surely Friday
evenings were always busy. Therefore a larger number
of medical staff should be laid on to satisfy the simple
law of supply and demand. Such logic appeared to
bypass the health service, however. The truth was that
whatever hour of whatever day you were unfortunate
enough to find yourself in Accident and Emergency, it
always took many lifetimes to be attended to. Even if
you were the only bugger in there, and were bleeding
to death.

To prevent patients seeing through this, hospitals
have devised a cunning holding system. First, you sit
in a dire waiting room surrounded by the pissed and
dying, and someone vaguely secretarial comes round
and asks how you injured yourself and how many
pints you've drunk. Second, several days later, your
name is mispronounced and you get to walk through
to an additional confinement area. Third, and just
when you really are about to die, you are pointed

towards a cubicle with a vinyl bed covered in green paper, and are told to try to hang on in there if you possibly can. If especially close to pegging it, you may be loaned an aspirin to help you on your way. Fourth, and this is when you are about to float into a welcoming tunnel of light, the curtain is pulled briskly back and a hassled nurse asks if you are Susan Jenkins. When it is apparent that you might not be, and therefore don't need to have your damaged breast examined, the curtain is returned to its rightful place, much to the relief of the spider which has spent several hours constructing a web across its surface. Some indeterminate time later, presumably when the pubs and clubs have all closed and the doctors have staggered back to the ward, a medic walks in, performs CPR on you, and then asks what, if you can remember, you came in for. Whether you can recall or not, the doctor will say 'Mmmm' and 'Hmmm' quite a lot while you are speaking, tell you it's probably not broken, and advise you to see your GP. The doctor's surgery will then allow you to be examined some four or five days later, and will refer you back to the hospital, to avoid having to prescribe any expensive medicines. Back in Casualty, you enter the system once more and survival of the fittest kicks in. Either you die in the queuing system as natural wastage, or else survive, in which case you end up perfectly healthy, just in time for the same junior doctor you saw previously, who is still on the same shift, to irritably ask you to leave as you are clogging up the health service.

When Roger had suitably aged from a man in his early forties to one in his late eighties, a doctor suggested he walk to X-ray. Given his condition, this was easier said than done, and Jake asked whether there was a wheelchair available.

The doctor appeared a little taken aback. 'A wheelchair?' he asked.

'Well, this is a hospital.'

'All the same.'

'Look, is there anywhere we could find one?'

'There might be one lying around somewhere. Ask one of the porters.'

'Which porters?'

'Or a nurse.'

Jake and Roger decided to forgo the vague possibility of transport, and headed slowly and carefully in the direction of X-ray, which was marked out on the floor in red tape. It hadn't been a bad car crash, but it hadn't been a good one either. Few crashes, in fairness, are beneficial events. Of the two, Roger had clearly come off the worse for wear and was in considerable pain. Jake was fine, if a little stiff. At X-ray, they joined a queue, which led to another waiting area, which then took them through to a holding room, before they finally got to join a tailback of variously injured people waiting to have high-intensity light shone through their bones.

The radiographer was a chatty man who had obviously failed to notice he was working for the National Health Service. He had a stab at deciphering the doctor's hieroglyphics, but decided to ask Roger directly what had happened.

'We were driving home after a stag do.'

'Drinking, eh?'

'No.'

'And you crashed?'

'Hit a parked car.'

'So it's your neck we need to look at, is it?'

'I'm in agony,' Roger replied miserably.

'And your friend?' He turned to Jake, who had followed Roger into the business-end of the X-ray room. 'Were you in the car as well?'

'Yes,' Jake said. 'But I'm fine.'

'Really? No neck pain?'

'None.'

'You must have a strong neck.'

'I think it was because I wasn't wearing a helmet.'

'A helmet? You were on a motorbike?'

'A car. My friend here wears a helmet when he drives.'

The radiographer hovered with an X-ray cassette in his hand, about to position the machine, and then stopped. 'A helmet? What on earth would you want to do that for?'

'Saf . . .' Roger couldn't bring himself to utter the word.

'No wonder you've got whiplash. Heavy helmet on your head like that. All that forward momentum dragging your neck out of joint.'

Jake smiled. 'I guess I'd better leave the room while you nuke him.'

'Jesus,' the radiographer said, shaking his head. 'A helmet? And what about the rest of your injuries? The foot? The finger? Looks like it's bleeding to me. Do we need to have a look at those? I mean, what exactly has been going on here?'

'They're fine,' Roger muttered. 'A previous incident.'

When Roger had had his photo taken, they headed back to Casualty and placed themselves at the end of another line-up of misery. As they sat and waited, the exact events of the crash were still playing on Jake's mind. One second they were trundling along at barely twenty, and the next they had swerved into the side of a parked car.

'But I still don't see why you panicked,' Jake said as they sat down.

'I thought that kid was going to run out at me.'

'What kid? I didn't see anyone.'

Roger's eyes were animated, as he relived the moment. 'He was there all right. By the side. Behind a car. Waiting to run out into the road.'

Jake scratched his head. 'If you say so.'

'I say so. He was there.' Roger closed his eyes and sighed. He appeared to be shaking slightly, maybe through delayed shock.

'I still didn't—'

'Forget it,' Roger said quietly.

Jake took a sideways look at his colleague. Roger wasn't so much an accident waiting to happen as one which was very much in progress. 'But why didn't you just stop, instead of veering into the side?' he asked.

'I tried, but I missed the brakes.'

'Missed them? How the hell did you miss them?'

'Got my bandaged foot stuck under the pedal.'

'Christ. So why then didn't you swerve away from the other car?'

'My broken finger.'

'What about it?'

'Caught it on the steering wheel. Had to use my left hand, which was on the gear stick, so I was off-balance.'

All of this was news to Jake. He had been busy recovering from possibly the world's worst stag night ever, when suddenly the car had come to a grinding, banging, shattering halt. The air bags had failed to deploy, presumably because they weren't travelling fast enough, but the Volvo had essentially done its job. Roger hadn't been entirely lucky, but he would live, albeit with a neck brace for a couple of weeks.

Several hours later, a junior doctor was woken from an expansive ten-minute kip, squinted at Roger from behind insomniac eye bags and told him he would probably be OK. 'Try not to head any footballs, get into any rugby scrums or do any dangerous sports,' he advised unnecessarily between yawns. Roger said he would see what he could do, and hobbled out of Casualty with Jake before either of them succumbed to natural causes. Jake dropped Roger home in a taxi, sighing as it pulled up outside his own house.

Technically, it was Saturday already, and in a few short hours he would be woken from a heavy unconsciousness to botch some more household improvements in between bouts of unrestrained sexual congress.

Male Prozac

Saturday 7:44 a.m.

Kate's brain:	Check bedside clock. Open the curtains.
Jake's brain:	Noises. Light. Movement. Fuck.
Kate's brain:	Gently wake boyfriend.
Jake's brain:	Open one eye, look at watch. Saturday, some time before eight. Fuck.
Kate's brain:	Clear throat. Shake partner, poke him gently in the ribs.
Jake's brain:	Resistance is futile. Another day being of denied Male Weekend Rights. No beer, no fried food, no sport.
Kate's brain:	Resistance is futile. You are mine. Shake harder.
Jake's brain:	Battle is being lost. Open eyes and try to appear hard done by.
Kate's brain:	'Jake, what do you fancy doing today?'
Jake's brain:	Silent answer, Fuck all. Girlfriend-edited version, 'Whatever you want.'
Kate's brain:	'Well, I've got a surprise for you.'
Jake's brain:	Oh fuck. Please, not more sex.
Kate's brain:	'I want you to look out of the window.'
Jake's brain:	This is an elaborate trick. Remain in bed. On no account look out of the window.
Kate's brain:	'Come on, lover boy, have a peek.'

Jake's brain: OK, the lawn needs mowing. Or the fence has blown down. Or the shed desperately needs shifting six inches to the left. Put me out of my misery. 'What is it?'

Kate's brain: 'It's no fun if you don't see for yourself.'

Jake's brain: It's not going to be a lot of fun anyway. Go through the motions. Remember, there is no chance of winning this battle.

Kate's brain: Great. Any minute now and he's going to get a shock. Phase Two is about to begin.

Jake's brain: Climb out of bed grumbling, and slump against windowsill. All right, the lawn seems fine. The fence is in one piece. The shed is ideally located. Nothing so far. Hang on, what the fuck is that?

Kate's brain: He's seen it. Eureka! Now to reel him in. 'So what do you think?'

Jake's brain: I'm thinking, where the fuck did that come from?

Kate's brain: 'We've got three channels of sport, some movies, and, you know, one or two other treats.'

Jake's brain: This is going to cost me. 'But we're trying to economize.'

Kate's brain: 'Look, if my man can't sit down at the weekend and watch some football while drinking a few cans of cold beer, what can he do?'

Jake's brain: Difficult point to counter. Remain silent. Think about things. Probably best not to argue your way out of this one.

Kate's brain: 'And the man said that the satellite dish can pick up over four hundred channels from thirteen different countries.'

Jake's brain: Including Holland?

Kate's brain: 'Including [wink at boyfriend] Holland.'

Jake's brain: Not the world's worst situation. Immediately overlook all potential ulterior motives – the payoff is just too good.

Kate's brain: Gotcha! Boyfriend to become hooked on new male Prozac substitute – *Pornbeersport*. Will be happy with his lot. Complacent, self-satisfied, content; i.e. won't spend time fretting about girlfriend not going to work. Plus, it's Big Spender next week, and maybe this time he won't moan too much.

Jake's brain: Find remote control. Find remote control. Find remote control. Find remote control . . .

You've Been Framed

This was getting too close to the truth, Pauline decided. From now on, they would have to stay out of the Bridgeton area. She would mention it to Simon when she saw him next. She knew that it was a risk worth taking, as all risks were, and that one day she would get caught by her husband. It was only a matter of time. But again, just when things seemed to be getting complicated, a spanner was taken out of the works. As she monitored her husband struggling to clamber out of his clothes and into bed, she realized that there was no need to panic just yet. Roger's car was in the garage for a protracted period of refurbishment at the insurance company's pleasure, and he wasn't likely to be spending a lot of time sampling the delights of Bridgeton's nightlife. She smiled to herself, picturing the faces of the people her husband would be advising on accident avoidance. Over the following days, he would be hobbling around factories with his neck in a brace, a heavily strapped ankle hampering his efforts, pointing out potential hazards with a broken finger which had now started bleeding.

As much as Pauline could see the funny side, it was by no means her aim to laugh at her husband. They rowed from time to time, but she loved Roger now as much as she ever had. Seeing him in pain brought her no comfort. When Jake had brought him home from the hospital she was upset not to have been the one caring for him. What she did behind his back was an act of real betrayal, which sometimes came home to roost.

She slid into bed next to her husband and vainly tried to find an undamaged piece of him to hold on to. Presently, she reached around him for the remote control and flicked the TV on, which lay at the end of their bed, with its ever-ready light eager to please when conversation flagged. *Casualty* was on and she relaxed from her husband's cautious embrace to view it more clearly. *Casualty* was one of her favourite programmes. Roger craned his head to see, and swore as his neck fought against him. Finally, realizing what the programme was, he let go of his wife and sat up on the edge of the bed.

'What?' she asked.

'Oh come on, Pauline, we've been through this before.'

'Your ideological dislike of my viewing preferences?'

'No. Just this one.' He sighed. 'The whole programme is one long wait for someone to get hurt.'

'Nonsense. It's good quality drama.'

'And after all I've been through this weekend. I think I've seen enough of hospitals.'

'But *Casualty* is fiction.'

'Is it?'

'Yes.'

'How do you know?'

'What are you getting at, Roger?'

'Nothing,' he answered, cradling his head in his hands. 'Look, you know I can't watch it.'

'I'll see what else is on.' Pauline selected another channel with an irritable flick of the remote control. 'Oh Christ, another one of your favourites.'

Roger glanced back at the screen. 'Shit. *You've Been* bloody *Framed*.'

'Come on, let's hear the usual,' Pauline lamented, flopping back on the pillow.

'It's the same principle. People come a cropper and we sit around and laugh at them—'

Pauline interrupted the lecture, laughing loudly as a fat woman fell off her bicycle. 'But it's funny,' she said, giggling again as the woman tried in vain to disentangle herself from the bike.

'No it isn't.'

'Lighten up, Roger, please.'

'It's not just squeamishness. You know the reasons.'

Pauline softened. 'I know,' she said reluctantly. 'OK, we'll switch it off.'

Roger was about to concur when he remembered something from the TV listings. 'Actually, there's a war documentary on BBC Two,' he said, moving gingerly into position in front of the box.

His wife turned sharply to face him. 'You mean you want to watch people getting hurt, injured and maimed now, so long as it's not on one of my programmes?'

'This is different. These are people who are *already* maimed. They died fifty years ago. What I can't stand is the waiting for something bad to happen that you get on things like *You've Been Framed*.'

'But the people on *You've Been Framed have* already been injured.'

'We don't know that,' Roger replied.

'Yes we do. Otherwise we wouldn't be watching it. And, generally, they aren't injured. Not on your scale of things. They just fall over when they're dancing or something.'

'We're sitting there waiting for it to happen, though.'

'But we don't know *what* we're waiting for. Fat-woman-on-a-bike could just have accidentally flashed her knickers for all we know. And that Spitfire there,' Pauline said, pointing to shaky black and white footage of a Second World War dog fight, 'might, if we freeze the instant now, be about to shoot an enemy plane down, do a loop the loop, drop a bomb, explode . . . anything. Where's the difference between that and any other TV programme where you can't guess the outcome?'

Roger was silent for a while. His wife would never see his point. It was the not knowing that killed him. And programmes and films that were built on the anticipation of injury or accident stretched his existing anxiety uncomfortably tight. It was OK for her. She wasn't pathologically accident-prone. Her life wasn't like one extended episode of *You've Been Framed*. She wasn't haunted by a small piece of footage which played again and again inside his mind, and refused to go away when he turned the TV off and switched out the lights each night.

Safety Scene #10

Interior of a car. We are moving through a built-up area. We see the rear-view mirror, in which is the reflection of a black man's face. We pan down over the dashboard. The speedo reads 45mph. The steering wheel has a blue oval Ford badge at its centre. Beneath this and to the left we see a gearstick. It is long and slender, with a shiny knob. This also has a Ford emblem on it. A man's hand appears in shot, grabs the gear lever and changes down. The engine whines and the revs rise. Above, further left, his hand moves to turn the radio up. At face level, we see from his expression that he likes this song. It is Blondie, 'Heart Of Glass'. He speeds up, before braking late to take a junction. We see through his eyes as he checks quickly left and right, before screeching out. The weather is fine, and there is little other traffic on the road. On his windscreen is a sunshade sticker, which reads, 'Radio One MW275-285'. He whistles to himself, and turns right at a roundabout, into an estate. 'Heart Of Glass' ends, and a Pink Floyd tune begins. The man reaches out and lowers the volume. A quick left, and then a short sprint right. He accelerates and shifts from third to fourth. Suddenly there is a child. Cut out to the wheels. They skid. Rubber stains the tarmac. A bang. The child is lifted onto the bonnet, hits the windscreen hard, rolls back off, out of sight. Everything is still. We see the man's hand move and select neutral. There is a muffled scream behind the car. Then the engine note rises again, a harsh, tinny sound. He moves the gearstick into first. The steering wheel turns. The car pulls off again at speed. We race through the housing estate, until houses become trees. In the countryside, the man stops the car in a lay-by. We pan up to his eyes. He sits and stares at his own reflection. His head is shaking slowly. We see his hands slowly move up and cover his face. We fade out.

Evangelical

If you were an industrial safety inspector, one thing might strike you as odd. Despite an entire career spent visiting workplaces the region over, what you would rarely have witnessed was any bugger doing any work. Inspections would comprise empty factory after empty factory, workers lounging around reading papers, listening to the radio and hiding in offices. Now if you knew that a company produced millions of litres of orange juice or thousands of pallets of washing machines a year, wouldn't your suspicions be ever so slightly raised by the fact that over, say, ten years you were yet to observe anyone even contemplating any manufacturing? Or failing that, wouldn't you jack your job in at the earliest opportunity and run off to join one of the companies you inspected? What was the point in walking around industrial units all day when you could simply do what every worker you had ever met did, which was sitting around on your arse drinking tea?

Obviously, managers the world over appreciate that a quiet factory is a safe factory. And for his part, it was clear to Jake that safety inspections were a farce. The workers being inspected knew they were a farce. The Safety Team knew they were a farce, and knew that the workers knew they were a farce. The workers knew that Jake knew they were a farce, and Jake knew that the workers knew that he knew they were a farce. So everybody was happy. Everyone – with the exception of Roger – had seen through it and had drawn a farcical truce.

And this was how the truce worked. In order to accomplish things, employees had to perform hazardous endeavours from time to time. Such actions went strictly against employment guidelines. If a member of staff injured themselves/destroyed the wing of a building/blew up a passer-by then the employer would be liable. However, for workplaces to remain financially viable, tricky procedures such as manufacturing, engineering and research and development had to be carried out on a daily basis. Thus it was in everybody's interest that dangerous practices were performed routinely.

Between the need for danger and the need for safety lay the Safety Team. It wasn't the Safety Team's objective to encourage safety, however – far from it – it was the Safety Team's objective to encourage the *impression* of safety. This was achieved by regular safety inspections. So regular, in fact, that employees could virtually set their watches by them, which was the very point. For if it hadn't been for the four months' advance notice companies were routinely given of the impending visit of the inspectors, all sorts of hell would break loose. If an outsider were to witness the sheer recklessness with which half of industry was carried out, most factories and chemical plants would be shut down.

Over the weekend, Jake appreciated that this marriage of convenience was growing stale, and now the rules were about to change. Someone was in genuine danger. And not just anybody. This was a woman he had once lain on top of, a woman who had stared into his eyes for the briefest of moments, during which a lifetime's information seemed to have been exchanged. It would be difficult to change his operating procedures just for one person, however. He would have to be seen to be fair. From now on, surprise safety visits were actually going to be just that. No advance notice to allow employers the chance to advise dangerous workers to take the day off, or to rush around sellotaping ineffectual notices up. And Peril and Sons, who had so far enjoyed only mild rebuke every time they scraped a new member of staff off their walls, were going to suffer more than most.

On Monday, Jake swore at the new motto, *Security Equals Safety*. As ever, the numerical evidence lay beneath it. *Last year, 13,011 vegetable-related accidents were reported to ROSPA*. He walked to his boss's office, wondering how the fuck you could possibly get injured by a vegetable, and, if you did, why the fuck you would own up to it. He found Geoff and told him he would be happy to accept the minor pay award, and that, from now on, he would be giving safety in Bridgeton a firm kick up its arse. It was going to be his single-handed responsibility to make the town a safe area to live and work, and he would be coming down hard on anybody not playing by the rules.

As Geoff shut the door after Jake's energetic departure, he looked decidedly worried and cursed himself for offering the pay rise. The last thing the world of safety needed was a kick up the arse. The way things stood, there was a delicate status quo, Geoff conceded, thoughtfully stirring his cup of tea with the wrong end of a pencil. Tilt this too far in the wrong direction and there would be fewer accidents. And fewer accidents meant less need for Hazard Prevention personnel, and hence lower funding for his department. Neither of which was good for a manager seeking a cushy payoff and early retirement.

Witness

Jake's curiosity could be contained no longer. He had tried ringing Phil twice already, but with no luck. Surely he had the results of the tests they had performed on his uncle by now. He picked up the phone and dialled again. This time, it was answered.

'Phil? Hi. It's Jake.'

'How're you doing?'

'Good. Look, I was just wondering whether you could fill me in on the results of the exhumation.'

There was a brief pause. 'I'd like to, Jake, honest, but it's not that simple.'

'How do you mean?'

'We found things that . . .'

'What?'

'Maybe we'd better meet up and have a chat.'

Jake swallowed, and bit his lip for a second. 'I'd rather you just told me now,' he said.

'Can't,' Phil answered, 'not over the phone. Look, tell me where, and we'll get together.'

'Do you know the Hog's Head?'

'Next to the Goose?'

'No, you're thinking of the King's Head. It's opposite the Laughing Cavalier.'

'Which one?'

'The older one with the grimy windows.'

'Oh right, a couple of doors down from the Fleece?'

'That's it. But on the Maypole Inn side of the road.'

'Got you.'

'Can you make the end of the week? Saturday? Noon.'

'Yeah, give or take.'

'No, I mean noon. Dead on.'

'I suppose . . .'

'You'd be doing me a major favour. I can't explain at the minute.'

'Sure. I'll see you at the weekend.'

'Twelve sharp. Bye.'

'Bye.'

He would have to wait a few more days.

On Saturday Jake sat by the jukebox in the Hog's Head and examined his loose change, wondering whether Phil would remember the right pub. Finding a fifty-pence piece, he reached round and rolled it lazily into the slot. Almost without looking, he keyed in the Big Spender code. Then he slouched to his feet and sauntered out into the car park to begin the inevitable. This month, for the first time in a long series of down-ward months, they were in the black. With no petrol, insurance or other car-related expenses, Jake had actually retained a small proportion of his salary. Having said this, it had been a short month, more like three weeks really, as the previous Saturday had been late and this one was early, technically speaking. Still, the principle was there somewhere, lurking.

Kate remained in a state of denial. She had brokered a compromise – they would only spend half of their remaining cash this month, and she would think about considering the possibility of maybe trying to find a job. Jake had reluctantly gone along with her suggestions, mainly to avoid his girlfriend attempting to seduce him, but now he had played his master stroke. He checked his watch. 12:04. Time to regain the initiative. As he strolled back into the pub, Kate was positioned in the usual place of their courtship ritual. He walked over to her and planted a kiss on her powdered forehead.

'Hey, Big Spender,' she said, smiling.

'Hi,' he answered, sitting down and glancing around for the cavalry, which had yet to arrive.

'So tell me again, big boy,' she encouraged, squeezing his thigh, 'what's the scores on the doors?'

'Thirty, give or take.'

'Any ideas?'

Yes, a fucking watch for Phil Ryder, he said to himself. 'Not really,' he replied.

'Well, how about this. Some more lingerie.'

'More? You bought a load last time.'

'A woman can never have too much underwear.'

'You never seem to wear any though.'

'I don't see you complaining,' Kate smiled, squeezing his leg again.

I never get the bloody chance, one part of his brain whispered to another. Again, Jake told his thoughts to remain quiet.

'We could go to Marks—'

'Phil!' Jake shouted in relief, noticing his friend enter the pub. 'Over here.'

Phil spotted them and came over. 'Hello, Kate,' he said. 'What's happening?'

'Hey, Phil. Oh, you know, nothing really. Nothing at all. Nope, nothing. Not one thing.'

Phil once again felt someone retreat unnecessarily from his police intuition. 'Drink?' he asked.

'Just got them in,' Jake answered.

As Phil headed to the bar, Jake broke the bad news to his girlfriend. 'I'm really sorry,' he said, trying to summon up a convincing impression of regret, 'but we'll have to knock Big Spender on the head today. I need to talk to Phil about Uncle Norbert. I think he might have some news.'

'What kind of news?'

'Bad news. They've been investigating his death.'

'Right.'

'So I guess I need to find out all the upsetting details. Why don't I catch up with you back at home, and I'll fill you in there?'

'Saucy,' Kate said, winking at him.

Phil returned and Kate finished her drink and left. Jake drew a sigh of temporary financial relief. 'Thanks,' he said.

'For what?' Phil asked.

'Long story.'

'Jake, I've been doing some thinking,' Phil began, leaning forward. 'Tell me if these two facts are true. First, that all the best-looking blokes are gay.'

'If you say so.'

'I do. I read it somewhere. And second, that all lesbians are ugly.'

'For the sake of humouring you, yes. So what's your point?'

'My point is, if these two premises are vaguely true – that all the best-looking blokes are gay, and all lesbians are ugly – then surely half-decent blokes like me should be swimming in attractive females.'

Jake took a thoughtful swig of beer. 'Still no luck, Phil?'

'Fuck all. Literally. Don't know where I'm going wrong.'

'Me neither.'

'You? What about Kate?'

'Between you and me, things aren't really working out.'

'No? You seem OK.'

'We're not. We're skint, Kate refuses to work, and is

demanding sex morning, noon and night. To cap it all, she's bought me a fridge full of lager and insists I watch porn and football virtually non-stop.'

Phil drew a deep breath and shook his head slowly. 'Sorry to hear that,' he said. 'Apart from the sex bit. And the beer. And the porn. And the foot—'

'It's not half as much fun as it might sound.'

'I'll take your word for that.'

'And she's also started some serious flirting with a computer nerd on the net.'

'How serious?'

'I don't know. But I'm going to do something about it as soon as I can.'

'What are you waiting for? If it was my girl-friend . . .'

'It's not that simple. I can't contact the wanker without Kate finding out. I need her to make the first move.' Jake scratched his nose irritably. 'Anyway, what was it that you couldn't say over the phone?'

'Oh yes. That. The inspector was sitting next to me, and I didn't want him hearing everything.' Phil put his feet up on the chair next to Jake's. 'You know we've been searching for the witness – the tramp fellow . . .'

'Eric.'

'Yes.'

'And?'

'We've found him.'

'What does he say?' Jake asked eagerly.

'Not a fat lot.'

'No?'

'In fact, we're not that sure he ever went missing.'

Jake leant forwards. 'What do you mean?'

Phil drained his pint. 'Get me another one of these and I'll tell you.'

Leo Sayer

Phil told Jake a couple of things about his uncle which unsettled him. As they talked, a quick pint turned into a slow half-gallon. After a minor pub crawl which barely scratched the surface of Bridgeton's vast number of drinking establishments, a decision was taken to go to the town's only nightclub, albeit with one abstention and one incoherent reply. Certainly, the general consensus was that more beer could only be a good thing.

Utopia was as sticky and packed as any Saturday night could be. Condensation hugged the mirrors, beer lurked in the carpets and sweat clung to faces. It was a miserable place where the town congregated to, in no particular order, drink, dance, fight and fuck. Jake rang his girlfriend en route, asking if she wanted to join them. She declined the offer of spending quality time with two obvious inebriates. There had also been an aspect of mild sulkiness in her refusal, and she had complained about a general lack of Big Spender activity, which Jake chose to overlook.

Inside, Phil decided to comb the nightclub for

myopic women as Jake headed for the bar. When they met up again several minutes later, Phil was decidedly upbeat. 'Guess what?' he asked. 'I've seen someone perfect. And she's got a friend.'

'Oh no,' Jake answered. 'I'm not getting palmed off with one of your rejects. I mean, the ones you actually like are bad enough, but their ugly half-cousins are usually frightening. And besides, in case you've forgotten, I have a girlfriend.'

'Who you're not getting along with.'

'That's a side issue.'

'Look, there they are!' he pointed. 'Past the bar, by the toilets.'

Past the bar, by the toilets, two girls glanced up in unison. The shorter of the two nudged her friend. 'The one on the left,' she said, 'has been staring at you for the last ten minutes.'

'What do you think?'

'From this distance, not good.'

'Let's steal some more drinks and see what else is on offer.'

'Oh Christ, they're coming over!'

'Shit. I know one of them.'

'Which one?'

'On the right. Taller guy. Fair hair. A bit skinny.'

'What's he like?'

'Let's just say intriguing.'

'In a good way, or in an intriguingly ugly kind of way?'

'Oh he's far from ugly. No, there's something there that makes you want to know more.'

'Well, here goes nothing. Smile. You never know, they might be rich. Sara,' Sara replied non-committally as Phil held out his hand and sheepishly introduced himself.

'Hello, Safety Man,' her friend said as Jake did the same.

Jake glanced up from his shoes, surprised. 'Hi. It's Louise, isn't it? Didn't recognize you.'

'Without my lab coat on?'

'Something like that. And anyway, how do you know I'm not wild and dangerous?'

'The people you hang around with, the clothes you wear, the things you say, the things you do, the lectures you give, the way I've already noticed you scanning round for fire exits—'

'That's a bad habit I acquired from a friend—'

'Lots of things really.'

'OK, it's a fair cop.' Phil and Sara edged away towards the bar. 'Anyway, what makes *you* so crazy?' Jake asked.

'Only the things I do at work, home and in play.'

'But apart from that?'

'Coming to dodgy nightclubs.'

Jake ran his eyes quickly around the heaving, sweating, low-ceilinged room. 'Yeah, it's ropy all right.'

'A good laugh though. I mean, look at the state of some of the punters.'

'That's the thing about a small town. The good bits are crap and the crap bits are good.'

'I have no idea what you mean.'

Jake rocked back on his heels a little unsteady. 'That would be the Leo Sayer.'

'What?'

'The all-dayer.'

'So who's your mate?'

'Phil,' he replied. 'Nice guy. A copper. Sounds a contradiction, but there you go. We grew up together.'

'So you've always lived in Bridgeton?'

'Went to school here, moved away for about six years while I went to university in Leeds.'

'Jesus, that was a long course,' Louise shouted over the din of the music.

'Something like that.'

'Why did you come back, then?'

'On a night like this, no idea.'

'No, really. Why?'

Jake gulped a mouthful of beer, a couple of unwelcome images stirring. This was not a topic he talked about, and the recent reminders in the form of fish fingers and saw blades had made him edgy. 'You know . . .'

'Did something go wrong while you were away?' she asked, nodding at his left hand. He appeared uncomfortable, and was rubbing his stubble with his palm, occasionally pushing the stump into the small cleft of his chin.

Jake thrust his hand in his pocket self-consciously. 'Not necessarily.'

'Well, what happened?'

He wasn't worried about her intrusiveness. She was drunk. In fact, he was glad of her candour. What he couldn't stand were the people who didn't ask. He opened his mouth and let the customary spiel flow out. 'One year in Leeds, after my degree, I was working for my landlord, helping him do up houses. We were sawing lengths of wood with a power saw. Ronnie, his name was, didn't notice that I had my hand close to the blade. He slipped, and went right into my finger, chopping straight through the bone.' The curious always winced at this point, and Jake imagined a squeamish tingle passing through them. Louise appeared unmoved, no doubt having witnessed enough amputations at Peril's to last a lifetime. He was quiet for a second. He knew how it must appear. A headline written across his forehead. *Man Loses Finger in Accident, Turns to Safety*. In reality, this had been no accident, but he'd never told anyone that. It was just easier to feed people a story they wanted to believe. He decided to change the subject. Move on, that had been his philosophy so far. Move on and make yourself forget. 'Anyway, what's your excuse for living here?' he asked.

Louise stole some of his drink. 'The usual. A boyfriend. Then when we split up, he moved on and I stayed. I'd already made some friends, and then I fluked an R and D job at Peril's.'

'I'm not sure fluked is the right word.'

'Spare me the lecture.'

'It's just that bad things happen there. And for what? Fireworks, which people stand in wet fields to watch light up the sky for a couple of seconds.'

'That's the point. Not everything has to last, you know. And transient things are always the most exciting.'

Jake remained silent, thinking, watching Louise when he didn't think she was looking. He had been on top of this girl. Silent words of intent had been exchanged between their eyes. He had experienced the aphrodisiac of near death and the raw desire of fear. And now he was talking like his dad. 'Couldn't you just make the fireworks a little less, well, explosive?'

'Look, some of our products are already so crap that retreating twenty-five yards after lighting them is a lot more dangerous than stuffing them down your pants. But as fat-boy Robert Peril is constantly telling us, it's the flagship lines that keep the company in business. And for ever more exotic fireworks we need to experiment. There's no magic equation for summoning up the perfect rocket or the most ferocious banger.'

'I guess not.'

'And you know what else?' Louise asked, tipping a little more of Jake's drink into her glass. 'I love it. It makes me feel alive.'

She certainly looked alive. Jake battled a powerful urge to pull her tight against him. After a few seconds, he said, 'I dreamed about you the other night.' Louise stared at him. Jake gazed into his plastic glass, watching the flat lager swill in time with his body as he swayed.

'What did you dream?' she asked.

'Just that there was someone in this world who was worth . . .' Jake stopped, appreciating that the lager in

244

his system was beginning to speak for him. He would try and go it alone, without alcoholic interference. He took a deep, sobering breath. 'Who was worth taking a . . .' Phil put an arm around his shoulder. Jake glanced up. Sara had returned, and was tugging at Louise's dress. Louise's eyes bored into Jake's for a second time, before their friends intervened.

'This is going nowhere,' Phil shouted. Sara was talking into Louise's ear. Jake felt himself being dragged away. 'She's not interested. Let's get out of here.'

'But—'

'Look, I've been blown out and I want to make a quick getaway.'

'OK, just let me—'

Phil was insistent. 'If we leave now, we can be at the station before the night security.'

'Meaning?'

'Meaning, get your coat. You know what I told you this afternoon about your uncle? There's something else I want you to see, in my office.'

Jake smiled helplessly at Louise, who shrugged back. As they left the club and the cool air attacked their perspiration, he wondered whether Phil had done him a favour. Maybe he had been about to make an idiot of himself. But there was no time for such delicate considerations. Phil was walking at a pace which belied the shortness of his legs.

Inside his office, Phil opened a drawer. 'Now everything I've told you today is not to be repeated,' he slurred.

Jake nodded an exaggerated, drunken affirmation.

'Here,' he said, 'have a look at this.'

Phil passed Jake a yellowy brown file. On the outside was a label which read 'Robert Walsh'. Jake opened it up, puzzled. 'Who's—?'

'Bob. The mortician, from Dabner and Sons.'

Jake leafed through the pages. Some were pink, others white, a few were yellow and almost transparent. Most contained scribbled notes or dense type. 'So what's Bob been up to then?'

'Recently, not a lot, as far as we know. However, and this might interest you, as his record suggests, he has several previous convictions for breaking and entering.'

'You think he's the one?'

'I don't know. But it's possible.'

'Have you interviewed him yet?'

'Not yet. I'm just interested in whether he's managed to get his hands on Norbert's keys.' Phil slumped back in his chair, suddenly tired. 'We're bringing him in soon though.'

Safety Scene #11

We see the interior of a busy factory. There are several conveyor lines speeding cartons of orange juice from large metal vats towards a small cluster of workers. Close-up on a man in his early forties. He has a rolled-up cigarette behind one ear, and is listening to a walkman. A small badge on his blue overalls says 'Dave'. He lifts a box of twelve cartons from the back of the packaging machine and bends down to place them on a pallet. Pan out. Behind the factory staff are three warehouse doors, covered in thick strips of grubby plastic. Periodically, a forklift truck enters at speed and picks up a pallet of juice. Pull out further. A high gantry surrounds two sides of the factory. A painter and decorator is on an extended ladder making small repairs. Focus back on Dave, the orange-juice packer. We hear the tinny rattle of his Walkman music. A forklift truck breaks through the plastic door-covering, beeping its horn as it does so, and heads towards Dave's pallet. Dave is in the way. The shiny metal forks head towards him, and the driver sounds his horn. Dave is oblivious. The driver slams on his brakes, swears at Dave and waits for him to finish what he is doing. We see the decorator, who glances down at the commotion from his position thirty feet above the concrete floor, the ladder shifting slightly as he changes position. The forklift picks up the pallet, loads it on top of three others, raises them all up into the air and leaves the factory floor. Dave adjusts his headphones, and as he does so, feels the cigarette behind his ear. Close-up on his mouth. He licks his dry lips. We watch him turn around, cigarette in one hand, and head for the plastic-covered door. Exterior view. The forklift driver is in the vicinity of the entrance, and is reversing quickly, with his load fully extended to a height of twenty feet, occasionally sounding his horn. Back to Dave, whistling towards the door.

Suddenly, there is a colossal bang.

Modern Injury Paranoia

Monday 11:07 a.m.

On the bus to the factory, Jake scoured the accident report. The details were unpleasant, and he couldn't help but feel partially responsible. After all, it was his job to ensure that workers were protected from danger.

Norbert's death had changed his views and had, for the first time in his life, made him squeamish. It was becoming embarrassing. He was having to look away from the screen during safety lectures, and had missed two consecutive meetings of the DangerClub. Of course he told himself that hazard-prevention films were different, that they were camp and funny, with their flimsy sets, innocuous conditions and appalling consequences, but still, the principle remained. They were laughing at injury, whether real or imagined. His TV viewing was also suffering, and this was more difficult to excuse. Three or four times in recent days he had to turn over during satellite films which involved car crashes, fights, long ladders, sharp objects or anything else the least bit entertaining. He sighed to himself. At this rate, he was fast going to turn into Roger. Each time the bus ground to a halt Jake shuddered along with it.

The trouble was that the overkill of violent imagery in films, video games and on TV had affected Jake in two contradictory ways, which were occasionally in danger of pulling him apart at the seams. First, he was becoming numb to violence which involved others. Second, and particularly in the light of Norbert's experience, he was increasingly fearful that violence could affect him. He closed the report and stared through the window. It was raining and condensation lined the windows, distorting the world outside.

Close to the factory, Jake stood up and pushed the bell. He was unsteady on his feet, the sweaty morning air choking him, before the doors opened and the rain splashed him back to life. As he walked towards the factory, ultra-safe modern cars sprayed through puddles and he found himself thinking about his childhood, bouncing around in the back of his dad's Allegro, his nose pressed against the glass, sharp metal door-knobs surrounding him, the interior trim looking as if it had been bolted together over a careless lunch-hour. Truly, things had changed.

Danger was an abstract concept in those days. Accidents generally happened to other people. Ensuring you didn't die in a road accident consisted of remembering a series of generally untrue notions made up by blokes in pubs. No one wore seatbelts, and the universal advice seemed to be, 'In a crash, try to get thrown clear, if you can.' Jake smiled a thin, rainy smile that the preferred seventies option, should you have the choice, was to hurtle through the windscreen and scrape along the tarmac. People also said that babies generally survived crashes better than adults because their bodies were relaxed. So as well as being thrown clear, you should also try not to tense too much.

Cars with air bags and steel cages continued to swish past as Jake reached the factory gates. It was a symptom of modern injury-paranoia that vehicles were now sold not for their performance or looks but for their safety features. Jake's piece of German machinery had, apparently, been 'A Safe Car in an Unsafe World'. NCAP ratings were splashed across posters. Ad campaigns starred smiling families of crash-test dummies. People like Roger bought solid, heavy Volvos to increase their probability of surviving accidents, largely to the detriment of people in lighter, flimsier vehicles. This was the way of the world. Safety for me; you'll just have to take your chances.

When he found him, the MD of Diamonte Orange Juice Ltd was upset about the accident. He was about to be a lot less happy, however. Jake told him that unless the injury-rate plummeted, Hazard Prevention would think about closing the factory. The MD was taken aback.

'You can't just shut us down,' he protested.

'I don't see why not,' Jake replied. 'This is the third big accident this year.'

'But lots of jobs are dangerous. You going to close down all the coal mines as well?'

'Tories have already beaten us to it.'

'And no one has to work here if they don't want. They know the risks.'

Jake opened the report and had another quick scan of the summary. 'Knowing the risks is one thing. Driving a forklift truck with an inappropriate load and having it topple over on you is quite another.'

The MD rubbed his face. 'I'm as upset about it as you are, Jake,' he said, 'but what can I do? We operate a factory. We need forklifts. The driver had been told never to reverse with a fully extended load, but still he did it. And now he's in hospital in a bad way. I don't see what else we could have done.'

'Fine them. Anyone driving inappropriately gets docked a day's wages. That'd do for a start.'

The boss scratched an eyebrow. 'You know, that's not the worst idea I've ever heard.'

'Thanks.'

'No, I mean it. Look, I'll give it a go, see how we get on.'

As Jake left Diamonte Orange Juice and headed back towards the bus stop, he began to think that maybe safety wasn't so difficult after all. People just needed an incentive to focus their minds. Common sense and perspective were the main things. What was more difficult, he appreciated, was the atmosphere that was increasingly developing at home. *Pornbeersport* was wearing off, his tolerance to the medication rising alarmingly. And as he began to emerge from the haze of the treatment regime, glaring problems were raising their ugly heads.

Jake reached into his coat pocket, searching for change. He pulled his phone and work gloves out, rummaged around in the lining, and discovered a couple of warm pound coins. He replaced the phone, and as he folded the thick protective gloves, he noticed that one of them needed repairing. It had become damaged, maybe on a site visit. He held it up in front of his face and jolted to a stop. A finger was missing. He placed the glove against his left hand. Glove and hand were identical in shape. He started walking again, the bus stop in sight. Rain poured down his face but he didn't wipe it away. They had reached him. At last, they had found him. They knew where he worked, what car he used to drive, and where he lived. And now they could get inside his house and amputate the fingers of his gloves. Jake stood in the queue and shivered.

Inspecting the Inspectors

Back at work, Jake opened his desk diary and let out a muffled cry. This afternoon was the one occasion he dreaded more than almost any other. It was the event that every Hazard Prevention Officer had secret nightmares about – the internal inspection. Roger entered, tripped over the carpet, banged his head on his desk and knocked a pile of papers onto the floor. Trying to salvage some dignity from the situation, he hobbled over to the bulging Injury Report Book and jotted down what had just happened.

'Would you mind?' he asked Jake.

Jake shrugged, then signed that he had witnessed the accident. He drew a long breath. That it had come to this.

Bridgeton Hazard Prevention ran a democratic system of self-inspection. Jake, Roger or Geoff spent four months as internal officer, and then passed the dubious and unpopular honour to the next in line. At the moment, Roger was in charge. Jake risked a glance in his colleague's direction, praying that he had forgotten about this afternoon's check-up. Fat chance.

Roger was rubbing his forehead, wincing as he did so, and flicking through a large volume entitled 'Preventing Hazard in Hazard Prevention'.

On the advice of the last internal inspection, the rollers of each swivel chair had been removed. It had been suggested that, in the wrong hands, a chair that moved could be positively lethal. As a result, several times a day and through force of habit, Jake pushed optimistically away from his desk towards the window and rolled nowhere. All this activity succeeded in doing was to plough a series of incisions through the carpet, which Roger regularly managed to trip over.

Jake rubbed his face and awaited the inevitable. Roger had pinned a new motto up in celebration of the imminent check-up. *Carelessness Always Catches Up With You*, Jake read. He began to gain the unhealthy feeling that Roger was sending him subliminal messages. Maybe the whole point of the posters was to fuck with his brain. So far, so good. In fact, as he thought about it, the whole business of internal examinations began to raise a series of troubling philosophical questions for him. First, who inspected the internal inspectors? Jake, Roger and Geoff inspected each other, but nobody seemed interested in inspecting the three of them. What if they were doing it wrong? And if they were, who could tell them so? Was there an ultimate inspector of everybody? And if so, did they ever have accidents themselves? In which case, were they then demoted and inspected by a higher, safer authority? Or, rather than being hierarchical, did it simply just go round in pointless circles of not much fun? And, most importantly, was the rest of the world laughing at all this?

The door opened, and Geoff poked his greyness through the aperture. 'Two o'clock for the assessment, is it, Roger?'

Roger glanced up from his manual with unusual

seriousness. 'Technically, Geoff, I'm not supposed to say. This is meant to be a surprise inspection.'

Geoff's uninspiring demeanour appeared to drop a notch. 'It's just that I've got to pop out later and I've got two written in my diary.'

'That's what I've got as well,' Jake added. 'We agreed the date ages ago.'

'Look, I'm not saying it isn't going to be two,' Roger said, bending down to retrieve some of the papers he had knocked over. 'But I'm also not saying it is.'

Geoff retreated and sat in his office, watching the clock shuffle towards two o'clock. He straightened a couple of files, and hid his pencil sharpener, paper knife, scissors, drawing pins and stapler in a drawer. Jake glanced around his own desk, and while Roger continued to read up on the rules, similarly tipped anything remotely dangerous into his briefcase, which he then locked. It was one minute to two. Roger's digital watch began to beep. The appointed hour had arrived, and a hush descended upon the town's Hazard Prevention Unit.

Roger stood up, stretched, and walked ominously over to Jake. For a couple of hours, the normal rules of their working relationship would cease to be. Jake shivered. Roger cleared his throat.

'As you know, Jake,' he began, in a manner which suggested he'd been practising, 'it's my duty as internal—'

Jake decided to fast forward to the bad news. 'Just get to the point.'

Roger paused dramatically, sensing the absolute power of his situation. 'I want the rollers put back on the chairs.'

'But Geoff said we had to take them off.'

'They're turning the carpet into a stumble hazard.'

'Well Geoff's not going to like it. And he's the boss.'

'As current internal officer, I out-rank him in matters of office safety.'

'And in the real world?'

Roger stared into Jake's face and was silent for a couple of seconds. 'Come on, Jake, I don't like doing this any more than you do.'

'I doubt it.'

'But it's got to be done. If we're not seen to be safe ourselves, who's going to put their trust in us? Besides, there's another serious problem with this office.' He paused again. 'The safety posters above your desk.'

'What about them?'

'First, you stick them in with drawing pins.'

'But I never even touch—'

'And second, and more serious, I've decided they're a fire hazard.'

Jake glanced up at his noticeboard. 'You're joking,' he answered.

'Do I look like I am?'

Roger was bleeding slightly from his black and white grazed forehead. He was hobbling around with his ankle in a cast. His neck was in a brace, making it difficult for him to meet Jake's eye, and his index finger was thickly bound. Jake declined to answer.

'I know there are lots of flammable papers in the office. It's just that yours are directly below a convection heater. You never know what might happen.'

'But it's electric.'

'So?'

'Well, it isn't as if flames are suddenly going to burst out of it.'

'That's not the point.'

'Well what is?'

'That I want something done about them.'

Jake momentarily and inaccurately sensed victory. 'Right, we'll stop putting them up, and I'll bin the ones already pinned there.'

Roger cleared his throat. 'I've got a better idea. I want you to mount them. Get some non-glass, nonflammable, shatterproof frames from somewhere, and slot them in those. Simple.'

'And suppose one of them falls on my head?'

'Fill in a report.'

Jake swore under his breath. In a few short weeks it was his turn to play inspector. Revenge would be sweet. He would make Roger take the posters back out of their frames and mount them above his own desk to mess with *his* head every day.

'And your bike parts,' Roger continued. 'They're a fire hazard as well.'

'What?' Jake asked, incredulously. 'They're fucking metal. When was the last time that an aluminium seat post burst into flames?'

'I mean, in the event of a fire, that they might block an exit.'

'How? They're not exactly going to get up and run for the fucking door.'

'They just might.'

'This is bollocks.'

'Anyway, I'll give you a couple of weeks to sort those things out. In the meantime, I'd better start on the rest of the building.' Roger walked out with an air of minor triumph.

Jake sat and loosened his tie. He thought momentarily about using it as a tripwire for his colleague, but decided Roger didn't need the help.

Down the corridor came the noise of muffled shouting from Geoff's office.

Everydayness

Kate was on the Internet when Jake arrived home uncharacteristically early at five thirty. He was still tense, and felt that his whole life was being inspected one way or another. His house was clearly being monitored, as the glove incident testified, and even his car had been tracked down and sabotaged. He was being toyed with by faces from the past that he'd rather forget. He was getting the message loud and clear. Obviously they wanted to scare him, but then what?

And work was no longer a refuge. Roger was scrutinizing him from the inside. He bolted the front and back doors and closed the curtains before sitting down on the sofa. Kate made no comment.

He tried to lose himself in cable TV. Its charms were wearing thin, however. There were only so many adverts you could see, only so many football matches, only so many films, and only so many beers you could drink. As soon as something becomes easily accessible, it loses most of its pleasure. The same was undeniably true of his girlfriend. She had said it herself on increasingly frequent occasions. 'It's just the *EVERYDAYNESS* which is killing me, Jake.'

In sharp relief against the mundane daily sameness of their lives, Kate was changing, and almost on an hourly basis. No one stays the same, but usually you can keep up. With Kate, the Tour de France would have had difficulty staying abreast of her twists and turns. Jake no longer saw the shifts of direction coming until he was already committed to a certain course of action. For her part, Jake was sure Kate would say that he was a long straight road, a perilous mountain road which had been stretched taut at some point, pulling all of the excitement out of it. But these days she was fluctuating so much that Jake hardly knew what to do with himself. Nymphomania had superseded near frigidity, microwave classics had been replaced by curiously inedible cuisine and an obsession with her boyfriend's unhappiness during weekends had turned into a quest to convert him into a sport-obsessed couch potato. Jake was at a complete loss.

One constancy remained. If anything, Kate was spending more time in chat rooms than before. He wondered whether he was about to get his opportunity to play some games with TRADER68. Something seemed to be building. There was an expectancy, a quiver of possibility about her of late. While Jake sat on the sofa spending quality time with four-packs of lager, hiding from his enemies, Kate tapped away almost incessantly. In between bouts of typing, she appeared bored and listless, and occasionally they would argue. Truly, *Pornbeersport* was wearing off from both sides. Increasingly an atmosphere was developing, and tonight Jake had a particularly bad feeling. Kate appeared to be trying to goad him. He asked her if she was OK.

She sat down heavily at the other end of the sofa and sighed. 'And what the hell do you mean by that?'

'This always happens,' Jake said quietly.

'What?'

He turned to her. 'You get bored, you want me to entertain you, I fail, we argue, you cheer up.'

'You call this entertaining?'

'I call it inevitable.'

'Meaning?'

'Over the last few days you haven't seemed happy until you've provoked me into showing some anger or emotion.'

'I shouldn't have to provoke you into showing emotion.'

'Yes, but you do.'

'It's the only way you demonstrate any feelings for me.'

'That's nonsense.'

'Is it?'

'Yes.'

'Well, when was the last time you showed you cared for me?'

'Just now, when I asked you if you were OK.'

Kate paused, a line of argument running out of steam. She tried another. 'You just seem so distracted at the moment, so uninterested.'

Jake drained his can, and muted the TV. 'I thought you were happy,' he said.

'That's the trouble with being happy,' Kate answered. 'You don't think much.'

'And when you're unhappy you think too much. Either way . . .'

Kate was silent for a few moments. One glaring sign something was definitely brewing was that, until recently, a protracted two-hour period of Hmms and Maybes would take care of Jake's side of many conversations, whereas now she seemed to require active participation from him. He had to think about his answers, and actually listen to her words rather than merely guessing the tone. One other notion had occurred to him over the past weeks as well. Every Big

Spender pound they squandered served only to separate them. They had bought a bigger sofa so they could sit further apart, moved to a larger house so they could occupy separate rooms, put furniture in the spare room so they could sleep alone if they argued, acquired a second TV so they could watch different programmes, renovated the downstairs bathroom so they could shower unaccompanied. And when it came down to it, all the money that paid for these luxuries turned out to have been borrowed anyway.

Kate stood up. 'I'm going to watch some TV,' she stated, marching out of the room and banging upstairs. Jake frowned and opened another can, appreciating that all too often living together doesn't necessarily mean loving together. His stump itched and he scratched it hard. When he did this, he often felt like the finger was still attached, and that he was grinding his nail down to stop it growing too long. He continued to rub, savouring the impression that his finger was intact. A drop of blood escaped the skin surface. Something somewhere was about to give.

Enquiries

Malcolm Dabner replaced the receiver and shouted for Bob to come and join him. Bob replied that he would like to, in theory, but was just at the tricky Draino stage of the current embalming. Malcolm sat and fiddled with his pen, rehearsing his words. He was reasonable friends with one of the local coppers, who had just filled him in on some of the details. In fact, as he thought about it, he was reasonable friends with a lot of people. Rarely, however, did they edge any closer than that. A step nearer to Malcolm, he readily appreciated, was a step nearer to the grave. Even in the pub, at the shops, on the bowling green, in his social circle, death clung to him.

Bob appeared at the door, bloody and sweating. He rubbed his forehead with the back of his hand, and a small trace of the cadaver's essence smeared across his brow.

'Sit down, Bob. You're not going to like this.'
'What?'
'We've got to dig that headless fucker up again.'
'Again?'

'We buried, it seems like . . . we buried the wrong man.'

'You're joking. Who says?'

'The police.'

'How the hell do they know? Couldn't exactly hold an identity parade the state he was in.'

'Those forensic tests, apparently.'

'Ah. Right.'

'And there's one other thing.'

'Boss?'

'Talk to you – the police . . . they want to talk to you, Bob.'

'What for? They haven't found out about that JCB, have they?'

'I'm not sure.' Malcolm leaned forwards, his face grim. 'But there's one thing I am sure of. If you've been up to any of your other old tricks again, you can kiss your job goodbye.'

Bob shifted uneasily. 'What are you getting at?'

'You know what. The thing with that is . . .' Malcolm gave up on another unpromising start to a sentence, and tried again. 'Look, when I took you on, I was well aware of your record. Half the town was. I was willing to give you a chance. And if you've started again . . .'

'I haven't, boss. Honest. That's behind me.'

Malcolm stared hard into his face and took refuge in pomposity. Bob avoided his eyes. 'I think it's best the police handle this now.'

Bob stood up and slouched back to his corpse. He made a mental note to ditch the keys he'd stolen from the bag of effects lying next to the headless stiff in the morgue. He was agitated and the contrasting serenity of the cadaver irritated him. He took a wide-bore needle and rammed it firmly through a prominent artery. That was the trouble with having a past. When you hoped you'd successfully buried it, some fucker came and dug it up for you.

Barnsley

The thing about London was that it was just so bloody expensive. Admittedly, there were things to do and places to go, but getting to them was a night out in itself, and staying at them was a task for a stern wallet. Barnsley. That was the place. The cheapest town to live in England last year, apparently. A pint of beer was still under the glorious one-pound-fifty mark, fish and chips could be had for a couple of quid, and thirty-five grand would get you a decentish house, depending on your outlook. Barnsley. The name had poetry in it. He said it again and sighed, as an exiled Brazilian might whisper Rio de Janeiro.

It was nine forty-six and he was late. A tube strike had almost stopped the city in its tracks. Barnsley didn't have a tube system, which now seemed like an added bonus. He picked up his pace. It wasn't good to be late for your most important client. The office was still a quarter of a mile away, and as black cabs crawled past in the enhanced traffic, he thought fleetingly of hopping into one, before dismissing the idea. Instead, he resolved to walk faster, and ten minutes later found himself in front of the British Library. Inside, he paid a fee of four pounds, and took a key up to the second floor, where the language rooms languished. Mr Keithly was already in the corridor, briefcase in hand, running the sole of one shoe back and forth over the hallway's thin carpet. He looked up and smiled.

'Got all the documents,' he said, raising his case to his chest and patting it affectionately.

They entered the small, poky windowless room and sat down at the minute desk, their knees almost touching. Mr Keithly opened his case and pulled out a wad of papers. As he handed them over, he said, 'Now, you're sure all this is legal?'

'Legal, just about. Moral, probably not.'

'And presumably moral crimes still go unpunished?'

'That's the beauty of them.'

'Good. Well, let's get this bloody thing done.'

There was an air of endeavour about the language room. Papers were exchanged, figures discussed and a calculator periodically abused.

'You know, I still can't get over your rates. No hidden charges, I hope?'

'None. Everything's free. All I ask is thirty-three per cent of what I save you.'

'Will a cheque do?'

'Cash. Always cash. Surely you understand that.'

Mr Keithly, a well-lunched man in his early forties, came close to blushing at his own naivety. 'Cash – of course. Sorry, I wasn't thinking. After all, it's only money.'

'Let me give you a general piece of advice, Mr Keithly. The way to become rich is to think of money as a person rather than an object.'

'How so?'

'As soon as you say "it's only money" you're on your way to neglecting it. Your cash is a living thing which needs to be nurtured and loved.'

'I see.'

'You have to put it above your family and friends.'

Mr Keithly nodded vigorously, his chins wobbling in appreciation. 'You know, I hope you don't mind, but I've recommended you to another couple of my colleagues. Did Mr Davison get in touch?'

'I met him yesterday.'

'Same place?'

'No. One of my other offices.'

'Which one?'

'The one next door.'

Mr Keithly laughed. 'Great system you've got here. I guess that's how you work so cheaply, with no over-heads to kill you.'

'This office costs four pounds per hour. I wouldn't call that cheap.'

'Anyway,' Mr Keithly replied, changing the subject, 'have you got those receipts you said you could lay your hands on?'

'Yes.'

'Where did you get them?'

'Trade secret.'

'But they're kosher? I mean, no one will know?'

'OK, keep this one under your hat. I print my own. I obtained three cash registers – different makes and models – which were being dumped by a supermarket. I can alter the dates and amounts on all three machines to match the circumstance, and if I change paper rolls, can make them appear new, old, knackered, whatever you want.'

Mr Keithly whistled. 'Now that really is a nice scam. And presumably I can claim for anything I want?'

'Within reason.'

'How are you on expenses claims?'

'Could be persuaded, for the standard thirty-three per cent.'

'This just gets better. So I'm going to pay fuck-all tax this year, my accountant is effectively charging nothing, and both of these losses can be offset by fiddling my expense claims with a load of your receipts. Just wait till the rest of the guys at work hear about this. I want to kiss you!'

'You kiss me and the Inland Revenue will fuck you,' he said, smiling.

Mr Keithly laughed and pulled out his wallet. 'There you go, three hundred notes. And here, have a meal out or something on me.'

The man took the fee and the twenty-pound tip and curtly replied, 'I don't believe in eating out. But thanks anyway.'

'Either way, pleasure doing business with you, Mr . . .'

The man stood up, pocketed the notes and accepted Mr Keithly's outstretched hand. 'Flint. Norbert Flint.'

Actors

Tuesday 4:31 p.m.

IM GONNA DO IT
  YEAH?
  CANT TAKE NEMORE
  WHEN R U GONNA TELL HIM?
  NOW!!!! IM ACTUALLY GONNA DO IT NOW!!!!
Kate typed. WISH ME LUCK

Ten seconds later came the reply. B BRAVE/ U CAN
SUCCEED/ SOON B 2GETHER!!!!!

Kate checked her watch, logged off and walked into
the hall. She squinted at herself in the mirror. Floating
freely down telephone wires, you could be anybody,
she smiled, and her reflection grinned back. It didn't
matter – your appearance, age, ability to cook, anything – no one could see you, no one could judge you.
That was the beauty of it – even ugly people were
beautiful on the Internet. Not that she was ugly, she
appreciated, examining her face in profile. Far from it.
But technology gave you the chance to reinvent yourself, away from the scrutiny of others. You could be
the person you wanted to be, rather than the person
you had ended up.

Before she had become hooked on chat rooms, Kate hadn't been happy with her life. She had slipped into a certain domesticity and felt that adventure was eluding her. Giving up her job had been a bad idea, although not bad enough to merit getting another one. Her empire had shrunk drastically, from organizing misleading vacuum-cleaner demonstrations in shopping malls, to pacing the front room ignoring the dust. But chat rooms provided space. You could visit the world simply by sitting on your arse and pressing a few buttons. And what's more, instead of travelling as Kate Archer, unsatisfied house-girlfriend, you could journey as Kate Archer, dynamic sex machine.

Of course what went for you, Kate readily appreciated, went for others. For all she knew, TRADER68 could be a bed-wetting mummy's boy. The photos could be fake. He might count his computer as his best friend. He might spend his evenings wanking over *Robot Wars*. All of this had concerned her. Until she talked to him on the phone. Then she knew. In chat rooms he was one thing. On the phone, quite another. And that was the irony. The Internet had set her free, but had also stopped her short of being able to decide about him. Sending short phrases with dubious spelling could only take you so far.

Gradually, they typed less and talked more. Except when Jake was around. He was unlikely to have been too chuffed about some of the words she was using. But TRADER68 – Paul to his friends – had several beautiful qualities which were lacking in her boyfriend. An endearing innocence. A gentle sense of humour. An easy-going shyness. And, above all else, huge piles of cash. Financial consultancy with a few shrewd investments along the way meant that Paul was, in his own words, swimming in money. What was the point struggling to stay afloat, when you could be bathing in the stuff? she asked her mirror image, watching her eyebrows arch.

Kate became almost moist as she thought about Paul's Big Spender possibilities. Fuck thirty-two quid of a safety inspector's pittance if a financier had thousands knocking about at the end of the month. Fuck being told what you could and could not spend if you had a partner who lavished gifts on you. There were no two ways about it. She was going to have to ditch Jake, the boyfriend she had ended up with, and begin living the life she had always promised herself. She headed upstairs and started sorting some clothes. As she did so, she made a mental list of points to put across to Jake in an hour's time. Rule Number One of ending a relationship – make the person you are leaving feel it's their fault.

When Jake arrived home, he found his girlfriend waiting for him in the hallway. For once, she was fully clothed and didn't express any interest in sex. Next to her were a couple of rucksacks and a suitcase.

'Where're you going?' Jake asked.

'My mum's,' Kate replied.

'How long for?'

'Until I can find somewhere to live.'

'What do you mean?'

Kate opened the case for the offence. 'Your constant penny-pinching is making living with you impossible.'

'But we have to cut back, we're—'

'And I feel guilty just for buying enough food for our tea.'

'I didn't mean to make you—'

'And you never do any work around the house.'

'I never do anything other than—'

'And you never seem to want to make love any more.'

'Well, naturally my enthusiasm is waning, seeing as we do it about three times a—'

'And you don't seem to appreciate my cooking.'

'I make a good effort to—'

'And you make me feel bad because I can't find a job.'

'I didn't realize you were actually looking for—'

'And frankly you're becoming a bit of a safety bore.'

'It is my job, and I do have to—'

'And I've met someone else.'

Jake stopped. 'Who?' he asked, pretending to be taken aback.

'Just someone.'

'Just who?'

'Someone I met.'

'Where? You never go out.' And then he made a show of the penny dropping. 'You've met someone on the Internet, haven't you?'

Kate was silent, looking at the floor, having run out of rehearsed lines of argument.

'So who is he?' Jake had a fair idea. Some wanker called TRADER68.

'He's . . . well, he works in finance.'

'And?'

Kate glared up at him, anger in her eyes. 'And what?'

It was Jake's turn to examine his footwear. 'And nothing.'

'Look, if it's any consolation—'

'No. It's no consolation at all. Whatever you were going to say. You've met someone else and you're leaving me. What could possibly be of any consolation?'

Kate didn't answer, and while they stood together in the narrow hall with her possessions between them, Jake wondered whether he was handling his girl-friend's news well. Clearly things weren't working out. The relationship hadn't been on an even keel for some time. A premature end was therefore in his interest, and he should be pleased. He could lie in at the weekends. Financially, he would be better off. He could resurrect his bachelor lifestyle of pleasurable sloth. The bed would stay unmade. He could visit the many pubs of Bridgeton as often as he pleased. He could eat edible food again. He could buy flat-packed items of furniture, and just leave them unassembled for as long as he saw fit. The garden could go to ruin, the drive to leaves, the fence to hell. He could adopt even more of Norbert's penny-pinching schemes. The telephone would ring again. He could start a savings account. In the evening, he could scratch his arse while lying horizontally on the sofa drinking beer and listening to music. He could dedicate his life to becoming more like Homer. Friends could call round at any time of the night or day and be guaranteed a makeshift party. And yet, and yet ... the hazy daydream of so much pleasure was gnawed away by an unpleasant thought. Kate had been unfaithful to him. 'You've slept with this wanker, have you?' he demanded, suddenly realizing the implication of what she had told him.

'No.'

'Oh come on.'

'Honestly, I haven't.'

'You're leaving me for someone you haven't even slept with? What kind of madness is that?'

'So now you want me to be unfaithful to you?'

'Of course not. But how do you know you're going to get on?'

Kate thought about Paul's large throbbing bank account. 'Some things are more important than sex.'

'That's rich coming from you after the last month.'

'Look, I'm going to stay at my mum's and get my head together, before I go leaping into bed with a total stranger.'

'A stranger? You mean you haven't even met him?'

'We've talked every day.'

'This gets worse. You're leaving me for someone you haven't even met?'

'I know enough about him to realize that I . . .' Kate left the sentiment hanging. 'And anyway, I am meeting him, next week.'

'And then what?'

'We'll see how it goes from there.'

Jake put his hands on his girlfriend's shoulders, and stared into her deep brown eyes. 'Kate, this might turn out to be a bad decision. I know we haven't been getting on well, but, you know, I don't want to see you fuck up.'

Kate shrugged his hands off. 'And that little speech is supposed to make me want to stay? That's the best you can do?'

To be honest, it was. Much as it rankled with Jake that another man was stealing his girlfriend, he could see that it was maybe for the best. He walked into the living room and slumped onto the sofa. He swore at the computer, which was still on. A couple of minutes passed. He could hear Kate crying. A taxi beeped, she gathered her belongings and left the house, the front door still open after her. Jake sat and stared at the muted TV, watching actors faking emotions for his benefit.

In the early hours, Jake had an idea. Tomorrow morning he would type a short message into Kate's beloved chat room. It was time to meet TRADER68.

Hardcore Txt

trader68 was L8. Jk scand t large room of intnet cafe. no sign. theyd agreed 2 mt @ 6, + trader68 wud b wearing a red baseball cap. there were no txt msgs on his fone 2 say y he was L8. Jk checkd his watch + felt vxd that s'body wud stand his g/f up. ok, Jk wud stnd her up, but that was diffnt. he ws allowd. it ws expectd. they were in luv. @ least til yestaday.

18:25 and stll n'thing. 2 kill a few mins, Jk used t PC he had paid 2 use. he clickd on t web + enterd K8's chtroom. 2 his surprise, trader68 was there, sending msgs. the cnt!!! Jk typed /where r u?/

trader68 replied /here!! in the meetg place!! where r u??? :< ☹ /

Jk stopd. so he ws here, in the same plce. but he couldnt c ne hats. he sat up higher and scand t room again. n'thing. /i cant c u/ he enterd.

/cant c u either/ came the ansa.

/wot r we gonna do?/ Jk askd. there ws a pause, then his fone beeped. Jk read t msg. /i can hear u!!!/ it said. fck fck fck, Jk swore to hmself. sht bastd wnk fck. trader68 ws gettg t upper hnd, + he regrettd giving him t numbr t day b4. he duckd down behnd hs terminal, then swtchd t fone off + turnd to t PC. /now let me hear u/ he keyd.

/how???/ came t reply.

/cough/ Jk instructed. he straind his ears. the msg sped thru fibre optic cbles, ws bouncd off a satellite, raced back + appeard on a vdu 2 or 3 metres away. there ws a muffld cough 2 his lft. Jk span around 2 c where it came from. there were a few possblties, 0 of whom matchd trader68's fotos. /again/ Jk instructd.

/no. your turn. I wanna hear u again. am v ecxited/ trader68 replied.

JK swore agn. fck wnk sht cnt. he ws unnervd + didnt want 2 b flushd out. he sat and thought. wot he really wantd ws to c trader68, size up t opposition and get t fck out. this wasnt going well. then he hd an idea. /fone running out of battery. let me txt u instead via internet. got s'thing saucy 2 say. v much lookng fwd 2 meetg u/ he typed.

/ok. u knw the nmbr/

/forgot. send again/

trader68 duly obliged + his fone nmbr appeard on t screen. Jk snt a txt msg to it. he stood up + watchd. 10 secs later a fone beeped + he followd t sound. 2 males ca. 25 + 30 were poss.

/dont understnd/ trader68 replied. /snd again/

Jk typed 1 more nonsense msg. /whr ksk uu cj ® xx 128 ?!!?/

there ws another fone noise + Jk focusd intently on t 2 males. he could now c 1 of them had a mobile. Jk walkd 2wards him, 2 make sure, passing close, b4 returng 2 his PC. right then u mther fcker, he whisprd 2 himslf, steal my g/f would u? lets c how u like this. 4 stations to his left ws a hrd faced bizniz woman who had been annoyng Jk by tlking incessntly on her fone. /trader68 – maybe nows t time/ he entered into the chtroom. he glancd @ t woman, who had finally ended her call. /think i c u. like what i c. your turn. i'm in t row infront o' u, wearng drk suit, scarf, glasses. come on over. thrill me!!!!!!!/

Jk pressd retrn on t k'board + sat back in his chair. 2 or 3 secs later, 1 of the males got up + began to swgger past him in t drction of t woman. Jk stared @ him. he ws late 20s, possibly stll pubescent, + ws flushd w anorak expectatn. the mther fcker had been using fake fotos. K8 ws going to get a big shock soon. + now the SOB ws gonna fnd out wot real women thought of flirting nerds.

As he left the semi-lunacy of the Internet café, Jake felt great. He had used modern technology to send electronic messages thousands of miles to bring two annoying people sitting yards apart into conflict. And it had been quite a showdown. He only wished he could tell Kate about it. She was unlikely to see the funny side though.

TRADER68 had waltzed over to the woman he believed to be the very ready and willing Big Spender, his joystick probably already firm, and had planted a kiss on the back of her neck. Serious Business Woman had been less than enthused by the prospect of an un-authorized anorak taking liberties. In one beautiful move, she swung her mobile phone, which was a clunky piece of mid-nineties equipment, rapidly behind her head, and slammed him in the face with it. From Jake's vantage point in the crowded Internet room, TRADER68 stood in utter shock, close to tears. Serious Business Woman had merely resumed her typing. TRADER68 then retired to his terminal looking both perplexed and wounded, and, to Jake's delight, had entered another message, asking whether violence was absolutely necessary on a first date. In what he later decided was his master stroke of the whole affair, Jake replied on Big Spender's behalf that violence was how she liked it, and to come over and give her a good slap on the arse. The look of sheer perplexity on his face as Scary Business Woman, having received another unwelcome geek visit, calmly ceased her typing, stood up and kneed him in the bollocks was an image Jake would savour for the rest of his life.

Jake pedalled home with a sense of justice coursing through his veins. Kate was soon to discover that she had been duped, a misdemeanour he felt he had corrected somewhat. And rather than lower himself to the appropriate course of action when confronted by someone who had just pinched his girlfriend, Jake had managed to get someone else to beat the wanker up.

Upgrade

Phil was sitting at his desk, in the same office they had visited after the nightclub a couple of weeks before. He cleared some papers off a chair to make room for Jake, and appeared unusually serious.

'It's been upgraded, Jake,' Phil said gravely.

'What do you mean?'

'Murder.'

'You're joking.'

'I'm not. My boss says it's what we need, good for Bridgeton, you know, if we catch a real live murderer. We don't get many of those around here.'

'That might be, but who's to say Norbert is a murderer?'

'My boss.'

'So someone vanishes without a trace, and they're automatically a killer?'

'When they leave a corpse behind, yes.'

'So what are your lot doing?'

'Every fucking thing we can think of. Poster campaigns, re-enactments and even good old-fashioned detective work.'

'Re-enactment? You're going to stage the event again?'

'Oh yes.'

'What's the point?'

'There isn't one. But it makes it look like we're trying.'

'You don't even know what happened. I mean, I've read the reports. There's fuck-all in them. And how do you envisage re-enacting an RTA? With a dummy? And stunt cars?'

'You've got a better idea?'

'Yeah. Don't bother.'

'Oh come on, you're just being logical and sensible now. That kind of thinking would never get you to chief inspector.'

'Suits me. So when's it happening?'

'Next Saturday morning, when there'll be lots of people around.'

'You want to stage a traffic accident on a busy Saturday morning in town?'

'Me? No. My boss? Yes. And he told me to notify the Hazard Prevention Unit, which effectively I've just done.'

'Oh Christ. Bang goes my lie-in.'

'You'd only enjoy it. Think how much fun this is going to be instead.'

'And what about the bloke from the funeral place?'

'Bob? We've questioned him and searched his house.'

'And?'

'Not a fat lot. Well, a couple of dubious things, but not sufficient to prosecute him.'

'Like what?'

'I can't really say. You know that, Jake. But I think Dabner and Sons are doing something fishy. Bob's a bit of a character. We tried to do him a couple of years back, but he scraped his way out.'

'And what about the break-ins?'

'Forensics are working on it. But there's no real evidence yet. Whoever's doing it is being very careful. We'll just have to sit tight and hope they have another go.'

'Great,' Jake sighed. 'That'll make Elizabeth feel better.'

Cycling Is Seventeen Times More Dangerous than Driving

Louise climbed into her battered Fiesta and pulled out of the Peril factory car park, her seatbelt hanging limply against the door frame. Generally, Louise believed that a little recklessness went a long way. Listen to safety bores, and you would never do anything interesting. Ten people a day die in car crashes, she had heard. There are roughly thirty million motorists in our country. Not bad odds. Besides, seatbelts lull you into a false sense of security. Better to drive with your eyes open and not be protected than rush around thinking you're invincible.

As she took a roundabout at some speed, Louise appreciated that, for most people, travelling to work was the most dangerous part of the day. If you were employed by Peril and Sons, however, driving – even without a seatbelt – was a haven of safety in your daily routine. But making fireworks had a lot going for it. To begin with, Louise's father hadn't shared her enthusiasm. He complained that it wasn't challenging work for a bright girl with a degree in engineering. Louise had disagreed. 'Dad, it's rocket science,' she said, 'and things don't get much more challenging than that.' The argument ended there. She approached the edge of the industrial estate, and began to navigate her way through Bridgeton, using its pubs as compass points.

With the wages she was saving, Louise decided that she would soon be trading her 900cc Popular Plus for something altogether more thrilling. Something more thrilling would not be difficult to achieve. She changed down to third as the Fiesta's alleged engine struggled with a negligible hill. Over the crest, she passed a cyclist who was almost able to keep pace with the car. In her rear-view mirror, she recognized him. It was Safety Man Jake. Louise eased off the accelerator, allowing him to catch up. She decided to be bold and ask whether he fancied going out for a drink some time. And then she chickened out, and floored it. After thirty seconds of hesitation, the engine began to respond. In the meantime, however, the non-plussed cyclist had started to overtake Louise's car, unaware of who was driving. As he drew level, a lorry appeared around the bend. There was very little room for all three of them. The lawnmower engine spluttered and surged, just as Jake was about to pass the car. Suddenly, he was in danger of being crushed. Louise braked as the truck sounded its horn. Jake braked as well, and then, realizing that he was about to die in the confusion, swerved across the road, just ahead of the juggernaut, and skidded to a halt on the opposite pavement. Louise kept her head down and pulled slowly and gradually away from the scene, all the time cursing her indecision. Fortunately, Jake had been too busy concentrating on the approaching calamity to recognize her. At a safe distance, she turned round. He was shaking a fist in her direction. Attempting to lip-read, Louise thought she detected a couple of fucking twats and maybe the odd stupid cunt or two.

A few hundred yards later, Louise reached the ring

road, slightly flushed, and asked herself what she was so scared of. She was an adult. She had coped with the opposite sex more or less successfully for a number of years now. The very reason we were here and were attracted to each other was to meet and reproduce. So why should it be so fucking difficult? Why should she half die when she met an attractive man who seemed genuinely interested in her? Why should she then conspire to get him killed? Surely the single fear she had in her life – that of relationships – wasn't so acute that she should now nudge potential suitors under the wheels of passing lorries?

Louise glanced in her mirror once more. Jake had faded from view and she tried to picture his face. She had only met him a handful of times before, excluding minor road-rage incidents. There was something unsettled about him which appealed to her. He went around giving dull advice to stop people hurting themselves, and yet she could tell that his heart wasn't really in it. Although he obviously cared, at the same time there was a reek of mutiny to him. He was a gentle soul who didn't want to be gentle. He seemed to struggle to appear tolerant. It was in his eyes. Blue, pale like the rest of him, knowing, penetrating, thinking. And then of course there was his arse. Louise smiled as she pictured his cute backside. Maybe cycling was good for you after all.

Having and Not Having

News of Norbert's unique approach to taxation soon spread. Mr Keithly passed the word to his colleague Mr Davison, who whispered it to Mr Langers. Mr Langers tipped the wink to his associate Miss Peters, who let Mr Beavers in on the scheme. Mr Beavers gossiped to Miss Fish, who enlightened Mr Johnson. Mr Johnson let the cat out of the bag when chatting to Mr Chan, who put Mr Richards in the picture. Mr Richards faxed Ms Chambers, who notified Mrs Clent, who advised Mr Walker. Mr Walker hinted to Mr Khaira, who mentioned it to Mr Goram, who sent a text message to Mrs Edwards, who emailed seven of her closest co-workers, both inside and outside the company, who all forwarded details to a number of their acquaintances, most of whom returned the favour and distributed the information to friends and family. In a few short days, almost everyone who had ever had a tax bill and wondered if they should be paying less, or had been seriously considering fiddling their work expenses but without the means of doing so, had contacted Norbert to arrange a meeting.

Norbert, meanwhile, put romantic thoughts of Barnsley out of his mind, and London remained a small region of the country where the normal rules of spending had been abandoned. Added to this, he noticed something almost brutal about the proximity of the haves and have-nots, who were isolated from each other only by smoked glass and sculpted metal. But this, he came to see, was the city's very beauty. There was such a clamour from the haves to have more, and from the have-nots to have, that the situation was ripe for exploitation. Sure, other accountants bent the rules, but Norbert was going to go a lot further. Rules weren't there to be bent, they were there to be broken. And as a man who was already dead, Norbert wasn't particularly worried about the consequences of his actions. After all, what worse event could happen to a person than being killed?

Accommodation had been a problem, and remained so. With no references, he was paying over the odds for a luxury studio apartment in Fulham, which was lacking only in luxury and studio features, was more a flat than an apartment and also didn't actually seem to be in Fulham. Although he had no proof of the latter inaccuracy, ignorant as he was of the exact geography of London, he resolved to borrow an *A to Z* and look into it.

In the evenings, Norbert sat on his bed-cum-sofa and weighed up what he had done, staring at the grubby cooker, off-white sink and stained toilet, which looked a long way short of luxurious and did nothing to raise his spirits. There were pluses to his current situation, and he tried desperately to elevate them above the suffocating tide of guilt which surrounded him at night. First, the fact that they always said You Can't Take It With You when you died. But Norbert had. He had taken it all. One bank card, from an account his wife hadn't known about, the account into which he had siphoned all the excesses of their life for the last seven years. Forty-two thousand, one hundred and eighteen pounds, seventy-one pence, plus interest, at the last count. And then there was the large bulk of shares he had acquired in a certain sector of the retail industry. Month after month of cost-cutting, haggling and competing with grannies had all been worth it.

More than the secret bank account and the shares was the fact that Norbert had escaped his wife. The marriage hadn't been working well for a number of years. The tension in the relationship had crystallized into the single issue of money. If he was honest, Norbert had been keen to flee for some time but had built a trap for himself. Leaving Elizabeth would have been biting the hand that fed him. Things had become so entrenched that he couldn't bear to admit defeat and go back to his old way of life. But a few weeks ago, he had found a way out. He had been able to walk away, literally, and still keep his self-respect. In fact, by being buried in a church, as his wife would doubt-less have insisted, he had gained a lot of previously unobtainable dignity. A vicar whom Norbert had never met would have talked at length of his many qualities and virtues. Death had bestowed an enormous benefit of the doubt on him which hadn't existed before.

These were the advantages. Virtually everything else fell into the other category, a huge, gaping cavity of regret and conscience. At first, Norbert had considered going abroad, reasoning that the more distance he put between himself and those he had left behind the less pain he would feel. But he didn't have a passport, and getting one would be tricky. So the exotic territory of London, by far the most foreign place in England, would have to suffice until he came up with a better plan. As he thought about it, staring miserably at the dripping sink, he realized that all forms of identifi-cation were going to be painful. Effectively, Norbert Flint no longer existed, which was testimony to the cleverness of his trick. To test this, he had ventured into Bridgeton train station the day after his death, heavily disguised in a woolly hat and sunglasses, and bought a paper. It was there, a single-column story: 'Local Man Dies in Horrific Crash, Funeral Wednesday'. For a second he had considered the Tom Sawyer fantasy of attending his own funeral, but had quickly seen sense. The best thing was to get thoroughly lost for a while.

Added to the very real sense of having to start again was the fact that Norbert had been unable to take his one prized possession with him. The distillation of a lifetime's experience in the field of not spending was now irretrievable, and this saddened him greatly. He could still be writing it, refining it each evening instead of sitting around and weighing up his lot. This was his *Das Kapital*, his *War and Peace*, his *Grapes of Wrath*. It was a call to arms which now would be heeded by no one. The manuscript would lie unread and undiscovered. His revolution had died before it was born and a whole generation of people would spend more money than they needed to. Norbert had wondered fleetingly whether he should write another one, but decided against it. He would either require a typist, who, at London prices, would bankrupt him, or a computer, which at any price made him feel queasy.

Norbert stood up and unfolded the sofa into its bed alter ego. Lying down with the duvet wrapped around him, he tried to make patterns in the checked wallpaper. Tomorrow was a busy day. Seven appointments from eight thirty to six. At least now he was working again. This would have to be the one salvation that saw him through, and stopped the almost constant pining he had for his wife.

DangerMoney

What would you do to prove you exist? How would you determine whether you are an actual living being rather than an insipid twenty-first-century lifeform afraid of the dark? What lengths would you go to to test your nerve? Run naked through the town centre? Drive past red lights at high speed? Walk around rough estates in the early hours? Be homeless for a night? Cut yourself with a blade? What?

And what if the following notions had become irrefutable to you? That we are ever more anxious about our own welfare while being numb to the suffering of others. That we have seen too much violence. That we can no longer be natural. That we are *sensitized*.

What if, for example, you had always believed that there was someone watching out for you?

Jake realized that his perception of danger needed challenging. Without living it, how would he know if he could cope should the occasion arrive?

But what to do? Should he confront his innermost fear, or simply face 'danger' in its indefinable and unimaginable form? What was he truly afraid of? There were the usual candidates. Drowning. Car crashes. Heights. Disease. Stabbing. Mugging. Burning. Hanging . . . they were too numerous to mention.

Eventually, in Leeds in 1992, he found what he had been looking for all his life.

Jake had bravely fought the efforts of Leeds University to educate the fun out of him, and had won. With a third in political history, he left college and began to search for jobs. While course-mates moved on, he stayed in his shared low-rent house and claimed benefit. Over the next year, he came to understand that a drinker's degree in history was not career gold dust. His parents begged him to come home but he remained in the city. There was enough defeat attached to his BA without moving back to Bridgeton. A new influx of people invaded the house the following October. Three were students, and one was an unemployed man. Kris was a cousin of the landlord, Ronnie, and worked part-time for him in return for free rent and a little cash. Ronnie owned about twenty properties in Leeds Studentville and Bradford Bedsitland, and while he was visiting Kris, asked Jake one day whether he fancied a job. He offered to cover his rent and give him a hundred quid a week, cash in hand. With little else available, and housing-benefit cheques still rolling in, Jake agreed.

Ronnie was only five foot five, but the general opinion was that you wouldn't fuck with him. Years of lugging fridges and washing machines into low-grade accommodation had made him almost as wide as he was high. Business was brisk, and he was having difficulty managing his many properties. He had one full-time painter and decorator – a scary bloke called Clem – and a brickie by the name of Dick. Both lived in Ronnie properties. But with Kris and Jake, he could cover some of the gaps. At the start, Jake spent most of his time collecting rent, dealing with minor problems, showing potential tenants around, fetching, carrying and helping lift heavy items of furniture. Increasingly, as he learnt the nature of Ronnie's business, he came to see the sheer recklessness of his endeavour. The thing was a mess, and Jake began to take more of a part in balancing the books.

The problem was the weird attitude all of Ronnie's cronies had to money. They did crazy things like double or quits on their day's wages. Ronnie would toss a coin, and Dick, Clem and Kris would go home with nothing, or twice what they had earned. He ran his empire in this way. Owning twenty or so houses, each with up to seven occupants, provided a healthy weekly income, even after expenses. But Ronnie wasn't thriving. He had a weakness. His dealing with his workers was just scratching the surface. The more Jake saw, the more he realized that Ronnie gambled at almost every level he possibly could, with suppliers, tenants, bookies, employees, dodgy blokes in pubs, anyone. He carried enormous sums of cash around in his pocket, but no one ever tried to turn him over. You didn't fuck with Ronnie.

Around six months in, Jake started fucking with Ronnie. It was almost impossible not to. The man had so little idea of his incomings and outgoings that a well-behaved saint would have been sorely tempted. More than the money, it was a touch of risk in Jake's otherwise safe existence. The job was far from interesting. Thievery raised the stakes. He came to thrive on it, and the more cash he stole, the more alive he felt. To expose yourself to a danger that was with you when you worked, slept, was in the very house where you dwelt – this was to experience a constant peril. Ronnie could virtually snap him in half if he so chose. Stealing from a man whom most people feared would therefore be a good test of his mettle.

But it was more than just an assessment of nerve.

Jake quickly came to see that he had finally found his challenge. It was an experiment, the definitive experiment. The first phase during childhood had gone as planned, but was now starting to raise issues. Had it purely been a piece of childish good luck? Had he been too young to conduct a worthwhile appraisal? Had he simply imagined the outcome? Twelve years of lacklustre subsistence had erased many of the key details. What was required therefore was the adult version of his childhood mission. And suddenly, the opportunity was within his grasp.

Over several months, Jake paid his student debts off, which accounted for around six thousand pounds, and stashed the rest in a bank account. It became his daily gamble. While Ronnie lost money hand over fist in haphazard and poorly judged betting, Jake took increasingly big chances. Of course he appreciated that if Ronnie found out there would be serious repercussions, but that only spurred him on. For the second time in his life he had encountered pure danger, and he liked what he found.

There had been one or two close scrapes, but Jake was digging himself in deeper every day. Sometimes he dreamed of being discovered, and it thrilled him to think of Ronnie's face, and what he would say, and how Jake would outwit him. Months passed, and the stakes became higher. It was like one long drawn-out game of poker, Jake bluffing his way through hand after hand, and Ronnie losing money in a slow inevitable tide. As with all gambles, there was a point at which to bail out, but it hadn't arrived yet. He was on a streak. The thing to do, Jake decided, was to wait until the first hint of suspicion, and then quit while he was ahead. After a particularly good afternoon, Jake returned to the house. Kris was waiting for him, and appeared serious. 'Ronnie's after you,' he said. 'Wants you urgently. Better ring him.'

He's on to me. He's fucking on to me. He's looked at

the books and he's on to me, were Jake's only thoughts. Suddenly he didn't feel so brave. It was September, and almost a year had passed since he began to challenge his perception of danger by stealing from his boss. He rang him, praying he was wrong.

He was. 'Jake, we've got a heavy lifting job that's going to need all of us,' Ronnie told him. Jake relaxed. 'Just bought a new place on Junction Road. Number fifty-two. Gotta lift some floorboards in and chop them. Go and hire some tools with Kris and meet us there.'

In the van on the way there, Jake took a serious decision. He would pursue his scheme for another month, just until he reached the fifteen-thousand mark in savings, and then he would scale it down. He had proved a point. You can put your well-being on the line day after day, but eventually your nerve goes or your luck runs out. Still, it had been fun substantiating the notion. He had bled a local hard man dry and lived to tell the tale.

Inside the new house, Clem and Dick were heaving thick floorboards up the stairs.

'At last, somebody to give us a fucking hand,' Clem called up to him as he passed them with the saw.

'You can fucking say that again,' Dick added.

Jake joined his boss in the main bedroom. Ronnie was pleased to see him. 'Right,' he began. 'We can get the job sorted. Give those two useless idiots a shout.'

When Clem, Dick and Kris were all assembled, Ronnie walked over towards the door. He was silent for a few moments, breathing deeply. His chest seemed to expand even wider, and he filled most of the door frame. Ronnie addressed them, his tone different. 'It appears one of you has been taking the piss,' he said. 'One of you owes me a large sum of money.' He turned and grinned at Jake. 'And we have a system for people who can't pay their debts.'

Jake glanced around. The others were monitoring his body language. He remained silent.

'Jake?' Ronnie prompted.

'What?'

'Don't fuck me about. I know it, you know it, in fact, we all do. About eighteen grand by Kris's reckoning. So where's my readies?'

Kris had been watching him. The bastard. Jake tried to put up a fight. 'I honestly don't know what you're talking about.'

Ronnie's face reddened. 'I think you bloody do. Now stop pissing me about. Where is it?'

Kris had been wrong about the sum. Including his debts, it was well over twenty grand. Jake made an instant policy decision to challenge his nerve even further. He had come this far. He would risk a sound beating for the chance of keeping hold of the money. 'As I told you, I haven't been pissing you about, Ronnie.'

'One more time, Jake, and that's it. I'm not a patient man, and I don't like liars.' He stepped forwards. 'Where's my fucking cash, you student wanker?'

So come on, Jake said to himself. Let's have some real pain. The stuff you see in films. Let me know how it feels. He remained silent, staring at his boss.

Ronnie turned to his second-in-command. 'What d'you think, Clem?'

'Fuck him.'

'Dick?'

Dick walked behind Jake and bent his right arm back towards his shoulder in a painful lock. 'Yeah,' he replied.

'Kris?'

'An eye for an eye.'

'That's right,' Ronnie said. 'You've taken something from me. I'm gonna take something from you. Clem . . .'

Clem picked up a hammer and a large U-shaped pin.

Ronnie dragged Jake's left arm away from his side. Jake felt the implacable strength that comes with twenty years of hard manual labour. A Black and Decker Work Mate stood in front of him. On top was a floorboard. Ronnie snapped Jake's ring finger out of its fist, and pushed it flat onto the piece of wood. Clem removed the heavy duty gloves which he wore constantly, and grinned at Jake. His left index finger was mostly missing. Out of the corner of his eye, Jake watched Dick rub the deep scar on his forearm and smile as well. Then Clem placed the U-pin around the finger, below the knuckle, and hammered it tight. Jake screamed as the blows came down, but Clem didn't hurt him. He tried vainly to snatch his arm away, but the hook held firm. He was securely pinned. His nerve suddenly deserted him. This was too real. It was actually going to happen. This was no longer a game. He begged. Ronnie was having none of it.

'You see, Jake, you fuck with me, I fuck with you. That's the way life is. You've got to pay for what you take. And then when you know the rules you can begin to give it me back.'

'Look, I can see the rules. Please. Ronnie, please. I'll get you the money.'

'Oh, I know you'll get me the money. But it's not just the cash you stole. That isn't what's important here. It's playing fair. You ask Dick and Clem.' He nodded to Clem who walked over and picked up the circular saw. He turned it on and revved it for effect. He brought it slowly over to the bench and held it over Jake's hand. Clem revved it up again, drowning his screams. It was an inch away. Jake pissed himself and yelled for help. Ronnie stepped forwards and took the power tool from Clem. Jake tugged at his finger. All his weight pulled away from the digit. The knuckle clicked. He was in danger of dislocating it. The Work Mate didn't move. It had been nailed to the floor. The warm fluid in Jake's trousers began to turn cold. He shivered. Still he fought. Bones and tendons were ripping away from each other. Ronnie dropped the saw another half inch. He felt the air from the blade on his finger. Standing behind him, Dick bent his right arm further up towards his shoulder blade, and Jake was paralysed with pain. Ronnie lowered the saw still further. The hairs of Jake's finger were sliced away. He looked at Ronnie. His face was alive. He met Jake's eyes and flashed him a grin through his shark teeth. And then he forced the saw into Jake's finger. The bone vibrated furiously and the blade slowed as it fought its way in, bouncing along it, shredding skin. Jake screamed. Ronnie pushed down to make a deeper cut. He was in no great hurry. Jake continued to scream. More skin was chewed away from the bone. His legs shook. He stared down. The blade was red. Ronnie pushed harder. Skin, bone, flesh, tendons and veins were all being severed by the jagged metal teeth. Clem, Kris and Ronnie were entirely focused on the bench. Jake forced the fingernails of his right hand into his palm. His shouts grew louder as the thick cutting edge ground towards the workbench. Second after second passed, the saw whining in unison. There was burning in the finger, like he was holding it in a lighter flame. Still the saw ate through the bone. And then came a violent and cold spark of pain. He pulled back, and felt himself slipping, falling away. His legs collapsed but he didn't hit the ground. Dick caught him, and lowered him to the dusty floor. He sat on his knees. His left hand was free. He held it up in front of his face. Blood was pulsing out of the stump. A hand-kerchief appeared. He glanced up. Kris dropped it in his lap. Ronnie stood over him. In his palm lay Jake's missing digit. Jake wrapped the hanky around his wrist and pulled it tight to lessen the bleeding.

'Right, say goodbye.' Ronnie showed him the amputated finger and Jake felt an ache in his left hand. Then he tossed the bloody finger to Clem, who walked into the adjoining toilet and pulled the lever.

Dick helped Jake to his feet. An unpleasant deadened ache began to give way to the white light of unadulterated pain. Sharp stabs of paralysis coursed through his hand. He was shaking and sweating and smelt of piss. He had one thought. Kill the pain. He would have to get to Casualty and fast.

'Come on, let's get you into the van,' Dick said.

Ronnie handed the keys over. 'Go in with him, Dick,' he instructed. 'Then bring the fucker straight back to me.'

They hobbled down the stairs and out into the street. Jake climbed into the van and slumped forwards. An indeterminate amount of time later, they neared Accident and Emergency, and Dick reached across and opened the door. 'Get yourself sorted,' he said. 'I'll be waiting out here. Can't fucking stand hospitals. And Jake, don't piss Ronnie about any more. It won't be your finger next time.'

Jake didn't go to Casualty. He walked through the hospital site, found a taxi-phone and dialled a cab for the train station. The bleeding slowed and the pain surged in nauseating waves. At the train station, Jake bought a packet of paracetamol and swallowed eight tablets. He used some of Ronnie's money to buy a ticket to Sheffield. Forty-five minutes later, he took another taxi to the Northern General. After an excruciating wait during which time alternately dragged and raced, he was given priority treatment. A cold anaesthetic dulled the agony. Two hours of minor surgery tidied the jagged wound. He was discharged overnight and told to come back in the morning. Instead, he caught another train, this time to Manchester, where he stayed with a friend. Dosed up on heavy-duty painkillers, his lesion began to heal and scar. A month later, and a delicate pink layer of skin had formed. Jake removed the bandages, and started looking for work.

With his finger, another part of Jake had gone missing. That secret bit of him that had always believed he should fear nothing. In the hours he had screamed in pain, a whisper of fear and caution had slunk into his body through the open wound. It had travelled through his veins and entered his system, where it refused to be dismissed. His eyes were coated with the dust of the amputation room, and saw things differently. Every opportunity had a hangover of potential disaster. No one was looking out for him. He wasn't numb to the suffering of others any more. Jake was no longer *sensitized*. He had confronted fear in its purest form, and had become an insipid twenty-first-century lifeform afraid of the dark.

Time Isn't Money

Norbert's one-man enterprise continued to thrive, and he came to the conclusion that more dead people should take up business. When you had ceased to be, you had no need for conscience, morals, laws or regulations. You could become a *proper* businessman, in the very purest sense. During the day, he manipulated the affairs of tax-paying customers, while administering free advice along the way.

Mr Davison, his seventh client of a fully booked Tuesday, was treated to just such an outpouring of common sense while they fiddled his expenses in a small rented room. Glancing at his watch and noticing the session was almost halfway through, he made what he later came to appreciate was a gross error of judgement, saying almost casually, 'Well, Norbert, time is money, I guess.'

Norbert put his pen down and glared at Mr Davison. 'OK. Let's dispel one myth for a start,' he replied tersely. 'Time definitely isn't money. If it was, the unemployed would be rolling in it. Prisoners would leave jail as millionaires. Queuing would make you

297

rich. Hanging about for hours doing nothing would swell your bank account. So time doesn't create money. It also doesn't equal money.'

'Right,' Mr Davison replied, shifting in his seat, wishing he'd kept his mouth shut.

'Look, waiters won't thank you for spending ten per cent extra minutes in their restaurant. Car dealerships don't accept hours as payment. Trying to open an account with Barclays by offering to donate some free time to them is unlikely to prove rewarding. So time is one thing, and money is quite another.'

'I just meant—'

Norbert continued regardless, not to be distracted from one of his favourite lectures. 'Besides, if time is money, and the love of money is the root of all evil, the love of time must also be the root of all evil.' He adjusted his tie and frowned. 'But you try telling that to horologists.'

Mr Davison fiddled with a piece of paper, feeling as if he was being told off for a reason he didn't quite understand.

'So the next occasion someone tells you time is money, tell them they can gladly have some of your wasted hours in exchange for a hefty chunk of their cash.' Norbert picked his pen up again, and continued where he had left off.

Mr Davison attempted to lighten the atmosphere in the tiny room. 'Still, with all this cash you're making me, think I'll go and have a nose around the sales. Feel like blowing some—'

Norbert frowned at him again. 'Sales? I have a problem with sales, Mr Davison, and so should you if you're going to manage your finances effectively. First, there are sales, and then there are sales. Most are just a sham. Some companies have permanent sales. A permanent sale is not a sale, by definition. Also, certain multinationals own several chains of competing shops. A sale in one of their chains might only bring prices down to the normal level of one of their other chains. You have to be careful.'

'Oh I will. Very careful. I'm only going to buy a few things to wear. They've got some cheap designer brands . . .'

Once again, Norbert ceased his auditing, and drew breath. Mr Davison decided not to offer any further opinions. 'Designer clothes I also have a real problem with, not least because the term suggests that normal clothes aren't so much designed as just thrown together randomly,' Norbert began. 'It's like saying that only posh, overpriced garments are lucky enough to benefit from someone sitting down and attempting to sketch them out beforehand. Which is the supreme irony because half of designer clothes look like they've been formed from a collision between the contents of two particularly knackered laundry baskets.'

'Right,' Mr Davison replied, vainly hoping that Norbert would stop lecturing him and actually get on with finishing his expenses form.

'Where I find designer outfits really dangerous, though, is in the very scary territory of children's clothes. Do you have any children, Mr Davison?'

'No.'

'Good. Now, one prominent company – surely owned by Satan – called Baby Pap or something similar, has combined two of the world's costliest pastimes – clothes and children. I mean, are people really that stupid?'

Mr Davison merely shrugged, remaining steadfastly silent.

Instead of returning his attention to the series of forms in front of him, Norbert's attention wandered elsewhere. Children. How good it would have been to have a child with Elizabeth. Elizabeth. Her name tortured him at night. He usually managed to forget her during the day, but this was now becoming difficult. It was four thirty, and an empty evening of bedsitdom was rapidly stretching out ahead of him. He craved his wife. What was she doing? What was she thinking?

Double Bagging

Elizabeth sat with her hands in her lap and sighed, staring at the cup in front of her. It was a strong, thirst-quenching brew, nothing like the tea travesties Norbert used to palm off on her. She glanced at the clock. Half past four. Another day of teaching distracted adolescents had ebbed away. Where the fuck was her husband? Perhaps he was sitting somewhere wondering what the hell he had done. Aside from wanting to castrate him, she hoped he was OK.

   Elizabeth's thought bubbles were shattered by several loud knocks at the door. She was instantly on edge. Although her house was now more secure, with deadbolts on the doors and locks on the windows, she was still painfully aware of her vulnerability. She crept to the window and peered through a gap in the curtains. It was Jake and she relaxed. Invaders rarely announced their visits by knocking she told herself, opening the door and inviting him in. She offered him a cup of tea which he declined. 'So what can I do for you?' she asked.

   'You know what? I went to see Mary the bad typist,'

Jake said, reclining on the sofa and fanning himself in the face of another heat onslaught, 'and she told me that Norbert had shares.'

'In what?'

'In an economy shop chain.'

'Which one?'

'Cheapstuff.'

Elizabeth took a seat next to Jake on the threadbare furniture. 'So if he's not dead, he could be cashing them in.'

'Exactly. His manuscript has a long scribbled section on retail companies and who owns who. It's massively detailed and very dull, but it bangs on and on about so and so buying out Omco, who then owned Safebury's, who went bust and changed their name to some other company. If he had shares in those companies it would make a lot more sense now.'

'And another thing. I've been thinking over the last couple of days. Wherever he's gone, and assuming he's alive, he'll need money. Now it's quite possible he had a bank account I didn't know about. I mean, he was secretive about our finances all the time. Except, of course, when he suspected I'd spent some money.'

'I guess I'd better ring Phil as well, see what they've discovered.'

'Bugger all, at a guess.'

'I don't know. They've issued posters for a missing person and stepped things up a notch.'

'Hundreds of people go missing every year. I can't see them doing anything special just because you happen to be friendly with a local copper.'

'But very few disappear leaving a dead person behind them. This isn't merely a vanishing act – this could have much wider implications.' Jake couldn't bear being slowly cooked by the large front-room radiator any longer. He cleared his throat and wiped his face. 'The draught excluders, the clingfilm, the central heating . . . don't you feel you might be . . .'

'What?'

'Well, *over*compensating.'

Elizabeth sipped her drink and revelled in the flavour that two tea bags per cup could bring. Again, by double bagging, she felt she was readjusting the balance of her life. 'Nonsense,' she replied. 'Anyway, Norbert might have had his faults, but he wasn't capable of physically hurting anybody.'

'I'm not saying he was. Something fishy has happened though. And the police are finally doing something about it.'

'Well, let me know.'

'I think I might go to the local Cheapstuff as well,' Jake added, chewing a fingernail.

'Why?'

'Norbert obviously spent a lot of time there. Maybe someone will know something.'

'Bit of a long shot.'

'It's crazy enough that it might just work.' He removed the sliver of nail from his mouth and flicked it surreptitiously at the carpet. 'As they say in films. Anyway, how are you bearing up?'

'Fine,' Elizabeth lied. 'The tablets are helping.'

'You know you can come and stay with us . . . with me, any time you want.'

'No, thanks, Jake. This is my home. The police have given me a panic button should the person break in again. And the place is still under surveillance.'

'So I noticed.'

'Is it that obvious?'

'Only to those with eyes.' Jake stood up. 'Anyway, gotta go. Cheapstuff close at five. Besides, I need some supplies.'

'I was sorry to hear about Kate.'

'One of those things. At least now I'm getting a square meal occasionally.'

'All the same.'

'I'll be in touch . . .'

Daylight Robbery

The following morning, Elizabeth stood in the kitchen buttering some bread. This had become a recent habit, a way of reminding herself of her husband. Although she still managed a glass of champagne at lunch, she also made time for a reflective chomp on her sandwiches. She had even bought some fish paste a few days previously. And, despite the terrible taste, she had felt some degree of closure when she ate it.

Today, smoked salmon was on the menu. Glancing at the clock, Elizabeth swore. It was time to inflict herself upon the youth of Bridgeton once again. She tidied up, had a quick look in the mirror, sighed and left the house. Twenty yards up the road was a parked car. Elizabeth thought she recognized its occupants, and waved at them. They ignored her. Several minutes later, her bus arrived and another day lurched into life.

Inside the car, a female police officer turned to her colleague and said, 'I wish she wouldn't do that.'

'It's a bugger trying not to wave back,' he replied. 'Instinct, isn't it?'

'I mean, it's hardly a covert surveillance operation if

the very person you're looking after points you out for all to see.'

'That's the prob—'

'Blue car,' the WPC said excitedly.

Her partner strained his eyes. 'K, was it?' he asked.

'Yep. There's two. Fourth letter first word, fifth letter second word.'

He wrote the letter twice on his pad. 'So it's C, something, something, K, something, D. And then B, R, something, something, K, F, something, S, something.'

'Any ideas?'

He examined the list of letters. 'Going to need another clue.'

'Fine.' The WPC drew an additional line on the hangman scaffold. 'There,' she exclaimed, 'green Mondeo.'

The officer followed her pointed finger. 'T.' He wrote it down and mouthed the letters slowly. After a couple of minutes, it clicked. 'Gotcha! Cooked Breakfast!'

'Arse. Never thought you'd get that one.'

'Too close to my heart. Talking of which, do you fancy—?'

'Hang on, I think we've got some action.'

The PC looked up from his pad. A shabby man in an overcoat and baseball cap was walking into the drive of Elizabeth Flint's house. Both police officers opened their doors and left the car, walking close to the hedge. When they arrived, the man was nowhere to be seen. 'Around the back,' the WPC whispered.

'You stay here, give me a shout,' the PC replied, creeping down the side alley of the semi.

At the back, there was no sign of the intruder. The garden was empty and the door was closed. The copper peered in through the patio doors. Nothing. He ran his eyes around the garden. The shed door was open, and he set off towards it. There was a noise and some movement. A figure darted out of the outhouse and sprinted towards him. He stopped, opening his arms, ready to rugby-tackle the man. The trespasser changed direction, and vaulted over the fence and dashed across a garden. The PC charged after him, and cleared the fence at the second attempt. By this time, the man was over the next and heading back towards the road. The officer began to slow. He had eaten too much fried food to get involved in athletic events. And he hadn't joined the force to hurdle garden fences. He changed direction and shouted to his colleague. 'He's making for the road.' The intruder negotiated another barrier and disappeared. At the front of the house, the PC caught up with his partner. 'You see him?' he asked.

'Hasn't been out this way.'

'I'll get the car. Radio for help. I think he's aiming for the park.'

A couple of hundred yards past the end of the road was a large wooded area of parkland. The WPC ran towards it, while the PC reached the car and asked for assistance. Then he started the engine and squealed the tyres down the road until he reached his associate. The WPC jumped in, and flicked the siren on.

'See him?'

'Nothing.'

'Fuck. Come on, where are you, you bastard?'

They turned left at the end and motored towards the recreation area. 'We've missed him.'

'Not necessarily. There's a path behind those houses, leads right into the woods.'

Jumping out of the car, both police officers jogged through the park gates, wildly scanning for signs of action. Three hundred yards behind them, the man they were chasing emerged from his hiding place at the side of a house, and walked in the opposite direction. He removed his hat and threw it over a hedge. Then he took his overcoat off and stuffed it in a dustbin. Another police car screamed past, and he smiled. He crossed the road and made his way towards the centre of town.

Country of the Damned

In his one-room studio, which, it now appeared, wasn't in Fulham at all, Norbert heated a half-tin of Kwiksave Economy Own Brand Beans, and toasted two slices of Kwiksave Economy Own Brand White Bread under the grill. Business was good. He was thriving, and wondered why he had never thought about working in London before. Apart from the noise, the overcrowding, the perma-roadrage, the prices and the inhabitants, it was great. The kettle half-boiled and he revived one of yesterday's lifeless tea bags in the tepid water. And the real pisser was that under different circumstances he could have employed one of his favourite money-saving schemes to relocate here. He remembered a paragraph he had written devoted to just such a situation.

Moving House for Free
There are two Golden Rules here. First, if it isn't nailed down, take it with you. Second, if it is nailed down, rip it up and take it anyway. Remember especially to remove the light bulbs. If necessary (i.e. the wife's common decency

prevails) insert old bulbs which no longer work in their place.

If moving a long distance, and you don't want to go to the exorbitant expense of hiring a van, try my free-delivery scam. Box your possessions up in suitcases. Go to your local rail station, and clamber on the relevant train with three or four cases. (In a worst-case scenario, it may be necessary to buy a platform ticket.) Leave via a different carriage door than the one you entered. Pre-arrange with your partner to meet the train at the other end, giving instructions as to the carriage number and location of said items. They can then step onto the train, and smartly off it, looking like a passenger, and request help with the heavy baggage. A porter will hopefully help them load the suitcases into their car. NB: ensure they don't tip the porter – this will defeat the object of the exercise. Repeat as many times as necessary, with empty suitcases returning in the opposite direction. Simple. I once moved almost the entire contents of my attic this way, and all for the cost of a platform ticket or two, without even raising an eyebrow of suspicion. After all, the chances of detection by railway staff are minimal, given that they are indifferent to their passengers to the point of actively hiding from them most of the time.

This was just one of several sections of the manuscript which Norbert could remember almost verbatim. He had spent so many years pouring his wisdom into it that its contents were scratched into his memory. And some of them were so filled with beauty and poetry that he wept a little as he recited them. The toast began to burn and Norbert pulled it out, cursing the excess gas he had used in the process. And then he had an idea. Maybe the manuscript wasn't beyond his means after all.

Over the next few minutes, the notion refused to retreat. After all, he knew exactly where it was. Other advantages presented themselves as his beans went cold. Documentation was the only other thing holding him back, and when he had that in his possession, he would be alive again! He could move abroad. And not just abroad. He could fulfil his lifetime's ambition. There was one region of the planet that Norbert had always ached for. It was there in any atlas, and he had stared lovingly at it, weighing up the boundless possibilities. Sometimes, he had run his fingers over the varied topography, the coolness of the page strangely at odds with the prevailing climate. He could see nothing except good times. His dreams would come true. He would be hot, wealthy and respected in the area of the globe he most admired. Yes, it was the Third World for Norbert.

If it cost ten pounds a month to feed a child, he reasoned, imagine how he could live if he cashed his savings and shares in! Surely he could afford a small African country for that sort of money. Five pounds a week would apparently provide a teacher for a village. He would buy a couple and have them spread his word. Twenty quid would get you a well. He would have a hundred, and would sell the water at a profit. And the exchange rates would be fantastic. The Third World was crying out for dollars, pounds and Deutschmarks. Before, the evils of foreign currency had overridden this logic – the ease of spending unfamiliar notes, being caught unawares because of tricky calculations, commission, haggling in an alien language. It was a minefield. But if you were a wealthy foreigner in a poor country, you were laughing. It was all relative, and he would be relatively rich. As the idea continued to grow, he could see that he had been wasting his time in London. Indeed, by moving somewhere terrible earlier in his life, he would have been affluent virtually from the outset.

Scraping his tea into the carrier bag which served as

a bin, Norbert began to plan. He left the flat. Tonight he was going to celebrate his ingenuity. Fuck beans on toast, it was time to push the boat out.

In the takeaway queue, he had his final brainwave. This was the salt on his fish, the ketchup on his chips. It was time for Eric to come out of hiding.

Company Policy

Jake locked his bike up outside Cheapstuff in Bridgeton's high street, which was ideally located between Poundstretcher and BulkBargains. There was a 'For Sale' sign above the shop window, and the owner was standing miserably at the till reading a newspaper. Jake introduced himself.

'Hello,' he said. 'I wonder if you can help me.'

The shopkeeper looked up. He was as scruffy as his store, severely beergutted and had stubble which aspired towards beardness. 'What with?' he asked unenthusiastically.

'My uncle used to come here all the time. A tramp-like bloke called Norbert.'

The shopkeeper scratched himself in two places at once. 'Oh yes. Norbert. Right ray of sunshine. What about him? Haven't seen him for a while.'

'He's de— he's sort of disappeared.'

'Disappeared?'

'Yes. And we've no idea where.'

He returned his attention to the newspaper. 'Maybe a detective would be more use to you than a shopkeeper.'

'The thing is, did he ever talk about going anywhere?'

'Netto. Aldis. Those sort of places.'

'I know it's a long shot. Was there anything else you used to discuss that might provide some sort of clue where he's gone?'

'Can't really say there is,' the shopkeeper replied, glancing up at a CCTV monitor which was showing nothing but empty aisles. 'Only thing we used to chat about was the prices of things. That and Cheapstuff.'

'Business not going well then?' Jake asked, nodding in the direction of the sign.

'Nope. I'm getting out. Anyone with any sense is. And losing customers like your uncle hasn't helped.'

'But at least you've still got your shop.'

The shopkeeper sighed. 'I don't own it.'

'No?'

'It's a franchise.'

'So who owns the franchise?'

'Omco.'

'Omco? Aren't they part of the Safebury's group now?'

'Not exactly. Safebury's and Landis merged, changed their name from Landis-Safebury's to Chatterbox, and bought Omco.'

'So your shop is owned by the Chatterbox group?'

'Nope. Hasbro bought them out.'

Jake rewound through the intriguingly tedious notes in his uncle's manuscript devoted to commercial tenure. 'But didn't I read somewhere that Hasbro was owned by Ardale?'

'Yeah. Which is part of Transcorp.'

'Transcorp which merged with UCS?'

'The very same. Which was bought by Nakasami.'

'Nakasami who went bust and resurfaced as Elite Holdings?'

'Yep. Who launched a hostile takeover of Spacec, and changed their name to Spacec Holdings.'

'So Spacec Holdings own the shop?'

'Up until last month, when StreetSmart bought Spacec Holdings.'

'StreetSmart who own all the other high street franchises?'

'Yes, all of my competitors.'

'How do you compete against the opposition if they're on your side?'

'I don't. It's against company policy.'

'So StreetSmart have got you by the short and curlies?'

'Actually, its shareholders have. StreetSmart is a cooperative, owned by punters like you and me, except with more cash, who sit around asking people to invest their money in shop franchises to make them more money. And I'll tell you who one of them was.'

'Who?'

'Your uncle.'

'I'd begun to suspect as much,' Jake answered, glancing around the poorly stocked shelves of the store.

'I'll tell you something funny as well, my friend.'

'What?'

'That old bastard owned more of my shop than I ever will. He told me one day – he had a wedge of shares.'

'No offence, but I always wondered why Norbert spent so much time in here.'

'It's obvious. Every pound he spent here was a pound which helped StreetSmart increase their share dividend.'

'But surely you've got shares in StreetSmart yourself?'

'Now there's the rub,' the shopkeeper said, scratching his arm. 'It's against company policy.'

A silence descended on Cheapstuff. Several miles away on the periphery of Bridgeton, shoppers were queuing to park their cars outside megastores and hypermarkets. Small shops like this one were going bust on an almost hourly basis. Jake thanked the shop-keeper and walked outside to reconstruct his bike. So his uncle had owned a large number of shares, and apparently wasn't dead. Surely there were ways of tracing share dealing. It was time to visit Phil Ryder again.

Reunion

At home the next day, Jake munched his mini-Shredded Wheats, scanning the box for something to read. The cereal was, apparently, good for his heart. This was welcome news, because it had been beating fast recently. He exhausted the ingredients list and nutritional info and flicked through a newspaper instead. Even the papers were full of it. Statistics, lifestyle trends, health data. '2.2% of us won't make 35,' an article proclaimed. Jake was thirty-three next year. He wondered whether he would ever see his mid-thirties. 'At the turn of the 20th century,' the piece continued, 'the figure was closer to 40%.' He glanced at another headline. 'We Are Getting Older,' it declared. 'Now, 68% of us will reach 65 years, and more will be women than men.' He turned the page. 'New data shows the UK infant mortality rate is unacceptably high compared with the rest of Europe. 6 babies per 1000 will succumb to accident or disease in their first year.' Virtually every story directly or indirectly concerned our own mortality. Towards the middle of the paper, an editorial told of the progress being made in slowing the ageing process. 'Not wanting to die is one thing, but wanting to live for ever is quite another,' it said. 'And it isn't death that worries people in general, just dying prematurely and painfully.' In the light of recent events, Jake was forced to agree. He looked up from his paper as the doorbell rang. Edging along the hallway, he peered through the spyhole. A uniformed man was on the doorstep. He pulled the door open. There were Fed Ex patches on his brown shirt.

'Package for Mr Cooper,' he said. The man handed over a small box and asked Jake to sign a form on his clipboard.

Jake took the item inside and carried it into the kitchen. It was reasonably compact and heavy, like a miniature bag of sugar. He grabbed a knife and slit the sellotape that was holding it together. He pulled out several handfuls of popcorn. In the middle was a jar of something. He cleared more of the packaging, and finally got a good grip. As it slid out, Jake read the label: Safebury's Pickled Gherkins. He unscrewed the lid and sniffed. Vinegar. He lifted a gherkin out and examined the green vegetable. He removed another and another and placed them on the counter, lining them up, wondering who the hell would waste their time couriering unpleasant snacks to him.

As he extracted a couple more, a small object at the bottom of the jar caught his eye. He walked over to the sink and tipped the entire contents out. There among the gherkins was a rubbery-looking finger. He picked it up and viewed it more closely. The colour wasn't right – it was pale and the nail was brown. But as he examined it, he realized something disturbing. It wasn't fake. He could make out a fingerprint on the surface. Some of the flesh had withered and deteriorated. And where it had been separated from its owner, the cross-section was rough, tiny pieces of skin flapping, the bone yellow. Jake held the finger in his right hand, close to his nose. It smelt of vinegar, but there was something else in the mix. A preservative, formaldehyde maybe. He pulled it further from his face. Perhaps it was a museum piece. It certainly appeared old enough. And then, as he continued to study it, he glanced at his own left hand, and a bolt of shock cut through him. As if he was about to place a wedding ring on his finger, he slowly moved the object towards his stump. He positioned it a centimetre away and screwed up his eyes. The colour was wrong but the thickness was similar. He slid the finger closer to his stump, careful not to let the two touch. That would have made him sick. He squinted again. The length was right. His stump ached. Jake shook his head. He felt ill. But they had thrown it away. He'd heard Clem flush the toilet.

Jake put his missing finger down and steadied himself against the work surface. It was happening. The other reminders had been gentle nudges. This was the big one, and would be hard to top. Things were about to get serious. He stepped back to the sink. Among the gherkins was a thin length of green plastic pipe, sealed at both ends with what felt like putty. He opened it. Inside was a small piece of paper which read, 'Expect a phone call.'

Jake threw the gherkins in the bin, and put the note into a kitchen drawer. He stared at his long-lost finger and wondered what to do. Should he bury it, pickle it or just chuck the thing? It was, he suspected, slightly too late to have it stitched back on. He decided to place it in the freezer until he could think of the right thing. Opening the door, he spotted the box of fish fingers which had been a recent present. Jake slid the finger inside and closed the freezer. Then he locked the house as securely as he could, and set about trying to think of a plan.

The Barnsley of Africa

The first few visits had not gone well, Norbert could now appreciate, as he sat on the second of three indirect trains that would take him the seventy or so miles back to Bridgeton. Although there was nothing inherently wrong with the plan he had come up with several weeks previously, its execution had left a lot to be desired. He had repeatedly put himself in situations which were, to say the least, unhealthy. This was to be his final visit, and he couldn't afford another fiasco. He had already purchased an economy-class ticket for Malawi. Although he quibbled with the airline's exact definition of 'economy', which, in Norbert's dictionary, would mean lopping a couple of noughts off, and then some, he had nevertheless parted with the cash and was packed and ready to go. He had consulted the statistics. Malawi was one of the world's ten poorest countries. It was the Barnsley of Africa. A pound would go a long way in Malawi. And they spoke English, were friendly and had a reasonable climate. All ideal for his needs.

One thing was lacking, however. He had already

found his passport, but required a visa if he was going to stay any length of time. Low on other forms of ID, his birth certificate would apparently seal the deal. And so, with only days until his departure, Norbert needed to retrieve the document. Luckily, it was easily accessible, in a chest of drawers in the spare room of his old house. Generally, on a Saturday morning Elizabeth was out shopping. Although he would dearly love to see her face one more time, on balance it was probably best that he didn't. She had suffered enough trauma recently. Norbert glanced out at the countryside they were trundling through. His wife. She was rarely out of his thoughts. If only there was a way of taking her with him.

To stop himself thinking like this, Norbert weighed up the cost of the expedition at hand. The wig had cost an extortionate fourteen ninety-nine. Not that as wigs went this was enormously expensive, just that for a single outing, the utilization-to-money ratio wasn't good. The wet shave had been eight fifty, and hadn't even removed all his facial hair. And the barber had held his hand out for a tip. Clothes too had dented his finances. As Norbert fingered the ticket in his hand, he appreciated that the less he thought about the cost of his rail fare the better. For that sort of investment he should surely own part of the franchise.

Norbert had devoted many hours to his appearance. Time was something he had plenty of, and it was vital that the disguise worked in daylight. After an eternity of faffing, he had been happy that he was unidentifiable as Norbert Flint. Long hair tied back in a ponytail, smart clothes, dummy glasses and a goatee beard. He even secreted a chunky mobile phone in his front pocket to complete the effect.

The train limped into Bridgeton station, a miserable two-platform affair that reminded Norbert for some reason of spaghetti westerns. Cutting through the empty ticket office and out into the street, he began to catch sight of his reflection in shop windows. He smiled to himself. It felt good, like crashing a perpetual fancy-dress party. He checked his watch and picked up his pace. The timing of the operation at hand was crucial.

Reconstruction

Close to the spot where it happened, Norbert slowed.
Two things were plaguing him. First, the fact that only
a matter of weeks ago he had been involved in a very
ugly event here, the image of which still refused to
fade. And second, and more worryingly, that there was
a good deal of commotion near his house. As he
approached, he decided to lean against the bus shelter
on the wrong side of the road and monitor proceedings
from a safe distance. Now and then he surveyed his
house as well, and watched vainly for signs of
Elizabeth.

If anything, more people were beginning to congregate close to his home. And then Norbert
recognized one of them. It was Jake. He was pre-
occupied, joking with a short police officer and a tall
black man with an apparent skin problem. Norbert
became absorbed in the surrounding activities. From
what he could determine, several men were having
great difficulty getting a badly dressed shop dummy to
stand up behind a bus. Eventually, the dummy was
tied to a long broom handle, which was used to prop

it up at a bit of an angle, its head slumping dejectedly forwards. There was something unnatural about its chiselled nose and moulded hairline, which stood very much at odds with a layer of stubble which had been roughly drawn on. Added to this, a can of lager was wedged in one of its inflexible hands, and a roll-up in the other. Next to the dummy, a police officer dressed in some of the shabbiest clothes Norbert had ever seen – and Norbert had certainly seen some shabby clothes – struggled to attach a false beard to his face.

Just as the exact implication of what was unfolding began to hit home, things became even more surreal. Part of the road was closed, and a lorry and a car drove slowly in tandem up to the dummy, before reversing carefully a few hundred yards back from the bus. There was much gesticulation and pointing among the healthy crowd of thirty or forty people which had gathered to oversee events.

Finally, when things were about to kick off, he spotted Elizabeth. She didn't look good. She had lost weight and her face had a heavy aspect to it which seemed to pull her features downwards. Immediately, Norbert wanted to rush over and throw his bony arms around her.

The demeanour of the bus-stop participants changed and Norbert decided instead to keep his distance. People retreated from the scene, some of them now just yards away from him. At a signal, the car and the lorry pulled forwards and built up speed. As they reached the bus, the tramp-like police officer pretended to grapple with the dummy for a couple of seconds, before nudging it into the road with the broom handle. The car knocked the dummy into the air, and the pole detached and shattered the window of a nearby parked car. The lorry, meanwhile, failed to hit anything at all and eased to a benign halt. The crowd, pleased with the show, edged forwards to inspect the damage and Norbert joined them.

'We'll have to do it again,' a senior officer instructed the assembled personnel. A small cheer went up, and a couple of spectators rushed off to move their cars from the general area.

Norbert heard Jake tell the officer, 'That pole's got to go.'

'So how are we going to stand him up?'

'No idea, but one fatality here is quite enough,' he replied. 'I mean, reconstructing an accident to jog people's memories is one thing. Skewering them with a fucking broom handle is quite another.'

'Yeah, and imagine where that would lead,' the short policeman next to him said. 'We'd have to reconstruct the reconstruction. Before we knew it, we'd have corpses piling up like nobody's business.'

'How about if Jimmy holds the dummy up as he wrestles with it, before sort of pushing it into the road?' the tall black man with the polka-dot skin suggested. A general nod of agreement went around the organizers.

'But that's not how it happened at all,' Norbert said to himself, shaking his head.

Norbert continued to move through the onlookers who were watching two uniformed men attempting to extract the pole from the interior of a car. By carefully edging along, he was soon standing just inches from his wife. He leant forwards and sucked her perfume into his eager lungs. It was all he could do not to squeeze her hand. Although the marriage had fallen badly out of kilter, there was always something about the smell of Elizabeth which felt right. It had been a secret language their bodies had shared while their minds refused to communicate. They had had a smell affair. He brushed against her, and felt the warmth of her hand against his. She half-turned, but among the crowd he was anonymous. He touched the material of her coat. It was coarse, and made her flesh seem even more fragile and vulnerable. Norbert continued to surreptitiously stroke her clothing. Then they were all asked to retreat twenty paces. A general murmur of good-natured disapproval seeped through the group, who retired the required distance. Norbert stayed close to his wife, edging back step for step with her. Over her shoulder, with her hair occasionally washing across his face, he once again watched the proceedings with enthusiasm.

This time, the car sped towards the bus, and the dishevelled copper feigned a fight with the dummy before tossing it in the general direction of the road, missing the vehicle by a considerable margin. The truck made a valiant effort to run the hapless mannequin over, and just managed to catch one of its arms, which came off and shattered into hundreds of fragments. In swerving, however, the lorry was forced to veer across the street, and managed to clip another parked car, which lost a door mirror and a substantial amount of paint. A second small cheer went up from the crowd.

As they surged forwards, Norbert was again able to hear the discussions between safety personnel and the police.

'Hardly a re-enactment, this,' Jake said. 'I mean, how many people's memories are going to be jogged by that fucking display?'

Two of the more senior-looking police officers conferred. 'You know that the super's got a bee in his bonnet about this one, Jake. We're going to go for one more.'

'Jesus. There's not much of the street left. What damage do you want to do this time?'

'As I said, once more.'

'Once and that's your lot. Otherwise Roger and I are designating the scene an urban danger spot.'

'OK, safety man. Keep your helmet on.'

As Norbert stood close enough to Elizabeth to feel her breathing, he felt proud that the Bridgeton police force was willing to spend so much of their time and resources reconstructing his death. Although they were woefully inaccurate in the details, they had still put a lot of effort into the thing. Not to mention money. He rocked forwards once more on his feet and brushed his wife, more firmly this time. What happened next took Norbert by surprise.

Elizabeth span round and screamed, 'Pervert!' at him.

Norbert glanced down. The mobile phone was sticking out of his coat pocket and poking into her backside. He looked up. She was staring at him. People turned their attention away from the quest for another re-enactment and glared at Norbert. A large man who looked as if he might count fighting among his hobbies stepped closer.

'You all right, love?' he asked Elizabeth.

'No I am not,' she replied with her best school-teacher indignation. 'This man here is bothering me.'

'Yeah, I've been watching him as well,' a woman piped up. 'Been touching her clothes and stuff.'

'A fucking pervert, eh?' the large man reiterated.

Norbert had to admit that he probably did appear a little deviant in his camouflaged state. 'No,' he replied. 'I was just . . .'

'What?'

He pulled his phone out as evidence. 'You know . . .' This wasn't going well. He needed to escape, and fast. But the crowd was too keen on trouble. There was simply nowhere to run. At least his wife was none the wiser. He would have to talk his way out, and never, ever come back to Bridgeton, whether in disguise or not. 'Really, I wasn't doing anything, I—'

The large man moved even closer. He wrapped one hand around Norbert's ponytail and tore off his glasses to punch him. The ponytail detached. The glasses were thrown away. His wife stared into his eyes. A hand gripped his coat. There was a change in Elizabeth's face. A fist rushed through the air and broke his nose. Norbert fell to the ground. Elizabeth fell down with him.

Wasting Police Time

Phil Ryder sat in the relatively plush office of his boss's boss's boss. The soles of his Dr Martens sank comfortingly into the carpet. Opposite him, Bridgeton's chief of police digested the long page of explanation that Phil had just finished typing. After several minutes, he looked up at him. 'So, let me get this straight,' he started, his voice loud and intimidating, even to a fellow copper. 'You're telling me that we re-enacted an RTA, and that the missing person who supposedly died in the accident was actually standing in the crowd watching us do it?'

'Something like that, sir, yes.'

'And why the bloody hell would he be watching us recreate the moment of his disappearance?'

'He'd apparently come back to see his wife.'

'Sir.'

'Sir.'

'And why had he apparently come back to see his wife?'

'He missed her, sir.'

327

'Missed her? Then why the bloody hell did he run away from her?'

'Seemed like a good idea at the time, I suppose, sir.'

The chief flicked irritably through some papers on his desk. 'Now, Ryder, you dug the tramp up, did you not?'

'No.'

'Sir.'

'Sir.'

'Then who the fuck did?'

'Dabner and Sons, funeral directors, sir.'

'You didn't use an exhumation team?'

'Didn't get the chance, sir. They'd already got him out.'

'And why the hell had they done that?'

'Just being helpful, sir.'

'Look, Ryder, this was a murder investigation. A big one. It cost a lot of money. We tracked bank accounts, shares, we did house to house, mounted surveillance, worked with Missing Persons, liaised with Taunsley, we'd even pitched for a slot on *Crimewatch*. And what do we turn up? An ex-accountant who leaves his wife, and then returns a few weeks later, and a tramp who doesn't look where he's going. And you know what that adds up to?'

'No, sir.'

'Not a fat lot, Ryder. Not a fat lot at all. This was going to be the big one, the one we hung our helmets on, the one that showed the ungrateful sods of Bridgeton that their police force is more than capable of catching murderers.'

'We could still do him, sir.'

'What with?'

'Breaking and entering.'

The superintendent appeared to redden. 'Into his own house? Can't fucking arrest a man for trying to steal his own property.'

Phil stared at his shoes for a second, racking his

brain. This was hardly commonplace criminal activity. 'How about wasting police time, then?'

'Any more suggestions like that, Ryder, and I'll fucking do you for it. This is not the result which is going to help Bridgeton sleep easy in its beds, or restore public confidence in the force.'

'I guess not. Sir.'

'But I still don't get how he did it. Have we at least established that?'

'Mr Flint has been most cooperative, sir.'

'I should bloody well think so.'

Pizzas

Jake sat alone in his front room, a splatterfest block-buster flashing away silently on the TV in the corner. He rubbed his chin with the remote control. Certain things were becoming evident to him. He was single and thirty-two. Women didn't necessarily flock towards men who worked in the field of Hazard Prevention. A house is unbearably small when you cohabit, and eerily big when you are the only resident. Clothes thrown on the bedroom floor don't get up and walk to the washing machine, before drying and iron-ing themselves and making their way back to the wardrobe. Pizzas all taste the same when you eat them every day. It is impossible to distinguish between what you are and what you are supposed to be if you watch too many films, read too many books, absorb too many adverts. There is no English phrase for *joie de vivre*. Washing up once a week still feels too often. Cups of tea grow mouldy and smell of sick if left long enough. Living without a car is difficult when you're used to having one. When it rains it doesn't necessarily pour, it just feels like it. Drinking beer at home doesn't really get you pissed. Nine fingers are better than eight. Five days to get hold of fifteen grand isn't nearly long enough. Ronnie doesn't have particularly good telephone manners.

He thought about his uncle. There were facts and then there were facts. Family weren't essentially better than anybody else. Norbert had been economical with everything except the truth. With the truth, he had been downright wasteful. Meanness with money can become meanness in love. Richness in life has nothing to do with richness in wealth. A bible of spending advice can help someone dig themselves out of debt. Faking your own death is a complete bastard of a thing to do to your relatives.

The doorbell rang. Jake stopped staring through the TV and walked into the hall. It was his uncle. He turned and headed back into the front room. Norbert followed him. The curtains were drawn, and empty beer cans and mugs cluttered up the place. Jake pointed to a chair.

'Thought I'd better come and see you,' Norbert started, sitting down. Jake remained silent. 'I think I owe a few people an explanation at least.'

'At least.'

'Jake, let me tell you about economy. It hails from the Greek word *oikonomos*, which literally means household manager. The science of economics is thus merely an extension of managing the household budget. Somewhere, something went badly wrong. The archetypal housewife had finite and limited resources to balance each week, so that good value in all things was at a premium. Where are women like this nowadays? If I had asked my wife to spend within tightly constrained means, it would only have encouraged her frivolousness. In other words, I had no choice but to become a house husband. And therefore—'

'What the hell are you babbling about? Please, spare me any more lectures.'

Norbert managed a weak smile. 'Let me continue. I don't blame you for being upset. Look, when I worked, all things pointed towards packing it in. The busier I was, the more time I spent earning money, the more I threw it away on conveniences. Who has time to shop for a bargain if they're using up all their time earning money? It was, I came to see, a self-defeating circle. Something had to be done.'

'Didn't exactly do you any favours though.'

'For a while it did. But then maybe I went too far. You see, I got completely caught up in it. I even wrote a book, an explanation for everything.'

'I know. I've read it.'

'You? How come?'

'Elizabeth gave it me after your funeral.'

Norbert's eyes widened. 'And what have you done with the thing?'

'Implemented its wisdom, mainly.'

'You've still got it?'

'Oh yes. Been quite useful. Especially the chapter on how to finish a relationship but retain your money.'

'I hope that didn't have any influence on Kate's—'

'No. It was already doomed really.'

'Do you mind?' Norbert nodded towards an unopened can of beer. Jake shrugged. 'Thanks,' he said, grabbing it, the tssschh of the ring pull penetrating the silence. After a few seconds, he continued. 'So the manuscript's OK. Fantastic. But anyway, don't you see that the more I discovered ways of saving money, the more I became entrenched in the quest for the ultimate cheap life? Even to the detriment of my marriage. Not for the first time, I had an idea and became obsessed by it.' He knocked back a mouthful of free beer. 'And there was the issue of pride.'

'Pride?'

'I went too far. I dug my way in deep, very deep, and in the end there was no way out. I couldn't just turn round to Elizabeth and tell her I'd been wrong all these years and was going to return to work as if nothing had ever happened. What would she have thought of me?'

'Probably a lot more than she does now.'

'True,' Norbert conceded, interlocking his hands around the can and staring mournfully down at them.

'Have you been to see her?'

'Not yet. The police questioned me most of yesterday. Today I've been getting my nose repaired. Thought I'd better leave it a while, let her calm down a bit. But anyway, the point is we'd become locked into something there was no escape from. Every single issue in our relationship revolved around money. What I've got to do now is convince her – and you, everybody – that I've changed, and that money doesn't matter. It's people that count.'

Jake had a sudden moment of clarity amid the clutter of his front room. A solution to his problems. In fact, he was looking straight at it. 'Norbert, there is one way you could at least convince me, and probably Elizabeth as well.'

Norbert edged forwards in his seat, eager. 'How?'

'It's just a question of how far you would go to help someone who was in need.' Jake outlined his plan and his uncle listened attentively. 'So what do you think?' he asked afterwards.

Norbert was quiet for a couple of minutes, deep in thought, weighing up the pros and cons. Mainly they were cons. 'You think this would work?' he said eventually, not really enthused.

'It would certainly do the trick for me. And I can't imagine Elizabeth not being impressed.'

Again, Norbert was silent, before mumbling, 'Let me think about it.'

Something else occurred to Jake. 'But anyway, you said you came round to give me an explanation, and I still don't understand how you did it.'

'It was cunning all right.' Norbert scratched his recent goatee beard. 'Oh it was cunning all right.'

Norbert's Accident

There had been no planning involved, no scheming or inventing. There merely existed an instant of time during which Norbert had appreciated that he could change his life for ever with one subtle, swift movement of his hand. He had seized the opportunity as he would have snatched a cheap tin of peas from a supermarket shelf. Eric the vagrant, half pissed and crossing in the opposite direction, had been badly run over. Norbert had missed most of the action as he rechecked the till receipt he was holding in his hand. The body came to rest in front of him. He took his coat off and wrapped it over the victim's torso. Looking up, he saw that the two vehicles involved in the accident had failed to stop. No one else was within a hundred yards of the accident site. In Norbert's back pocket, attached via a chain to one of his belt loops, was his wallet. Norbert unhooked the clasp and freed it, slipped one bank card out, and, working under the coat, attached the wallet to the headless man's jeans, sliding it into his back pocket. Next, he edged his keys into another of Eric's pockets. He salvaged his beloved price gun, and then the pièce de résistance – he pushed the receipt into one of the man's bloody hands and slid his calculator into the other. Clothes could have scuppered the plan, but, quite by coincidence, Eric was wearing almost identical garments to the ones Norbert often dressed in. It was gruesome, but a few seconds had suddenly freed up the rest of his life.

Eventually, people approached, cautiously, half looking, not wanting to see the full glory of the accident but not wanting to miss it either. A WPC must have been in the vicinity, because she was there quickly, warning the spectators to step back, radioing for a frankly optimistic ambulance and bending down to tend what was left of the man. She asked Norbert who he was, and Norbert said Eric Jones. He didn't know the tramp's surname, but had frequently heard his wife refer to him by his Christian name. As made-up-on-the-spot aliases went, Jones wasn't the worst he could have come up with. She wrote it down in a small notebook, slow, round movements of her biro lingering over the letters. Then she asked him what had happened. Norbert said he wasn't really sure. There had been a sound, a noise he had never heard before and never wanted to hear again, a kind of squishing, popping, spurting noise. The WPC didn't look too good. She was pale, and, if anything, losing colour. Norbert said that the headless man seemed to be reading a piece of paper, hadn't looked where he was going and had been knocked down by a car. Then, lying prone, his head had been squashed by a following lorry. Trance-like, the WPC wrote as if Norbert was dictating, and he was able to just make out the words 'head', 'squashed', 'not looking' and 'lorry' on her pad.

A police car arrived, and soon afterwards the sounds of an ambulance struggling through the traffic could clearly be heard. Norbert gave his pseudonym again to one of the new police officers, while the WPC was escorted away from the scene by the other. Eventually the ambulance arrived. The paramedics, having had a good look from the safety of their cab, sauntered around to the back of their vehicle and fetched a stretcher and a blanket. The new PC pulled Norbert's blood-splattered coat further over the victim's torso and chatted briefly with the ambulance men with a cheery and grisly bonhomie.

'Nasty one there, then,' he said.

'Not very pretty at all,' one of them agreed.

'Fancy a spot of resuscitation?'

'We'd have to find a mouth first.'

'Not to mention a head.'

'Probably stuck under the wheels of a lorry on the bypass somewhere.'

'That's a hell of a long airway to clear,' one of the paramedics replied. 'And you'd need a fuck lot of breath.'

The trio laughed quietly to themselves. Norbert retreated from the scene, and asked the WPC, who was resting inside a police car a few yards away, whether there was anything else he could do. 'No,' she said. 'Just let me know your address in case we need to contact you, and you're free to go.' Norbert made up an address and the WPC wrote it dutifully down. Then he walked to the nearest cash point and withdrew a large sum of money using his one remaining card.

He was free at last.

With freedom eventually came a problem, however. He had no documentation, no ID, no proof that he had ever been alive. His improvised plan came to him a fortnight after his death. While his wife sat in the front room and grieved, Norbert pieced it together. He would break into his house in disguise, and retrieve the pieces of paper he needed to exist. But, as he now readily appreciated, there was a gulf of distance between the plan and a successful outcome.

Things had deteriorated at the shed level on his first

visit. For some reason, his wife had locked it, and he had been forced to break in to retrieve the spare house key secreted there in an old chest of drawers. The noise having woken her, when he had attempted to unlock the back door, she panicked. For some unknown reason, she started banging a hammer on an old pan. If that wasn't enough to send you packing then nothing was.

The second trip had been at least partially successful. Rooting around during the day, Norbert had been able to find everything he needed except his manuscript. Of course he was aware that Elizabeth would notice someone had been rummaging about, and so he had covered his tracks with an empty can of Tennent's Special and a roll-up butt. Appreciating that Eric would apparently have gone missing, he had decided to let him take the blame.

The third visit had been worse, if anything. Using the supposed cover of night, he had successfully entered the house after removing a small downstairs window with a screwdriver from the shed. And then, just as he had given up ever finding his manuscript, and was saying one final and silent farewell to his slumbering wife's naked body, she had woken and damned near screamed the place down. He had no option but to run. To have taken his balaclava off and comforted her was impossible. His entire future lay in not being detected. And so he had sprinted to his hire car and driven miserably back to an area of London close to, but not technically within, the boundaries of Fulham.

Norbert had decided therefore to change tack. A new disguise was called for. And he would go in daylight while his wife was at work. The first attempt had been a dismal failure. Everything had looked good to begin with. He walked around the back, ready to enter and retrieve his precious manuscript once and for all. And then, out of nowhere, two coppers showed up.

Luckily, they were slow and unused to chasing criminals, and he had been able to make good his escape.

Finally, with just days until his departure to Malawi, desperation had set in. He wanted his manuscript and he needed his birth certificate. He turned up at the weekend, in daylight, hoping his wife was out shopping, intending to slip in and out invisibly, and never come back. Only, for some lunatic reason, the powers that be had decided to reconstruct his death, and, in a fitting end to his evasion, he had become rather too involved in the proceedings.

Slogans

At work the following afternoon, Jake stared up at the posters which faced his desk, and silently swore. This was his ritual, in the way that others might offer up a prayer to the day which lay ahead. A new catchphrase had been added to the list. *Risk It and Lose It*. It was accompanied by the information that *37 tea-cosy accidents were reported in the last national audit*. Jake wasn't sure who sent these short messages of joy to the unit, but they arrived regularly, in official governmental envelopes. Roger or Geoff then unpacked them, mouthed the words to themselves and pinned them up on Jake's side of the room, to keep him on his toes. This one wasn't funny though. Tea-cosy mishaps were usually caused by children being attracted to the bright colours and scalding themselves. The office clock to the left of the posterboard showed 12:08. The day was Monday. Four days until he lost another finger. Unless, that is, his uncle saw sense. He stood up and grabbed his coat.

'Where're you off?' Roger asked.

'Surprise inspection.'

Roger flicked idly through his diary. 'We haven't got any of those 'til next week.'

'I know,' Jake replied, gathering his cycling paraphernalia. 'That's the surprise.'

Robert Peril was less than pleased to see him. 'Jake, you're not due for a couple of months,' he complained, slightly bemused. He picked up the phone, ready to dial. 'Look, let me ring your boss, double-check our dates.'

'It's OK,' Jake replied. 'I'm only here for a casual snoop. Nothing official. And whatever I find, I won't report.'

Robert visibly relaxed, and replaced the phone receiver. 'So what's on your mind?' he asked.

'I still can't shake this R and D thing.'

'We've only had three accidents since you were last here.'

'Three? That's encouraging.'

'Yeah, we've been a bit quiet. Mind you, that's all about to change.'

'Why?'

'Between you and me, we're gearing up for the big one. We've been awarded a major contract to do Edinburgh.'

'Hogmanay?'

'Oh yes. We've had to promise them something special.'

'Like what?'

'The biggest single firework New Year's Eve has ever seen. We're beginning to up the ante. There's a lot riding on this.'

Jake thought suddenly of Louise. 'So R and D's going to be a particularly risky place for the foreseeable future?'

Robert rubbed his face. 'Jake, you know where we stand on this one. I don't want to go over it all again.'

'Worker protection, Robert.'

'Money, Jake.'

'Profits before people.'

'No profits, no people.'

The two sides of the argument hung in the air for several seconds. Jake appreciated the futility of his position. 'Do you mind if I have a quick look round then?' he asked.

'If it's all unofficial, fine. Help yourself.'

Jake walked out of the office, depressed by Robert's attitude, but excited by the possibility of seeing Louise again. In fact, this was the main reason for his visit. Peering through the perspex door, he caught sight of her. She was working alone in a small enclosed booth, typing numbers into a computer.

'Ah, if it isn't the Safety Man,' she said, spotting his approach.

'Hello, Danger Woman,' he replied.

Louise chose to keep quiet about almost running him over recently. 'You've sobered up since last time I saw you.'

'Unfortunately yes.'

'And to what do we owe this pleasure?'

'Who said anything about pleasure? I'm here to make sure you're safe.'

'Just me?'

Jake paused, wondering if his motive was so obviously transparent. 'No, everybody,' he lied.

'As houses,' Louise told him.

'Look, Louise, I thought I made a bit of an idiot of myself at Utopia the other night.'

'That's the general point.'

'No, I mean it. I was thinking, what time do you get off for lunch?'

'Any time between now-ish and two.'

Standing in the middle of a danger zone put his apprehension over his next question into perspective. Rather than skirt around the issue, badly out of practice as he was, he simply blurted it out. 'How about I buy you lunch?'

Louise glanced up at him, and then back at the computer. 'Fine, just let me finish this. I'll meet you in the car park. Ten minutes OK?'

Jake smiled and walked around the large laboratory with little concern for his personal safety. After faking a few clipboard notes, he left the department and headed outside to bask in the sunshine. Presently Louise joined him. She was wearing jeans and a tight vest top, and Jake summoned up every last gram of willpower to stop himself staring. After several weeks of hardcore Dutch porn, this was by no means an easy feat. They ambled off the industrial estate, towards a local café. As they walked, Louise turned to him and said, 'So come on, Safety Man, tell me what your worst faults are. What are you crap at?'

'Why?'

'I'm just interested.'

'And why are you interested?'

'Well, let's say you were thinking about investing time or effort in something. If that something was a car or a house, you'd get a survey done.'

'I suppose.'

'But when you meet someone, it's different. Let's say you were going to chat me up.' She ran her fingers through her hair. 'All you would do is regurgitate stories and anecdotes which serve to illustrate your good qualities. Now I'm not interested in what you think I might want to hear. I'm interested in what you don't want me to hear.' She dug her hands deep in her pockets. 'Like in a survey, where they only tell you what's wrong. Then, if you know all the faults in advance, it saves a lot of heartache in the long run.'

'A bit negative though. And I've got some cracking stories, some of which are almost true.'

'Exactly. Come on, let's have those faults.'

Jake stopped and faced Louise. 'I've only got nine fingers.'

'So I've noticed.'

'And I might only have eight by the end of the week.'

'How come?'

'Probably better that you don't know.'

'Why?'

'Because it's my job not to expose people to unnecessary danger.'

'Tease.'

'Some other time. Next week maybe, if I get that far.'

'So what else is wrong with you apart from finger negligence?'

'OK. Spending. I used to spend too much. Or rather, I didn't earn enough to match my outgoings. I'm not so bad now.'

'That doesn't really count. I want real, up-to-the-minute character flaws.'

'I find it nearly impossible to hug middle-aged women.'

'Not the worst thing ever.'

'I'm not very good at living with people.'

'Who is?'

'I don't like DIY.'

'Now we're getting somewhere.'

'I laugh at sick things.'

'Like what?'

'Like cartoon violence. Only when it becomes real, I . . .'

'What?'

'I lose my nerve completely.'

'Interesting. Any others?'

Jake started walking again. 'I'll let you know. OK, your turn.'

Louise removed her hands from her jeans and folded them just below her breasts. 'Oh, no. I never said this was a reciprocal arrangement.'

'But—'

'Just because I get a survey done on your house doesn't mean you're entitled to have one on mine.'

'Well, just a hint.'

'I can give you one fault, and one only.'

'Go on then.'

Louise opened the café door. 'I'm afraid of relationships.'

Jake stopped in the doorway. 'How afraid?' he asked.

A woman pushed between them on her way out. Louise refused to meet his eye. 'Very afraid,' she said. 'How about you?'

Maybe it was just too soon after Kate. Perhaps the best thing to do was to remain single for a few months, regain some perspective. Besides, he might imminently be needing to spend time in hospital. 'The same,' he conceded, stepping inside and closing the door after him.

Dust to Dust

The vicar put his hymn book down and glared at Norbert. Just a couple of months ago, he had buried him. He made a mental note that if Norbert Flint died again, he would insist on cremation, to do the job properly. And while church attendances were undeniably down, he could well do without the living dead clogging up his pews. More than this unholy resurrection, what bugged the vicar was the obvious disparity between the calibre of the man he had consigned to the ground and the one who now stood before him. He puffed his cheeks out and pleaded for inner patience, before resuming where he had left off.

'And without further ado let us sing hymn three-two-four.'

Jake wasn't keen on joining in. He wasn't in the least bit musical. Even singing in the bath was an ordeal for all concerned. But looking around him, he appreciated that he ought to at least give it a go. The rest of the congregation – Elizabeth and Norbert – similarly overcame their reluctance. A painful couple of minutes later, they were encouraged to sit down, while the vicar quoted some more verse.

Elizabeth was close to tears, and kept her head down. So this is what it feels like to be lonely, she thought to herself. Three mourners, none of whom really knew you, massacring religious songs in a draughty church. No family, no friends, no well-wishers, just a handful of people who felt guilty enough to come and endure the service. A vicar who had an axe to grind, and was desperately struggling to find positive words to say about a vagrant who shouted abuse at passing cars. Elizabeth had insisted that Norbert pay for the ceremony. After all, there was a debt of dignity owing. Eric had come to a diabolical end, had been buried under the wrong name, exhumed, buried again, exhumed again, and was now finally about to be put to rest. As in life, death had been unpleasant.

The police had been little help. There was a suggestion that Eric had been convicted of various minor offences in nearby Taunsley. Although the police were able to trace an old address through his criminal record, no family were laying any claim to him, having long since moved on. Elizabeth blew her nose. Her eyes were moist.

Norbert stared down at the cold stone floor, worn smooth by centuries of restless feet. The regret he felt about his whole adventure took a new turn. The implications of his actions stung him, as the vicar fabricated a dismal, half-hearted eulogy. With each word, Norbert could see that his deception had hurt another innocent being. His mouth felt awkward, his throat tightened, and a tear dripped onto the floor, where it was soaked up by the dust.

By the coffin, two undertakers bowed their heads, swaying slightly from time to time. Bob Walsh similarly monitored the floor. He had run his eyes over its even geography a hundred times before and yet still found new imperfections to peruse. He didn't listen to the eulogy. He had heard too many before. The vicar had a system, a structure to his sentences, which varied little according to the nature of the deceased. A bit like police interrogations really. They said the same things, used the same words, implied the same things each time. And, as he thought about it, if he was going to be hassled over things he clearly hadn't done, he might as well return to his former habit of breaking and entering. There was little point enduring such insults with none of the gain.

He turned his attention to the shoes of his boss Malcolm Dabner, who stood next to him. They were slightly muddy on one side, testimony to the fact that he had come and inspected the new grave himself, just to make sure they were burying the headless man in a large enough hole this time. Malcolm noted Bob's gaze out of the corner of his eye and spotted the dirt on his own footwear. This wasn't good. Still, were they about buried . . . they were about to bury the right man in the right plot, which was a blessed relief. Unlike his colleague, Malcolm did listen to the vicar's words. One day it would be his turn, and he wanted to know in advance what was likely to be said about him.

The vicar rounded off, and a final hymn was sung quietly in the large church. Presently, the coffin was carried outside by Bob, Malcolm and two others, and was lowered into the ground. Elizabeth threw a small clod of earth onto its shiny wooden veneer, and said softly, 'I am sorry for taking your name in vain.' Norbert hung his head. The funeral had been expensive, despite Dabner and Sons offering a very generous reduction for the large amount of business he had put their way recently. But money was irrelevant at times such as these, even, Norbert conceded, to people like him.

Reconciliation

With the curtains half drawn, flags at half mast, Elizabeth ushered her husband into the living room and pointed at a tatty piece of furniture. 'Make yourself barely comfortable,' she said. 'Not that I should allow you to even set foot inside the place.'

Norbert grunted a submissive and sullen reply. 'S'pose not.'

'But I figure I ought to hear you out before I throw you out.'

'Thanks. And I think you'll be surprised by what I've got to say.'

'I don't think anything will ever surprise me again.'

Again, Norbert gave a meek and submissive acknowledgement.

'Well, come on,' she said, 'I'm waiting.'

Her husband cleared his throat. 'I have the ability to change our lives.'

'*Our* lives? From now on, there's your life and my life. They are not the same thing.'

'Shares.'

'What?'

'I have shares.'

'We figured that much. Mary told us.'

'You don't understand,' he began, excitedly. 'The shares I've got are in StreetSmart. They've been taken over so many times that their dividends are worth a fortune. Do you know they've gone up a massive twelve hundred per cent in the last four years? That's twelve times their initial value.' Norbert was on the edge of his seat. 'I don't need to tell you that a lump sum from cashing in my life insurance a few years ago is now worth a very great amount of money.'

'Devious bastard.'

'And then there's the savings. Let me show you something.' Norbert took out a folded bank statement and passed it to his wife.

'Jesus. Is that right? Forty-three thousand?'

'Plus interest.'

'You skimmed forty-three thousand off our lives?'

'I'm afraid so.'

Elizabeth thrust the piece of paper back at her husband. 'Wanker!' she shouted.

'Look. I'm not telling you this to impress you. I'm just straightening everything out.'

'Any more?'

'There's the money I made in London.'

'How much?'

'Around six thousand, at the last count.'

'So we're actually quite wealthy.'

'Yes. And most of the house is paid for. So here's what I propose.' Norbert walked over and knelt down in front of his wife. 'A couple of years of luxury. We'll blow it all.'

'All?'

'Most of it.'

'And then what?' Elizabeth asked, unimpressed.

'I'll return to accountancy.'

'I'm sorry, Norbert,' she replied, 'I can't see you being anything except your old self.'

'But don't you realize what has happened to me?' he implored, staring into her eyes. 'It's like a Jesus thing.'

'What do you mean?' Elizabeth demanded mistrustfully.

'I revisited the scene of my death, only to be reborn.' Norbert's eyes were burning brightly. 'I am re-incarnated. Now I can change. Trapped in my old body I couldn't.'

'But you didn't die.'

'In many ways I did. To my family, to the church, to my friends, to my wife, even maybe to myself, I really did die. I mean, I was even fucking buried.'

'No. Eric was buried. You were poncing around Fulham.'

'Wandsworth, it turns out. Anyway, that's not the point. I *felt* dead. And as I think about it I've come to see that in some circumstances death can be a form of freedom.'

'From what?'

'From a life you've created but can't bear any more. From a marriage that you've ruined but don't have the courage to put right. From a person you love but can no longer make happy. From everything.'

Elizabeth was silent and Norbert stood up and stretched his legs, which had become stiff from too much grovelling. 'I don't know,' she answered after a while. 'I really don't know. I mean, I'd rather you had an affair than did what you did.'

'I did. A love affair with money.'

'And now it's broken your heart.'

'And yours.'

'It's done more than that,' she muttered.

'But it wasn't me. It was the cash.'

'You sound like a drug addict.'

'Well in many ways I was. The more I had the more I wanted, and the less it satisfied me. Tell me if that's not the classic refrain of an addict.'

Elizabeth ran her hand over the scruffy sofa, and

swept her eyes around the dishevelled interior of the living room. The decor had been new once, and all of the furniture pristine. And then Norbert had disappeared up his own wallet. 'Every addict ends up destroying the very thing he holds precious,' she said eventually.

'Exactly,' her husband replied. 'The truth was that I couldn't bear to spend money. The more I got, the less I could stand to part with it. Just having it in the bank made me feel happier than frittering it away ever could. I was ill.'

'And now?'

'I think I'm cured. And there's two things I can do to demonstrate it.'

'What?'

'First, I'm going to save Jake's life.'

'How do you mean?'

'You'll see. And second . . .'

'Yes?'

Norbert opened his jacket and took out a couple of tickets. 'Give me a couple of weeks and I'll prove everything to you.'

Comeuppance

Pauline appreciated that there was a degree of inevitability about her husband catching her at it. A husband always finds out in the end. He had nearly done so once already, but she had managed to hide herself away from the spotlight and ride it out. From that moment on, however, Pauline was aware that Roger had his suspicions. But what was she supposed to do? Give up on a good thing with Simon on the off-chance her husband would discover them?

What had surprised her though was Roger's reaction. Most husbands would have gone ballistic. There was an air of resignation about Roger which unsettled her, as if he hadn't understood the situation fully. She still felt the worst was yet to come, when the real implications of her actions hit home. In fact, to begin with, he had blamed himself.

'If I'd been a proper husband, you wouldn't have felt the need to go elsewhere for your kicks,' he had said sullenly.

This had been one of the things which hurt the most. What Pauline really needed, she came to appreciate, was to offset her guilt against some excessive jealous anger. But no. His lack of verbal abuse was deafening.

'Look, I've been spending time in pubs, clubs and

social centres with another man,' she had yelled at him, hoping to encourage his wrath. He had merely stared at her with silent regret.

She had even tried watching back-to-back episodes of *You've Been Framed*, *Casualty* and *999* in an attempt to goad him, but he had risen above it. That was, she saw now, the real problem with her husband. He was just too good a man for her.

Rat-running

'Can I talk with you a moment?' Roger asked, interrupting Jake as he flicked rubber bands at the safety posters above his desk.

Jake fired one last shot at *Live Safer, Live Longer*, which missed and hit *Gamble and Lose – You Choose*. He span round to face his colleague. 'What's up?'

'It's a personal matter.'

Jake was not overjoyed. He and Roger seemed to have drawn up an unwritten agreement on their first day not to mix their personal and professional lives. And since Roger didn't appear to have much of a personality, and Jake much professionalism, this had worked well so far. 'Yeah?'

'Things aren't good at home.'

'No? What's wrong?'

'It's Pauline. She's . . .' Roger looked down at the small patches of vitiligo on his hands. 'She's been going out with another man.'

'Shit. I'm sorry to hear that.'

'And I think it's all my fault.'

'How do you work that out?'

'She hasn't been getting what she needs at home.'

Jake hung his head. 'I'm very sorry,' he repeated, uncomfortable with the direction Roger was pursuing.

'You see, the thing is that I once had an accident. Not a bad one, all things considered. In fact, as accidents go, it was a rather good one.'

'What happened?'

'I was rat-running through an estate, and from nowhere, this boy runs into the road. Seven or eight, at a guess. Right over the bonnet. Didn't have time to do anything.'

'Was he badly hurt?'

'I didn't stop the car. I was someone else, in a film or something. If I kept going the moment wouldn't be real. I just drove and drove – didn't go to work – headed out into the countryside and sat in a lay-by shaking, staring into the mirror at my own cowardly eyes.'

'Roger? You're telling me you never reported it?'

'My eyes . . .' Roger was crying, slumped forwards, an arm hiding his face.

'It's OK,' Jake said, patting him gently on the back.

Roger jerked upright, angry. 'No, Jake, it's not fucking OK. I was a coward. I ran. A small boy got knocked down. I don't think he died, but he certainly got hurt. I did it. My fault. I could have helped him but chose not to.'

'But he might have been all right. Maybe he got up and walked away.'

'I doubt it. And that's the thing. I will never know. I read all the local papers the next day, turning the page, expecting to see "Boy, eight, Maimed by Hit and Run Driver". I watched the news. Nothing. I wanted to ring the hospitals. I *needed* to know. It was killing me, eating me up. Night after night and no word. I couldn't sleep, Jake. I couldn't do anything. Couldn't drive, couldn't work . . . I didn't know how badly injured the kid was, but I was utterly paralysed.'

'And then what?'

'A bad year or two. Depression. My vitiligo flared up for the first time and started to gnaw away at me. I drank. And every time I saw a boy who had a limp, or was in a wheelchair, or was injured in any way, I thought he was the one.'

'Jesus. I don't know how you'd get over something like that.'

'I didn't either. But you do. Bit by bit. You still sicken yourself, but after a while you forget why. There's just a general revulsion which lingers.'

'Do you think it's why you do what you do?'

'Hazard Prevention? Maybe.'

'How old were you when this happened?'

'Nineteen. Just about to go off to university.'

'And I guess you didn't drive a Volvo in those days?'

'Hell no. I had a souped-up Escort.'

'You grew up in Bridgeton, didn't you?'

'Yep. On the other side of town, out by the old aerospace factory. Why?'

'No reason. Interested really. I grew up over that way. Bit grim, wasn't it?'

'Yeah.'

'You know, Roger, I reckon that kid was probably all right.'

'I can't see it.'

'There was nothing in the papers, and I lived in that area. There weren't that many people round there. If a kid about my age – and he would only have been a year or two younger than me – had died or been confined to a wheelchair or whatever, we would have known about it. You know how bad news travels.'

'Do you think so?'

'Really. And my dad was a good friend of the local copper. I'm sure we would have heard if the police were looking for a hit-and-run driver. Everybody would have heard.'

Roger appeared a little calmer and his breathing was

returning to normal. 'I'd never really thought about that. I went off to university, and when I came back, moved to the other side. Still can't drive that way. If I have a site visit I skirt round on the ring road and then double back. Takes ages, but it's worth it.'

'I'm sure everything was OK,' Jake said again, smiling at Roger, who appeared slightly reassured. 'But, and I'm sorry for missing the point, what has all this got to do with Pauline having an affair?'

Roger looked up at Jake with astonishment. 'An affair? She hasn't been having an affair. No, something much worse than that.'

'What then?'

'She's been working in nightclubs.'

Jake was obviously missing something. 'And?'

'As a bloody knife thrower's assistant!'

'What?'

'You remember when we went out on Adam's stag do?'

'I could hardly forget.'

'There was a knife thrower, and his assistant wouldn't perform. Well, I thought I recognized her, but couldn't be sure.'

'Pauline?'

'Exactly. She clocked me, and tried to creep away from the stage. She thought I would see her. Jake, I never realized it, but all these years she's been craving danger and excitement. And all she's ever had from me are warnings and statistics and caution. I've driven her to put her life on the line in order to feel alive. And the worst part of it is that I have no idea what I'm going to do.'

Safety Scene #12

A boy is lying on his back in a road. Everything is still. Clouds float by and one, which at first reminded him of a cow, now seems more like a dog. He stands up slowly, dusting himself off. Must have been the car, he thought. He picked up his school bag and saw that his knee was grazed. Sounds of his classmates drifted through the placid air, and he walked towards them, a smile returning. So God really did exist. There was someone looking after him. And now he even had a graze to show for his adventures.

Inside the playground, he spotted his friend Phil Ryder. Look, Phil, he said, nodding down at his injured knee. Not bad, Phil replied. The teacher noticed him and told him that he was late. Sorry, sir, he replied. Better get that graze seen to, the teacher said. Go and see Mrs Aitkins in the staffroom. He walked into the cool building and stood outside the staffroom door, his knee stinging with satisfaction. Cigarette smoke and laughter seeped under the door. He rapped his fist on the hard wooden surface and Mrs Aitkins answered.

Yes? she asked.

Mr Roper said I should see you about my knee, miss.

Your knee? It's only a graze, boy. Still, I suppose we'd better get a plaster on it.

OK.

Right, what's your name?

Cooper, miss. Jake Cooper.

Ah, Rosemary's son. Handful of trouble, she always says. Come on then, let's get you a plaster, cover that thing up.

And as Mrs Aitkins brushed a small piece of grit away from the wound, Jake Cooper decided he had had enough danger for one day. Besides, it was true. He had proved it. Someone was watching out for him. Someone would always be watching out for him.

Jake sat at work and recalled these events, slowly shaking his head. He rarely thought about it now, but Roger had nudged the memory. He stared up at the posters which presided over his desk. They were dominated by the perennial favourite *Safety Is No Accident*. He mouthed the slogans from the surrounding smaller notices to himself. *Uncertainty Is Unacceptable*. Listening to Roger sighing as he turned his computer on. *Risk It and Lose It*. He pictured Norbert wandering the streets with nowhere to go. *Drinking Stops You Thinking*. He saw Elizabeth standing in front of a class of adolescent ingrates, counting down to her lunchtime champagne. *Gamble and Lose – You Choose*. He glanced at his half finger. *Live Safer, Live Longer*. Two days and Ronnie was coming to visit. *Security Equals Safety*. He needed a contingency plan. And then, as he thought about the very events which had shaped his life, he had a sudden urge to tell Louise something.

DangerLove

Jake left the office and unlocked and reassembled his bicycle. He had a few issues to get off his chest. If he was quick, he could catch Louise before she finished work. Climbing onto his bike, Jake pedalled warily across the Anger Management car park, avoiding any potential trouble. Usually at this time of day all was quiet, patients having disappeared home to wreak havoc there. Traffic through the town centre was heavy. It was quarter to five, and the streets were full of people making hasty dashes out of work to miss the rush hour. Not that Bridgeton had a proper rush hour, but it had enough vehicles and was sufficiently cramped to muster a damned good impression.

Cutting in and out of stationary and moving cars, Jake tried to get his story straight. He ran over a few of the things he suspected to be true.

Some people need to feel as if they're about to die before they can truly sense life. Others need to feel as if they're already half dead, afraid that if they live too much they will take one more step towards ceasing to be. Most of us hover somewhere in between, dependent on both prudence and adventure to keep us happy.

It's why we go to fairgrounds, to ride on machines that pretend to jeopardize our lives, knowing full well that they don't, otherwise we wouldn't go on them.

It's why death is sexy. It tells us that we're alive.

It's why we like scary movies. We pay to feel frightened. Obviously, we don't like actually being scared, we just appreciate the fact that we're not. And the best way to do this is to walk out of a cinema on a sunny day having sat through two hours of suspense and terror.

It's why we jump off tall platforms tied to long pieces of elastic. We want to imagine that we might die, all the time knowing that we won't. After all, bungee jumping isn't dangerous, it's just organized bouncing on a length of elastic.

It's why we drive go-karts, go mountain biking, do anything that slightly raises us out of the secure lethargy that goes against every human instinct we have. It's why extreme sports exist.

Jake jammed his brakes on as a car pulled out in front of him. Changing down, he slowly began to build momentum again, and continued to pedal and ponder.

Risk is a finite commodity. You only have so much of the stuff in your bones. Some have more than others. But eventually most people reach a point where they've used it all up. Fifty-year-old miners will suddenly refuse to plunge underground any more, having previously done so every day of their working lives without thinking about it. Frequent flyers will stop flying. After a while, it catches up with you.

Our adrenal glands are virtually dormant these days. We are no longer fighting for our survival on a daily basis. When you remove the struggle to feed yourself from the equation, suddenly you have the energy for pettiness. When you all but eradicate danger as well, what are you left with?

The things which are truly dangerous are the ones we do obliviously, with no Extreme Clubs or jargon-laden subcultures. Like walking home after a night at a club or cycling through rush-hour traffic or climbing ladders or . . . or . . . love. After all, what was love if it wasn't danger? It was every bit as bad for your health as any pastime you cared to mention. Suicides, broken hearts, stress, alcoholism, sexually transmitted diseases – love was the real villain. And yet even Roger was prepared to expose himself to such potential disasters in order to be happy. This is what he would tell Louise. He wanted to take a risk on her. He was willing to subject himself to the possibility of pain, misery and loss just to be with this woman he barely knew. He was happy to jeopardize a perfectly satisfactory life for the chance of loving someone. In fact, as he headed through the town centre dodging cars, he was even ready to chance a protracted wheelie down the centre of the road if that would help matters.

Safety Scene #13

Interior of a busy, well-lit and elongated room with a low ceiling. From the hazard warnings, perspex shields and unusual equipment it becomes clear that we are in a research facility. Workers are wearing overalls and full-face masks. We focus in on a male in his mid-thirties, long hair tied back. He is holding a large orange cylinder. Next to him, a female worker slowly decants a hefty volume of powder into the tube. Close-up on the container from which the powder is being poured. We see that it reads 'Extreme danger – Explosives!!!'

We pull out and pan round the room. There are fifteen or so other staff performing various acts. We focus on a young male who is holding a sparkler in his right hand. He is not wearing gloves. He lights the far end, and it shimmers into life. The camera pauses lovingly on its fiery effervescence.

Back to the original couple, who are carefully inserting a fuse into the cylinder. It is a very long firework, and they bed the fuse deep into its centre. We see the woman take handfuls of what appears to be sand, and pack it on top of the explosives. Meanwhile, we see her partner remove a heavy lid from a metal box, and lean it precariously against an adjoining wall. Inside the box are several other pyrotechnics of similarly excessive dimensions. We cut to the member of staff who is testing sparklers. The one he is holding burns unexpectedly quickly towards his hand. Pan up to his face. A brief look of concern. He tries to let go of the sparkler, but for some reason he can't. We see that it is caught in the material of his sleeve. Back to his face. Concern turns to panic. He is about to be burnt. He shakes his hand violently, and finally the sparkler comes loose, flying through the air. We follow its progress. We can hear it fizzing, and almost smell its metallic burn. The sparkler hits the floor and bounces. Cut to the two workers who have finished with their enormous firecracker and are in the process of laying it in the brimming metal box. The sparkler somersaults and lands in the box. Close-up. Two or three fuses spark into life. We see the metal lid a few metres out of reach. We hear the word 'Nagasaki' screamed through the room by the pretty girl nearest the box. Slow-motion footage of people running desperately away. We see that all efforts to escape are too late. An enormous thunderous bang, almost simultaneous with several others of equal intensity. People are jolted through the air. The walls blow out. All is still. We hear some muffled screaming.

Carnage

The tarmac of the industrial estate was flat and smooth. Jake struggled on in nineteenth gear, off-road tyres doing all they could to hamper his progress. Switching to twentieth, he stuck out his hand to let car drivers know he was planning to turn right, should any of them fail to run him over. Peril and Sons was just past the crest of a mild incline. He was sweating. Beads of perspiration slunk down his face. He could see the far corner of the factory where Louise would be working. Its windows were dark. Jake glanced at the front cog of his bike. The road hummed beneath his fat tyres. He looked up. There was a colossal noise in front of him. He slammed on the brakes. The research and development department of the factory was instantaneously enveloped by a thick, black, clinging smoke.

Closer to Peril and Sons, the extent of the damage was more obvious. Bricks were now rubble. The entire floor was visible in cross-section. A dividing wall reached only halfway to the ceiling. No windows were left. Even the perspex had been torn apart. There was little movement. Jake took out his mobile phone as he ran towards the building. He requested ambulances and fire engines through short breaths. Fireworks began to ignite and bang. A fire must be underway somewhere. There was no way he could enter. He stopped ten yards from the factory and searched through the smoke for anyone to pull from the debris. A couple of seconds later, workers filed out of the far door of the factory. Mainly assembly line and clerical staff. Clearly, the damage was confined to the R and D section. In the distance, Jake could hear sirens. Oh please oh please oh please oh please oh please not Louise.

Several people came and stood near Jake. The explosions were now too frequent for non-emergency personnel to enter the building. There was a surreal desperation. No one was sure that this could really be happening. The sirens grew louder, and the first fire engine screamed into the car park. Four firemen in protective suits rushed into the factory. Oh please oh please oh please oh please oh please not Louise. A second engine arrived and started to douse the remains of the research department in water. Thirty seconds later, a body was carried out. Oh please oh please oh please oh please oh please not Louise. Workers crowded around and Jake was unable to see who it was, except that it was male. An ambulance screamed onto the site, and two firemen emerged with another body, which was laid out on the tarmac. Oh please oh please oh please oh please oh please not Louise. Jake pushed through the onlookers. It was another male, who was at least twitching. He was wearing unusual clothing. More bodies were carried out and decanted on the grass, firemen dashing straight back into the factory where at last the fireworks had become too soggy to explode.

There was a small commotion to Jake's left. The first body to be removed from the rubble was moving. More than this, it was getting to its feet. Jake walked over for a better look and breathed a quick breath of possibility. The body was similarly attired to all the other victims so far rescued. At a distance, normal overalls and face protection. Close up, however, and there were subtle differences. More workers were removed. Oh please oh please oh please oh please oh please not Louise. The man pulled off his head protection and walked stiffly off with an ambulance driver. And yet . . .

More emergency crews filled the car park with angry sirens. Moments later, two females were pulled out, one on a stretcher. Oh please oh please oh please oh please oh please not Louise. Jake ran over to where they were dumped next to an ambulance. A cold panic squeezed his intestines. Louise. Her legs were kicking as she lay on the stretcher. Her head protection was charred and he couldn't see her face. Some of her hair was singed. Her arms seemed all right, and her hands were encased in large gloves. She began to fidget, and Jake heard her scream. A female medic checked her body for breaks, while another attempted to loosen the mask.

'Here, let me,' a man to Jake's right said, crouching next to Louise. It was Robert Peril. He reached around and sprung a catch which released the head gear.

Louise was shouting incoherently.

Robert stood up, his chubby face drained, and looked at Jake. 'I never thought . . .'

Louise continued to shout. Jake ignored Robert, unable to take his eyes off her.

As the mask was removed by the medic, her shouts suddenly became audible. 'Get this fucking thing off me!' she yelled. The woman next to her rolled over and squatted on all fours, coughing.

The boss of Bulldog Fireworks put an arm around Jake's shoulders. 'You see,' he said, 'your nagging finally did some good.'

Louise struggled to her feet, trembling. Jake stepped

367

forwards and held her. She was unyielding and rigid. 'What is this stuff?' he asked, tapping her arm with his knuckles, glancing over Louise's shoulder at Robert Peril, the sting of burnt hair in his nose.

'Survival suit,' he replied. 'Kevlar limb covers, full torso, bulletproof face mask.'

Jake grinned a thin acknowledgement of relief. A paramedic put his hand on Jake's back.

'We'll have to take her to hospital for a check-up. Are you a friend of the patient?' he asked.

Jake gazed into Louise's eyes. 'Something more than that, I hope,' he answered.

Louise managed a shaky smile. 'Something more than that,' she said.

Anger Management

This time there was no bravery. Jake had experienced real danger and knew what it felt like. He had no wish to go through it again. There would be no heroics today. Losing one finger was bad enough, but two would begin to look like carelessness.

It was Friday. In a carrier bag at his feet were three padded envelopes, each with four thousand pounds in them. Norbert had suggested, and Jake had agreed, that twelve thousand should be enough to buy Ronnie off. And if it wasn't, they could always get some more later today.

Two new posters had arrived that morning, and Roger had gleefully stapled them up above Jake's desk. The first one read, *There Are No Dangerous Situations – Just Safe Ones Which Have Been Neglected*. The second was equally cheery. *Make Well-being Your Priority; Make Risk Your Enemy*. He sat and fiddled with a biro. At the bank, Norbert had been remarkably calm. He reminded Jake of a prisoner about to be executed, who had finally accepted his punishment and made peace with the world.

Ronnie had suggested the time. Finally, after almost a decade, Jake had spoken to him five days ago. He sounded strained, jittery and menacing. He made it clear that if he didn't get his cash back, Jake would be losing some more flesh. Jake wanted to know how Ronnie had tracked him down. Apparently one of Clem's friends had seen his name in a Regional Safety Bulletin, and they had learnt his address from a computer directory of Bridgeton.

'And you sent all those joke things?' Jake had asked.

Ronnie tittered to himself. 'Clem's idea. Fucking genius. Got you spooked, I bet.'

'Something like that. So you kept my finger?'

'All this time. Clem pretended to flush the bastard, but he palmed it instead. We were gonna give it you when you got back from the hospital. Dick reckoned I should make you wear it round your neck 'til you paid up. I thought I should shove it up your arse, give you something to think about.'

'Nice.'

Ronnie's tone changed. He had been matter of fact until now. 'There's nothing fucking nice about ripping me off. No one fucks with me, OK? Especially not jumped-up student twats. I want my fucking money, I want it on Friday, I want it handed over at lunchtime, and I don't want pissing about. You do know what I'll do to you if you piss me about? Do you want me to tell you, arsehole?'

'No.'

'I'm going to put you in my fucking van, take you back up to Leeds, and me and Clem are going to fucking tear you apart. There'll be fuck-all of you left.'

At the time, Jake had no idea whether Norbert was going to save his life. 'But what if I can't get the cash? I'm broke—'

'Not an option, you cunt. You took from me and I'm having it back. You've got a steady job, a nice car, a house – borrow it from the fucking bank.'

370

* * *

Ronnie had given him no idea of where the money was to be exchanged, just that it would occur at lunchtime. Jake checked the office clock. 12:35. He stood up and stretched. He was nervous and hadn't been able to do any proper work all morning. Instead, he had typed up a few surreal accident reports. Several times he been on the verge of ringing Phil. But there was no way he could go to his friend and ask for police protection. He had, after all, stolen a large sum of money from a semi-legitimate businessman. That was the real bugger about the situation – handy as it was to have a mate in the force, he could do nothing for him when he needed it most.

Roger sat at his desk, oblivious to Jake's impending scrape with death. And although he had carried on as usual, there was something different about him, Jake fancied, since his recent confessional. Walking towards the window, Jake smiled at the lunacy of the situation. That Roger was the driver of the car, and that Jake had shaped his future in a single unthinking moment.

Idly peering out into the car park for potential action, he saw him. Ronnie was there. The first time in eight or nine years. He had lost some weight and some hair but he still looked mean. Ronnie was staring up at the window, but from the way his eyes darted about, couldn't see Jake directly. Jake was suddenly scared. He wanted it over and done with. Ronnie was standing next to a black car, and was running a long object back and forth over its surfaces. Jake strained his eyes. It appeared to be a pair of bolt cutters. He glanced down at the second finger of his right hand. Fuck.

As he watched more closely he saw that the bolt cutters were scratching the paint of the car. Ronnie was grinning up in the direction of the window. And then Jake twigged. The car was familiar. More that that, it was the one Jake had sold back to the garage.

Someone from Hazard Prevention or the Psychiatric Unit had obviously bought it. Ronnie was unlikely to be aware of this fact. He made a show of holding the bolt cutters in front of him. Then he turned around and smashed them through the passenger window. Jake couldn't hear the noise, but saw the glass fracture, remain intact for an instant and then pour into the car. Ronnie was enjoying himself, oblivious. He did the same to the rear window, and then chopped the aerial. He held it up, and waggled the second finger of his right hand. Jake made an instant decision to throw the cash down to him and remain safely inside. The man was a fucking lunatic. He snatched his bag and was about to open the window when Ronnie began to really go to town on the car. And then events changed direction. A large man from Anger Management approached him as he put the windscreen through. An altercation blew up. Jake slid back the glass and listened.

'My car. My car. My car,' the man screamed.

Ronnie told him to fuck off, while smashing the headlights.

'My new car. My lovely new car.' The large man reddened considerably.

Once again, Ronnie told him to fuck off and stop bothering him. There was an element of the touch-paper being lit. Ronnie grinned up towards Jake's office, and Jake, unseen, grinned back. The Anger Management patient stepped forwards and ripped the bolt cutters from Ronnie's grip.

'My car. My car. My car,' he repeated. He appeared to be trying to take deep, pacifying breaths. And then Ronnie swung a punch at him, catching him under the chin.

What happened next took Ronnie by surprise. The AM case grabbed him by the collar of his lumberjack shirt and brought the bolt cutters down on his head. Ronnie buckled and fell to the floor. And then the man really got stuck in with his fists and boots. Ronnie was taking a sound beating, and was bleeding from the head wound. The heavy tool pounded into his flesh time and time again, and Ronnie twitched with each blow. He looked unconscious, and still blows rained down on him. The Anger Management man paused, glanced at his car, and began to kick Ronnie hard in the chest. Squeamish of late, Jake watched until he was sure Ronnie was badly hurt, before calling for an ambulance. Roger was also monitoring proceedings. Within a few seconds there was the sound of a siren, and a police car arrived, doubtless already summoned by the Psychiatric Unit. Jake made a mental note to ring Phil Ryder when he got the chance. There were a few names he could mention, a few addresses, a few business practices, which might, as it were, help the police with their enquiries, and keep Ronnie out of harm's way. That was if he lived long enough to be prosecuted.

An unfit copper climbed out of his car and tried to calm the situation. However, things were beyond calming. A few more Anger Management patients had begun to congregate, and a visitor to the Tourette's Syndrome unit was swearing uncontrollably. Someone broke a window of the police car, and all hell broke loose. The other copper, a WPC, jumped out and radioed for help. A couple of fights erupted, and more cars were damaged. Three male psychiatric nurses ran over and attempted to restrain their patients, which only served to antagonize them. Ronnie was still on the wrong end of a thorough kicking. A bicycle hurtled through the air and knocked over the male copper. Two police cars screeched into the car park, followed by an ambulance. Desperately struggling into riot gear, several of the PCs were caught in the crossfire. A particularly psychopathic in-patient got involved, swinging punches at anyone he could. Two mean-looking coppers finally managed to extract their batons, and started laying into people. Another AM case turned up in a big four-wheel drive, and spying a parking space between two police vehicles, nudged his car towards them. A truncheon smashed through his window, and a PC threw an out-patient onto the bonnet. The driver revved the engine and began slamming his car back and forth into the two police vehicles, pushing them out of the way and scattering people in every direction. On the other side, a small group of patients emerged from the unit and turned a car over, before setting light to it for good measure. A fire engine entered the carnage, and was pelted with a wide and unusual range of missiles, from coins and shoes to wing mirrors, mudguards and bolt cutters. Another car was tipped over and ignited, patients whooping and hollering in delight. Roger whistled through his teeth.

'I always told you that car park was dangerous,' he said.

Jake turned away from the window and picked up the bag full of money. Somewhere on the other side of Bridgeton was a nervous half uncle. He walked out of the office and left via a rear door, having witnessed enough trouble for one day. Sometimes, he conceded to himself, violence is the only solution to your problems.

Norbert's Compensation Package

A week later, Jake stirred in the half light. It was early Saturday morning and he was aware only that he wasn't in his own bed, and that he wasn't alone. Next to him, there were occasional restless movements, and the bedclothes seemed to be slipping away. He murmured a semi-conscious curse.

Louise's brain: Jobs. Jobs. Jobs.

Jake's brain: Fuck. Here we go again.

Louise's brain: Jobs. Jobs. Jobs.

Jake's brain: Pretend to be asleep.

Louise's brain: Jobs. Jobs. Jobs. I need a new job.

Jake's brain: Pull bedclothes slowly back up body.

Louise's brain: Peril and Sons are out of business until the factory is rebuilt. Wake Jake.

Jake's brain: I am being prodded.

Louise's brain: 'Jake?'

Jake's brain: Mumble loudly, hope that will suffice.

Louise's brain: 'Could you get me a job in Hazard Prevention?'

Jake's brain: What? 'What, you?'

Louise's brain: 'Yes me. Why not?'

Jake's brain: 'Because it would be a bit like Roger becoming a stunt man.' Roll over, close eyes again.

Louise's brain: 'I mean, thinking about it, you being paranoid and

	implementing safety procedures saved my life. I'm interested in the topic now.'
Jake's brain:	Oh fuck. Another unemployed girlfriend. 'I'd advise you try for a different sort of job.'
Louise's brain:	'Why?'
Jake's brain:	'Anxiety is infectious. As soon as someone tells you their fears, they become your fears. Believe me, working where I do, it's a bugger.'
Louise's brain:	'Well, what else?'
Jake's brain:	Sit up, pay attention. 'I dunno. How badly do you need the money?'
Louise's brain:	'Not that badly, as it turns out. After saving my wages from Peril's and inheriting some cash last year, I've actually got a decent sum together.'
Jake's brain:	'Don't worry about it. Relax. Something else will come along.'
Louise's brain:	'I suppose.'
Jake's brain:	Awake now. No chance of dozing. A shag doesn't look too likely either. Suggest a dip in the pool instead. 'Fancy a swim?'
Louise's brain:	Check watch. Fuck. It's nearly lunchtime. Hard to tell with the blinds shut. Almost twelve hours since last shower. Must smell. Need to wash hair. Very lacking in make-up department. Cannot be seen in public with unshaven legs. 'Look, I'll catch up with you.'

Leaving the room, Jake bumped into his aunt in the hotel corridor and thanked her again. 'Don't thank me,' she replied, 'thank your uncle.'

'Half-uncle.'

'Whatever.' Elizabeth turned to walk away, but Jake stopped her.

'Come here,' he said, wrapping his arms around her.

'Jake, would you get off hugging me? What are you doing that for?'

He let go of his aunt. 'Just proving a point to myself,' he replied.

376

She regarded him suspiciously. 'And what point might that be?'

'That I have it in me to hug people.'

'You're weird,' she mumbled, smiling to herself as she walked away. 'Now there's a family trait if ever there was one.'

Norbert was outside, lying next to the pool, his body so white it was almost reflecting the sun.

'Thanks again for paying for our holiday,' Jake said, approaching and sitting next to him.

Norbert twitched slightly. 'No problem. Only if you could keep your minibar expenditure down to a minimum. You know, buy booze from the super-market. It's more economic that way.'

'I'll see what we can do. And thanks for agreeing to help me sort my debts out.'

'Like I said, no problem.' Norbert convulsed again. 'I'd rather that than give my hard-earned cash to a thug from Leeds.'

'Yeah, bit lucky what happened.' Jake squinted in the sun, the swimming pool of the expensive resort dazzling him as the light bounced off its surface. 'Finding it hard?' he asked.

His uncle, although lying flat, wasn't in the least bit relaxed. Jake could tell that, despite his recent generosity, this was hurting him. All eyes so far had been watching his reaction to each new bill that came his way. Mineral water, taxis, meals out and tipping had been especially painful. Everything else was merely a struggle. 'I'm doing the best I can,' he answered. 'Mind you, this is the easy bit. After you two fly home, we're off to Venice. Christ.' Norbert swallowed hard. 'And then Monte Carlo.' He appeared to grow even whiter and it hurt Jake's eyes to look at him. 'People have gone bust there.'

A waiter approached with a cold beer and a plate of sandwiches. 'Would you like to charge this to your room, sir?' he asked Norbert, putting the tray down beside him.

Norbert nodded. 'Room three-two-six,' he replied, taking a sandwich.

When the waiter had disappeared, Jake said, 'But you're next door to us. And we're in,' he examined his key fob, 'eight-one-seven.'

'Precisely,' Norbert smiled.

Behind his uncle, a couple walked arm in arm in the sunshine. One of them was tall and mainly black. His companion was petite and pale, but had caught a little colour over the previous couple of days. Jake called to them. 'Roger! Pauline! Over here!'

Roger and Pauline strolled over. 'Hey, Jake. What are you up to?'

'Not a fat lot,' he replied. 'Just winding Norbert up. How about you?'

Pauline consulted a piece of paper that she had pulled out of the back of her husband's shorts. 'Freefall bungee jumping, this morning. And then paragliding at three.'

Roger addressed Norbert. 'Hope you didn't mind us tagging along, Mr Flint. It's just that when Jake told me where you were heading, we thought . . .' he squeezed Pauline's hand, 'that it might do us the world of good. And big resorts like this have all manner of activities to keep you amused.'

Jake still wasn't sure what had got into his colleague. His adrenal glands must have wondered what the fuck had hit them. 'Bungee jumping?' he said to Pauline. 'I think I'd rather have knives thrown at me.'

'Oh, it's all OK,' she replied. 'Roger's consulted the statistics. Apparently you're three times more likely to die riding your bike to the shops than doing a well-supervised jump with a reputable company. And as for paragliding, because you're always over water, the probability of serious injury, excluding drowning, is slightly less than your average risk of melanoma if you spend . . .'

Jake stopped listening, and stretched out. There was only so much nonsense about safety that you could listen to. Roger and Pauline slunk away, and Norbert cleared his throat.

'Mind you,' he said, 'I'm thinking about buying some champagne tonight.'

'Jesus. Get yourself out of the sun.'

'No, I'm serious. I've got some good news which I haven't told anybody yet.'

'Yeah?'

'And I think you should be first to know, since you looked after it so well and followed its advice.'

'Followed what advice?'

'I just dialled our answering machine, and there's a message from a publisher.'

'A publisher? As in books?'

'Yep. I put myself to good use in the couple of weeks before we came here, Jake. Tidied my manuscript up, paid Mary to retype it — properly this time — changed a few things and added some others that occurred to me in London, and sent it to twenty publishers.'

'Don't tell me . . .'

'One of them is interested in it.'

'But how are you going to get tightwads to buy a book about not parting with cash?'

'Ah, there's the beauty of it,' Norbert said, stroking his goatee beard. 'Even misers will part with cash if they think it will save them money in the long run.'

Jake interlocked his hands on his chest. If he did it one way, his hands fit perfectly, and you couldn't tell. If he did it the other way, he was left with two spare fingers. Over the gentle lap of the swimming pool a few empty slogans echoed inside his head. *Stay alert and you won't get hurt.* He closed his eyes. *Anger is only one letter from danger.* He smiled and yawned. *Safety is a state of mind*. His breathing started to slow. And as the sun bore down on his skin, he began to doze, feeling the petty anxieties of the twenty-first century seeping out of his pores and into the dry Mediterranean air.

THE END

PAPER
John McCabe

EVERYTHING IS RELATED. . .

Scientist and part-time dreamer, Dr Darren White is losing the plot. Work has descended into a distinctly unscientific mess and his research is non-existent. Taking time out from discovering the last great theory of the Twentieth century, Darren begins an illicit investigation into Class A pharmaceuticals and fears he may be on the verge of murdering an irritating colleague. What's more worrying though is the sudden appearance of a Bomb in his Head, which needs diffusing, and soon.

Darren has tried everything to arrest his helpless slide: the catchily named Operation MWIMI (Make Work More Interesting) foundered on the rocks of his facial hair, and The Day of Rules turned into the most unruly of days. Nothing has really helped. And now he needs to get his life in order because he has met Neuro Girl, who doesn't look like the sort of woman who would stand for any bombs going off in her vicinity.

The more Darren searches for order, the more elusive it becomes, until the surprise contents of a stolen computer suggest that things are rarely what they seem. And when your only hope is that life isn't logical, then you know you're in trouble . . . don't you?

'ORIGINAL, ENTERTAINING AND COMPELLING'
The Times

'A FINE AND HIGHLY ORIGINAL THRILLER'
City Life

0 552 99874 5

BLACK SWAN

SNAKESKIN
John McCabe

'CARL HIASSEN MEETS JOHN O'FARRELL BY WAY OF
LESLIE NIELSEN. HI-OCTANE HI-JINX'
Mirror

Most people say that there's no such thing as a free lunch.
But basking in the Los Angeles sunshine, Ian begs to differ.
Thanks to a computer banking scam, he has set himself up
with meals for life. Until his cosy lifestyle is threatened by
an unexpected glitch. Desperate situations call for desperate
remedies. Even to the extent of returning to England and
pretending to be a mediocre scientist called Darren.

Darren doesn't know anything about this, but he soon will.
All he does know is that someone has stolen his identity –
and that nobody would do that unless they really had to.

And what follows is a prime example of why you should never
drag an innocent bystander into the mess that is your life. . .

'PAINFULLY FUNNY . . . PART MIKE LEIGH GRIMNESS,
PART HOLLYWOOD ACTION FLICK, EXPECT TO SEE THE
FILM OF THE BOOK IN A MULTIPLEX NEAR YOU SOON'
Heat

'A THOROUGHLY ENJOYABLE COMEDY OF ERRORS . . .
IT'S A PLEASURE TO WATCH THE STORY UNFURL'
Punch

'THOROUGHLY ENTERTAINING . . . HALF BILE, HALF
SMILES'
i-D

'FANTASTICALLY GRIPPING . . . EXCEEDINGLY SHARP,
ORIGINAL PROSE'
Arena

'I COULD SAY THAT MCCABE WRITES AS NICK
HORNBY WOULD IF NICK HORNBY WERE LOCKED IN A
LABORATORY FOR A YEAR. BUT THAT WOULD BE
GLIB. THE WRITING IS ORIGINAL, ENTERTAINING AND
COMPELLING'
The Times

0 552 99873 7

BLACK SWAN

STICKLEBACK
Jogn McCabe

It's Wednesday morning. You hate your job so much you haven't done any work for two weeks and nobody's noticed. You share an office with a sad and obsessed Trekkie whose computer manuals are encroaching on your workspace. Your breakfast routine has gone wrong. It's your 29th birthday.

So you have the worst hangover in the world and you're on the Number 11 bus circumnavigating the dreariest suburbs Birmingham has to offer. The bottle of red you've been necking is nearly gone and the passengers on the bus are freaking you out. You sip into the Jug of Ale for a pint.

And now you're trapped in the gents by a man-mountain with only one eyebrow and if you thought things could only get better, YOU WERE WRONG. . .

Stickleback is a novel about men's need for routine and what happens when life intervenes. A funny, poignant and fast-moving tale of office life, drinking, drugs, love, friendship, clubs, football, computer programming and the perfect financial heist.

'WITTY AND INCISIVE ABOUT THE PREOCCUPATIONS OF MODERN LIFE'
Observer

'NOT ONLY DO YOU HAVE A COMPULSIVE READ ON YOUR HANDS, YOU ALSO HAVE A FASCINATING PROFILE OF THE RITUALIZED MEDIOCRITY OF CONTEMPORARY LIVING'
Big Issue

'THIS FINE FIRST NOVEL . . . MAKES A VERY WELCOME BREAK FROM THE NORM'
The Times

0 552 99984 9

BLACK SWAN

A SELECTED LIST OF FINE WRITING
AVAILABLE FROM BLACK SWAN

99917 2	FAY	Larry Brown	£6.99
99979 2	GATES OF EDEN	Ethan Coen	£7.99
99686 6	BEACH MUSIC	Pat Conroy	£8.99
99912 1	BIG SKY	Gareth Creer	£6.99
99925 3	THE BOOK OF THE HEATHEN	Robert Edric	£6.99
99945 8	DEAD FAMOUS	Ben Elton	£6.99
99935 0	PEACE LIKE A RIVER	Leif Enger	£6.99
99987 3	NO ONE THINKS OF GREENLAND	John Griesemer	£6.99
77082 5	THE WISDOM OF CROCODILES	Paul Hoffman	£7.99
99916 4	AMERICAN BY BLOOD	Andrew Huebner	£6.99
77109 0	THE FOURTH HAND	John Irving	£6.99
99936 9	SOMEWHERE SOUTH OF HERE	William Kowalski	£6.99
99874 5	PAPER	John McCabe	£6.99
99873 7	SNAKESKIN	John McCabe	£6.99
99984 9	STICKLEBACK	John McCabe	£6.99
99785 4	GOODNIGHT, NEBRASKA	Tom McNeal	£6.99
99907 5	DUBLIN	Seán Moncrieff	£6.99
99901 6	WHITE MALE HEART	Ruaridh Nicoll	£6.99
99919 9	NEEDLE IN THE GROOVE	Jeff Noon	£6.99
99849 4	THIS IS YOUR LIFE	John O'Farrell	£6.99
99862 1	A REVOLUTION OF THE SUN	Tim Pears	£6.99
99817 6	INK	John Preston	£6.99
77095 7	LONDON IRISH	Zane Radcliffe	£6.99
99645 9	THE WRONG BOY	Willy Russell	£6.99
99920 2	SWEETMEAT	Luke Sutherland	£6.99
77000 0	A SCIENTIFIC ROMANCE	Ronald Wright	£6.99